CASSANDRA

GODDESS OF HARMONY

Debbie Behan

Cassandra - Goddess of Harmony Published 2017
by Butterfly Kiss Books
Copyright © 2016 by Debbie Behan

Previously published under the title of
Lord of the Planets - Home Worlds
Published 2013 by Butterfly Kiss Books
Copyright © 2013 by Debbie Behan

First published as Lord of the Planets - Cloud Riders 2013
ISBN - 978-0-9874013-1-1

Cassandra
Goddess of Harmony
by
Debbie Behan

ISBN (pbk): 978-0-9954205-0-2
ISBN (ebk): 978-0-9954205-1-9

DEDICATION

To the wonders of the universe and
those who inspired me to follow my dreams.

CHAPTER ONE

Princess in a New Land

A couple of days ago Cassie had a home and a nanny that catered to her every need. Suddenly, her whole world had transformed and she found herself alone and miserable. Cassie's last memory of home was a hand covering her eyes and a smelly cloth held against her mouth. The fumes had burnt her throat.

She woke in a dark metallic crate; the sides felt like aluminium. It seemed no bigger than a packing box. She could feel that her ears were pressurised and she cried out as her body slammed into the sides of the container. It was obvious it was being unloaded.

'Ouch!' she screamed out as the container landed with a thump. Her bottom hit hard and she felt her *whole spine adjust, and not in a good way*. Cassie was unable to stand up in the confined space and she started to cry, not yet able to grasp what was going on. The drugs she had been given were still making her groggy.

Her sobs were so heavy that her lungs and stomach began to hurt from the deep gulps of air she was trying to suck in. Cassie tried closing her eyes, which didn't help either. Her head ached and she felt violently ill from the smell of herself being locked up for she didn't even know how long. She thought it might have been a couple of days by the way her stomach twisted with hunger and she was so dehydrated, her sobs were waterless.

She heard someone turning a key in the padlock on the door and she sat very still, waiting for a face to peer in at her. Cassie shook with fear as she listened to the sound of doors slamming as the vehicle sped off. It was only then that reality sank in.

I've been left to die.

Cassie's adrenalin kicked in; feral instincts made her howl like an animal. She lashed out with her legs, booting the section where she had heard the key used. It was stuck. Cassie curled her legs tight and pounded on the door. After using every ounce of strength she could muster, the door fell open.

She stayed inside for a long time, scared to look at where she was. She focused her eyes. The scorching sun stung and bit into her pupils as it shone inside the crate. All she knew was that she had been dropped off in bushland somewhere.

Cassie finally plucked up courage and ventured out, forcing her aching body to walk towards a dead tree that had toppled over nearby. Using one of the stumps that jutted out, she undid the knot that bound her hands together. Cassie wiped her face, stood up and realised that even though her body was stiff and sore she had finally been released from her captivity. She was happy to be alive. Free at last!

Cassie stretched, glancing around for water, a sign, or a road to follow. The vehicle must have veered a long way off the main road to get her to where she was, as there were only tyre marks in the dirt as far as she could see. *If I follow the tracks, will they lead me back to the road? Or is it a trick to take me further away from civilisation?*

Disorientated, she decided to head in the opposite direction, not trusting her kidnappers. The bush began to thin out until there were just sparse trees and bushes that poked out of the fine and powdery red dirt. She frowned as a whirlwind picked up the red sand, stinging her eyes and sticking to her clothes and body where she was perspiring.

'Great,' she grumped. 'Now I must really look a sight.'

She gazed down at herself, wondering if she did find a road if someone would pick her up. *I look and smell disgusting.* The wind whipped up again. She could barely see two feet in front of her and the heat in the wind was unbearable. *Have they dumped me in a desert somewhere?* She wiped the dirt off her face and hands but it just smeared and felt worse. Every step she took she forced herself against the strong wind. *How much worse can this get?* She trudged along, trying to find some sign of civilisation.

Cassie thanked the heavens when she finally stumbled across a road and found a sign. *Left will apparently take me to a mining town called Mt Newman, right to a town called Perth.* Mt Newman was only a few miles away. She wasn't sure how long it had been since she had eaten and there had been no sound of a car. Therefore, walking was her only option and she began to trek her way along the dusty, partly covered road towards Mt Newman.

The sun beat down on her fair skin and the wind scorched her arms and face. Sadness overwhelmed her as she realised she might die before getting to the town. Thirst took over her every thought as she pushed harder against the howling wind.

Keep moving! She kept yelling at her body. *Surely it couldn't be far now.* The thought swam around in her mind repeatedly.

She heard a car coming. A horn blasted. Turning in her dazed state, Cassie realised that she was walking in the middle of the road. The utility truck skidded to a stop. Pain screeched within her as she fell and rolled herself away from the loud motor.

'What the hell were you doing walking in the middle of the damned road?' she heard one of the men say as he checked her body to see if she had broken a limb.

Cassie shaded her eyes and saw another man leaning up against the truck with a smug look on his face. 'Just leave her, Kayden. How many times have spies tricked us like this? Get us to feel sorry for one of the enemies very own so we take them in, using them to expose us? Christ knows where this one's been. She's so filthy she'd probably give you a disease just touching her or maybe that's the plan. If we don't get sick they'll be sure they're on to something.'

'Shut up, Jason, she could be hurt. Just give me a sec.'

'You're a bloody vet! What can you do anyway? Let's get out of here and leave her to her own luck. Someone will be along shortly and they can deal with the scrubber.'

'And if you're right, we need to know what enemy camp she's come from.' He straightened her out, slid his arms under her and picked her up as if she weighed nothing.

'She's not getting in my bloody car,' Jason grumbled.

Cassie caught her breath and coughed but the dryness stopped her from talking. She wanted to tell them to leave her alone. Instead she just stared helplessly at the one called Kayden.

'Help me get her in the car, Jason, and stop being a jerk.'

Jason moved to the back of the utility truck, unclipping the canvas cover and dropping down the tailgate, helped Kayden pick her up. 'Put the dirty wench in the back of the truck then. There's no way I'm putting up with that smell all the way home.'

The two men were rough when they put Cassie down. Her head ached as Kayden shoved a rolled-up towel under it.

'You know, she might have been one of Ma Baker's girls and at one of those parties they have out here in the bush. Never seen her before though.'

'If she is could I really be that lucky?' Jason slapped his side with renewed vigour.

'Whatever, stud! We at least need to try to find out what we're dealing with here first. It's one of our hottest days and she won't last long out here in the condition she's in.'

Cassie passed out.

When she came to, she was in a horse stable in a barn. She was lying on hay and she was itchy everywhere it touched. It was dark and she was freezing but at least the moon was full and giving her some light. Next to her she could see a bottle of water and three biscuits on a plate. The thought crossed her mind that they might be laced with drugs but she was far too hungry to care. Nervously anticipating her fate and yet unable to stay awake long enough to do anything about it, she fell back to sleep.

When she woke again, she had a horse blanket on her that smelled worse than she did. The plate had gone but the bottle had been refilled. Giving thanks, she drank the water in gulps. Cassie jumped and put the bottle down when she heard steps. She scurried into the corner and tried to hide: her meeting of the two men had not made her comfortable about being around them at all. Her body froze as the man called Kayden moved towards her and dragged her out, his fingers digging into her arm.

He threw her out of the stables and turned a freezing-cold hose on her. She rolled into a foetal position out of instinct to stop it stinging the cuts. He kept asking ridiculous questions that made no sense and even though he was a bully and hurting her, she made no sound. Cassie had watched movies about mistreatment. He kept it up until she was clean and he realised she wasn't going to participate in his line of questioning. He helped her up and lead her back to the stable. He tossed a clean pair of jeans and a shirt at her and said impatiently, 'Get dressed. I'm taking you back to wherever the hell you want to go. But you're not staying here.'

Where does he think my home is? It's at least three days travel from this place! Cassie was cold and confused but didn't want him hurting her anymore so she did as she was told. He watched as she removed her wet clothes. She could feel his eyes burning into her, enjoying her embarrassment. She turned her back on him. *God, so humiliating.*

'What are you hiding from? If you aren't who I think you are then you have to be the other and I'm sure you've stripped off for many a man! Could this just be another part of your act to get me to think you're actually a lady?' he scoffed. 'A lady would not have been wandering around in the middle of the road trying to get anyone to stop and take pity on her.'

Cassie shot him a heated look and threw off the rest of her clothes without care. He had made her so cranky she would let him look at what they'd done to her! She turned and he had a full view of her.

'Happy?' she scowled.

Cassie heard him swear. 'Where the hell are all those bruises from? Jason said he didn't hit you with the car.'

'What do you care how I ended up with them? Leave me alone.' She turned her back to him. She wanted to tell him how she really ended up so banged up but was angry at his reaction. The look on his face made her feel ugly and instead of confiding in him, she just wanted him gone.

He stomped out cursing. It confused him. She'd looked so innocent as she stood naked in front of him but her refusal to answer any of his questions infuriated him. What was she playing at? Cassie dressed, slouched against the wall and closed her eyes.

* * * *

Damn it. I passed out again. Why? She wondered.

She woke up in a bedroom this time, her stomach rumbling from hunger. Cassie had no idea how long she had been asleep but she needed to find some food. She went to get up but her legs were tired and could not keep her in an upright position. She collapsed onto the floor with a thud. 'Cripes,' she groaned.

The door flung open and Kayden came in and lifted her back onto the bed.

'You're weak. How long has it been since you ate?' he asked impatiently.

She gestured that it had been maybe two or three days.

He seemed irritable that she had barely spoken two words since she arrived. 'Look, I'm still not sure if this is all just an act and I'll definitely not play bloody nursemaid to any woman. If you want to eat, the kitchens outside this door. You might as well quit the performance and go get it yourself or starve.' He stood looking angrily down at her. He made Cassie so mad that she swung her legs over the bed, attempting to stand again and ... whoops!

Cassie woke up back on the bed. There was water and a sandwich next to her that she choked down, ignoring her dry throat and gulping water with every bite. She lay back, thankful that at least her hunger was satisfied. Feeling better, she gingerly moved from the bed and headed for the bathroom. Out in the main room it surprised Cassie to see Kayden reading in an armchair. She thought he hadn't seemed educated enough to be reading with all the cursing he did.

Kayden looked up.

'Can I use your bathroom?'

He pointed to a door and Cassie nodded. She looked back at him as she closed the door. Immersed in his novel and he took no notice of her. He looked different under the light shade: not so cruel at all.

The toilet led into a shower. Cassie found a clean towel. She looked in the mirror and was shocked at her appearance: the hose-down he gave her didn't clean her face or her hair very well because she had rolled herself into such a protective position. Red dust had caked onto every strand of her hair and Cassie's normal golden-blond colour was dirt-stained a reddish-brown. Her face had red dust patches and her clear hazel eyes looked dark and dull from the mascara that had run from her tears. She could see why the men had thought she was untrustworthy. She looked a fright.

She turned the tap and scrubbed herself clean. The spray bit into the cuts and battered against the bruising on her skin although just to feel dirt-free was worth it. It made her feel much better. Reaching for a towel, a wave of light-headedness came over her and she leaned against the wall. Exhausted, she slid down the tiles and sat on the floor, hugging the towel, waiting for her energy to kick back in.

Did I faint again? Maybe I did. She heard footsteps and the voice of Kayden cursing her. He stood Cassie up and she could feel him shake her and curse some more. She remembered very little after that.

* * * *

The room glowed with the first signs of dawn. She pulled back the covers and noticed she wore a big shirt that Kayden must have put on her. She also noted she was still alive which proved it was unlikely he intended to hurt her.

At least she now knew why she kept passing out. When Cassie had washed her hair she had felt a big lump and a cut on her head that stung under the water. *I must be concussed.*

Her body still felt tender and sore, yet she felt stronger since the pain in her head had eased. She padded out into the kitchen in bare feet and made a cup of coffee, and the call of fresh air had her walking outside to drink it. The porch had a chair that she bypassed, preferring to walk out into the yard to have a good look at her surroundings. Kayden's farm wasn't fancy—nothing like the immaculate gardens and grandeur of the castle Cassie had once called home—but it was quaint and peaceful. There were dirt tracks leading away from the house in different directions. The trees and shrubs were sparse and the red dirt and big boulders that covered the landscape reminded her of her first look at this country in which she had been dumped. Kayden had the largest barn she had ever seen and a few horses were nibbling on feed behind a high-gated fenced area. *How long has it been since I've done this?* Not in many years had she been able to stand out in the fresh morning light and view anything. From her bedroom her view had been very limited and even the open window never gave her such a complete feeling of freedom and love for what she was now seeing for the first time. Even though her parents were not there, she still felt a little nervous about being outside. At home she would have been beaten for an action such as this.

Cassie contemplated how a twist of fate had led her here, to this farm, with the strangest of men. Not that she had met many; well, up close and personal, only her father. Kayden had mistreated her but it was nothing she wasn't used to, yet at other times he was kind and his eyes told her she could trust him. He was so different to the men in the movies she had watched and the magazines she had read. She had thought all men were womanisers, wanting everything their own way and doing anything to get laid, yet she had picked up none of this behaviour from him. She wondered if he would put her on a plane home if she told him who she really was. *God, no!* She would have to carry her secret alone. She swept her eyes around the landscape. There was a power, an unseen energy pulling her to this spot, this farm and to Kayden. This was where she knew she needed to be—for now anyway. She found a log to sit on and sipped her coffee, watching the glow of daylight up the sky and gasping at its beauty.

'How lucky is the person who lives here? This would be so pretty to wake up to every day.' She talked quietly to herself as she had done for years. There was usually not a soul to hear her.

A sound behind Cassie made her jump. She stood up and faced Kayden who was standing behind her, looking at her with a strange expression.

'Yes, very beautiful to wake up to.' The sunrise reflected in his eyes.

'Sorry, I didn't mean to wake you. I just woke feeling better and wanted to see where I was.'

'You have a slight accent.' He eyed her a little suspiciously after hearing her speak more loudly and fluently.

Cassie put her head down, wishing she hadn't spoken. *Now he has that 'I don't trust you' look back in his eyes again.* 'My name is Cassandra but most people call me Cassie. I'm not from around here.' She took a sip of her coffee and ignored the uncomfortable tension that fell between them. 'I want to apologise for passing out on you. I have a huge lump on my head and it stung under the shower,' Cassie said, flinching as she touched the tender spot by accident.

Frowning, he walked towards her. 'Let me see. Keep still!' He was somewhat gruff but not scary anymore and his fingers, strangely enough, were very gentle as they parted her hair. 'You may need a stitch but it seems to be healing alright. Do you normally heal quickly?'

Cassie shrugged. 'Don't know. I've never had a cut before.'

He let her hair fall back. 'You'll have a little scar but it will be well hidden under all this hair.' He squinted and held a hand over his eyes, viewing the sunrise. 'Sit. Don't let me disturb you. I just have to go check the paddocks before breakfast. Unless you want to come and have a look around, get out of the house for a bit?' he asked in a more civil tone.

Surprised at his change of mood, Cassie jumped at the offer. 'To get outside anywhere would be a treat. Can you wait until I get some shoes on and tie up my hair up?' She ran inside, excited. *Check the paddocks. What does that mean?* Her thoughts ran wild as she dressed. *Who cares? It gets me out of the house.* She smiled.

When she came out to join Kayden, she noticed that he seemed to have a happier look on his face. He wasn't smiling but he definitely wasn't grumpy. He stood by a utility truck with the door open, and closed it after her when she jumped in. A little way down the dusty track he pulled up at an open field where horses grazed under lovely flourishing trees along a pretty stream. *No red dirt here,* she thought, amazed at how this area was so different from the rest of the landscape she had viewed so far. They walked along the stream. Cassie watched as fish darted in and out of the rocks, the clear crystal water flowing over them like moving glass.

Kayden went over to pat and check a couple of the horses. He lifted the hoof of one and pressed it, talking quietly. 'That's looking better, boy,' he said, letting its leg go and patting its mane again. Another couple of horses were ready to foal and he frowned at one of them. 'You better come with us, girl.' His tone was calm.

He went back to the truck and grabbed a bridle. After harnessing the horse, he led it around and dropped down the back of the high-sided trailer. Once the horse was safe on the trailer, he checked a few more horses and then they headed back.

It was obvious Kayden wasn't a real talker which suited her just fine. The last thing she needed right then was someone wanting answers she could not even get her own head around yet.

Kayden took the pregnant horse back to the stable and bedded her down for the day. 'I'll have to watch her carefully today,' he said, making Cassie jump with just the sound of his voice. He'd been so silent since they left (unless he spoke to the horses) and it took her by surprise. Until now, his voice had always had an annoyed tone, implying that she was intruding in his world. Even though he had not yet sent her packing, she had been waiting for it. 'Mother's ready but it looks like the foal needs turning. I'll tend to her after breakfast. I'm sure you can amuse yourself while I'm busy.'

'Can I watch? I've never seen anything get born before.'

He raised his eyebrows curiously and then shrugged. 'If you want to. But don't get in the way or you're out of here,' he grumbled. The tone of his voice said clearly that she was once again walking a fine line and to do as he said—or else.

Cassie smiled meekly and he turned away, but not fast enough. She was positive that he had nearly smiled back. The way he straightened his shoulders however and walked briskly out made her wonder if she had imagined it. Cassie practically ran to keep up with him as she followed his long strides back into the house. After washing their hands they went to the kitchen. Cassie felt awkward being around someone who seemed to fill up every room he walked into. He was unusually large, she thought, although she hadn't seen that many men in the flesh to compare him with.

Pulling a pan and utensils from drawers below the bench, he started cooking bacon and eggs. He threw her a loaf of bread. 'Here, you can cook the toast,' he said casually. This time his voice sounded a little more human. Yet all it took was a dumbfounded expression on her behalf and the annoyed look was back on his face.

For goodness sake, why can't I keep my stupid face from showing any expression? 'I'm sorry. I didn't mean to look ill-mannered but I haven't cooked before. If you show me, I'm a quick learner.'

His eyes darkened and creases lined his forehead as he frowned, making her cringe and take a step back from him.

'I don't know where you came from or why you had to turn up on my doorstep but I was hoping you could at least feed yourself. Even the bloody animals know how to do that.' His flat tone let her know he was more frustrated with her than upset. He threw two pieces of bread in the toaster and pushed down a lever. 'When it pops up, just butter it,' he added a little sarcastically as he held up the knife and the butter. 'You do know how to butter bread, I assume?' He went back to cooking the bacon and eggs.

Cassie grumbled under her breath and she saw his face tighten at her response.

He pulled out two glasses from the cupboard and filled them with juice, handing them to Cassie, gesturing for her to put them the table, while he dished up. The tension was choking but he did pull out a chair for her. She guessed that maybe he was just worried about the horse out in the barn and that she was not the problem at all.

It was hard not to watch his every move. Cassie had never been so close to an eligible male before and she loved the way he folded the egg and bacon into a sandwich and held it in one hand while his other gripped the paper he read. His fingers were long and strong and they put a tingle through her as she imagined curling her own fingers around them. She shook her head and glanced down at all the food on her plate. She tried to eat but her stomach filled after just a few bites. She thought about the last few days. By the date on the calendar in the kitchen she knew it was day four since she had been taken from her bed. It had seemed a nightmare and yet there now seemed to be so much to be grateful for. Even the little bit of kindness she had received from Kayden was more than she had ever had. Cassie didn't want him to take her home as he had threatened and yet if she kept annoying him, she would end up there for sure. Already, Cassie liked his quiet existence and wished she could stay a while until she learned to do things for herself. Somehow though, she doubted this man had patience for anything other than his horses. She focused back on her plate of food. She had barely touched it and Kayden had already cleaned his up.

Cassie was on edge, wondering if wasting the food he had cooked for her would be enough to tip him over the edge and make him cross at her again. He'll most likely stomp out to the stables without me, she thought. Tears sprang to her eyes that she tried to wipe quickly away.

Cassie heard his paper move and his eyes peered around it at her. 'What's wrong now?'

'My stomach, I still don't feel well. I know you hated having to cook it for me and now I'm wasting it.'

He shrugged and went back to reading his paper.

Damn. He's so hard to fathom. She dropped her shoulders and breathed out heavily. Now she realised how tense she was, she really had to stop feeling so uptight. *Maybe it's me and not him at all.* She leaned back in her chair, drinking her juice and looking outside. The tree near the window had lovely lilac flowers that lifted in the breeze, making a carpet of petals around the trunk. Yes, it was beautiful here.

She picked up the dishes. One thing she did know was how to wash a dish: she had seen that done plenty of times when she was a child.

Cassie followed Kayden out to the stables when he was ready

and he sat her up on a bale of hay, putting a hand on each side of her and leaning in close. She could smell the delicate spice of his aftershave and his body, so near, was a bit unnerving. His eyes closed as if he too was taking her into the depths of him. Cassie heard the horse make a weird noise and with a quick movement he stood up, glancing towards the noise. The moment was gone and his old self was back.

'Remember, one peep out of you and you go back inside,' he warned. 'Sit still and don't move.'

Cassie watched as the horse dropped onto the floor, obviously in a lot of pain. Kayden was at its side within seconds, sliding a big long glove onto his hand that went all the way up his arm. Then to her surprise, he slipped it inside the animal. She was horrified for the poor thing. *She's making the worst noises!* Even though she was unsure of this strange procedure, she kept herself perfectly still and quiet, her eyes barely blinking as she observed a miracle: a foal slid out and lay with its mother.

It wasn't long before it tried to stand. *Not even a human baby is this smart!* Tears ran down Cassie's face as the little fellow wobbled and tried to get its balance. Kayden looked around and she felt his eyes on her for a minute as her heart went out to the tough little fellow. By the time she'd ripped her eyes from the newborn, Kayden had turned back to the mother and continued working on her.

After it was all over he led them both into a clean room and hosed the little one down. Cassie watched as the mother nudged him to keep him moving. When Kayden finished, he said they needed to leave them for a while; that the mother needed rest.

It was well into the afternoon by the time Kayden woke Cassie, asking her if she'd like to go for a swim. She was glad to go and cool off but after checking her watch, she wondered what had happened to the last forty-eight hours or so. She recalled that the paddock had been covered in fog when they took one of the horses back and after they returned home, Kayden had made her a hot drink.

Did he drug me? Thinking she had lost her marbles, she put the thought aside. She must have her days mixed up. One seemed to run into another on the farm. She smiled and took up his offer. It was stinking hot inside and sweat had dampened her hair and pyjamas so she quickly changed and bounced out the door, excited to be doing something other than sitting there in the heat.

At the waterhole, Cassie looked up at the rock wall that stretched far above their heads. The sun was in a perfect position to highlight the ferns that grew from the crevices between the big boulders. Closer to the water's edge she could see reeds growing, staining the water yellow. Farther out, the water seemed to change to a royal blue that ran into indigo in the depths. The water smelled clean and was lovely and refreshing to wade in. She had to suck in a huge breath to stop from shrieking after jumping in as her still-bruised and aching body hurt with the pressure against her skin.

Kayden picked that moment to move past and he accidentally rubbed against her. She flinched and groaned.

'Sorry,' he apologised, looking down at her bruises. A look spread across his face: a mixture of pity and horror. She looked down at her body and could hardly blame him if he thought she looked disgusting: she felt ugly.

She swam away to hide from him behind some reeds and lay back, floating in the cool water, relaxing her mind, trying not to think about looking like an elephant lady. *They will heal,* she repeated, trying to console her vanity. She remembered that she was with a person who really didn't seem to like her very much anyway. She had to stop worrying. *All I have to do is be good for a little while and not anger him. Then once I get stronger, I can just disappear into the night and his life will be back to normal.* Happy with her new thoughts, Cassie closed her eyes and imagined her room at home and her wardrobes of clothes and shoes. If only she had been good then she would not be here in pain, trying desperately to survive.

She felt a splash. Kayden was trying to get her attention. 'Do you swim?' He splashed her again playfully, appearing to be in a happier mood.

'I'll race you to the other side,' Cassie challenged him, lifted her head out the water and eyeing him competitively.

'Let's see what you've got.'

Making it to the other side was easy but coming into the last couple of metres on the way back, Cassie slowed. She had nothing left. Kayden flew past her and stopped. He was looking back as her eyes started to close and she slipped under the water. Cassie could feel him grabbing her and lifting her out and even though her body had let her down, she still felt and heard everything going on around her. It was somewhat scary not being able to open her eyes and she hoped the feeling would pass quickly. She felt him throw a towel around her, place her in the truck and put something under her head before it all went black.

* * * *

It was dark and she was back in bed when she woke. *Damn it, not again. This guy's going to think I'm such a girly-girl, fainting all the time. Way to go and make an impression, Cassie girl!* She sat up with a start, wondering what was happening to her and felt two arms pull her back down. Kayden had been lying with her and was still holding her. *Mmm, nice.*

'I don't know what's wrong with me. I'm so sorry,' she apologised in a whisper.

'You're still weak and just overdid it.' He was leaning on his elbow, watching her. 'I hope you didn't mind me staying with you until you woke but you gave me quite a scare.' His voice rolled over her like warm honey.

She smiled shyly. 'I um ...' She wanted to say she had never lain with a man before and that it was nice but the words were stuck in her throat.

He reacted to her blubber as if she did not want him there and he mumbled a curse, getting off the bed. 'You're right, of course. I shouldn't have presumed. I'll keep my distance and take you home as soon as you're okay to travel.' He stood at the door for a minute, maybe waiting for her to respond, but she was speechless.

That isn't what I meant it to sound like at all.

'I guess you're hungry. I'll call you when dinner's ready, seeing as you can't do anything for yourself.'

Cassie wanted to crawl back inside of herself. Kayden glared at her before shutting the door and leaving her on her own. She lay for a while thinking, pushing aside his cutting remark.

She had woken up in his arms. He *was holding me. Me.* At that moment a horrible thought changed her happy mood. It dawned on Cassie that he might still think she was one of Mar Bakers girls. Maybe he had wanted to have his way with her, only she had rejected him. *No wonder he was cross. A woman rejecting him he could handle, but by a would-be tramp?* After all, that's how he saw her. She couldn't lie there thinking of what he thought of her any longer. It was making her nuts. She flung the blanket off getting up. *If he wants me gone tomorrow, then maybe I should make a run for it tonight while he's sleeping.*

With this new plan in mind, Cassie decided to go all-out to be polite and throw him off the trail. *Not that he'll care when he wakes and finds I'm gone.*

Kayden turned around as she appeared at the door, looking her up and down with an almost-smirk crinkling the sides of his mouth. Cassie looked down and saw that she had only one of his T-shirts on.

'I didn't know where my clothes were,' she said timidly.

He returned his gaze to the frypan. 'You're not anything worth looking at, girl, so don't kid yourself. It hardly worries me what you wear. Anyway, I had to wash your clothes. They should be dry soon—and don't say it,' he said sarcastically, 'You have never washed clothes before.'

This man sure sounds as if he dislikes me. So why is he cooking for me if he really feels that way towards me? Why am I still here? None of his unusual behaviour was making sense and even if it did, she had no answer for him. Cassie was ashamed to tell him she had never had to wear anything twice. She just walked over to the table and sat down quietly. 'I'm sorry,' she apologised and hoped he wouldn't growl anymore.

When he made no further comment, she glanced up to watch him as he confidently moved around the kitchen. He was so big, well over six feet, yet seemed so graceful. His hair was dark brown tonight, yet in the sunlight it had red highlights. His eyes were hazel and changed colour with his moods. He had the longest eyelashes Cassie had ever seen on a man. Sometimes he watched her through them and she felt like he could see right into her very soul. His features were strong and masculine but when he smiled, which was not often, he looked so very young.

Tonight he had his shirt off and wore only his singlet because he had been with her. She smiled as she realised she was wearing the shirt he must have had on. Somehow it gave her a warm glow as she imagined him taking it off and carefully putting it on her to get her warm. They had been swimming so he would have had to remove her wet clothes. Cassie shook the silly thoughts from her mind, knowing he would never really care about her like that. *Maybe he just thought that I'd reward him with sex if he was nice enough to me.*

A sneak peek revealed his tattoos. One looked like Pegasus, the mythical flying horse, which didn't surprise her, seeing as he liked horses so much. He bent into the drawer to pick out a pair of tongs and his masculine body rippled as he moved. For a nice-looking man, he was sure angry towards women. *What a total waste! Oh well, not long now and he will be on his lonesome again.*

The sound of a motor disturbed Cassie's thoughts and she looked out the window and saw a four-wheel drive pulling up. Doors opened and closed. She heard a couple of voices: one was very familiar. They were joking around as they walked towards the house.

Kayden moved as quick as a flash at the sound of them. He threw a steak sandwich in front of her and shot her a look that told her to stay where she was as he went out to talk to them. Cassie ate quietly and when she finished she put the plate in the sink and went back into the bedroom.

Kayden must have taken them to see the new foal as it was quiet for some time. When they finally came into the house, she could tell they must have been drinking because there seemed to be a lot of staggering and slurring going on with the one she did not know. As the night progressed they started playing cards and taking shots, getting noisier and noisier. Cassie pulled the covers over her head.

As inexperienced with people as she was, she knew it wasn't right for a young lady to be in a house with drunken men.

She drifted off to sleep but woke as the door flung open. She saw Jason gawking at her and laughing. 'Kayden should have told me you were still here. Seem I rescued you, I reckon you owe me a kiss,' he said, lunging at her.

He flopped in a sitting position on the bed next to Cassie and lifted her to him. She tried to pull away from his drunken breath. He had a firm grip on her though and started to kiss her, muffling Cassie's calls for help with his lips. She pulled away, jumped off the bed and hit him across the face.

'Come on, girlie! What's your problem? I just want a kiss.' He got up and grabbed her again.

She yelled at him, 'I don't want to kiss you.' She called out to Kayden but he did not respond, making her so mad she shoved his friend up against the wall, smashing a stand, just about putting him through the plaster and brick partition.

She ran out, noticing Kayden was lying on the couch, passed out. She slapped his face for getting her into this position. Cross she had to show her evilness, used that which she suppressed. Now she would have to leave him. Leave this life she had grown to like so very much. He stirred and sat up. The other one also began to wake, hearing Jason moan. She fled and outside she heard Kayden cursing as he stomped in to see what she had done. *It's time for me to find other living arrangements*. Not only was she in a house full of men who drank and thought she was a spy or one of Mar Bakers ladies, but she had just hurt his friend. Cassie bolted out the door and kept on running. Somehow she ended up on the track that led to the horses. At least there was water there and she could freshen up and get a drink before she found her way back to the highway.

It took a while but she finally made it. The big one with the sore hoof was lying on the ground and didn't move when she went near him, so she curled up against him and cried herself to sleep.

* * * *

It was daybreak when Cassie woke to the sound of an engine and froze as the horse stood up and left her exposed. She darted over to the river, tried to cross the slimy rock surface and slipped, cutting her foot and squealing out in pain. She kept moving until reaching the other side and then ran again. She was just about to look behind to see if she'd been cunning enough to get away when hands grabbed her roughly and swung her up into a pair of arms.

'What the hell are you playing at? Stop struggling or I swear I will tie you up.'

Cassie realised that Kayden was holding her and the fear subsided. She stopped fighting to escape as he carried her back over the creek. At the truck he grabbed a bag from inside the cab, sat her on the back and patched up her foot. He was very gentle and careful with her and Cassie calmed down and started to breathe normally again. When he had finished, he lifted her chin and put some cream on her split lip she got when fighting Jason off.

Her face felt puffy and tear-stained but she didn't care anymore. He had passed out allowing his friend to do as he wished. Her eyes filled up with anger at him. 'I was calling for you. You shouldn't have got so plastered that you couldn't look after me.' she hissed.

'I am not your carer, Cassie. Someone like you should know what to expect if you want to stay in a house full of men.'

'What do you mean someone like me? I've never even been around men. How was I to know what to expect?'

Kayden sucked in a breath and sighed. 'How old are you?'

'Nineteen. Why?' she asked.

He seemed angry but controlled his voice. 'You seem very young for your age and the way you look. You're telling me that you've never had a serious relationship?'

'None.' She shook her head, feeling miserable and upset. 'But that doesn't mean I'm stupid and don't know what feels wrong.'

'Maybe you should realise that the grass is not greener on the other side and whatever happened or what tiff maybe you had with your folks you should suck it up and go home. How long have you been around this area for?'

'Since the day you found me. I was just kind of left.'

He looked at her sharply. 'What do you mean, left?'

'Near where you found me. My parents sent me away. I'm a very bad person.'

'You're lying. Stop it. Tell me the truth,' he cautioned her.

She choked back tears, outraged and indignant. She lifted her chin, squaring her shoulders and trying to control her voice. 'I'm not fibbing. I heard my parents say they wanted me gone permanently. Next thing I know I woke up in an aluminium container of some sort, my lack of memory making it obvious they had drugged me. I travelled for a couple days by plane and afterwards by car. The container is there, near where you found me. I'm not a liar!' She watched his disbelieving glare with tears streaming down her face. 'They hated me, like you do now—and your friend does—and I don't know why you do! I've done nothing to you except be useless at taking care of myself.' She jumped off the back of the truck in frustration, wincing at the pain in her foot. 'Ow!' she squeaked, holding both hands to her reddened cheeks. She plopped on the ground, rocking back and forth, nursing her foot and her hurt pride.

'You must know your story is bizarre and totally unbelievable.' He put up his hands in a frustrated motion. 'However, I'm inclined to give you the benefit of the doubt and check out your story. But trust me when I say that if there is no container, Cassie, and this is just to get my sympathy ...' Kayden didn't finish. He just picked Cassie up and put her in the car. They drove back in silence. Cassie became nervous when she saw that the other car was still out the front. She held her breath and started to shake, not wanting to go inside.

Kayden could feel her fear and growled, 'It's okay. I won't let him touch you. Just settle down. Do I have to treat you entirely like a damned child? You act like you're bloody ten years old.' He picked her up, annoyed again, and she wrapped her arms around his neck, not letting him go. She didn't care how cross he was; he was safer than the others were. He laid her on the bed and pried her arms from around his neck. He shook his head. 'I still doubt your wild story, Cassie. However, if you're telling me the truth and want my help, you will stay here until I get back. If you're a liar, maybe it's best if you were gone when I return,' he said and left her.

She heard him talking, the noise of car doors opening and closing and the engine of the car starting up, after that silence. Cassie was glad they were all gone and now alone, hobbled to the bathroom to freshen up. She knew he told her to stay in the room but she smelt like the horse and needed a shower. Finding another shirt in the wardrobe, she put it on and lay back on the bed. Her foot was sore so she took his advice and decided to stay off it.

It was some time before she heard the car pull up again. Only one door opened and one set of footsteps came inside as the car drove off. Cassie could hear Kayden pacing in the sitting room and knew he must have found she wasn't lying and was wondering what to do with her now. She was just about to get up when he opened the door and came in. You could have fried an egg on his face; it looked so hot and red. He seemed a little calmer as he changed the dressing on her foot.

'I told you not to move. You've opened it up again.'

'I had to go to the bathroom. While I was in there I showered as well,' she said bravely.

'I noticed you've cleaned up. You smelt like a horse when I brought you home,' he joked.

Cassie giggled and he smiled back and kept fixing her foot. It was the first time he had even attempted humour and it was refreshing to see him actually smile at her. His face was so handsome when he did.

He didn't speak for the rest of the day; he just lifted her wherever he wanted her to be while he worked through his jobs. They checked on the new foal and fixed a couple of fences before cleaning the stables. He was a hard worker and never seemed to stop. Cassie understood that he was so used to being on his own that having her around must have been why he seemed so frustrated. He was just a loner and happier to be by himself.

That evening they sat on the porch drinking coffee while they watched the sunset. Listening to the night creatures as darkness came made Cassie brim over with questions. The sounds filling the air were foreign to her. She questioned Kayden and he told her what they were. It was the first time they had really had a conversation that was more than simple politeness and it was nice just to listen to his honey-smooth voice that made her feel warm all over. When he was being just like that she could listen to him forever. He picked out the sounds for her and not only named the insects that made them but also gave her a description of their colours and shapes.

'Your country is very different from what I have ever known.' She turned and looked at him curiously. 'Where am I? What country is this?' Kayden seemed to get annoyed again and Cassie reacted by cringing away. 'Don't worry, I don't need to know.'

It was a long time before Kayden answered. 'You really don't know?' he asked.

Cassie lowered her eyes and felt stupid for having to ask. 'I saw a sign when I first arrived that said Newman or Perth. I wasn't very good at geography and those places don't ring a bell.'

'You're on a farm a little way out of Mt Newman in Western Australia.'

'Australia!' Cassie was wide-eyed and shocked. 'Kangaroos and koalas Australia?' she asked, not quite believing what he was saying. 'Why would they send me so far?' Hot tears streamed out of her eyes now she knew that there was definitely no going home. 'They sent me down under.' She stood up and paced. 'And probably hoped the desert or the crocodiles would get me. They really wanted me dead!' Cassie stopped moving as the impact of where she was shattered the last bit of hope she had left. She flopped back onto the seat next to Kayden, wondering if panic attacks could kill because right at that moment, her heart was racing like a freight train, almost too fast to breathe.

Kayden slid his arm around her. 'You are very convincing but your story is so unbelievable. How could someone do that to their own? Are you sure, Cassie, that you haven't just run from a bad experience and are trying to get shelter? I promise if you tell me I will help you. I just need to know the truth.'

Cassie shook his arm off and pulled away. 'Kayden, I repeat: I am not a liar and I do not need your help,' she fumed. 'I'm better now so let me make your life a lot easier and relieve your conscience. I'm not scared to go it alone nor do I need a babysitter anymore. This is my new life now, not yours. I'll make it just fine on my own. I'll head off to that Newman town tomorrow and that'll be the end of it. Now go away and leave me alone. I hate them and I hate you,' she sobbed and turned from him, wishing she never had to talk to him again.

Kayden sat for a minute, before getting up and walking back inside the house, closing the door. Cassie hated her family for what they had done to her and now she hated him. He had never believed a word she'd said and right then she didn't care. I'm really on my own and I'll show them all I can make it, she thought as she finally went to bed. She punched the pillow before cuddling it.

It was late in the night when a big crash woke her. It was so loud she jumped out of bed and stood frozen to the spot. There was another loud grumble and a shrieking crack that lit up the room. That one had her moving and she ran out of her room and flung open Kayden's bedroom door. She stood there, breathing fast and hard.

He sat up, looking concerned and sleepy and rubbing his eyes.

Cassie whispered, 'What's that noise?'

As she said it, the house shuddered with another loud crack. She flew over and jumped at him, wrapping herself around him and trembling, waiting for the roof to come down around them. He lay back down with Cassie still clinging to him like a vine to a tree. 'It's just an electric storm. Don't you have them where you come from?'

Cassie shook her head and clung to him as the sky crackled again.

'Shh. Go back to sleep. It won't hurt you, silly,' he said, a bit jovial but sleepy.

He relaxed and breathed heavily, letting her know he'd gone back to sleep. Every time the noises cracked, they shot through her and there was no way she could sleep. She clung on to Kayden, not releasing her grip until the noises quietened down. It was only after she settled that she realised he was stroking her hair which helped her to doze off.

When Cassie woke up much later she was on her own. She sat up, remembering the storm and feeling silly about being scared. She scrambled out of his big bed and looked for him. He was having a coffee and reading the paper. She looked at him a bit shyly. 'Sorry about last night and the whole storm thing,' she said, embarrassed, as she slipped into the bathroom.

'Watch that foot. Don't press on it too hard,' he cautioned and she hopped the extra few steps to prevent it opening up again.

Cassie came out of the shower to find he had fried a couple of eggs for her. She ate while he cleaned up his plate of food and finished reading the paper. He said he had already gone out to the paddocks and she felt sad that she'd missed seeing the foal this morning. It was her last morning here and she would have liked to say goodbye. Kayden was most likely wanting to get his rounds out of the way early so they could leave directly after breakfast. She suddenly regretted saying she hated him and was leaving.

Chapter Two
Truth Unfolds

Kayden put his plate down and lifted her onto the table. She flicked the suds on her fingers at him. He grinned and after taking the oversized bandage from her foot, said that it looked good and today she just needed a band-aid. After putting a plaster on, he slid her off the bench. They heard a car pull up and Jason walked in with a box. He had a black eye and Cassie shrank into Kayden as he came closer.

'My sister packed up some of her old clothes for Cassie to wear and she also put some girl stuff in there for her.'

Kayden laughed. 'Nice shiner. Sorry about that.'

'I deserved it.' Jason glanced at Cassie. 'Now she's in the light and I'm sober I can see she really is just a little cutie.' He grinned. 'We thought you were … it doesn't matter, I just came to apologise.'

Jason didn't seem like the scary person she'd thought he was at all. In fact, now he was being nice she could see it was all one big misunderstanding. 'Sorry for throwing you against the wall. I guess we're even, hey?'

'And about that, how did someone as fragile-looking as you manage to throw ninety-five kilos across the room?' Jason asked.

Cassie put her head down and knew they had probably guessed her secret. Nervously, she glanced up at Kayden, trying to judge what he was thinking. His face gave nothing away.

'I told you I was really bad,' Cassie choked out, upset, and strode to her room to figure out what to say next. They wanted an explanation and what was she meant to say? 'Sorry, guys, I'm a freak of nature'? She started to close the door behind her but Kayden followed her straight in.

'Stop running, Cassandra and tell me what's going on. I can't help you if you keep hiding secrets from me.'

'I've been telling you the truth but you never believe me. I'm bad, Kayden. There's a power in me that will come out if people try to harm me. That's why they sent me away. My dad says I'm evil and I promised myself I wouldn't use it here. I tried not to but ...' Cassie stopped, breathed heavily and whispered, 'I have never been kissed before and it felt yuck ... and he touched my breast.' She blushed brightly at the thought.

Kayden looked at her, surprised. 'You're joking. I can maybe believe you've never been in a relationship before but to tell me at nineteen you've never been kissed, come on, Cass. That's a bit much to swallow for even one as gullible as I am where you are concerned.'

Cassie sighed. She hated how he questioned everything, believing only things that had solid proof. Well, maybe she liked it too. He was no pushover and as frustrating as that was she pushed on. She had to start trusting someone and Kayden was definitely someone she was starting to trust. 'All my life I've been kept a prisoner in my parents' home to prevent others from finding out my secret. My family are, let's say, very wealthy and high in status with the community. I was their freak daughter who they hid from their social world. My only contact ever with a male was with the gardener and chauffeur although I was never allowed out of my room to talk to them. I just watched through my window. Honest to God, you are the first man that I've ever been game enough to talk to. I would be in so much trouble right now if we were at my home.' She sucked in a long breath and let it out. 'I do try so hard not to use the evil in me but it just happens when I get angry. I thought I could control it but I felt scared. I'm so sorry.'

Kayden's eyes went dark again and his expression was frozen. He looked like he was going to explode.

Cassie panicked. 'Please don't hurt me. I won't ever bother you again. Just take me to that town. On the other hand, I can walk if you prefer. Please don't do what they did to me. I'll find somewhere to live on my own so that nobody will ever get hurt again. Please, just give me a chance to prove I can change.' Tears ran down her face. She was petrified, imagining what he might do to her.

Kayden sat with his head down. He was clenching his fists so hard she saw his knuckles turn white. He relaxed them. He had not restrained her yet so she took the silence and calmed conditions to mean he was letting her go. She stood up nervously to leave, only to feel his hand slip into hers gently and pull her back down.

'Cassie, stay with me a while and talk to me, please.'

Cassie sat with a gesture of agreement. 'You're not mad at me, then?'

He shook his head. 'Not at you, Cass.'

He immediately put her at ease. Cassie had never had anyone ask her to talk before, only ever been talked at. She suddenly realised what it must feel like to have a friend, to have someone who wouldn't just yell, stomp off and ignore her, but wanted to know more about her. It was unsettling but nice.

'Why didn't you use your protective power on me when I hosed you and was mean to you?'

'I don't know. I was scared but I knew somehow that you were only angry with me, not out to harm me. Although, now you know the truth, I'm not so sure. Other signals from you are confusing me,' she said honestly.

'I'm hardly going to hurt you for doing what comes naturally to you, Cassie.' He pulled out a hanky and passed it to her. 'Why, if you are from overseas, haven't you a stronger accent? You speak as if you have been living here for years.'

She dried her eyes and sniffled into the hanky he gave her. 'My nanny was an Aussie and was the only one who was ever kind to me or even talked to me. Everybody loved her and I tried to model myself around her so that others might like me too. That's how I knew about the outback and kangaroos, because she would sometimes sneak me into the garden and tell me stories of your land.'

'What's your surname?' His eyebrows curved questioningly.

His question made her catch her breath and she talked quietly. 'They want me dead. Please don't send me back.' She started to freak out.

'Settle down!' he growled. 'Cassie, here in Australia, once you are eighteen you are old enough to make your own decisions on where you live. Nobody can send you anywhere you don't want to be now that you're nineteen. If I can trust you enough, girl, to listen to your unusual tale without chucking you out on your ear, the least you can do is start trusting me in return.'

Kayden was right. *He could have tossed me out days ago.* She screwed the hanky up in her lap timidly. 'Wyatt—Cassandra Wyatt. My parents are connected to royalty and live in a castle in England.' she said, shaking, hardly able to put her thoughts into words.

Kayden had a serious expression: his eyes locked onto hers and his forehead creased with concern. 'I know you're scared but if these people did that to you it's not only illegal and wrong, but immoral. You must trust me and that means doing as I ask.'

Cassie slowly nodded. 'Okay. I want to trust you but what are you going to do?'

'Firstly, I'm going to verify your identity as you have no papers. After that Jason and I are just going to do some research to see if they've filed a missing persons report in case the authorities are involved. We will need to cover any tracks if they have.' He stood up, his height looming over her. 'In the meantime, just in case you are being watched, I don't want you to go anywhere, even to answer the door. Don't make me tie you to this bed, Cassie because I need you safe until I can get to the bottom of this. If you want my help you'll do as I say. Do you understand, Cassie? Am I making myself clear?'

She shivered at his livid tone of voice although she felt it was not so much directed at her as it was about her. She was hardly going to disobey him. She had nowhere else to go and he was right: she had no papers and was here illegally. She really did need his help. Cassie just hoped she hadn't put Kayden in danger by staying with him.

What if the kidnappers come back to retrieve my dead body and follow my trail here? Although, somehow guessed that Kayden being so astute, would have already thought of all those things. Long before she had, as if he was used to handling such matters. Well, the way Cassie saw it, for now this home of his felt safe and so did he. Especially now that Jason had apologised and was treating her like a lady and friend now. Not a spy or whatever else he had her pegged for.

'I promise,' she said, leaving her fate in his hands. Looking at them, she could tell they were very strong and capable hands at that.

Kayden held Cassie's shoulders and made her look up at him. 'If you run from me again, Cassie, unlike them, I'll be able to find you and trust me: I will not be so kind next time.'

Feeling tough and confident for the first time ever, she shrugged off his hands. 'Okay, I get it. I'm in big trouble with authorities if I'm found here without a visa. I trust you, Kayden but if you let me down I swear I'll fight you and anyone else who tries to stop me having this freedom that I've grown to love. I promise that whatever this thing is in me it will come out to play.'

Amusement spread across his face. 'Just stay put, girl. Nobody is going to take your freedom ever again. Not if I have anything to do with it.'

Cassie heard him talking to Jason before they sped off in the car. She lay back on the bed, trying not to fear what might lie ahead. A big part of her had started to trust Kayden. She had to give him a chance. Cassie had finally had a taste of something real in the last few days and for once in her life she finally wanted to live, to explore this new land with or without this stranger she had just met.

Smiling, she stood up, happy for the first time ever. 'I really want to live,' she giggled. Her mind drifted to the foal and the birth: watching it, Cassie had felt like she was being reborn too and the feeling exhilarated her. She felt excited and even though had promised to stay put the feeling to share her joy was too strong. Cassie wanted to see the foal, feel its soft coat, smell its newness and run with it; yes, run with the foal.

Finding some old gumboots to keep the wound on her foot from getting dirty, she forgot about her pledge to Kayden about leaving the house. As her wild abandonment at this new life overtook her she trudged off down the dirt track towards the horses. When she made it to them they were all drinking from the stream except for the big one she had slept beside. It came up and nudged her for a pat.

It looks like I've made a friend. Cassie smiled cheerfully.

He followed her over to the little foal that she bent down to cuddle. She could smell his baby milky breath and feel his soft curly fur against her cheek. He was so sweet and not at all wobbly now. He was frisky and jumped around her as if he wanted to play. He nudged Cassie before he galloped off so she playfully ran after him, laughing as he spun around and came back at her. She laughed and rolled on the ground as he knocked her over. 'You'll cop it now,' she stood and hugged him, feeling the happiest she'd ever felt.

She heard a noise and spun around. Kayden was standing behind her, looking annoyed but also with a grin in his eyes. 'I told you to stay! What part of that did you not understand?'

'I put on boots so my foot didn't get dirty.' She stuck her foot up in the air.

'I can see that. I'm not sure if they go with my T-shirt that you're wearing as a dress. Couldn't you find anything in the box Jason brought over?'

Cassie cocked her head to the side. Does that mean he cares what I look like? She thought eyeing him curiously, feeling strange warmth radiating from him. She grinned. 'I've never had to dress myself before. My minders always did that. Maybe you could show me how you prefer me to look. I would be most happy to please you.' She smiled and curtsied teasingly.

He shook his head. 'That last sentence is definably something a princess would say, only I'm not someone you have to impress. Now, tell me why you were out here. What was your plan? To steal one of my horses and run?'

Cassie was surprised he would think she had come to take one of his horses and put her hands on her hips, indignant at his accusation. 'I don't know how to ride a horse, silly! The baby one made me disobey you. He beckoned me with his cuteness. I just wanted to touch his hair and smell his newness. I wasn't running, you big bully,' she answered with attitude and a sense of humour to lighten the fact that she had been thoughtless in her actions and was trying to cover it with a bit of wit. She dropped her arms and grinned.

'Don't get cheeky with me, young lady!' Kayden stomped over to her, picked her up as if she were a lightweight and put her up on his big horse before jumping up behind her. His movement was so quick she barely had time to take a breath. He held on to her and her hands tightened around his arms as the horse moved forward and trotted towards the house. It was a weird feeling. However, the more she relaxed back into Kayden's frame, the more the horse's rhythm became bearable and she began to feel comfortable.

He felt her ease and loosened his grip around her waist. Closer to the house he asked if she wanted to go a bit faster and she sat up, shaking her head. He laughed cunningly. 'I have you.' He pushed the horse into a gallop.

She felt so fragile, sitting on the horse as if she was going to go flying off. After a little while that also became easier. She enjoyed the wind on her face and the freedom of going somewhere quickly without the restraints of a shell around her, as there was when travelling in a car. He pulled the horse up, held her around the waist and slid them both off before sending the horse back to the paddock. Cassie was still laughing when they went inside to where Jason sat with a laptop, staring at her.

'Yep, it's her alright.' He swung it around for Kayden to see her picture. 'To save face, her parents have posted the picture for anyone knowing her whereabouts but it can only be viewed from their country. They haven't gone worldwide with it so Australian authorities would never know who she is or even that she's disappeared.'

Jason looked at the picture of her parents and the castle from which she had disappeared. Cassie felt the room spin and Kayden's arms go around her. He sat in the recliner with her, stroking her head whilst talking quietly to Jason. Cassie felt warm and comfortable and Kayden's attentiveness made her feel better. She finally sighed heavily, releasing the thoughts of home and smiling at the gentle soul holding her.

'That's the way, princess. The past is behind you now. Let it go.'

Cassie nodded. He stood up, placing her gently back in the chair. 'You need to eat. It's getting late. Come on, Jason. You can give me a hand while our princess rests up a bit more.'

'Oh alright,' Jason griped. Glancing at Cassie, he winked. 'If I have to!' he continued his playful objection.

Cassie quietly contemplated her future with Kayden. They knew she was a princess and it looked as if they were going to let her stay. She decided she could to learn to cook and take care of them; earn her keep that way. Unable to see past today and pleased that she still had a roof over her head she figured she could relax here for a while until she decided what to do next. No good over-thinking your situation, girl, she told herself as she glanced towards the men.

'Is there time for a shower?' she asked, a little embarrassed that she was too useless to help with something as simple as getting a meal ready. *How long will they put up with me if I'm unable to do even the basics?* She felt annoyed for being so useless. It had never occurred to her that one day she would need domestic skills. A princess in her land never needed such capabilities. When they were on their own she would ask if Kayden would teach her. Kayden's voice interrupted her thoughts.

'Wait,' he said, rustling around in the box of clothes Jason had brought in and pulling out a dress and some matching underwear. 'Try these.'

Cassie shyly took them. *Boy, how embarrassing to have clothes chosen for me in front of Jason.* Still, she had asked Kayden to tell her how he wanted to see her dress. As much as she appreciated his help, in front of the guest it was a little humiliating. Swallowing her pride, she smiled politely and almost ran towards the bathroom to hide the crimson that crept into her cheeks. The hot water streamed over her and the heat washed away her trivial cares. Light-heartedness sent another wave of emotion over her as she remembered how Kayden had told her that she was old enough to live wherever she wanted.

Overwhelming joy surged through her knowing that she never again had to return to her homeland or to her horrid parents.

Cassie's feet barely felt the floor she was so delighted. Everything was now out in the open. They'd accepted her for who she was. Putting on the new underwear and frilly pastel-coloured dress, she decided it was maybe a little too snug. However, it did show up her shapely figure and as she spun around she admired the cut of the skirt, watching it spin out as she twirled in front of the mirror. Brushing her hair, she clipped it up and was amazed at what a difference the small amount of fresh air had made to her complexion. The pasty look was gone, replaced with a slight tan and colour in her cheeks as if she had just applied foundation and blush. She threw her dirty clothes into the basket and made a note to ask Kayden how to use the washing machine in the morning. She opened the door and both of them turned and seemed to freeze.

'What?' Cassie looked down and second-guessed what she had on.

Kayden coughed. 'Looks fine, we just haven't seen you dressed up before. It's just a boy thing.' He turned around grinning and continued cooking.

Jason nudged him. 'Never looked that good on sis.'

Cassie shrugged and walked to the kitchen. Being around men was a challenge. She now understood the reasoning for the title of the book she had seen advertised once stating that men were from Mars. *Maybe I should have read it.* She grinned to herself. 'Want some help?' she asked.

Kayden took her hand and steered her back to the table. 'You just sit way over here until Jason's hormones settle down,' he laughed.

Cassie cocked her head to the side and wondered if she would ever understand the way they talked. She had no idea what she had to do with Jason's hormones and didn't want to embarrass herself further by asking a question that she should probably know the answer to at her age. Yes, she thought, and girls my age raised under normal circumstances, would talk and giggle together and go to real schools and would know all about men by now. She sighed. *How uneducated I feel.*

Cassie eyed Jason as he chatted to Kayden in the kitchen, allowing his charismatic nature to shine through. His age was hard to pick. His fair hair was long, yet shaped, framing his face perfectly. He was clean-shaven and his fair skin was flawless as if he were no older than his early twenties, yet his stunning blue eyes showed her that like Kayden he was an old soul and had been around for a long time. Her eyes were drawn to his male shape that was buffed and toned. With such good looks she wondered if he did any modelling although he hardly looked the type to strut his stuff in front of a crowd. She smiled at the thought.

So many questions I have. Yet if I ask, will they want more from me in return? Cassie decided that time would reveal all. Tonight was not a time to dredge up old lives, but the beginning of a new era, with new memories to make, far more memorable than those left behind.

Kayden and Jason brought dinner over and during the meal, Jason was so nice to Cassie that she hardly remembered what he had been like in his tanked-up state. She finally felt as if fate had played a part in finding these two men who seemed to like her. Listening to them made her heart feel at peace. She was filled with gratitude as they included her in every topic as if they were actually interested in what she had to say.

'Hey K, we should take the princess for a ride up to the Wittenoom gorges tomorrow. What do you reckon, man? She'd love it if she hasn't been outdoors before.'

Kayden shook his head. 'She still needs a couple of day's total rest.'

Jason's face lit up and the smile he directed at Cassie was stunning. 'Hey, if it's the foot you're worried about, K, I can carry her easily. Problem solved.'

If Cassie were aware of the impact she was having on him she would have blushed at his blatant advances. However, Cassie's natural innocence left her merely flattered that he was being so sweet.

Kayden however, was no fool. He frowned at Jason's sneaky offer and seeing that Cassie was unaware of his mate's undertone, intervened. 'She's been pretty banged up, Jase. Her bruises are getting better; it's the head wound that's worrying me. Until she stops getting dizzy and passing out on me she goes nowhere.'

'What bruising?'

Kayden motioned for Cassie to show him, noting her timid look. 'It's okay, Cassie. Believe me; Jason is very familiar with injuries. I want him to look at your head too, just to make sure you're healing alright. My forte is horses. A second opinion will ease my mind.'

Jason checked her head and she felt him running his fingers lightly over the area and along the cut that was healing but still tender to his touch. 'The cuts healed but there's still is a lot of swelling. Maybe she should still be lying down.'

Cassie shook her head slowly. 'No way, I've spent my whole life in the bedroom. Kayden said if I take it easy I can move around, just so long as I lay down if I start feeling tired. He's been taking really good care of me.' She smiled at Kayden, who winked back at her.

'Okay, but if you want my advice I'd recommend total bed rest. But that is if I was here looking after you.' He chuckled and Kayden shook his head, keeping his eyes on Jason with a look that made him quit mucking around and finish the examination. He checked the bruising on her thighs and freaked out. 'You should have told me we hit her, K. You poor little thing,' he said, sitting back down. 'You're damned well black and blue. Christ, I must have really hurt you when I jumped on you the other night. No wonder you screamed.'

Kayden raked his hand roughly through his hair. 'It wasn't just from that, idiot. Our princess had never been … um … kissed either. Sorry, Cassie but he needs to know. Didn't you feel her?' All of a sudden he sounded grumpy.

Jason looked at Cassie with regret, before turning to Kayden with a puckered brow. 'In my defence I was smashed and come to think of it, yes she did freak out when I French kissed her. I thought she was having me on. Anyway, I have already apologised to her. Stop trying to make me feel worse.' He looked back at Cassie. 'You forgive me, hey princess?' He slid off his chair and knelt on the floor, holding her hand between his in a begging gesture.

Cassie touched his face with her free hand and smiled sweetly. 'Jase, it's okay, let's just put it in the past. I looked a mess when you found me. It's perfectly understandable you would have considered me to be of a feral nature. Please believe me when I say many of my bruises are from my trip here and the rough handling. I think they forgot to put, "Handle with care" on the outside of the crate and instead it said, "We will pay you double to throw this one around".' She giggled, trying to lighten the moment and not wanting the subject to ruin a perfectly enjoyable night.

Jason's eyes softened. 'We've been so cruel to you, thinking you were just a plant sent in to spy on our group. This has happened to us a few times before and I'm afraid you've borne the brunt of other liars who came before you. I hope you can forgive us,' he said sincerely.

'Group?' Cassie asked, confused.

Kayden cut in. 'Later. Let's just enjoy a truce and talk about details another day.'

Jason kissed the back of her hand, treating her like a true lady and showing her how he felt about her now. It was a nice gesture and Cassie giggled at his smooth charm. Glancing back at Kayden, she could see in his eyes that he wasn't completely sure about trusting her yet.

Chapter Three

Entertaining Companions

Cassie had been on Kayden's farm for a couple of months. All of her bruising had gone and she felt happier than she had ever thought possible. She was even learning how to cook although Kayden only let her do the easy parts, like stirring the pots and helping him roll out the dough for bread rolls and so forth. Mostly she sat at the bench and her job was to chat and keep him amused while he prepared the meals. Kayden still grumbled about having to do everything for her even though Cassie knew he actually enjoyed taking care of her more than he let on. When he took over a chore that she could barely get her head around or when she made a fuss of his male ease at doing it, his face would break out into the cutest smile.

Cleaning the house was the only chore he left her to learn on her own. She was fascinated that even after so many months there was still one monster that hid in the laundry and refused to work with her. The dreaded washing machine! As she told Kayden, it seemed to have a vendetta against her. He just laughed when she told him that it had big teeth that snarled at her and kept eating the washing.

Much of their time on the property they spent outdoors, like today. It'd been a nice day. Kayden had taken Cassie for a ride on his horse, Zoltan, for a couple of hours. They stopped near a lovely stream that flowed with fresh, cold water so the stallion could have a drink. Kayden left Zoltan by the water's edge and walked Cassie over to a log to sit and enjoy the view. They both laughed at Zoltan who seemed to be making a big deal about how to get close enough to drink without getting his hooves muddy. Finally, he drank the water and settled down. Kayden had only just begun to broach the subject of Cassie's unusual gift when a sound by the river stopped him in mid-sentence. Both swung their heads toward the noise.

A pack of wild dogs had advanced on Zoltan while he drank. They were creeping up and around him, poised and ready to attack. A large, black, longhaired mutt came from behind a bush and snarled. With the pack leader making his move, the others closed in on Zoltan. Frightened, the steed made a loud noise and reared up, thrashing his hooves in their direction. Kayden had already jumped up and let out a call to scare the dogs and at the same time, ran towards Zoltan.

Cassie's senses came alive with the danger. Without thinking she threw up her hands aiming them towards the pack. The impact of the power she sent towards the snarling animals hit them like bricks, hurling them backwards, slamming them into the trees and bushes over the other side of the stream.

They made yelping, painful sounds, leaving her feeling bad as they scurried off. The ones on the other side of Zoltan ran from the fear that they felt from the rest of the pack's agonising howls.

Kayden already at his horse and Cassie noted his speed was so much faster than a normal human's or maybe in the confusion it just seemed that way because she was shocked. She had gone and used her power again when she knew it was bad to do so. Yet as it did prevent the attack, she thought Kayden might not be too cross with her.

Cassie was shaking and rocking, waiting for the punishment she usually received from her parents for using the curse she had been born with. Instead, Kayden shocked her by picking her up and swinging her around. 'You little powerhouse! Remind me never to stir you up and get you angry at me.'

'You're not mad?' Cassie felt stunned by his reaction.

'Mad? I've been waiting to see what you could do and I was starting to think your altercation with Jason was a fluke. That was excellent!' Kayden hugged her before hoisting her back onto his horse. 'Let's get Zoltan out of here before the mutts come back,' he said, still excited at what he had just witnessed.

Cassie was still dumbstruck. Kayden's reaction was not what she would have expected. She had grown up feeling ashamed of her powers and knew the use of them was forbidden. Yet amazingly enough he wanted her to use them and had actually been waiting patiently to see what she could do.

Kayden's voice interrupted the thought she was reaching that maybe there were others like her that he knew of; that in this country her curse was normal. 'Can you use your gift at will or only to defend yourself when you feel threatened?'

She shrugged, not used to talking about it so casually. 'I have no idea. I was a child last time I tried.'

They stopped again a little further up the track.

'This spot should do it.' Kayden helped her off Zoltan.

He chose a spot where soft grass and pretty pink and white wildflowers carpeted the ground. Pulling off his backpack and laid out drinks and snacks for them, chatting as he organised their food. He could see how freaked out she was so made an effort to make her feel comfortable about what she had just done.

It was working. As they ate Cassie told him how she had feared using her 'gift', as he kept calling it and how for years it had only brought shame on her folks and given her nothing but grief.

'You should be proud of who you are, Cassie. Talents such as your's should never be squashed.'

She smiled. 'You're the first person who hasn't hated me for what I just did.'

'That's because you lived with people who obviously had no idea how special you really are, girl.'

Cassie giggled. 'I think you're just being kind,' she said before looking more seriously at him, remembering. 'You understand because you are a bit like me. Am I correct, Kayden? I just saw how fast you moved to get to Zoltan.'

He nodded. 'Yes, I too have gifts but yours absolutely fascinate me.' He took a swig of his drink and pointed. 'See that old tree over there? It needs chopping down. Can you knock it down?' he asked.

She thought about the tree, put her hand up and nothing happened. 'Nope, looks like you're just going to have to use an axe,' she chuckled.

Kayden shook his head, amused, and cupped her face in his hands. 'Cassie, concentrate and think of someone or something that makes you angry.' He urged her on, removing his hands and pushing her hair back from her face so he could watch.

Cassie thought about home and how her parents made her angry. She could suddenly feel her insides power up. This time when she threw her hands at the tree it was with emotions deep within her and the tree shattered into sawdust that floated through the air and settled around them. She sat up straight, shocked that she could direct it so well.

Kayden kissed her hands. His eyes and voice filled with emotion. 'You're so valuable. I can't believe you just walked into my life and that you've been happy to stay.'

Cassie smiled at him as his eyes sparkled. His gaze, behind those long lashes, captivated her with secret thoughts. In some kind of trance she felt a magnetic pull towards him as if he was linking them together somehow. She could feel, just for an instant, every emotion he was feeling and by the look on his face she felt sure that he was also feeling her.

Did I really feel his strong feelings for me or did I just imagine it? Cassie felt bewildered as Kayden stood and started packing up the remains of the picnic lunch, closing off from her and acting as if the exchange had never happened. *I guess if he did, we would be still here in each other's arms.* Feeling a bit young and stupid for wishing they would be together, she sucked it up. If he was only ever going to look upon her as a friend, Cassie intended to be the best one he ever had.

A funny thought struck her. Maybe he was worried that she might zap him like she did to Jason. *My thinking is probably way off. As if a strong male like him would be scared of a pint-size girl like me.* Followed by an even worse thought. *What if I am just that to him? A girl, a princess, too young and not womanly enough for him?*

When they arrived home after their ride they saw that Jason had come for a visit and had been waiting at the house for their return. 'I've come to ask the princess if she'll accompany me to town on a dinner date,' he said, smiling sweetly.

'Whatever saves me from looking after her.' Kayden's mood changed. He became aggravated and impatient with them both and dismissed them as if he had put up with enough. He practically pushed them out the door together.

Cassie was so surprised at Kayden's reaction. The final hope that there would be more to their friendship crashed around her. The fact that there had been no protest and he hadn't cared about her being in the company of another man at all got her dander up so she swallowed her hurt pride and went with Jason. He was charming as always and chatted all the way into town. He had become a good friend and it wasn't long before he'd eased her anguish about Kayden and they started to enjoy themselves.

As much as Cassie adored Jason, he was not Kayden and many times during the night a little part of her strayed, wishing it was Kayden she was on a date with. How mean and insensitive is that? she thought pushing it to the back of her mind and concentrating on Jason again, becoming attentive for as long as her brain would allow before diverting again.

They had a banquet of different flavoured foods that Jason made her try. She loved the way he constantly made the effort to educate her in Aussie culture to help her fit in. He told her silly jokes that made her laugh through most of the courses so she ate heartily without complaining about everything she put to her lips.

After dinner he held her hand and walked with her through the streets, showing her the different styles of double-brick housing in those parts and how they were fully air-conditioned to handle the rugged and harsh West Australian heat waves which were common up north and explaining how the strong-framed houses are constructed to hopefully withstand the cyclonic months where rain, floods and terrible winds ravage the landscape.

When they arrived home, Jason said that he had enjoyed himself and kissed her cheek, thanking her for the lovely night. He was a prince among princes but he was not Kayden and Cassie felt bad that she hadn't felt anything more than friendship as he held her hand and kissed her goodnight.

Kayden was in bed. Not wanting to wake him, Cassie tried to undress in the darkness of her room and jumped straight into bed. Kayden heard her and stomped to her room, pushing the door open. Cassie sat up and saw his heated look.

'If you're going to go out until all hours the least you can do is be courteous and keep it down. Next time do your damned kissing and canoodling in the car, not on my front porch,' he said, gnashing his teeth and stomping back into his room.

Kayden had riled her up, provoking her to stomp irritably into his room. 'He kissed my cheek, mister! Don't think I'm one of your horses you can farm out to your friends for entertainment just to give you a break. Next time you don't want me around, say so! I will gladly prefer to sleep in the barn for the night.' She scampered back to her room in a huff and threw the blankets over her head, feeling just as moody as he was.

* * * *

Cassie woke up early. The light was not yet peeking over the horizon. She rolled over and moaned. *God, what a nasty piece of work I was last night.* The way she had retaliated towards Kayden was childish and uncalled-for. *It is his house and I should have more respect. No way does he bring girls here and flaunt them in my face.* She knew she could be so damned hot-headed sometimes.

Feeling bad that they were fighting, she sneaked into his room. It wasn't the first time she'd gone to him to apologise and she felt a little nervous in case he might reject her. After all, she had upset him. Sliding under the covers, she hugged him remorsefully.

'Sorry,' she whispered and was so glad he pulled her closer and hugged her back.

'I've been waiting for you, little one. Thanks for forgiving me,' he whispered.

Contented to have their friendship again, they fell straight back to sleep.

When Cassie woke, still embraced in Kayden's warm arms, the sun was pouring through the window. He must have felt her wiggle, preparing to get up and readjusted his hold. It felt so warm and natural that she settled back into his arms with a sigh.

'Don't go,' he said in a husky voice.

His lips found hers. The kiss was so soft and tender that Cassie thought she was going to pass out from the sweetness of his mouth. Her breath quickened and her body was strangely wrapping around his. His lips moved from hers and smiled, his eyes sparking like chips of bottle-green glass, the brown in them intensifying the colour. She knew she was under his spell and didn't ever want him to stop.

'Was that a better first kiss?' he smiled and his eyes still danced as he watched her.

God, does he want me to answer that? She had never felt anything so divine.

Kayden gazed into her eyes and she followed them as they settled back on her lips. She melted under another of his kisses and this time the feeling gave her tingles all the way down to her toes and her mind liquefied, the feeling, sensational. Her body was having extraordinary sensual desires as his tongue moved deeper inside her. She heard him groan as he hardened against her, matching her slow movements. The urge to have him naked and feel his raw passion made her feel light-headed. Her lips missed his as soon as he pulled back and rolled away from her.

'Come with me, princess. I have to check the horses before the morning gets away from me.' His voice was deep and shaking. Cassie wanted to drag him back to her lips. Grinning and pulling her up, they walked back to her room. His thigh pressed against her, the strong taut muscle and the feeling of his masculinity made her insides tremble.

'Get changed and I'll meet you at the car.' He looked down at her with a tormented expression. 'Cassie ... you're just so beautiful,' he said, kissing her again. When their lips parted he lifted his head up and she saw him close his eyes as if he was struggling too.

She sighed. 'The horses—they need you, don't they? I can feel you almost communicating with them.'

He smiled. 'How do you know that?'

'Womanly intuition. I'm right, aren't I?'

He nodded. 'Well, if you know I'm being dragged from you, you also know not to keep me waiting. Move it, princess!' He slapped her gently on the behind and chuckled as he shut the door.

He left Cassie feeling dazed and unable to function. As her heart slowed, she began to register what she had to do and quickly dressed in jeans and a T-shirt. She went to the bathroom and splashed water on her face, which still tingled from the sensation of his kisses before racing out to join him.

The horses were grazing when they arrived except one that moved with a slight limp towards them when they pulled up. Kayden grabbed his bag out of the car and worked on its hoof. Unable to fix it completely they brought the mare back to the stable which was nearly full of horses he'd treated lately. This won't be their last run, she thought as he readied a couple of stallions to go back into the paddock.

That morning was the first time she had ever made breakfast. Cassie setup a makeshift table on a bale of hay and told Kayden not to expect this kind of service every day or she would have to start burning it and make him come and help again.

He rolled up the morning paper and tapped her with it, encouraging Cassie to retaliate and attack him and sending them both rolling in the hay together. Cassie loved the way his eyes glazed over just before he kissed her again. The sensation of his hold and those yummy lips didn't last. At that exact moment, the horse Kayden had been attending kicked up a fuss about its sore hoof. Kayden pulled them both up out of the hay, drinking down his coffee and focusing his efforts back on the mare.

* * * *

Cassie started sleeping in Kayden's bed but he never took their relationship any further. After a couple of weeks she realised he didn't want her the way she wanted him so she didn't go in to him anymore.

Cassie understood by his lack of commitment that she was just company and a bit of fun. She needed to snap out of the fantasy she had of them being a couple and realise that he would never want more than friendship. What he offered her was more than she had ever had. She had to stop being selfish by wanting more.

Chapter Four
Sleeping Beauty

Cassie had become a big part of Kayden's life. Even so he kept his work secret and just put her out to it.

'Is she asleep, Kayden?'

He nodded. 'Yes, our sleeping beauty will be out until we get back. I hate doing this to her, Jason.'

Jason shook his head. 'Then tell her about us and see if she will join us. Rules are rules. Unless she joins us it has to be this way, bro.'

'Yeah, I know. I need to talk to Zoren. She has powers that could really help us up there.'

'In that case stop procrastinating and sort it out. You're the boss and a female on our team is not an issue for us, dude—but it is for you. I have known you for centuries, man and never seen you so twisted up about a female. You shocked me when you never moved her on. You could have rid yourself of her that first night. Shit, you could have left her for the car behind us to pick her up that first day but you saw her, even then. You really saw her, hey?'

'Give it a rest, Jase. Yes, yes and yes to it all. My problem is whether she'll handle taking orders from me. You know how I get when the mission takes me over.'

'Yeah, we know. You can become a real prick if we stuff up but we get it and understand. You have a big responsibility up there and it drains you guiding us through it. But if she's meant to be one of us, she'll get it as we do.'

Kayden laughed. 'You don't have to be quite so Goddamned honest.'

'Just keeping it real, dude. Hey! The guys are pulling up,' Jason said, watching out the window. 'We better get out of here unless you want them finding out about your sleeping beauty before you're ready to bring her out of the closet. I can't imagine with a mission in progress that you feel like explaining your new secret weapon.'

'Good point. Not in the mood to clash with the boys tonight,' Kayden said, getting up, kissing Cassie on the cheek and smoothing her hair back. 'Sleep tight, little one.'

Jason chuckled. 'Crikey, you have it bad, man. Have you slept with her yet?'

'Jase, I'm not going there with you.'

'So, I take that as a big fat no. You're losing your touch and your balls, man.'

Kayden pushed the stirring lug out the room. Jason laughed so hard Kayden had to cover his goddamned mouth. 'You could wake her. Quit your crap, Jase! I mean it.'

Jason put his hands up. 'I give, okay? Cool it, dude.'

Woody, Conor and Ethan had already started getting the horses ready when Kayden and Jason reached the barn.

'What's on, boss?' Conor asked Kayden.

Kayden looked around at his men. Woody, Jason, Conor and Jason's brother, Ethan had been riding with him for as long as he could remember. They were a good, steady bunch who knew him like the backs of their hands. He roughly scraped his fingers through his hair, wondering if he could really join up a female. How would she add to the mix when none of them including himself could stand a female being around for longer than a few months? Yet here he was, considering the crazy notion. Cassie was different though and he wanted them to get to know her first. Yet every minute he had with her was precious and to share her was not easy for him to cope with. Even the night she spent in town with Jason nearly did him in.

He had been a hair's breadth away from marching into town, throwing her over his shoulder and bringing her home when he'd heard Jason's car in the distance. He grinned at how jealous he'd became, yelling at her like it was her fault any guy would want to be around her. Due to having such little self-esteem she had no idea how truly adorable she was. He'd felt like a real heel when she came to him and apologised. *Apologise for what? Being the most beautiful woman on the frigging planet? Yeah right! Wait until this lot see her.* He sighed deeply and felt sure he would lose her if he didn't make her his by then. He groaned deeply, knowing just how badly he wanted to.

He eyed Jason as they hounded him as to why the boss never partied with the stars or stayed out late after a mission anymore. How long Jase could keep his mouth shut was also an issue. Kayden had to admit though he was impressed with his loyalty.

'Boss, you in there?' Conor asked, waving a hand in front of Kayden's eyes. The action and look of concern snapped Kayden out of his thoughts and back into reality.

'Sorry, man, mind's elsewhere tonight, unlike you, hey?' he said, slapping Conor on the shoulder. 'Just a rescue mission, guys, in and out. I've already plotted the course so we're good to go.'

'What princess has Aurus kidnapped this time?' Woody had guessed it already.

Woody was more astute than the others and his powers went well beyond those of the rest of the team. Truth be known, Kayden knew he could send Woody on his own and just his presence alone would frighten the crap out of Aurus although he knew Zoren would freak out if he split up the team. They had their allies but they also had their enemies. Getting a chance to pick one of them off would be their adversary's greatest joy and sending a team member alone was a sure way of getting him killed.

Putting the bridle on his horse, Kayden turned to face Woody. 'Princess Eda was visiting friends and on her way home, ended up a little lost and went through Taurus's constellation without permission. We all know how much Aurus loves a princess and her being on his land without authorisation is a good excuse for him to abduct her.'

'You mean give him time to seduce her?' Jason commented, only saying what the rest of the team was thinking.

Kayden winced knowingly and agreed. 'What he is doing is within their laws and yes, he knows it. After all, he caught her on his land. When we get her out I hope she's learnt this time.'

Jason jumped up on his horse. 'Poor Perseus must be beside himself. How many times has he rescued the chained princess? Normally when she wanders off he finds her just chained to a rock and he easily saves her. However, this time there is no rock. It's Aurus from Taurus. As we know, Perseus recently made a pact with Aurus. It must be frustrating for him not to be able to charge in there and grab the princess he has sworn to save, no matter who has her.'

Kayden mounted his horse. 'Agreed. He sounded disheartened when I spoke to him but cheered up when I told him the parents had come up with a plan. King Cepheus and Queen Cassiopeia have cut a deal with their neighbour, Cetus. They will let him court their daughter if he helps them get her back. Aurus loves to go whale hunting with Cetus, so Cetus is giving us permission to barter for him. He will refuse Aurus access to his whales unless the princess is returned.'

Woody mounted his horse in one slick movement. 'I didn't know Cetus has a thing for the Princess Eda. He has always hated her.' He sounded surprised.

'Love and hate walk a fine line. Cetus is apparently beside himself with jealousy that she might be canoodling up to Aurus and falling for his charms. The king tells me he is almost feral—wants to blow Aurus and his constellation out of existence.'

Conor and Ethan punched knuckles and back-flipped onto their horses. Woody, Jason and Kayden cracked up laughing.

'They must have spent hours behind our backs practicing that one,' Woody commented, still looking amused.

'Show-offs pulled it off too,' Jason added.

'Come on, guys. I know you want to impress the ladies up there but you'll turn us into a frigging circus act.' Kayden choked away the laughter behind his discipline. Still amused and enjoying the time with his team, Kayden instructed Zoltan to take the lead. Zoltan felt Kayden's every thought and needed no prompting as he trotted off in front.

Kayden's mind wondered back to Cassie again. She was never far from his thoughts because just as Zoltan had picked him all those years ago, so had the new foal picked Cassie. Kayden could see this resemblance in the way the Zoltan's offspring could understand Cassie, even as young as he was. The talent she held within her even now, without training and before she'd gone through the transition into immortality, he found remarkable and in fact a miracle in itself.

Kayden wondered if she even understood she would become immortal. It angered him that her parents had done her such an injustice. *The kid's going to feel messed up for a few weeks, never mind the change she'll undergo physically.* He fretted silently for her situation. Kayden and Jason had discussed at length when they would break it to her. She wouldn't be aware of anything magical thanks to her ignorant and cruel parents. For a woman it was hard as it was rare afterwards for them to carry children. They both knew Cassie was only just starting to feel confident and happy again and the last thing she needed was for another blow to hit her just yet. His poor, innocent sweetheart had her work cut out for her once she came into her own but come hell, rain or shine, he intended to see her through it.

Zoltan trotted out to the paddock towards the portal where the clouds would take Kayden and his team up into the sky and to the stars above. Tonight Kayden was in a good mood and had allowed talking until they reached the paddocks, unlike other nights when he would cut the chatter as soon as they mounted their horses.

'So, our mission, guys, is to make the deal, deliver the Princess Eda back to her home world, the constellation Andromeda, and get back here before dawn,' Kayden reiterated.

'What, no drinks with Cetus?' Woody glanced at him and frowned. 'What's the rush, boss?'

Jesus, this secret is really doing my head in. How do I tell them it's because I have a beautiful woman in my bed? Even the thought of her being in his bed—her smell, her hair falling across the pillow—made him hard. Jeez! Get a grip, man, he thought, moving in the saddle, trying to get himself comfortable. He had to get back to his woman and no way did he want booze on his breath. He already felt guilty enough linking her to him and keeping her in a comatose state while they were gone. 'Sorry, mate, have a horse in foal.' *A little white lie won't hurt.* Kayden sucked in his breathe as he heard Jason stifle a laugh that the others didn't notice.

'Jeez, boss, we could have organised Conor's brother to horse-sit. Damn, it has been ages since we caught up with the duke. We men were hoping to get in a bit of whale watching and maybe have a mermaid or two for a bit of variety. Sex in the water, K, you can't beat it.' Woody and Conor pounded fists.

'Guys shush, another time. Enough please. Tonight, we save the princess and drop her off. End of story. Now the lot of you quiet down and quit bitching or you know what happens on the way up if you don't.'

There was not another peep out of them. Kayden could make their trip damned uncomfortable and they knew it. He felt bad he was spoiling their fun. Hell, a couple of months ago he would have been the one insisting on a visit to Cetus's constellation but Kayden had no choice. He had to come clean about Cassie with them, but not now. He wanted to talk to Zoren first. *I'll ring him tomorrow. He'll understand that it is important for Cassie to feel completely happy before I put all this on her.* The last few days she had been quiet, somewhere else. He hoped she was not thinking about leaving him. He cursed himself for kissing her and ruining the trust she had in him.

The trip was long, giving him too much time to think about her face, her lips and God, that incredible body. *I am in love, a goner, from that very first day.* She'd been naked and bruised but still the most gorgeous woman he had ever seen. He knew it embarrassed her as he watched her change. *But God, I couldn't believe how perfect she was. Her silhouette was divine, her movements angelic. She captivated me right there. Jesus, why am I unable to commit to her? Just come right out and say it: Cassandra Wyatt, I love you. So simple. Jase is right, I have to grow some balls and tell her how I feel. Tell her what my team and I do.* Kayden closed his eyes, remembering the feel of her as she rode with him and shivering, thinking how electrifying it would be to have her there right now.

Woody's whistle ripped through his thoughts. 'Hey, boss, who was that you imagined with you? Have you a hottie you're not telling us about?'

Conor coughed, nearly choking himself. 'Christ, if she's real you better stop hiding her, man.'

Oh shytzer, Kayden thought. The magic must be so strong up here that my guarded thoughts have seeped through to them. Damn it. I'd better get the princess out of my head while we're up here. Being so close to the team with all this magic is amplifying my feelings. Shit, shit, shit! If they think I have someone they'll want to hang out with me when we get back. They'll use any excuse not to go home until I give.

Jason turned to them. 'He ain't got anyone. Just one of Mar Bakers girl's. She's new. You can all visit anytime you want. They're open twenty-four seven. Get your heads back in the game and stop pissing him off.'

Good save, Jase. Man, I owe you one.

Chapter Five
To Love Someone

It had been a few days since there had been any fog in the paddocks so it was all back to normal. Cassie wanted to ask Kayden why the fog made her sleep so many hours and while she slept, why her dreams were so bizarre. *Maybe it is just my head injury still healing.* She shrugged inwardly, helpless in knowing the reason behind it as she helped Jason set the table for dinner. The three of them had been having a lot of fun and why that thought had just popped into her head surprised her. Although maybe it's just the stress of loving someone I can never have, she reasoned with herself, eyeing Jason as he joked with Kayden. Maybe I could try to love someone else to take my mind off him. Jason is a sweet and caring person. Maybe …

'Hey, girl, where's your head? I just asked what you were doing on the weekend. I was thinking about having friends over for a BBQ. You interested?' Jason asked, putting his arm around her and grinning. 'Will you come?'

Yes, it's time I moved on. She felt that Kayden didn't need her hanging around like a lovesick puppy. She nodded. 'Sure, love to.'

Jason looked happy with himself as he helped Kayden finish dishing up. After his invitation, the air between Kayden and Cassie was thick. Maybe he guessed she was giving up. However, she thought, that should make him happy, not annoyed. *As soon as Jason goes, I'm going to sort this out. If he doesn't want me here anymore, he only has to say.*

Before Jason left, he placed Kayden and Cassie's hands together.

'What are you waiting for, K? Just let nature take its course. Even on my date she couldn't stop thinking about you, mate. If she knocks you over the other side of the room just suck it up and get back on the horse, so to speak.' He laughed and left.

Cassie stood and went to clean up the dishes from the table. 'Jason is no fool but he really had that all wrong. You should have told him you only see me as a friend, Kayden.'

'Is that what you think, Cassie?'

'Kayden, please. I slept in your bed for two weeks and you barely touched me after we kissed. I know you think I'm just a bit of fun to have around and that is fine. Honest. I would sooner keep you as my friend than not have you in my life at all. Forget about Jason's stupid comment but next time just tell him the truth so he drops it.' She tossed her exasperation at Kayden.

'Cassie, sit down and talk to me. I can see I've hurt you and we need to talk.'

He pulled out the chair next to him for her to sit.

Cassie stayed standing at the bench, unable to talk to him so close. 'Kayden, you have nothing to apologise for. It was my first kiss: always the most unforgettable, no doubt. I'm new at all this and impressionable.' She tried to smile, doing what she could to prevent him from seeing how truly wounded she was from his rejection. 'I'm young and sure I'll find another that will make me feel as you did. Only hopefully next time they will feel as I do too.' She wrung her hands in the tea towel, not wanting to sound ungrateful. Pulling it together, she gave him a nice polite smile. 'Although I have to admit you will be a hard act to follow.'

He glared at her, speechless. Under his gaze, she felt embarrassed for saying so much. She hurried outside to get some fresh air, cursing for being so open and still feeling his eyes that had burned into her as she spoke. *What's wrong with me? I should have just let it go. Now he's probably packing my bags for me as we speak.*

She heard his footsteps and the screen door open. Her cheeks burned with shame for speaking up and if she could have willed it she would have opened up the floor and let it suck her into it. She was so glad it was dark.

'Cassie, please let me explain,' he said, slipping his hand into hers.

She sighed, trying to find the words to stop him worrying. It was so humiliating. She glanced quickly at his kind, worried face and wished she could find something clever to say to put it behind them. 'It's life, Kayden, so don't feel bad. My whole life has been just like this. I love, I care, I get hurt but guess what, I survive. None of this is your fault. It was only a kiss.' Cassie felt drained, unable to take away his worried look.

He put his finger to her mouth. 'Hush, little one. Now it is your turn to listen to me. When you came to me, I hurt you terribly, both physically and mentally. Every day I suffered, watching you smile through bruises I helped cause and patiently waiting for me to believe in you. When we had proof that you were not a threat you forgave my arrogance and I swore to myself that if you stayed with me I would never hurt you again. Now, through my promise I have hurt you once more.' He held both her hands and faced her. 'You are the most desirable woman I have ever seen. I want you so badly that at nights I fear to touch you in case I can't stop. If I make love to you it might not be pleasant; you know how strong I am. I'm not normal, Cassie. The longing and hunger for you is primal. I've never felt like this before and it may make me lose control. I can't bear it if I scare or God forbid, hurt you. I really am sorry, princess. I should have told you how I felt. It has confused you, making you think I don't feel as you do.'

Listening to him, Cassie understood how easy it was to get your wires crossed. She had never thought that one of her minor fears had been one of his major ones. She couldn't blame him for not talking to her about it. After all it was she who had pulled away and refused to discuss it, instead preferring to believe she was unworthy of anyone's love and that that was the end of it. Cassie wiped away the dejected tears that had run quietly down her face. 'There is a first time for every woman in the world, Kayden and they all survive. I'm not normal either if you hadn't noticed. Maybe we will be perfect, maybe not. If we don't try then how will we ever know? If you hurt me, I have the power to protect myself.' She cocked an eyebrow at him and amused at the thought, said, 'Would you really prefer my first to be with someone else ... maybe Jason?'

He growled loudly and pulled away from her, stomping across the veranda. 'Like hell! Don't even kid about him, Cassie!'

She enjoyed his jealousy. It was what she needed to hear at that minute to prove just how much he wanted her too. 'What are we going to do, Kayden? If you can't bring yourself to be with me ...'

Before she could say one more word he had her in his arms, kissing her, letting go of his jealous passion finally. He pulled his lips from hers. Breathing heavily and on the way to losing control, Kayden lifted her chin and looked into her face, seeing her raw and innocent love for him. 'Not like this, Cassie. Will you come to me tonight?' His voice was deep and honey-smooth.

She nodded and left him on the porch, both of them wanting it to be special.

As Cassie stepped out of the shower that night, she heard Kayden cleaning up the rest of the dinner dishes so she knew she had time to dry her hair. She took her time while Kayden showered and brushed it until it felt soft and silky. Finally happy with the look, she giggled nervously. 'He won't see me in the dark anyway,' she whispered into the brush before putting it down.

Cassie stood in her bedroom with a towel wrapped around her and all she wanted was his skin against hers. The moonlight lit up the room and now she stood before him, her eyes flowing over his nakedness as he laid waiting for her. He stood and she caught her breath, seeing how faultless he was. He lifted her into his arms and lay with her on the bed, his lips burning with passion. That's when she knew it was the second kiss she'd never forget.

Her body surrendered to his loving attention until she could take no more and begged him to give her his all. He groaned so deeply and the sound shuddered through her like shock waves as his urgency finally gave way. She could feel his loveliness pushing and teasing, moving slowly and gently until lust overcame the strangeness and they were finally one. They both smiled and then the wild abandonment of all their fears opened up the heavens and deep in her soul Cassie knew there would never be another for her.

CHAPTER SIX

Kayden Confides in his Princess

When she woke to the alarm, Cassie hit the snooze button and stretched, feeling the aches from her very first night of passion. Kayden still had her wrapped in his arms. He shifted and moaned in his drowsy daze, looking for her lips. Melting under his passion, she couldn't believe the feeling he was stirring in her again: deep within her a lustful feeling made her forget the tenderness she had felt when she first woke. She shuddered as he deepened the kiss, letting her know he wanted her again. *God, how can anything feel so good?* She had never thought desire could make her slip into an out-of-body experience where tenderness vanished, replaced by a state of dizzy pleasure.

Disturbed by the alarm, Kayden grinned mischievously and reset it. He went and ran them a bath. When he came back he picked up his lover as if she was a fragile flower and slipped them together into the warm suds where he sponged Cassie from top to toe. Never in her wildest dreams had she imagined that bathing with her man could be so enjoyable.

When they finally arrived at the paddock to check the horses there was a strange mist in the air. Cassie, although still a little shaky and in a dream-like state knew from countless other times what came next and sighed as she knew the rest of the day would be stolen from her. The day she had only just begun was now a vision put on hold. As she watched her man she knew he would be bringing back horses with them. They would then go back home and he would find her something to do while he stole away alone into the barn for a while, doing whatever. He would be jumpy all day. Next would come the strange ritual of having a late-afternoon sleep, only she knew she would not wake until the following morning. Kayden would wake her and following a rather large meal he would sleep on and off all day as if he had been out all night.

Cassie frowned, imagining as she always did that he had been sneaking out to get laid elsewhere. It was the only explanation. In the misty sleep she would sometimes hear car doors and an engine starting just before Kayden would come in and wake her. After last night though he had no need to go there. Or at least he better damned not, she thought as she stomped after him, waiting for the ritual to begin.

Arriving back at the stables Kayden's mood was sombre yet edgy.

Here it comes, she thought.

'We have a problem,' he said as they put the horses into the barn. 'Can you start breakfast, princess? I'll join you in a minute. I just have to check on something.'

He saw the look of fright and betrayal flash across her face. Cassie quickly looked away, knowing it was going to happen again today. *He's going to spoil everything we've just found and for what? Fog? Another woman? What did that stuff do to him? How can I fight mist?* She felt helpless to respond.

'I know you don't understand, princess but I promise to explain everything after breakfast. I just have to make a call, alright?' He looked at her, pleading.

Cassie smiled weakly and left him to break it off with his lover or whatever. *He told me he loved me.* She had to believe that she was worthy of love and trusting him was part of it. Jeez, I am so insecure, she thought, feeling silly. Give the guy the benefit of the doubt!

Kayden could feel the tension in Cassie. Throwing his arm around her shoulders he led her over to the seat on the porch. 'We need to talk, sweetie.'

She almost preferred not to know his secret in case it spoilt the night they had just had together. She didn't want to know about his mysterious behaviour in case it was another woman. There was no other explanation for what he'd been doing all this time while she was conveniently made to sleep.

'Cassie, this has been a very confusing time for me. I've wanted to tell you so many things and to ask you something so important but I had terrible trust issues. I thank my lucky stars you have stood by me through it all. When you find out what we do you will understand why.' He sighed heavily. 'I'm not making much sense, am I?'

Cassie kicked at the stone near her foot. 'I know you're gifted because when we kiss your power tingles,' she smiled. 'In a good way though. And I've seen and felt the power within you. I also know when the fog comes you use your powers to make me sleep while you go to your lover or whoever. I often hear horses or a car leave when I'm in the sleepy haze. I figure they drop you off or your friend is leaving. When I saw the fog this morning it crossed my mind you would be leaving me again tonight and maybe last night was—' Tears of torment ran from her eyes and she wasn't able to finish.

Kayden smiled and kissed her tears. 'There is definitely no other woman so get that out of that beautiful mind of yours now. I love you, Cassandra Wyatt.'

He hugged her and after a while she pulled away. 'Then if it is not another woman, what have you been doing?'

Kayden sat back in the seat and had a faraway look in his eyes. 'There is so much more, Cass. Please don't freak out.' He went quiet and reached for her hand. She could feel how nervous he was by his hot and sweaty palms.

'What about if I ask the questions and then I will only take in what I need,' she said, feeling that might break the ice.

He nodded.

'Okay, so you have this big farm but you don't seem to be growing any produce on it. You have friends living nearby that Jason refers to as a group and sometimes team. So my first question is, what do you all do and why do others want to infiltrate your group when you never seem to get together and do anything?'

Kayden listened. 'We—me and the guys—don't need to work as we are more than provided for and want for nothing. We have two farms side by side. Cassie, like you we all have powers and have been chosen for our abilities to do very special work. You could say we are an elite band of soldiers, a select group. I am their leader—the commander—and the horses we watch over are precious to us. They are our magical rides that take us to our missions.'

'That's why I hear horses? Is that what speaks to you, the fog, like in the scary movies?'

He shook his head, amused. 'The fog lets me know that Zoren, my boss needs us. The fog is actually a low-lying cloud called an Altostratus Praecipitatio storm cloud. It gives us access to a portal.'

'A portal? Like a gateway to other planets like in *Stargate*?'

'Well, sort of. Only we go by horse and use the clouds. But we only travel as far as the stars.'

'Wow! This is much cooler than any movie! Even Zoltan your horse is special. Like the tattoo of Pegasus on your arm?'

He smiled and showed her the tat. It was a horse with wings and under it in very small print was the word 'Zoltan'.

Cassie giggled. 'Boy, and you thought my story was out there! This I will have to see to believe. Yet I know you and know you would not lie about this sort of thing. Still, I have the right to think it's fantasy until I see it with my own eyes. Okay?'

He nodded and agreed.

'So, you're a group of trained soldiers with extraordinary gifts. I get that but what do you do? It must be pretty top secret,' she asked inquisitively.

'Yes it is, sweetheart. What we do can never be spoken of in front of any other person ever. You see, here on earth in astronomy, celestial spheres defined by exact boundaries are classed as star groupings or constellations and have been studied by humans for centuries. As children you're taught to look up into the sky and find shapes such as the Milky Way, the Three Sisters, the Teapot and the most popular, the Southern Cross, better known as the Crux.'

'Yes.'

'Well, powerful leaders have ruled the star constellations for many lifetimes. The rulers fight and bicker over many of the same things we do here on earth.'

'Politics, power, sex and greed,' she added.

'If we left them to destroy each other, the loss of the celestial spheres would create a universal change to the solar system. Planets and our own earth's gravitational force would change and we could collide with other planets, their moons or even the sun, any of which would be fatal to all life on earth.'

He stood up and stretched. Cassie took the hand he offered her and they walked towards the car park where she could hear the sound of a car coming in the distance. 'We are called the Cloud Riders, Cassie. We are the peacekeepers of the constellations, sent to ensure that law and order's restored at all costs. If a star is unable to be controlled we have the ability to extinguish the problem. You've probably seen shooting stars. That is them trying to run. They never succeed but they do try.'

'So, if Zoren is your boss and lives up there how does he contact you?'

'Zoren communicates with Zoltan my horse and after that Zoltan communicates telepathically to me. Remember that night you ran from me and went and lay with my horse? He told me you were there and I knew you were safe. I needed to sort out Jason before I came to get you so he laid and waited with you and kept you warm. Then when you went to play with the foal he let me know you were there playing but not unhappy. He was keeping an eye on you for me.'

'I remember he came straight up to me,' she said, thinking about that day. Two cars were turning into the driveway. 'How many are in your group?'

'There are five of us because there are five corners to a star. To destroy a star all we have to do is position ourselves at each point and the energy between us puts its light out. Then we either vaporise it or leave it in the outer hemisphere where it will do no harm.'

'My powers only come to me when in dangerous situations. Where do you draw yours from?' Her eyes were like saucers.

'I draw from "**Spirit**, the bridge between body and soul," and take rightful place at the top of the star. Flanked on the right is Woody, "*Air*, intelligence, creativity and superior." And on the left is Jason, "**Water,** emotion, motion and adaptability." On the last two points, on the right is Ethan, "*Earth*, stability, grounder and potential." And on the left is Conor, "*Fire*, strength Blood and Life-force."

'So, you and your men will go riding tonight to protect a constellation of stars that are misbehaving, so to speak.'

'Yes. Zoren has given me the mission and we ride tonight. That's why I wanted to get you used to riding with me. I want you to join us if it doesn't sound too frightening.' He stopped and faced her, holding both of her hands. 'Cassie, I know your head is spinning as I haven't had near enough time to settle you into any of this but I would be honoured if you came for a run with us. Just come with me on Zoltan. We will take extremely good care of you. I'm hoping you love it as we do and want to join us, but no pressure. This is an easy mission so it will be just a leisurely trip first.'

Cassie shook away the feeling she may have been dreaming again and felt way out of her comfort zone. 'Kayden, I think you have it wrong. All I can do is blow things up. What you do is far beyond my powers. Please don't take me because you feel concerned about leaving me alone. You can always trust me with your secrets as I know I can trust you with mine. Just know I will be fine and am happy enough to wait here for you until you get home.'

He ran his hand through his dark locks. 'Cassie, I'd have kept this a secret and never asked you to be a part of it if I didn't believe you'd be of great value to us. Look, the boys will be pulling up any minute and I've run out of time to discuss it much further. I need to speak to the team and fill them in on the mission. Just trust me for now and come with me, Cass. Throw caution to the wind and let me show you a whole new world that I know you will more than fit into.'

'Where would I fit into you're group. Spirit, Air, Water, Earth and Fire, there are no other signs of significance. I am the odd man out.'

'You my sweet Cassandra will tie us all together. You forgot about "**Faith**, unity, love and harmony." That will be your place in our group and is something every one of us has been missing. Please believe you belong here with us.'

'Believing in someone after what my life was like is difficult, but I do trust you. But Kayden Hunter of the Cloud Riders, I don't know you yet, so the jury is still out on that, but will try if you think I can be of value.'

'That's all I can ask, is to give this new life a go. What have you to lose?'

She nodded. 'My life is in your hands, Kayden and has been since you found me. Before then there was nothing. I guess I'd be crazy not to come and see if there's a place for a freak like me in your world.'

He came close and she could almost feel the power running through him. 'You're my little freak now and your place is by my side, Cassie, for as long as you want to be there.'

CHAPTER SEVEN

Joining the Team

C assie watched as the rest of his team pulled up in two black, four-wheel drives. Cassie had seen pictures in some of Kayden's motor magazines and the vehicles looked the same: overhead spotlights, crash-proof steel surrounds and bodies raised high with huge chunky tires.

Jason jumped out first and put his arm around Cassie while moving her closer to the men as they got out of their vehicles. 'Cassie, this is Woody.'

Woody was so tall Cassie had to shade her eyes with her left hand to see him while she shook his hand. His vibrant red hair outlined his head and his stunning green eyes seemed to burn into her very soul. He was astonishingly handsome.

'Hi Cassie, nice to finally meet you.' His grin lit up his eyes even more.

'Thank you, Woody. Glad to finally meet you too.'

'Cassie, this is Conor. And last but not least, my brother, Ethan.'

She smiled, shaking his hand as if she already knew him. Ethan resembled and sounded so very much like Jason, only he was a little shorter. Conor — well he was so different from the others she couldn't help but stare at him. She was fascinated by his head that was shaven and smooth as a button. Cassie wondered if he would be offended if she rubbed her hand over the glossy patch. It was the first time in her life she had ever seen anyone up close with absolutely no hair. He also had many tattoos and she found him so interesting she wanted to just stand and soak him in as he politely made conversation.

While Cassie chatted to Conor, Jason dropped his arm from around her and punching his brother, said, 'Let's see what the big guy's gawking at.'

Kayden was showing Woody a diagram of some sort. They moved over to get a better look. He eventually called Conor and Cassie over. Cassie felt awkward. She knew nothing of what they talked about. She decided to give them space and sticking her hands in her pockets, she leant up against one of the cars, watching in silence. It was confusing to her that Kayden had not once glanced in her direction or made any effort to include her in the conversation.

Cassie was so used to him holding her or being wrapped up in his arms that she felt a little lost. She eyed the five men: just the size of them overpowered her. She began to think Kayden was embarrassed to show that they were together or maybe a little ashamed of her. She looked down at her simple jeans and T-shirt. Her hair was tied back and she was wearing no makeup. She guessed she did look a little like a frump. *What has happened to me?*

Cassie felt annoyed with herself as she always took such pride in her appearance, even though she usually did just hang out on her own all day. She took a deep breath and closed her eyes. She was totally letting her insecurities creep back in again so she glanced out over the property, trying to pull it together. She was definitely freaking out. Maybe she should just tell him no, that she wasn't ready for any of this, he and his arrogance included. After all they had only slept together last night. Maybe he did it so she wouldn't go to Jason.

Her heart jolted, thinking suddenly that he might not feel as she did. Had he said what he did to get her to work with them? Her mind was swimming with every conceivable negative thought. She shook her head, trying to settle her nerves.

A load cheer brought her attention back to the new members of the team as she attempted to shake off how neglected she felt. First she studied Ethan as he stood with his arm around Jason, chatting. He had similar features to Jason. Both were blond-haired, blue-eyed, model-type men. Ethan had more tattoos and he was not clean-shaven. He had a five o'clock shadow going on that was quite trendy yet his expression was a lot more serious.

Conor, although bald and clean-shaven, had a cheeky grin. He had tattoos down both arms like sleeves as well as one that curled a little up his neck that looked very sexy. His eyes were hazel and almost as bright and happy-looking as Kayden's but his build was short and stocky. Yet in saying that, he would still have been around six foot; he just looked shorter because the others were all closer to Kayden's height which had to be around six foot five or maybe a bit more. All she knew was that they all towered over her and made her feel pint-sized. *Jeez, what am I doing here with these people?* She was nowhere near their league.

Woody laughed and attracted her attention. He leaned on Kayden and had to be at least a couple inches taller than he was. Christ, the guy is a giant, she thought. And yet there was a delicate sweetness about him. Maybe it was the red curly hair and bright green eyes. His creamy-smooth skin was sprinkled with cute freckles; across his nose they made him look distinguished. Whatever she saw in him it drew her like a moth to a flame and in that instant he made her feel like she could trust him with her life.

Yes, they were all smoking-hot men, she concluded as she looked down and drew circles in the dirt with her foot. *They must have girls swarming around them.* She would pale to the likes of the women these men normally hung with or dated. No wonder she was getting the cold shoulder suddenly. If the ground could have swallowed her daggy self up she would have been happy. She glanced back at Kayden who was joking and enjoying his mates. A flittered glance in his direction had her compelled to compare him to the others. He was drop-dead gorgeous. Out of all of them, he was definitely the pretty boy. *Christ, no wonder he is ignoring frump-girl.*

They all started to walk over to the stable and she was asked to follow. Inside the horse stable the bales of hay that she normally sat on were pushed out of the way. They all stood on a platform that was lowered into an underground room. Cassie's nerves were rattled and she wished Kayden would hold her as he normally did when she was doing something new. She decided to be brave and just suck it up.

The room was full of wall-to-wall computerised screens that showed every angle of the sky. By the looks of it there were eighty-eight modern constellations showing at any one time and the computers and satellites tracked all activities. However, tonight the focus was apparently on the Milky Way.

One of the satellites had picked it up in the southern hemisphere. Cassie recalled looking at the night sky and seeing dark patches or cloud-like shapes within the Milky Way. These were referred to by astrologists as the Emu in the sky yet here, with the equipment used, this Emu in the sky was real and was in charge of the stars that made up the Milky Way.

Cassie eventually stopped being gob-smacked and concentrated on the topic of conversation. At the sound of Kayden's voice, she drifted back to the conversation and focused. She was glad Kayden had said this was to be just a trial run for her. When this mission was over there would not be another for her. Kayden, as their commander, was acting as he did when they first met: superior and bossy. If this was the way he was going to act during working hours she wanted no part of him or the job.

Kayden, for Cassie's sake, explained the controversy a little more thoroughly as he knew she'd be unaware of the rulers or of the long-running dispute. He had already told his men to prepare for a longer meet. However, he would try to hurry it along so they could eat before heading out.

With a pause, he eyed Cassie, 'Aldebaran and Conom have sent a loyalist called Teyar to a Wolf-Rayet star. This is a massive, hot star omitting huge amounts of helium, nitrogen, carbon and oxygen and will easily overpower the Emu in the sky. Consequently they would be able to take charge of the huge group of stars within. This would give Aldebaran and Conom a big advantage in their war against Orion if the loyalist Teyar succeeds. They would surely overpower Orion's Belt with that many stars in their army. This would give the sky's most evil wizard far too much control in the galaxy so the mission is to intercept and talk down or destroy the Wolf-Rayet star advancing on the Milky Way.'

'Why does this Aldebaran and his friend Conom want to take over Orion's Belt from Orion?' Cassie asked.

Kayden glanced at her the way a teacher would look at a student who had just interrupted his class. 'Many centuries ago, Aurus the ruler of Taurus, gave his old friend Aldebaran his own star and named it after him. Aldebaran is an evil wizard and has for many years detested Orion for hunting with his two dogs, Canis Major and Canis Minor on Taurus for cattle without permission.'

Cassie had researched the mythology of the Taurus star sign some years back for a home schooling project. She recalled learning that if a princess wandered into the bull's sight Aurus would capture her. She also knew of the legendary two dogs but the tales she had thought were just myths. She figured if it were true then Aurus the ruler of Taurus must be centuries old. Immortal, she pondered. For a few seconds her eyes glanced around the room at the faces before her. Could they be immortal too? Is that why they seemed so young yet their eyes told her so much more? To her, they had that same old soul deep within them and the eyes of ancient warriors. The mind boggles; she shook the thoughts from her mind and refocused back on the meeting.

Kayden continued. 'Conom is a warlord and the supreme sovereign of the star constellation Monoceros. Conom used to be good friends with Orion. They would go hunting together on Taurus with Orion's two dogs, sneaking into the constellation without permission. However, a dispute broke out over equal shares. Conom turned on him, angry when Orion would not distribute the kill evenly, causing a massive argument and an eventual falling-out between the two. Aldebaran saw the opportunity to get rid of Orion by teaming up with Conom so he befriended the warlord and now they fight against Orion to take over his bounded region. If they succeed, they intend to split Orion's constellation between them and restructure the stars. Orion is now constantly under threat and he fights to keep his kingdom in the sky.'

Kayden glanced at Cassie with a strained look and then back to the boys. 'The universal change would only affect a couple of planets and do very little damage to the star system so Aldebaran is moving ahead with his plan as planets are nothing to him. He sees them as nuisances, always rotating and getting in his way. Not only is he dangerous with his powers but his armies alone have caused massive devastation to the ones who have opposed him. Zoren wants this war stopped and is counting on us to get some intel from the renegade star Teyar once we capture him.'

Cassie understood now. The Cloud Riders' job tonight was to seek out and find the star Wolf-Rayet and capture or extinguish it before it had time to do any real damage to the Milky Way. She was trying to digest this new way of life. She felt like they had dumped her into another world. Kayden's coolness towards her was not helping Cassie handle what she knew would be ahead. She was feeling very scared, vulnerable and in way over her head.

After they finished working on strategies, Woody wanted to see what Cassie could do. They all went outside and Kayden selected a few tree stumps that she could use to show off her skills. She had been trying to practice and hoped she didn't make a fool out of herself since it was the first time she had their attention. Her hands shook as she put them up at Kayden's command but nothing really happened, there was just a slight light force.

Kayden's voice cut the air. 'Cassie, focus and stop mucking around,' he growled in a grumpy, impatient tone.

She closed her eyes, willing herself not to zap him instead! When she opened her eyes she threw up her hand at the stump instead of him. As they all focused back on the trees, their mouths opened wide as not just one but all three of the stumps blew to smithereens. All that remained was a grey powder that swirled up and into the sky above.

'Yahoo! You go, girl!' she heard the men say as they high-fived each other.

Woody whistled and put his arm around Cassie. 'I'll be making sure I don't get you angry, little lady,' he chuckled.

Kayden shrugged. 'Told you she was powerful,' he barked as he spun around and walked inside with the team following closely behind him.

Woody kept his arm around Cassie as they walked in with the others and pulled out a chair so she could sit with him at the table. He was attentive and likable, sort of the way she had expected Kayden to be treating her. 'Where did they find you? K and Jase must have had a bit of trouble trying to capture you with those powers.'

Cassie's smile was a little fake as she tried to keep her unhappy thoughts in check. She felt bitter and confused at the way Kayden had spoken to her and then stormed off even though she did what he had asked. She thought about lying and then a prickly heat ran over her skull as she watched Kayden still ignoring her.

Maybe this will get his attention, she thought. 'They ran into me with their truck and then threw me in the shed, dirty, hungry and thirsty, rendering me helpless until I gave in.'

Woody burst out laughing and Kayden threw her a petulant look for saying it but at that point she didn't care and ignored the frown he gave her.

Woody turned to Jason, who also looked a bit guilty. 'Tell me the truth, where did you find her?' He seemed insistent.

Cassie was surprised that they all knew nothing about her. When she'd made the statement, she thought they all knew at least some of it so she hadn't been expecting Woody's reaction. She thought that they may have been able to joke about it and she could show Kayden she was able to have fun with the past, but it was going terribly wrong. She did not want Jason to feel bad again. He didn't deserve her stupid attack. After all it was Kayden she was really mad at.

Jason put his head down. 'Like she said, man. But we had no idea at the time just who she was.'

Woody was angry. His face reddened and his eyebrows furrowed together, making his eyes look dangerously red. 'You two have no idea how to treat a lady.' He put his arm around Cassie protectively. 'You're coming home with me when we get back so you can see that some of us are actually civilised and humane.'

Cassie looked over at Kayden's grumpy face and seethed, then smiled sweetly up at Woody. 'I might just take you up on that offer.'

Kayden slammed out of the house and Jason went after him. She felt bad she had turned it into a tit-for-tat fight and excused herself, going to her room. She stayed there until the meal was ready and only came out because Woody insisted she did or he would carry her out. He was still all smiles, so obviously not scared of the monster Kayden.

Kayden and Jason were sitting at the table, talking and laughing when Cassie came out, obviously over their bad moods. Woody was attentive and chatted to Cassie non-stop, ignoring the electrifying tension every time Kayden and Cassie locked eyes. She was getting more and more upset and as soon as she could, she excused herself and walked out for some fresh air. It was dark now and with all the might she could muster, she fled into the night. Running like the devil was after her, she didn't once look back. She figured it would take Kayden a while to react as he would think she had run to the horses and would be thinking he would pick her up on the way. It seemed likely they had to go into the paddock to get to the portal anyway.

As Cassie pushed her legs to get her further away she contemplated how crazy she was to get involved with a man who had two heads. She would get over him and this would all become a nightmare that one day she would forget. She had no idea where she was going. This was where the cars came from and she hoped it would be the way out and onto a highway. The opposite direction took her straight to the horses so unless she wanted to be found, that was not the direction to be going.

She ran, walked, and then ran for many hours before exhaustion got the better of her. She found a tree to curl up against and slept. She knew they would be on their mission and no one would be looking for her now so she could rest here for a while.

Cassie woke hours later and cried for the man she had fallen in love with who had obviously bedded her without remorse and with the intention of using her powers for his strange cause. Cassie reflected on the shows she had watched and the many novels she had read about such behaviour. She was young and green and thought it was love he shared with her but it must have just been lust and greed.

She awkwardly stood and pushed on, her mind and body numb from being so stupid and thinking he cared about her. She heard trickling water and looked around. The vegetation was a little greener and as she pushed through the scrub she found a river. The sun was high in the sky now; she knew it was at least mid-morning. It shone on the water making it sparkle and inviting. Cassie took off her clothes and went for a refreshing swim that rejuvenated her aching legs.

When she emerged from the water and dressed, gone were the tears and sour mood. She had replaced them with a more positive and determined attitude. She would go and find a life for herself, one that didn't involve conniving men. She had a plan—sort of—and to accomplish it included pushing every sad feeling she had deep inside. That definitely meant no more feelings of such raw passion. Cassie slipped on her shoes with determination as she built a wall inside her heart that would keep the last nineteen years of her life from escaping. *Today is the first day of the rest of my life and I'll be damned if I will take that frightened, broken child with me.*

She scowled, then strode off with purpose. She followed the river that eventually thinned out to a trickle before leading her straight onto a road. Cassie understood how dangerous it was to hitchhike. Young women like her disappeared, more often than not turning up dead or worse: drugged and shipped overseas and sold off as slaves. She shrugged, knowing exactly what that was like. She knew that things like that could happen even from your own bed.

CHAPTER EIGHT

Lessons in Life

Squaring her shoulders and holding her head up, she put out her hand and began to beg for a lift as car after car drove straight past her. She was only walking now and she had lost all motivation when she heard a car slow down. She stopped and looked inside the window, finding a kindly elderly couple inside.

They introduced themselves as Ruby and Jim. Both seemed very sweet and told Cassie they were on their way to the city of Perth, right where she wanted to be. Jumping in, she pushed the last of her past behind her. Cassie confided that she had come to Western Australia for a holiday and even though thugs had mugged her of all belongings, she loved this part of the country and had decided to stay. She was on her way to Perth to get a job and make a better life for herself.

Her story moved Ruby and Jim. They felt sorry for the young woman they had befriended and offered her lodging in their home.

Ruby was a grandma. The silvery-grey hair that she had pulled firmly back into a bun highlighted a weathered face, imprinted from a hard-working life. Yet there was a kindness in her eyes. It was new to Cassie and it drew her in, making her feel very special. Jim was a jovial gentleman who opened the door for Ruby and always held her arm when they moved anywhere. They were the perfect couple who told Cassie they were up for their fortieth wedding anniversary. Cassie pushed the thought away that they could have been Kayden and her, many years from now. She reminded herself that love—his love—was something she had left at the river with that terrified girl she had once been.

Ruby and Jim lived in a suburb called Belmont within walking distance of a shopping centre. The next day Cassie headed off, determined to get work in one of the many stores. To her surprise the first shop she walked into had a vacancy and she began full time work in a stylish dress shop. It was okay, although there was always a constant nagging inside her that she should be somewhere else. Where though, she didn't know.

Ruby and Jim had a grandson named Alex who came to the house quite regularly. Ruby told Cassie she thought he had a thing for her but no man was ever going to enter her heart again so she kept her distance. Alex was your tall, dark and handsome stereotypical male who probably had women swarming all over him and as far as Cassie was concerned, they could have him.

One night after dinner he asked Cassie if she was interested in a job where he worked. Alex was the floor manager at the casino and an opening had come up that he felt would suit her. She smiled politely and asked him for details. She figured anything would be better than watching people dress all day while telling them how great they looked, hoping to snag a sale. She shuddered at the thought of doing it too much longer. Alex told Cassie they were looking for a games manager. All she had to do was organise the staff on the gaming tables and sometimes help the events manager with the casino entertainment.

'You seem to have a flair for enjoyment,' he said. 'You're always so bright and cheery that it would be refreshing to have someone happy around the office. The job is yours if you want it but no pressure. I'll give you a couple of days to think about it.'

She chuckled. 'I hardly need a couple of days to think about getting out of that dress shop. Washing dishes would be more exciting than turning up there every day. When do I start?' Cassie asked, flattered he had thought to offer it to her.

Fate Meeting

C assie had been working at the casino for a few months and had a good rapport with her work mates and the regulars, even knowing them all by name. Towards the end of the shift her instincts alerted her that she was being watched, yet detected nobody unusual as she glanced around the noisy crowd. Being used to overzealous drunks perving on her, she shrugged it off and continued with her walk of the floor.

It was a good night with the casino in full swing and the room packed with gambling patrons. Flitting from one game table to the next, Cassie made sure the dealers were handling players tactfully and that they had their game faces on.

She stopped at one of her favourite tables. The patrons there were having a good night. She kidded around with a couple of the big players, soaking in their good mood before moving on. Then she felt the eyes on her again.

Why is it bothering me? Cassie was used to others watching her and she normally relied on the bouncers to keep a lookout for troublemakers and move them along for her. However, the eyes she felt on her were becoming disturbing. Scanning the gaming floor more carefully this time, she gasped as her eyes rested on a man from her past. Leaning against the railing with a drink in his hand and a slight grin on his face was Woody.

Oh my God! That was the only immediate thought Cassie's brain could manage as she stood frozen to the spot, her hand up to her mouth, not taking her eyes off him as all the memories flooded back to her. Pain ripped across her chest, squeezing her fragile heart as if it were in a vice. The colour drained from her face and the room began to spin. An agonizing electric shock surged through her as all the emotions she had squashed deep inside her surfaced. She felt herself fighting her way through blackness, then nothing.

When she came around, Alex was talking to her. 'Are you hurt anywhere, sweetie?'

Cassie frowned. The raw memories were tumbling into her new world while she fought to reseal the opened door within. She tried to get up, pushing everyone away from her. With one quick movement Alex had Cassie in his arms, looking overly worried as he carried her into the office and laid her on the couch.

'You've just passed out and until I get you checked, Cassie, you do as you are told and rest,' he said, getting a cold cloth and dabbing her forehead.

Cassie was being ungrateful so she let him fuss, glad there was no Woody in sight when she woke up. Facing him again just now would be unbearable to say the least. She didn't like it that Alex seemed a little too concerned about her and realised his feelings for her were more than those of just a workmate.

'I've called an ambulance, Cassie. Can you hear me?' Cassie heard Alex say. She slowly opened the eyes that wanted to stay closed to hide her embarrassment over collapsing in front of everyone.

'Please, no ambulance. I'll be fine. I just need to rest a minute.'

Alex rinsed out the cloth in cold water again and let the coolness of it sit on her forehead. 'I just want them to look at you. They're here now. Please do not fight me on this, Cass,' he said, still troubled.

The ambulance team came in with a bag and checked her vitals. They agreed that Cassie had just fainted and suggested that she should visit her local doctor for some tests as soon as it was convenient.

After they left, Cassie wondered if she really saw Woody or if she had just imagined it. She sat up, drinking the coffee Alex made for her and apologising for the embarrassing display in front of his patrons. 'Sorry to scare you, Alex, I just ...' And it was then that Cassie realised how she still held her secret past sacred, as her voice even now would not allow her to whisper his name.

Alex sat next to her. 'Did it have anything to do with that guy with the red hair who caught you before you fell? He put up a hell of a stink. He wanted to stay with you but I had him removed from the premises.'

Cassie couldn't talk about it even to Alex who she considered to be a good friend. So she did what she had to and lied. 'No, I don't know who he was, I just felt dizzy. My fault totally. Not been sleeping well lately.' She stood up. 'I really would prefer to go home now. My shift's over and I think I just need an early night.'

Alex smiled sweetly and patted her hand. 'At least let me take you home so I know you got there safely.'

Cassie nodded, not really wanting to face walking outside alone and maybe running into any more of her past tonight. They walked out to the car park together and Alex kindly opened the car door for her and even did up the seat belt. Cassie lay back, letting him buckle her in. She was so exhausted she didn't even protest when he insisted on walking her to the door and laid a goodnight kiss on her cheek before he headed back to work.

He was very sweet, she thought as she walked inside and flopped on her bed. He even offered to sit with her for a while. She frowned. *Yes, sweet, but does he have ulterior motives?* Unable to deal with thoughts of a future with any man Cassie had politely rejected his offer, preferring him to leave her alone to think.

Her cover was blown and the memories were now tearing her heart apart. All these months later she had to face up to the fact that she had not run away from him at all. She still kept her love for him deep inside and it was now killing her to even think his name. *Kayden, the love of my life! How am I going to do it again?*

She groaned, knowing how hard it was to forget the first time. Now, just seeing a friend of his had set her world upside down. What would she be like if it had been Kayden himself? She groaned again, punching her pillow. *Damn him!* Tossing herself over onto her stomach, she started to sob. She cried all night until there were no more tears left to cry, not getting out of bed until around midday when she felt a bit better.

Cassie rationalised the whole situation and decided that just because she had seen his mate, Woody, didn't mean that Kayden would look for her. She kicked herself again as these memories alone showed her how innocent she had been, unable to see until now just how one-sided the relationship had been. She had practically thrown herself at him and today could almost feel sorry for the guy for having such a wimpy puppy begging for his love.

Cassie stood in front of the full-length mirror. *If he never came to you before, girl, he won't now. Get it together and forget him.* She scowled at herself. *Now, stop being stupid. He never loved you and it's time you faced up to it and started a new life.* Cassie smiled at her grumpy face and knew this time she had no intentions of squashing the memories she held. She was older, more self-assured and deserved respect. *It is time you opened up your heart, woman, and found a new love.* Cassie kissed her fingers and pressed them to her reflection in the mirror. 'You deserve better than to allow yourself to be treated so poorly,' she whispered, feeling energised with the talk she had given to herself. *Yes, today I may give Alex a chance to fill the emptiness I carry.*

Cassie picked up her jacket and handbag and headed for the door with a new spring in her step. She had been just an immature girl when Kayden found her and she had let him be mean to her, just as she had allowed her parents to be mean to her. But not anymore! She had friends now, a good job and a nice place to live with a loving couple who genuinely cared for her. Thinking this, she felt strong as she set off for work. If she was ever to see them again she would be polite but that was all they deserved from her. *My time living with hurt is over.*

Alex was happy to see Cassie although he frowned at the dark rings under her eyes. 'Maybe you should take a couple of days off, Cassie. We can manage around here.'

Cassie opened her purse and dotted powder around her eyes. 'There, good as new. I'll be fine.'

He shook his head and laughed. 'You're worse than me. Just remember the job's not worth your health. If you change your mind, just come see me.'

Over the next few weeks Cassie worked hard and for many hours a day. It took her mind off the reality that had finally sunk in: she realised she had been right in her thinking that if Kayden had any feelings for her he would have come for her long before this. She viewed her options: one being to go and face him, kick him in the shins, maybe yell at him for being so damned hard to forget. The more level-headed option was to settle contently back into her job and the new world she had created for herself. She chose the second as the more sensible.

Cassie relaxed a little more around Alex, allowing him to be more attentive than usual. One night after work as Alex walked her to the car she let her guard down and threw caution to the wind. They had become very good friends over the months and walking arm-in-arm with him felt very natural to Cassie. She started to think that maybe giving Alex a go wasn't such a bad idea. She certainly felt comfortable around him. Cassie chattered and laughed with him and knew that tonight, if he asked her on a date, she had every intention of accepting. They stood by the car against which Alex would usually lean, talking to her. Only tonight without warning, he took her in his arms and kissed her.

It was unexpected and at first, Cassie tensed. He nearly pulled away but she put her arms around him so he would stay. His lips were warm and the kiss was different from what she remembered a kiss felt like but she didn't hate it. She lingered, letting herself relax to give him every opportunity to make her feel the passion she had once felt. After a few minutes it felt sweet: not passionate, just sweet. He pulled away and looked at her through loving eyes and she felt sad, knowing her feelings weren't the same. She wondered if she would ever feel true emotion again.

'Alex, please,' she said. 'I just can't. I'm not ready yet.' Tears sprang to her eyes.

His heart sunk because she didn't feel the same way he did. But he felt worse because he had upset her. 'I'm sorry, Cassie. I shouldn't have forced you.'

She blushed. 'We won't act all funny next time we see each other, will we? I'd hate this to change things between us. You're my best friend.'

Alex kissed her forehead. 'Don't worry, I'll get over the rejection.' He grinned, trying to lighten the moment.

'I'll see you tomorrow. However, I won't be wiping it from my memory banks, Cassie. If you think I'm giving up on us any time soon you'd better think again. Just the fact you let me kiss you makes me know you care about me and that's enough for now,' he said, sounding like he always did and making her grin. He stuck his hands in his pockets and headed back to the casino.

Cassie watched him walk away and wiped more tears from her face. 'What is wrong with you, girl?' she said, annoyed with herself. She went to open the car door when a hand closed it and a familiar arm wrapped around her waist.

'You still love me, don't you?' She heard Kayden's voice.

Cassie tried to wiggle out of his grip and hit his chests with her fists but he held her firmly, bringing his head down to claim her lips with the passion she so remembered. Within seconds her body stopped fighting and betrayed her. It melted into him with unleashed lust.

He pulled back and held her, looking into her love-soaked eyes. She tried to pull herself together and speak but no words came out. *How does he do this? After all this time, he thinks he can waltz back into my life and reclaim my body.* She lingered, viewing him through the stupid eyes she knew must surely be giving away the feelings she still kept for him deep in her very soul.

He took her hand. 'We need to talk.'

Feeling her surrender, he placed his arm around her as they walked in silence: two lovers who had run out of words and were waiting until the minute they could be back in each other's arms. Cassie followed like a lamb to the slaughter as if she had no will of her own. His power over her was making it obvious that if he hadn't come to take her home she would surely die from a broken heart if they parted this time.

He took her back to his suite at the casino. Here he sat her down on the bed before pouring them a drink. She swallowed it and savoured the burning sensation as it ran down her throat, trying desperately to bring herself back to her senses. Neither of them seemed able to do what they should have been doing—talking.

Kayden moved to Cassie. He took her empty glass and tossed it aside. He scooped her up into his arms and kissed her again. This time there was so much love in that kiss that tears ran from her eyes. Kayden felt them and lay down with her on the bed, letting her cry it out in his arms. He held her close while she let the hurt of what he did to her leak from her eyes, one tear at a time.

Calming finally, she lay quietly, feeling how very nice it was to be back in his warm and comfortable arms. The feeling of belonging made her realise she had been so childish, running away and not trying to work it out with him. She must have hurt him terribly too. Why he was here with her now was beyond her.

Finding her voice, she looked up at him and saw that his cheeks were wet from the emotions she had shed. 'I'm sorry. I was just a girl and too inexperienced to understand. I thought your indifference meant you did not care enough for me and had just used me. I can feel now that wasn't true. Was it? How have you been able to forgive me?'

He looked so emotionally distraught with his bloodshot sad eyes and miserable expression that her heart broke for the ordeal they had both put each other through. 'Cassie, I did treat you terribly and because I slept with you once I expected you to be grown up enough to feel and know that meant I loved you. I was a fool. Only recently someone made me realise that you had been locked up all your life and had no experience with men or any kind of love at all. I scared you away and deserved every bit of hatred you threw at me. Even so, I love you with all my heart. I have come here today to beg your forgiveness and to ask you to come home with me. I promise I have learned my lesson and I will never be so careless with your love again. If you send me away I will go. But I beg you, give me another chance?'

Cassie searched his face for any kind of trick. All she could see was raw love and feelings. 'I've made a new life for myself here, Kayden. People respect me and I enjoy having my own money to do with as I please without having to ask for it.' She shook her head and sat up.

His arms dropped from her as if he were unable to hear the rejection and needed them to hold himself together.

Cassie moved from him and walked into the bathroom to splash her face and think. When she came out she had made her decision and smiled at him. 'But all this means nothing without you.'

Kayden jumped up and swung her back up into his arms. 'You little sneak! I thought you were telling me it was over. My heart was in my throat and I could hardly breathe.' He swung her around. 'I feel so happy I don't know what to do with myself.' He was laughing and placing little kisses all over her face and neck.

Cassie laughed with him and hugged him back. 'Let's go do something together. Build a new memory—a good first one. Let's go on a real date. I'll take you to my favourite spot.' She grinned, wanting to pinch herself to check that he was actually there.

Kayden wanted nothing more than to take her on a date and as he slid her down he kissed her one last time before getting himself in check and taking her hand. 'So, this is our very first date? I like that. I am all yours.' He bowed and gestured for her to lead the way.

As they arrived at Kings Park, Cassie explained about the nights she had spent there with her friends. She pointed out the beautiful views of the city to the left, South Bank to the right and positioned in the middle, the casino where she worked. Cassie pulled up and getting out of the car, walked arm-in-arm along the path she had walked many times while dreaming of this very moment.

She took Kayden to the Whispering Wall and after sitting him at one end she walked all the way to the other. Kayden eyed the size of the seat that was shaped like a horseshoe and his fear of losing her nearly caused him to move from where he was told to stay and go to her. Cassie called out to him, distracting him from his thoughts. 'The distance is so far you will not be able to hear a quiet voice but by leaning your ear against the wall just a whisper carries. Try it, just lean in,' she called to him. Pressing her own cheek to the wall she whispered. 'I love you.'

Kayden whispered back, 'I love you, too. God, how I love you, honey.' His voice broke and Cassie could hear him breathing heavily, trying to pull it together. Then pressing his face to the wall again he said, 'Please, come to me. I can't stand you to be so far away from me. Never again, Cass.'

They both stood up and began walking, meeting halfway and signifying how they were going to be in their relationship this time round. They strolled over to the wishing well where Kayden poured his heart out and bent down on one knee, kissing her hands, promising never to make her feel unimportant to him again. Her spirits lifted at his heartfelt confession and lifted again further along at the lookout where he wrapped his lovely big arms around her as she was pointing out all the fun places she'd been.

'You must have had many men take you on dates here. I get jealous just thinking about it,' he said, a little quiet and sullen.

Cassie didn't answer him. She too, was feeling resentful of the many women who had frequented his arms since she'd been gone. She changed the subject, not wanting to spoil their night with silly jealousies. Instead they sat and revealed harmless scattered details of their past few months without each other. Wrapped in each other they sat on the soft grass watching the sun come up.

'You know, Cassie, we never went out on a real date. This is perfect!' He grinned, pulling her up from the grass and into his arms. 'I had a great time, princess.' He held her close.

She felt the power of his feelings. 'I did too.' She grinned back at him.

'I was your first kiss, your first love and I know this sounds selfish, but I wish I had been your first date as well,' he said as they strolled back to the car.

* * * *

Cassie said, 'Just one more stop for coffee before our date ends. There is someone I want you to meet.' They pulled up at her home and he looked at her with eyebrows furrowed so close together by a frown that she almost giggled at him. 'Come inside, I want you to meet the two people who have been my dates to all the lovely places I've told you about.'

'I can't, sweetheart. Let's go somewhere private. I can't take it just yet, meeting the other man or men in your life. I'm really not up to it, princess.'

She ignored the protest, gesturing for him to follow. 'You'll enjoy meeting this man. Trust me. There will be absolutely no tension,' she said, opening his door and dragging him out of the car and inside the house.

Ruby had heard them pull up. Cassie chuckled to find her still in her dressing gown, already organising coffee. Jim was at the table reading the paper with his tracksuit on.

'Hi guys,' Cassie smiled. 'I want you to meet the man I intend to spend the rest of my life with.'

Ruby thought she looked absolutely radiant as she made the introductions.

'Kayden Hunter, this is Ruby and Jim, my friends and companions who have been my dates to every event I've had the opportunity to go to.' Kayden looked at her, stunned. 'Yes, you were also my very first boyfriend date,' Cassie giggled and stretched up to kiss his cheek.

Kayden's grin said it all. Cassie could tell by the sparkle that washed over his eyes how happy she had just made him. Up until that point, Kayden had no idea his lover had kept herself just for him and Cassie could see his fragile heart soar.

Ruby hugged him and made him feel welcome. 'Our Cassie has brightened up our world but we knew it wouldn't last forever.'

Jim stood politely. 'So you're the man she ran from. I'm so glad you've finally found her. We worried that she would end up an old maid because she wouldn't go anywhere without us oldies,' Jim confessed, shaking Kayden's hand.

Cassie glared at Jim, shocked. 'How did you know? I never said a word!'

Jim laughed again. 'Walls here are thin and you talk in your sleep. You called out to Kayden most nights. Sorry, darl, you never fooled us for a minute.'

They sat and drank coffee while Ruby cooked them a big breakfast. After they ate, she helped Cassie pack. Even though they were sad to see her go they were happy that she had found her soul mate. It was then back to the casino so Kayden could check out of his room and Cassie could say goodbye. When she found Alex, Cassie swallowed hard as she choked out her gratitude for his friendship. She sobbed in his arms as they held each other for the last time.

'It's okay, Cassie love. I knew when I kissed you that there was another man somewhere who had your heart but I did love that you tried to kiss me back.' He grinned, brushing her hair from her drenched cheeks.

'I'm sorry it wasn't you, Alex. You know I adore you don't you?' she hugged him again.

Taking her by the chin, he forced her to look up at him. 'As I adore you, my friend, but if he stops making you happy for even a second, you come home to me, you hear?'

Cassie nodded.

'Now come and let me meet the man who is stealing you from me.'

Cassie cheered up. 'You'll like him, Alex. He's so much like you at times. When I first met you it was hard not to hate you for it.' She giggled, making him smile at her.

'You know I should be mad at you for leaving me in the lurch like this but your happiness means more to me, pumpkin,' he said, touching her nose and hugging her under his arm as they walked back towards Kayden.

Alex took it really well and she knew she would miss him most of all. When he shook hands with Kayden he asked him to look after her and bring her back for a visit from time to time. He sounded more like a big brother than her sort-of ex. She thought how sweet a man he really was.

* * * *

Kayden drove in silence, worried for Cassie as she sobbed silently into her hanky. Coming back into her life had been one emotional roller coaster and he swore to the heavens that he would make it up to her. An hour later Cassie dried her face, squared her shoulders and turned, watching Kayden as he drove.

He turned and squeezed her hand with a nervous tremble. 'Any regrets?'

'Only one.' She touched his face tenderly and wished she hadn't been so hasty in dragging him out of his room at the casino. She had been a little anxious at the time but now all the goodbyes were over all she wanted was to be in her man's arms.

Kayden saw in her sweet, loving face what she was thinking. He thought if he didn't change the subject he wouldn't be able to stop from pulling up, kissing those luscious lips and doing anything he could to ease her sadness.

He grinned. 'I know exactly what that regret would be and I've been wondering the same thing. Why would you buy a Mazda?' His comment was out of left field and Cassie started to giggle. Her infectious change of mood thrilled Kayden and he laughed with her. He felt pleased he had taken her mind off the sadness she had been feeling and he listened intently as she explained that her car had all the newest mod cons including sunroof and what she felt was one of the best surround-sound systems. She turned on the CD player and a Fleetwood Mac song blared out from the speakers, making him laugh.

'So you like the older-style music?'

Cassie grinned. 'I know. Who would have guessed? I've found out a lot more about myself too. I love eggs but not the bacon. I like baths with many bubbles and the smell of scented candle shops draws me in like a moth to a flame. And best of all I like to just sit and watch a really fast action movie but the bad guy always has to lose or I don't like it so much.'

They pulled up, Kayden still highly impressed by her revelations. Cassie sounded full of life and had worked hard while she was away to learn a lot about herself. He felt proud of the woman she had become. Gone was the nervous, fearful Cassie and in her place was a desirable seductress who had him so wound up he could hardly wait to get out the car to hold her again. Kayden walked around to Cassie's side of the car and when he had her standing, leaned her back against the car. 'And now we are home, what was that one regret you started to tell me about?'

Kayden closed his eyes as she pressed her body against his. She didn't need to say a word. She had him under her spell and he shuddered with longing as he felt her stretch up. He bent down to meet her honey-tasting mouth. He could feel her power humming sweetly through her and as he deepened the kiss it tingled throughout his whole body, sending such a sensual feeling through him that he lost control. With a swift movement he scooped her up into his arms and carried her inside. That is where they stayed until the sun came up the next day, happily in each other's arms. They dozed off every now and then but it only took one or the other to move and they would be hopelessly lost in each other again.

At daybreak, Kayden wished he could stay in bed with her forever. The horses needed tending to though so he dragged himself out of bed. He could no more leave her this morning than he could have yesterday once he had seen her again. He needed her close and he lightly kissed her like a feather tickling her skin. He loved the way she wiggled and smiled before her gorgeous eyes fluttered open.

'The horses.' She stretched and yawned. 'Give me a minute revol enim.' She chuckled and ran into the bathroom. He slapped her backside playfully as she ran past.

'Give *you*, "lover mine". When did you learn to reverse words?'

'Casino code,' she chuckled again. 'Teg siht knurd tuo fo ym ecaf,' she called out before closing the door.

Kayden grunted as he pulled on his jeans, still trying to work out what she said. He grinned as she walked back into the room and quickly began dressing. 'Get this drunk out of my face?'

'Very good, tiger! I'll have to make them a lot harder if I want to swear at you.' She chuckled again as he grabbed her and tickled her.

'You better not, sweet cheeks or you will be in so much trouble.'

Cassie picked up her runners and bolted for the door. 'Evah ot hctac em tsrif emosdnah.'

Kayden was after her in a shot, enjoying her new game and the confidence she now oozed. He snatched her up and ran with her out to the car. ' "Have to catch me first, handsome" was not near hard enough but good try, sweetheart.'

She was smiling at him and he stood frozen with her for a second or two, unable to believe that just a day ago he had been in total misery and torment for months. Yet in one day this angel in his arms had turned his life around yet again. 'Have I told you yet today how much I love you?'

'Yes, but I'll never tire of you saying it.' She smiled and in that instant the sun swept across the sky and lit up the golden highlights in her hair. Her skin shone with a glow like that of the goddesses from the heavens and he thought she surely was sent by the gods themselves for him to take care of and to protect.

It was no surprise to Kayden when he took Cassie to the paddock and the horses all remembered her. He could feel them soak in the angelic vibe she was projecting. He knew her powers had grown and with work, he wondered if she knew just how powerful she could become.

Kayden slapped the dust off his pants as her feeling of joy shuddered through him. He had never disconnected from her so he had still been able to feel she was okay. It was the only thing that kept him sane while she was gone. He knew it was wrong but letting her go completely was something he couldn't handle. Getting the gear he needed out of the truck, his eyes diverted back to Cassie as she squealed and laughed, making him quiver as her vibration hummed happily through him. He knew he had to connect her to the team and it made him speculate on what would happen when he added the woman she had now become into the mix. He could only hope that she would give off a different, less seductive vibe. It tormented him that they might feel about her the way he did.

Throwing a towel over his shoulder, he let out a quiet growl. He wanted no competition. Yet he knew he wanted her with him all the time now so no amount of debating was going to change what had to be done. He knew he just had to wait and see how it played out. Taking a deep breath and rolling his shoulders, he went to tend the horses, barely concentrating as his eyes kept fixing on his woman. She was mind-blowing and the more excited she became the more her happiness pulsated through him, putting him in high spirits too.

Cassie suddenly noticed a strong poised tan horse eyeing her from a distance. She noted he was younger than the rest and yet stood tall, proud and patient waiting his turn. His pure black mane and tail softly outlined his perfect shape. She patted him and turned her head to the side. 'Surely you are not the baby foal.'

He nudged Cassie, wanting to play and have some fun.

Cassie laughed. 'I don't believe how quickly you've grown. Kayden what did you call my horse?'

'Starburst.'

'Love it! Hey Starburst,' she patted him. 'You're not the baby no more, are you, boy? Okay then let's see what you got.' She grinned mischievously and started to run at full speed away from him before stopping quickly and darting back at him. He reared up, making her laugh as he made a chuckling sound in the back of his throat and then took off. He was so cute. Cassie followed him to the river where she ran around the trees to get away from him and they played hide and seek—only he was too big to hide and kept making her laugh when he tried.

There was a screech of tires on the dirt and dust flew everywhere. Cassie stopped mucking around, wondering who it was. Out of the dust, Woody came running down the hill, gathering Cassie up in his arms, laughing and very happy to see her. She felt flattered and flushed crimson at his attention which made him laugh more.

'I knew that if he was this happy it had to be you. Welcome back, Cassie girl.'

Another car pulled up just as quickly and Jason, Conor and

Ethan opened their doors and headed for them. Woody still had her in his arms and he raced back up towards them and slid her onto her feet. 'See, I told you she was back.'

They all took it in turns hugging her while Jason went crook at Woody for not waiting for them. He had apparently just taken off out of the house when he felt his boss's emotions.

'I saw her playing with Starburst and knew it was Cassie.' He was still grinning at her.

Kayden finished checking the horses, came up and slid his arm around Cassie protectively. 'That's enough, boys, she's taken,' he said, smiling down at Cassie and keeping his arms firmly around her, letting them all know in no uncertain terms who she belonged to. Cassie was delighted that he was finally able to show his love for her without hesitation or thinking that it might damage his leadership.

'You look fabulous, Cass.' Jason gave her one of his cute boyish grins. 'City living definitely agrees with you, girl.'

Cassie knew she had changed and it had been almost overnight. On her twentieth birthday she had just woken up different. Her body shape had changed from stick-thin to voluptuous and shapely. Her hair had grown in length and golden highlights lightened up her usually dull, lifeless locks.

She grinned, flabbergasted at how much attention she was getting. 'It's called growing up, Jase. It had to happen sooner or later. I was a bit of a nerd last time you saw me.'

He chuckled. 'Well, I didn't like to say it then but shytzer, you were hard work. To think you even had to learn how to cook toast. Can you boil a kettle yet?' He joked with her and she laughed.

'Cheeky beggar, it looks like I have a thing or two to prove.' Kayden tried to protest but she put her hand up to stop him. 'It's a friendly little bet we have then, Jase,' she egged him on.

He glanced at the boys and they all nodded. 'Okay, girl, you're on. A fiver out of each of us.'

'Double it and you are on.'

'So we sit back and do nothing and you cook.'

'You got it?'

'And if it tastes like crap and we have to end up cooking ourselves, you pay us.'

Cassie put out her hand. 'Deal!'

He shook it and they all went back to the house, laughing about the burnt offerings they would get for their ten bucks.

Back at the house, Kayden listened to the men and only entered the conversation when he was directly asked a question. His eyes were fixed on his woman who drifted with ease around his kitchen. The aroma of what she was cooking wafted over to him and he wanted to go hug the honey who was making him feel so happy. She was cooking for him and for them. How could this be?

She wiped the back of her hand across her forehead unconsciously and flour-marked her flawless complexion. He wondered if she'd be mad if he went out there and kissed it off; he would have broken his promise to stay seated. As if she felt his thoughts she sent him a surge through their connection and he shuddered at the lovely emotion she sent his way. He wanted to tell her he was cheating and could feel her but somehow he felt she already knew because it was working both ways. She smiled, confirming his thoughts and then went back to making the last batch of pancakes. Finally she asked for the table to be set and there was a mad rush as juice and coffees were organised while she placed the food in the middle of the table. The men sat down, grabbing toast and piling omelettes onto their plates.

As Cassie came over to place some more dishes on the table, Kayden pulled her onto his lap. 'What have you done with my helpless little princess? Who is this grownup impostor?' he laughed.

Cassie grinned happily. She could only give thanks for the day when two loving angels picked her up and took her into their lives unconditionally. She had learned so much more than how to cook: she had learned the most important lesson of all—how to treat a man— and she would never forget the experience it had been watching the love Ruby and Jim had for each other.

'You better taste it first.' Cassie smiled and kissed Kayden's lips softly before getting up to finish serving.

Ethan tasted his omelette and at the same time stuffed a pancake in his mouth and grinned. 'She's definitely a keeper!' he said, devouring more pancakes.

After breakfast Woody and Jason did the dishes. There was a rule that those who cooked did not have to help with the dishes and Cassie liked that rule already. Kayden sat with his arm around her, contented and relaxed while they talked to Ethan. Cassie was having a bit of fun with the whole 'brother' thing. She had no brothers or sisters and was surprised when Ethan admitted he was the elder brother.

'I thought Jason was older,' she said and received a playful scowl from Jason for saying so.

Ethan explained the height difference, saying he was more like his dad's side of the family in appearance: slightly shorter and stockier. Ethan gestured towards Jason. 'He may be taller than me but I can still hold my own.' He grinned mischievously at Cassie, his blue eyes alive with a challenge. 'I can take him down any day.'

'I heard that. You're on later, short-stuff.' Jason's voice came from the kitchen.

Conor sat back down, giving Cassie a chance to admire his tattoos. He told her that every time he had a new woman, he'd add to his body art. 'I just love the pain they cause me,' he said. He grinned at her reaction, showing her his most recent tattoo of a skull and a black rose. 'See, like this one, her looks were as perfect as a rose but she was all dark and evil in the bedroom,' he said and Cassie, not used to bedroom talk of any kind, flushed crimson at his honesty. He laughed at her shyness. 'She's cute, Kayden,' he said, slapping his leg where the tattoo sat proudly. 'But have we got our work cut out for us toughening her up enough to put up with us five blokes!'

Kayden pulled Cassie back into his arms. 'She's perfect just the way she is and she needs no educating from you lot.'

Cassie nuzzled into Kayden's body, enjoying having a protective man to care for her. He had become everything she dreamed he would be. She couldn't help but lap it up a little.

Woody and Jason finished in the kitchen and sat at the table shuffling a pack of cards.

'Who is in for a hand or two before we hit the road?' Woody glanced straight at Cassie with a smirk.

She put her head down, amused. She thought that with his red curls and his emerald eyes that shone like gems, he looked all mischief. Cassie knew that he had seen her at the gaming tables and surely would know there were some skills hidden within her. *Surely he isn't thinking he can beat me?* The challenge was too good to refuse. Cassie squeezed Kayden before jumping up with enthusiasm. She grinned when she heard Kayden's muffled chuckle. 'I'm in,' she said, joining them at the table.

Kayden knew only too well what Woody was up against and came to join them. 'Count me in. Wouldn't miss this for quids.'

'We're in.' Ethan and Conor pounded fists.

Kayden pulled his arm from around Cassie so he could take his cards.

Jason and Woody wore the same playful expression.

'Let's see what the new girl's got.' Jason's eyes were wide as he dealt.

'You're one of us now.' Woody nodded for her to pick up her cards.

Cassie picked up the hand and smirked. 'Just don't expect any sympathy when I win.'

'Bring it on, girl!' filled the air as the games began.

A few hours later, Kayden called it a night after Cassie had won again. 'That's it, guys. She's too good for us tonight. Get some shuteye and we'll finish this off another night.'

'Bad luck, guys,' Cassie stirred them up as they left. 'Maybe next time I might let you win a few.' She was happy she could hold her own.

Jason hugged her. 'Nice to have you home, Cassie girl. It was fun,' he said as he left.

Woody kissed her cheek on the way past. 'I learnt a few tricks off you tonight. Until next time, sweetness.' He inclined his head in a gentlemanly fashion.

Ethan and Conor leant in and kissed Cassie's cheeks at the same time. Arm-in-arm they left in good spirits and singing.

'That was fun. Whipped them good and proper,' she said, waving them goodbye.

Kayden grinned. 'Yes it was a good night, sweetheart. You had them eating out of your hand. But just remember they learn fast. It may not be so easy next time, my little cardsharp.'

She stretched and yawned, resting against him as he guided her to the bedroom. 'I still have a few tricks up my sleeve. They may need to be a lot sharper when I'm not so tired,' she fell backwards onto the bed exhausted.

Kayden shook his head at her. 'Did anyone ever tell you that you are a hopeless night owl?' he kidded as he changed her into one of his shirts to sleep in.

She giggled at him grumping at her. It felt like old times and she was just so happy to be home.

* * * *

It was still dark when Kayden guided her out to the car the next morning to check the horses. He had already made her a coffee that he put into her hand before taking off down to the paddocks. Cassie sipped the coffee and by the time they arrived, she was feeling awake and chirpy. The light was just starting to push across the sky when they pulled up, although low cloud cover was making visibility of the hillside poor. They both looked at each other, knowing what that meant.

'Sorry, sweetie. I was hoping we would have a bit more time together before this happened.'

'Your boss wants you?'

He nodded and hugged her. 'I promise I have locked up the big bully that upset you last time, sweetheart. Will you give me another chance to prove to you that I've changed?'

'I know you love me now, Kayden. I'm older, wiser and stronger and even if you growl at me and make me furious, I will stay just so I can growl back at you when the others have all gone home,' she said, trying to soften the moment that brought them both unpleasant memories.

'I hope you do, Cass. I don't even care if you zap me to kingdom come. Just stay with me, alright?'

'You'd better wear a safety vest in that case because one step out of line, buster and you're toast,' she joked.

He ran a hand gently down her face, loving that she had really forgiven him. 'Just make sure you don't aim below the belt or there will be definitely no make-up sex,' he stirred her back. He stopped for a second and glanced back at her, smiled and tipped his head in an old-worldly gesture before he headed back down towards the horses.

Cassie smiled happily as she turned to Starburst who was already bucking and wanting to play. After a bit of fun with him she sat on the grass and her little friend stood beside her. They both knew the fog meant something big. 'Pity you can't come with us, boy. Maybe when I get more confident they might let me take you.'

He snorted and nodded.

They both watched Kayden and Zoltan. Kayden was standing still with his horse, both eye-to-eye. Kayden nodded, reached out to his horse and patted it on the nose and the horse nuzzled him back.

'They must be speaking telepathically, Starburst. Do you think we'll ever be able to do that?'

Starburst made a noise again and nudged her.

She patted his nose, still watching Kayden. 'Yes, boy, I know we sort of do now but not like them. I can't hear your thoughts yet but I promise I will try. Can you hear what they are saying, boy?' she asked. 'Kayden's using Zoltan's magic to help him link me to the rest of the team isn't he?'

He threw his head up and down and stomped a foot.

Cassie giggled. 'I take that as a yes.'

Kayden had barely moved from where he stood while checking the horses. They just came up to him one by one and once he had looked them over, they disappeared back into the fog. It was thicker now and almost eerie and soundless. Even Starburst stood quietly beside Cassie unless she spoke.

When Kayden came back to the truck with the selection of horses, he pulled Cassie to her feet. 'Feel like a little ride in the clouds with me this afternoon?'

Chapter Ten

Life Above and Beyond

C assie had only just come out of the shower when the men turned up. As she dressed and dried her hair, Kayden and Jason made breakfast while the others sat around discussing what a buzz they got when Kayden linked Cassie to them.

Cassie came out to a loving new family that ate and chattered happily together and the good mood continued into the day. Kayden never left her side and even downstairs in the satellite room where he was unable to hold her, he kept gently pulling her close to him while he spoke.

Kayden told them how the star constellation the Three Sisters, who were three very powerful white witches, had meddled in the war, conjuring up a little witchcraft to help Orion's cause. The wizard Aldebaran and his mate the warlord Conom, had since found out and had just deployed three super-strength comets to take out the Three Sisters' home worlds and wipe their existence from the galaxy.

Kayden addressed his men, telling them to make sure that if Cassie needed extra power, they were to give her what she needed if it came down to her joining the fight.

Cassie felt a sensation of power run through her. She realised that this must have been coming from them all and she started to understand why it was imperative to have the team connected as one unit. They all supported each other and for now it was her they were helping. She was terribly grateful. This whole adventure was daunting, yet she didn't want to look weak before Kayden or his men. She straightened up, shaking the fear from her thoughts.

'That's enough for now. We need to rest before we take off.' Kayden hugged Cassie possessively, understanding the concern and fear she would be feeling, this being her very first mission.

All the beds and couches in the house were taken up as if they had done this many times before. Cassie realised how difficult it must have been for Kayden to keep her a secret for so long. She thought it was very sweet as she nuzzled into him on the bed, glad this time he would be taking her with him. She felt Kayden draw her closer to him as he sent them all into a fog-like sleep together. Her last thought was of how remarkable he was because of the control he had over their minds.

When they woke, they joined the others on the porch and sipped coffee while waiting for the horses to ready themselves. The boys passed around the golden bridles as Zoltan led the other four horses out of the barn. Cassie's eyes were wide with amazement as they lined up and stood like soldiers themselves in a perfect row with their heads held high. She could hear Kayden giving orders telepathically to Zoltan who in turn passed the orders to the others.

Woody leant against the house next to her, feeling her confusion. 'Did you know your man's mystical name is Ahearn? He is owner and lord of all horses. His gift allows him to communicate with them all; however he only chooses to speak to Zoltan. His horse controls the entire herd.'

Cassie was fascinated as she stood taking it all in, not wanting to miss a thing.

Woody grinned and ruffled her hair. 'Now watch and learn, princess. You will have your own horse soon.'

Woody bridled his horse. Once the golden bridle was in place her mouth gaped open as she watched his horse magically grow wings and armour of multi-coloured beads and pearls covering its entire body. It was the most beautiful transformation she had ever imagined possible. She had watched movies about Pegasus and seen animated mystical kids' programs but this was enchanting. Cassie quietly watched as Jason, Conor and Ethan slipped the golden bridles over their horses' heads and the same thing happened. The four winged horses now stood, glowing with soft-coloured pearl armour. Each horse was identifiable by a marking of coloured pearl that swirled along their sides like a tattoo, entwined in the mother-of-pearl armour.

Cassie sucked her breath in at the beauty of it. When she finally breathed out, it was with the biggest smile. Kayden grinned back with a relieved sigh.

Woody and Conor mounted first and instantly a bright glow surrounded them. When it dulled, it left them dressed in black leather pants and boots with white T-shirts. The T-shirts had slashes across the chests, exposing a lot of skin and even though the glow had gone, their bodies were still illuminated, making them look angelic and very handsome. Swords and daggers had also appeared and the two men watched her face, gauging a reaction.

Cassie jumped up, clapping with excitement. 'Goddamn, you guys look hot!' She almost danced over to them, poking at Conor's skin to see what he felt like and then stroking his horse. 'Feels like real pearls,' she said, gently touching the wings and trying not to spook the horse.

Woody and Conor high-fived each other. 'You heard her, mate, we're hot.' Conor was grinning.

Turning back to Kayden, she put both hands up to her face, now concerned. 'Jeez! I hope my clothes don't change to that outfit.' She was aghast and unsettled. 'What a peepshow. Hope you have a plan B.'

Kayden put his hand up and in it he held a jacket. 'One step ahead of you, sweetheart. We've never had a woman with us before so I've told the guys not to look in case I have to cover you up.' He didn't sound too convincing as to what would happen.

While he bridled Zoltan, the men grumbled that Kayden was spoiling their fun but as instructed they all turned away politely while Kayden lifted her onto his horse. Cassie watched as everything around her lit up; the glow was quite intense. There was a moment of nothingness like she was floating, and then the light dulled and she glanced down, quickly making sure she was covered.

'I look like Cinderella, only they forgot to add all the material. These horses are so naughty.' She put her hand up to her mouth, stifling a laugh.

Kayden was in a trance as he watched her transform into the most gorgeous creature he had ever envisaged. Cassie's gown was of the softest, sheerest of all materials: totally unearthly. The top of the dress was cut low and definitely showed off her perfect shape, making her perky and seductive. The dress fitted faultlessly, showing off her gorgeous slim waist, opening to reveal soft leather sandals that were laced and criss-crossed up to her thighs and showed off her long and shapely legs. *Damn! Does she even have knickers on with this?* It slit right up her thigh. He glanced back up at her face and hair. She looked like a model with perfect makeup and soft and silky hair that swept up into white-beaded clips. No way was he covering any part of her up. She was more than a little hot and the men would perve but so could he. It was in his arms that she would be.

Cassie turned pink with unease as she looked down at the scanty dress she had on. However, her shyness eased as she saw the approving look on Kayden's face. 'You look like an angel, honey. You look beautiful,' Kayden murmured, mesmerised.

The rest of the team turned and gave her a few complimentary whistles.

'Wow,' Woody commented. 'Who would have guessed a female would look that good? I would have insisted one come along every trip!' he said, trotting his horse up beside them and poking her in the arm as she had done to them a few minutes prior. 'Just checking she's real.' He chuckled, moving away, copping a playful punch from Kayden before he mounted the horse to sit behind her.

The glow he produced put a tingle through Cassie and he felt her quiver. The way she looked he wanted to make her do more than that. He smirked at the thought. When the bright glow subsided, Cassie twisted in the saddle and grinned. 'You're not just hot, babe, you sizzle.'

That's my girl, he thought. Still likes me best. He grinned back at her and gave her a quick peck. 'Now, let me focus, sweetheart or we'll never get to our destination.' He shook his head and tenderly pulled her back against him as he took the reins and trotted Zoltan back to the paddock where the portal to a new world awaited her.

Before they went through, Cassie turned with eyes lit up in anticipation. Her face relaxed and her lips parted slightly. 'I'm ready to see your world this time.'

'You're one gorgeous looking woman, Cass. How I'm ever going to concentrate tonight, I have no idea.'

She giggled and wiggled comfortably into him—maybe a little closer this time—and he groaned quietly and closed his eyes, knowing her well enough to know she had deliberately done it.

'You little devil woman,' he whispered and the depth of his tone tingled through her. They both laughed quietly at their secret bit of fun as Zoltan headed toward the portal.

Silence fell around them and a strange sensation of going into another dimension took over Cassie's thoughts. She watched as the clouds began to swirl into blue, green, red and purple laser-like shapes. A pattern emerged and changed; the colours twisted and turned into star shapes until finally a hole appeared in the centre of the star. She felt mesmerised as the colours all swirled into one, enlarging the hole until there was no star left, just a swirl of mixed colours and the opening which they glided through.

She whispered how incredible this was to Kayden. She'd never dreamed anything like this existed. They came out on a cumulonimbus cloud that extended up thousands of metres, and while gliding within the cloud, magic flashed before her, the explosion of pastels puffing out around her like cotton candy, soft and calming. After a while the colours ran together until another star shape as bright and pretty as you could imagine formed before them. The centre swirled as they moved closer to the opening; the circle enlarged and they flew out the gateway into the atmosphere where the stars were.

Cassie blinked her eyes, adjusting to the brightness and clarity that burst into her vision. Once her focus was clear she took the opportunity to look around, curious to see what earth looked like from up there. Gone were the clouds they had come on, replaced by a pretty night sky that sparkled and glowed with planets, moons and stars. The atmosphere was clean and fresh: it stimulated the senses.

Kayden pointed out the world they had come from and as Cassie thought, from up there it was just a shining dot in the sky. The galaxy of stars that were many thousands of miles apart sparkled like diamonds. The close stars looked just like planets, only not completely round; actually they were slightly bent out of shape. The only common dominator was that all of the stars up close to her had a glow around them. This glow highlighted to her the five points of the star that the guys used to position themselves when putting out the star.

She understood now how Kayden and his men could easily find their mark when taking control of the star. Kayden had told her she would develop many special gifts once he took her over, even controlling the way she saw things. His talents certainly went far beyond those she had ever dreamed another person could have.

Cassie suddenly felt a bit overwhelmed that he had chosen to love her alone, out of so many who would certainly be proud to stand beside such an exceptional man.

As they moved closer, the glow around the stars faded. Cassie was now able to see everything on the star with clarity.

Kayden's mind cut off her thoughts.

The horses' magical powers allow your eyes to transform so you can be this close and not suffer any glare. This is the same magic that also helps us breathe and keeps our body temperature constant. Once you adjust, Cassie, your own powers will take over and you will be able to do it on your own without the horse's help. I must stress though that even while you can live up here, once the horse is de-bridled, you will find your powers weakened.

Cassie watched as they neared the stars of the Three Sisters. She thought how easy it was to pick the constellation from up here. They flew around the three stars while Kayden checked something out. He was quiet, not telling them what he was looking at and she thought the no-talking rule really sucked, especially when she wanted to ask so many questions.

She watched quietly and saw a current that seemed to crackle and spark out blue lights between the three stars. Kayden, obviously satisfied, moved them towards the middle star. As they flew closer, Cassie's eyes widened as she saw the size of the enormous castles below them. Around the grounds, funny-shaped critters ran about forming lines and they stood like soldiers waiting to receive them.

Kayden tightened his grip on her and seemed nervous for her. *When we pull up, stay with Woody and do as he tells you, okay sweetheart?*

It seemed they were landing. She figured she could talk now and hoped it was alright. 'What were the blue laser lights linking the three stars?'

The sisters rule a star each. This star we are landing on belongs to the eldest sister, Adora. She is running a current between her two other sisters trying to build up a golden cloud of protection. If she can formulate enough power it should deflect the Comets if we run into trouble.

'Nevertheless, I can hear it in your voice. You sound sceptical.'

Unfortunately yes, this is their only form of defence and I'm pleased they're at least trying. But no, it looks doubtful that the power will build up enough in time. The connection still looks weak to me although it may give them protection against hurtling debris.

The horses landed and Kayden jumped down, allowing the soldiers to escort him into the castle. The funny-looking soldiers had armour and helmets, yet looked like something out of a *Star Wars* movie. Cassie wondered if someone else on earth had tapped into this planet to get the idea. The more human-like ones were about her height or shorter, but stocky and their skin was a dark purple. They all wore breast plates and three-quarter length pants with a robe over the outfit. She also noticed their heads seemed far too big for their bodies. The weirdest part was that they only had one eye which blinked constantly when focusing on her, as if she was too bright to look at for too long.

The team jumped off the horses and stood around having a chat while Woody came over to lift her off Zoltan. Cassie put her hands out and shook them, a bit freaked out as to what would happen if she dismounted.

'It's okay, you know, we are in the world of magic now. You won't suddenly disrobe, sweetie.' He sounded amused by her reaction.

Relieved, Cassie giggled and let him take her off the horse. The guards still surrounded them but little critters broke past their barrier, pushing and shoving to come over and touch her. She felt as if she was royalty or something the way they gushed and bowed in front of her. They began to surround her so Woody pulled out his sword and scared them away from her.

'They've never seen a woman with us before and you're glowing like an angel. The powers you have are strong anyway, amplified up here and they can feel them humming as I do. Only royalty hold such powers. That is making them inquisitive to meet you.' He was leaning back against his horse, watching her.

Cassie looked down at her skin that was illuminated brightly, with concern.

Woody grinned, showing her that he understood her thoughts. 'It's okay, it suits you and not everyone will feel the hum. It surprises me that the small dogitter creatures are picking it up. They are a lot more perceptive than I thought.'

A funny-shaped hairless blue dog with six legs came up. He made a funny squeaky noise and seemed to drop his head and look shy. He made Cassie forget she was a little different. Against all these creatures she didn't feel kooky at all. She bent down and patted it and the hexagon critter ran around in circles and came back, making her laugh. It acted excited and looked as if it were about to jump up on her when Woody grabbed Cassie from it, placing her down beside him and scared it away.

'Sorry, Cass but you never know what powers they may have. They all look cute till they change.' As he said it, the thing grew a big head out of its little one and snapped at him. It was clear to her it was annoyed that she was snatched away. Woody just laughed. 'She's mine, buzz off.' He shooed him away.

Cassie couldn't stop laughing as Woody scooped her into his arms and held her up so the others were unable to reach her. He made a game out of it, making the critters jump around his legs, making squeak and hooting noises.

Jason came over and scared them away. 'Quit stirring up the dogitters, man. You know it pisses the boss off.'

'Bloody pests wouldn't leave her alone and anyway I like her laugh. Stuff him.'

Jason grinned and rubbed his forehead. 'Jeez, man, I hear you. She has us all by the balls looking like this but his mood's high. Let the rest of us just enjoy it for five, will you?'

Woody smirked mischievously as he put Cassie down. 'Until later, giggles.'

When Kayden came back to them his face was expressionless but his eyes held an 'I told you so' look in them. 'The sisters have put measures in place and as I thought they are not hopeful but were pleased to see us arrive. Adora asked us to join her and her sisters for a celebration dinner if all goes well.'

Woody rolled his eyes and pounded fists with Jason. 'Remember last time, man? We drank so much the horses barely knew their way home from the intoxicating smell.' He laughed. 'I'm in.'

'Me too,' Jason agreed.

'We're in,' Ethan and Conor spun around and joined in.

'Me too. I reckon after all this weirdness I'll need a drink or two. I'm there with you guys on this one.' Cassie breathed out heavily.

Kayden lifted Cassie up on Zoltan. 'I'm only gone a minute and you've sided with my men already!' He jumped up behind her. 'Looks like majority rules but I have to warn you, princess, they have already heard about you from Zoren so be prepared for an initiation into their world. It should be some night.' He grinned and wrapped an arm around her waist. He bent close to her ear. 'I have a little initiating I want to do with you on our own so save a little of that fun for me, gorgeous.'

Cassie wiggled up against him. His breath was hot against her as a pleasurable sound escaped his mouth. 'You are so bad, girl!'

She giggled. 'That's just me giving you a sample of what's in store for you, my yummy toh revol.'

He threw his head back and laughed and the enjoyable sound he made in this world of magic floated around them. The others stopped chatting and swung around.

'Hey man, what's the joke? It must be a doozy for you to laugh before a mission,' Jason said as he mounted his ride with one easy motion.

Kayden was still looking amused. 'Private, boys. Ready?'

They nodded as they too mounted their horses, still surveying their unusually happy leader.

Kayden bent down and whispered, 'Yummy hot lover, hey? With you, my love, to keep that title will be an honour.'

CHAPTER ELEVEN

Introduction to the Stars

Commanding the horses and team was not easy this trip. Cassie's nerves had accelerated her powers and she was giving off an exquisite current. Woody and Jason were way too close, chatting to Cassie. Woody said something funny to her and she giggled at him, causing Kayden's hackles to come up. Shit! One girl and four damned competing males to fight off every time a man wants attention, he thought moodily. Stuff them. They can go get their own bloody woman. This one's mine. Mine! He grumbled within and almost sent them the message through telepathy. He was feeling so protective of his woman and wrapped his arm around her possessively.

Enough chatter, guys. Settle down. We're nearly there.

At the mention that they were nearly there, Cassie stiffened and her heart pumped far too quickly. She was scared and the men could feel it and were obviously keeping her mind off it. He kicked himself for getting all bull-headed and jealous.

You okay, sweetheart? He relayed just to her.

She nodded.

Just remember, my men and I are used to handling these situations on our own. Therefore if you find a glitch with your powers, don't sweat it. It's not as if we're up against a Supernova. We have you covered, okay, honey?

'What's a Supernova?'

Novas form from the death of an extremely massive star generally many times heavier than our sun. The star core reaches a certain mass or density limit and then explodes and the outer crust breaks away and travelling thousands of kilometres a second, destroying anything in its path.

Her silence told him that she got it and it was just one more bit of information he knew she would store away in that astute mind of hers. He found her so very intriguing the way she processed data, never needing further discussions. It was as if the lessons learned unlocked another part of the universal knowledge already deep inside her. She did it often and it fascinated him.

You knew that all ready though, hey, princess?

She leaned back into him. 'Yes and much more. Yet I'm not sure how.'

Kayden squeezed his goddess, certain now that this was what she was. However, using his gift of selected telepathy that controlled who he could send his thoughts to and what he kept personal, he decided not to reveal this thought to the team or her for fear he might frighten her further. Her little heart was pumping louder and faster by the minute. 'You belong here, princess. It's the magic inside you,' he whispered in her ear.

She turned her head slightly and he saw that her eyes reflected deep into her soul, ancient knowledge flickering within them.

Kayden had no idea why she had been sent to him yet he knew instantly that he would have to show great patience for what lay ahead in their future. Yes, he thought, settling her back in front of him as they arrived at the coordinates. He would go to the ends of the universe to keep her safe and protected.

As soon as they stopped, Kayden could feel that something was wrong. Moving his men and their horses into combat positions, he viewed the intruding Comets. He was picking up a different sound behind them. Ethan had extra-sensitive hearing up here and seeing his back go rigid confirmed that there was a disturbance behind the Comets.

Ethan, what you hearing, man?

He signalled three, plus something scattered behind it. Kayden waited for him to pick up what it was before he reacted. The rumbling and the speed of the Comets were disguising a threat they both knew was coming but until it came closer they were both clueless.

Zoltan, get your stallions ready for anything. If this goes down the way I'm feeling it will the Comets are not our only threat.

Ethan picked it up first and signalled Kayden.

Okay, men, we have a problem. Ethan's just picked up that the Comets are magnetising and dragging meteors—some the size of a cricket field—with them. It looks like Aldebaran and Conom have broken the treaty with Zoren. This is not only a deliberate attack on the Three Sisters but us as well.

The team all looked surprised but not one of them showed fear, just pure and workable anger toppling into rage. Rage was not good.

Okay, I'm feeling you men, just settle. Anger is good—use it but don't lose it and rage out on me. Last time you took some good with you so chill, okay? With all the missiles he's sending our way it'll be tough but we also have an advantage. In the wizard's vision of this attack he mustn't have foreseen our secret weapon. None of us knew Cassie would be on this trip. Let's just say that tonight is as good a time as any to introduce evil himself to our demolition specialist.

The men all signalled with thumbs up that they agreed that Cassie was going to be some force to be reckoned with. Cassie didn't move a muscle but her hackles were up, prickling the hair on Kayden's arm where he held her. She had sat up straight from the minute they arrived, statue-perfect, alert as an alley cat ready to pounce. Her power was taking over her fear and replacing it with readiness for what lay ahead and he could feel her heart pacing comfortably now, her energy spiking and humming through him. Kayden analysed it and for what was coming he knew he needed much more from her.

Zoltan, reposition the squad. Give me double the parsec between the two teams. Jason and Conor, your target is the Comet on the left. Woody, you and Ethan handle the one on the right. Cassie will pick up anything floating in between. Well, we love a challenge, men and this is a doozy. Keep your wits about you; watch each others' backs. I'll be monitoring the debris. Keep yourselves tight with your ride in case I have to pull you out of the way of some rubble.

They nodded and signalled when they were ready. Kayden

could feel them all link and start building their magic.

Woody, I need you to control the team's power tonight. I have to concentrate on getting Cassie ready. You've got the control.

Woody gave him the thumbs up as Zoltan moved the horses as instructed. Knowing that the men knew what to do, Kayden placed his hands on Cassie's shoulders. He hated the thought of even doing this. He knew he needed to give her a couple of sessions with Woody to teach her how to use her gift without anger but for now he had to work with what he had. He firmed his grip on Cassie's shoulders, not enough to bruise but enough to cause her an uncomfortable throbbing. Sorry, but I need more than I'm feeling from you, princess—time to get you angry, he thought, hating this part. *You still dream about Alex's kisses, don't you? He must have been good to keep you away from me so long.*

Cassie swung around and glared at Kayden, her blue eyes burning through him like lasers. Man, even angry she was as sexy as hell! It took everything he had to not pull her into his arms and kiss that look off her face. He had to cut her to the core or they were all going to lose their lives here tonight. He had no choice: it was either this or give a very dangerous command. Admittedly, it would save their lives but he couldn't guarantee the lives of the other good souls who might get in the way. Right now Kayden had no intention of even considering that. Yes, the situation was critical and his men knew it but if he gave the order for the guys to cut loose and kick it into overdrive, they would have to draw the power they needed from evil instead of good. He cringed at the thought, as he'd have no control on what they ended up destroying. There would be no stopping them until their power source dried up. *Man, what a mess!*

Kayden looked around, annoyed, wondering if Zoren was watching the balls-up this mission had become. He hoped he was giving his people a good serving for their incompetent reporting. Now good and cranky, he focused back on Cassie, his eyes glowing, face taut and temper flaring.

Don't look so damned innocent, Cassie. You called out to Alex in your sleep last night. Jeez, I could have slapped you. He was hardly the only one either. I saw you with Woody before, giggling in his arms. You were flirting and wanted him too, didn't you? Please don't give me that look of purity. It won't work on me this time, bitch! You think I'm bloody stupid enough to think you kept that hot body just for me for all those months? Please! He rolled his eyes, growling out the final words through gritted teeth.

Cassie was crimson with rage. It was a cheap shot but Goddamn it, not a total lie. He was so jealous when he thought of her with another that it did his head in. She screamed out and her hand came up to swipe his face. Kayden grabbed her wrist, going nowhere near that hand and pointed it to the Comet.

A thunderous bark roared out of him. 'Use it … now!'

Kayden could feel Cassie's anger as she threw her hands at the fireball hurtling towards them. The bolt of light that shot out of her hands hit the invader and blew it to dust.

Goddamn it, she was everything he thought she could be and more. Kayden loved her so much right then that he could hardly breathe. He could feel her excitement buzzing through him for what she had just done but it was too soon to celebrate as it was far from over: that had been only a small part of what was coming.

'Cassie Wyatt! Pull it together and help the boys or they are going to die! Clear those damned meteors now!' Kayden barked the new order at her, pointing to what he needed cleared out the way. While she cleared a path he watched Woody and Conor who were already on the other Comet. A large piece of meteor was heading straight for them from an angle they'd missed. *Shytzer, too late for me to pull them out.* He straightened his posture with threatening intent, keeping up his grumpy facade. 'Cassie, help Woody!' he commanded in a tone that pulled her out of her rage to listen to him.

Her head swung around, she glanced in the direction he pointed and with lightning speed thrust both hands at the huge ball of dense and impenetrable rock, lifting it away from them before she blew it up far from where it could do them any harm. Kayden looked up and saw nothing left but soft flakes of blackened soot that blew over Woody and Conor in a dirty cloud, her delivery and execution faultless.

As she cleaned up other smaller meteors around them Kayden left her line of sight to check on Ethan and Jason. They were really struggling to get a grip on the Comet as they fought the meteors hurtling at them with velocity. The unstable axis had them spinning and changing direction every millisecond. Kayden knew his men were running out of time. He had to see if Cassie could stop it, except he could feel her powers draining as she began to enjoy herself. She was so immersed in what she was doing, thoughts of the nonsense he fed her were not fuelling her anger any longer.

He stretched his neck, cracking it each way and psyching himself up, seeing that he needed her one last time. *Zoltan, pull Jason and Ethan out and have the horses stand by for clean up.* Kayden pointed the location. Zoltan let out a sound that was almost human and thrashed his head: he was also feeling Cassie's power and it was spiking his adrenalin too. Kayden snatched Cassie's arm as it went up for another strike, careful not to go anywhere near those hands.

'You ever two-time me again, Cassie and I swear I will make you pay so badly those bruises you had when I first met you will look like bloody fingerprints. Do you understand?' he snarled and she nearly pulled out of his hands she was so livid. 'Cassie.' He controlled his voice but kept it firm and commanding. 'You can give it to me when it is over but Jason needs you so do what you came here to do and blow shit up. We need you to take out the other Comet as there is too much debris surrounding that one. It's totally out of control and getting far too close.' Kayden let her hands go, praying she threw her anger toward the whirling invaders and not him. He really felt he went too far that time. Her eyes were pits as she glared at him.

The danger was closing in. Woody and Conor just about had their Comet out and were readying their horses for clean up. Even if Kayden called them to come and help this side, they would never get here in time. He watched with bated breath as Cassie flung him one more glare that would kill. All of a sudden he felt her draw from him.

How the hell was she doing that? She had somehow linked back to Zoltan and him, snatching power from them both. Kayden slumped as he was temporarily drained and he knew it was going to be a huge hit this time. As that thought left his mind he could only watch and wait as Cassie pulled what she needed and threw both her hands up together with massive force. Silver streams of lightning shot out from her in every direction.

What the hell! Kayden hollered in his mind to his men. *Did you see that guys?*

The men all nodded, punching the atmosphere with their fists. The explosion was so fierce Kayden had to hold himself and Cassie with everything he had left or they would have blown off Zoltan. Even after the strike, the noise still thundered around them. The impact was so intense she not only blew the Comet out of the sky but also cleared a path of meteors with it. In one blast, she had just about cleaned the entire field.

'Superlative,' was all Kayden could think to whisper out. *In all my life, I have never seen anything like it*, he relayed to the others, amazed. After the intensity of the power surge, Cassie went limp in Kayden's arms. Her mind was still alert but she was drained and exhausted, needing time to recharge. *Way to go, sweetheart, you did really well. Just relax now. The boys can take it from here.*

Holding the biggest treasure the world would ever see, Kayden sat contentedly, knowing his team had kicked butt. It took everything he had left not to shout, punch the air, cry, laugh and take the beauty in his arms, making her feel the joy she had just given to him. There was not going to be one part of her luscious body that he would not kiss and thank as soon as he had her alone. But for now she needed some calm time to recharge. When the men were done, Kayden knew he could draw on the power of their adrenalin rush to make Cassie feel better.

Chapter Twelve

Radar

ow, did I do that?

Cassie's mind raced as she slumped back against Kayden, her body numb and exhausted. Kayden held her and that was all she could feel. His arms had wrapped around her the minute she leaned into him and she could feel him now as he sent happy little sparks through her. Calmness flooded her mind as she watched the rest of the team complete the mission. The men and their horses were literally glowing and they started spinning like tops. The speed of their spinning formed a cyclone of colourful lights and the men inside were now a blur. The colourful cloud they projected was charged with electrical bolts that began to smash through the meteors, disintegrating anything and everything in their paths. They continued to whirl and the force of their spinning suddenly became stronger as they linked themselves together with a charge, similar to what she had seen from above when they had arrived at the Three Sisters. Whatever magic it was it was disintegrating whatever was caught in the middle, blowing it to fairy dust that sparkled all around. The colourful fragments reminded her of being inside the clouds—exquisite and so very pretty. Cassie now understood the Cloud Riders' power. Her method was quick and deadly when she was mad enough but the rest of the team were beautiful to watch; it was absolute perfection in motion. With the danger eliminated, they slowed and once the glow faded they sat on their horses and high-fived each other.

It was over and as if she had suddenly broken out of a trance Cassie's memory returned. She lurched forward and snapped her head around to face him, her angry eyes glaring at Kayden. He was grinning as if butter wouldn't melt in his mouth and he held his hands up in a protective position. 'Please don't hit me! I promise I'll shut up now,' he chuckled.

'That was such a dirty trick, Kayden. Don't think you're getting off that easy. That was really, really mean and now everyone knows about Alex. Couldn't you have just spoken the words instead of relaying it by telepathy? And I did not sleep with Alex or call out his name. Damn you, Kayden. Grrr ... you made me so angry, I still feel like I want to slap you.'

Her body shook, she was so infuriated. In one quick movement, Kayden spun her around into his arms and was kissing her. Cassie struggled against him until the passion of his kisses calmed her and his love was all she could feel. Her mind was now torn, wanting his lips to stay on hers forever but still angry that he had said all that in front of the team. Finally he lifted his mouth from hers and she lay helpless in his arms.

'Nobody else heard what I said to you, my lovely but I needed you to think they were all listening. That was a bad attack, honey and without you here today some of us may not have made it back alive,' he said with a serious tone.

She frowned and searched for his reasoning for picking that topic to make her angry.

He seemed to read her thoughts and smiled. 'I know you love only me, princess. I watched Alex kiss you and even though it nearly broke my heart, it confirmed your feelings for me when you didn't respond to him. Will you forgive me?' he said as he laid little kisses over her face until her frown turned into a smile. 'Am I forgiven, sweetheart?' He looked at her lovingly.

Cassie touched his face; it felt like touching soft petals. He was magical up here in the sky, and spellbinding. She didn't know he could select who he could talk to and now it was just between them, she forgave him with a stunning smile.

'That's my girl,' he whispered in her ear, kissing the lobe, making her shudder and giggle. 'I promise to make up for every mean word I spoke when we get home,' he said, sitting her up as the guys approached.

Yes, my love, and man, am I going to make you keep that promise! Cassie grinned at the thought and settled back against him.

Back in formation, they headed back to Adora's star, the eldest of the Three Sisters. As soon as they stopped, Woody grabbed Cassie off the horse and swung her around. 'You go, girl.' He laughed as the others came over as well for a group hug.

Kayden moved in when they finished making a fuss and rescued her from them. 'That's enough, guys, she's only little. You're going to squash her.'

Woody slapped him on the back. 'She may be little but she sure packs a punch and knows how to make a big entrance. Zoren's going to be blown away with what just went down.'

Jason was a bit vocal and aired his concern to Kayden. 'We could've been in serious trouble out there without Cassie. I know Zoren has other battles going on but he should get his facts straight before he sends us out next time. We could have left earlier and cleaned them out of the sky before they even became a problem. That was too close this time, K man.'

'I'll talk to him when he gets here. I just had a message through Zoltan that he watched it all on the satellite link and is pleased and impressed with our new addition. He wants to meet her personally. Let's just enjoy our victory and smooth out the wrinkles later.'

Ethan looked up and his blue eyes looked anxious as a shadow came over their heads. Cassie swung around to see what had struck him speechless and spotted a straggler meteor. She knew as well as Ethan did it was too late for them to get back on their rides or even to get out the way. She had to come up with something to make her mad and quick, so she thought of her dad swiping her across the cheek. Using the anger of this memory of her burning cheek, she threw her hands up and forced the meteor back. When she had moved it far enough away, she smashed it into dust.

Dropping her eyes back down, she looked straight at Ethan. She sensed he could tell if anything more was out there. He closed his eyes as if looking far out into the universe then shook his head. She watched his look of concern turn into a smile. 'I'm positive that was the last of them.'

'Good work.' Cassie grinned at him. 'None of us saw that one coming.'

He looked so much younger—even adorable—with the expression he wore after she praised him. He put his head down and a blond curl hung on his forehead; at that moment she could feel something so vulnerable about him. Maybe he felt he had let them down, not concentrating enough to pick it up sooner. That wasn't how she saw it. They were all fairly depleted of power and it would have been hard to pick up. She wanted to cheer him up so she nudged him. 'You deserve a drink for that one. Shall we radar?' she teased him, gesturing a hand and a small bow towards the castle.

Jason and Conor cracked up laughing and followed them down to the palace while Kayden and Woody put the horses away.

'That name had better not stick, girl or I won't be grateful at all that you saved us. He was a geek with glasses as I recall, bitch,' Ethan whispered to her.

'What name? I'm here only to serve the master, radar.' She giggled and moved away from him, holding on to Jason.

'Don't hide behind me, princess. Man, he is so going to get you for that.'

Ethan came towards her and she playfully squealed and held on tight to Jason, making him laugh and protect her.

Ethan leaned real close this time. 'Big bro is not always going to be around. You're going down, girl,' he said as he strode off in front of them, catching up with Conor.

'He's fun,' Cassie whispered to Jason.

Jason just laughed and let her hang off him as they followed Conor and Ethan through the grounds. They strolled past the gardens, if you could call them that. Here she took time to take in her surroundings. In place of grass there were mirrored mosaic tiles that reflected the soft pastels of the trees. In the centre of the area, large crystal sculptures of the Three Sisters stood proudly. At the statues' feet, crystal-shaped stars and moons formed their constellation as seen from above. On the other side of the path, glistening figurines of a mystical creature towered high above her, with the body of a lion and the head and wings of an eagle. Running around the entire castle was a lake or maybe an illusion of one. As they moved closer it looked as if the water was actually made up of thousands of diamonds or quartz crystals, glittering in the moonlight.

The bridge leading to the entrance of the castle, also a mixture of the glass and crystal, was held together with what looked like gold pillars and ropes. The colourful little critters running around the grounds stood out against the softness and calmness of the setting. Further into the grounds there were trees and plants, nothing like the trees on earth. The trunks were pure white and the leaves were multicoloured pastel. The shrubs that surrounded them were the colours of the critters that ran around, and brightened up the surrounds beautifully. The light from the two full moons that circled the star above suddenly hit the grounds at different angles, causing the colours to reflect against the glass and crystal and sending an array of colours shooting around them. It was a truly spectacular sight.

Finally Cassie felt as if she belonged somewhere. Amongst all the freakishness in this new magical world she was not an outsider anymore. There were plenty of weirder things going on here than she could even dream up. Cassie was sure destiny had played a big hand in getting her this far and she was thrilled that it had led her to Kayden and all of this.

Woody and Kayden caught up to them. Jason released his hold on Cassie so she could be with her man and turned to tell Woody how she had stirred up their boy Ethan.

Kayden thought it was funny. 'Little troublemaker. You know you've just made up a new game and he'll make you play it out.'

Cassie shrugged. 'I have an advantage.'

He grinned. 'Spill.'

She giggled. 'I'm sleeping with the boss.'

Woody nudged her. 'Don't think I won't kidnap your arse, young lady, if you stir up my boys too much,' he said in fun.

Laughter helped Cassie loosen up; being part of a team felt good. The men were entertaining and it was nice to have some fun for a change.

Kayden stopped walking and kissed her hands, holding them as if they might break.

'Okay, you two.' Woody broke up Kayden's efforts to woo Cassie further.

'Goddamn it, Woody, can't you give me a minute?'

'Did, and it's up,' he smirked, putting out his arm to Cassie. 'It's time to show our newest member how to party with the stars.'

She slipped one of her arms through his and the other through her man's.

Woody patted her hand, brother-like. 'Promise me if we lead you astray and get you into trouble that you won't blow us up until we get home. There we'll have somewhere to run and hide,' he said and smirked.

Kayden scowled. 'There will be no leading the new girl astray, Woody. Don't even think about it or you know what'll happen.'

'Okay, boss, I give. Please no stuffing around with my horse on the way back. I can already feel a hangover of massive proportions and will need my horse to be steady,' he said, putting his hands up and giving in.

As they walked through the castle, Cassie was enchanted by yet more mirrors and crystals that reflected light around the rooms. Golden moons, planets and star shapes were embossed in the blue tiles on the floor. The mystical-creature theme continued, carved into huge golden pillars that supported the roof as well as into the gold frames of all the furniture. Soft, plush, light-blue cushioning of all shapes, trimmed in gold, were placed on the dining chairs and used as scatter cushions on the lounge suites.

Walking around she let her fingers glide admiringly along the soft silks and the feathery cushions before continuing along the grooves of the furniture as she traced the creatures carved on them.

Kayden was leaning against one of the pillars watching her. 'The creature is a griffin. On earth the legendary monsters build nests up in the mountains of India. Instead of laying a normal egg they lay an agate one, a coloured semi-precious decorative form of quartz, hence the pastels you see outside, a symbol of the beauty they create. The griffin's instincts are to collect pure gold from the mountains where they live and will guard their treasure to the death. Their talons are so big that after they die the wealthy pay much for them, using them as cups to hold ambrosia—known as the wine of the gods. This world is the home of the griffins and the creatures are worshipped and adored by the Three Sisters who still control the majority of them. The griffins bring the gold they collect here and the sisters get it made into all the beautiful pieces you see before you.'

He pointed to a scroll hanging on one of the walls telling a story of old. 'The only menace to the griffins was the one-eyed Arimaspians. They would kill the griffins and seize the gold for their own greed. The Arimaspians are the purple, one-eyed critters you see outside. For their crime the sisters had them captured and brought here where they will live out the remainder of their lives, turning the gold they tried to steal into what you see around you. That is their punishment for killing so many of the winged griffins on earth.'

Listening intently, Cassie had unconsciously sat down. She quickly stood up, smoothing out the cushions when the Three Sisters made their entrance. She couldn't take her eyes off the women. They seemed to float into the room, their movements languid and elusive. Their evening gowns, although dissimilar in design, were all in a delicately spun sheer-gold material that flowed around them like lustrous silk. Gold jewellery dripped off their exposed skin and they even wore exquisite gold and quartz tiaras. They were the worshippers of the gold-loving griffins and were proud to wear the gifts the creatures bestowed on them for the love they received in return.

Kayden was by their sides within a couple of strides. The redhead was holding his arm possessively as he brought her over to Cassie, followed closely by the two other sisters.

'Adora, Kewana and Dyna, I would like you to meet Cassie Wyatt, my newest warrior.'

Adora was the one she had glimpsed today with the incredibly long, red hair. Now looking at them, she doubted if they had ever been to a hairdresser. All three had unusually long hair. Kewana's hair was straight like her sister Adora's but Dyna's hair was white and curly and fell in ringlets. It was the first time she had ever seen Kayden with another woman on his arm and she had to admit there was a part of her eager to pull that long, long hair and maybe even scratch those golden eyes out. She smiled as the thought popped into her head. *As if I would.*

Up here Kayden was her boss and had spent centuries forming bonds with these celestial rulers. She had to come to terms with stunning females hanging off him as he also had to get used to sharing her with the Cloud Riders who to him, were probably just as threatening: all bulked-up, handsome and very attentive to their newest member. His little comment, while in combat, laid testament to the fact that he was maybe a little on the jealous side. Good, a bit of payback, she thought as Adora dropped Kayden's arm and the Three Sisters stood in front of her, bowing to Cassie as if she was their queen.

'Cassie Wyatt, we are blessed by your presence and we are honoured you could join us.' Adora's harmonic voice pierced her guilty thoughts.

Well, maybe I might have been a bit judgemental. She grinned at them. These gals really are quite sweet, she thought as she decided to change her mind on the whole scratching and hair-pulling thing. 'Thank you, I'm flattered but really I'm nobody special. I'm just one of the team and to tell you the truth, just winging it until they teach me. I still have so much to learn.'

Adora took Kayden's arm again. 'K, sweetie, you neglected to tell me how honest and delightful she is.'

Kewana and Dyna each slipped an arm through Cassie's and

giggled. 'You sound just like us, Cassie. Let's go get you a drink so you can tell us all about yourself. You are our hero, cloud girl,' they said, dragging her into the dining room.

Woody went straight over to Cassie with a shot of starstarter that she drank straight down to help her relax as she followed him to the table. Kayden had already pulled a chair out that she gratefully took. The last thing she wanted to do was have to make up a story about herself. There was not much to tell and these chicks looked like they wanted to settle into a real girly gasbag. Woody sat on the other side of her and she breathed easier. Saved by my team, she thought and she watched as Woody poured them some Moonjuice. She had heard about it but not tried it yet. The boys had said it was nectar from the moons precious underground rivers. Depending on how far away from the sun, the moon brew could be quite potent or very soothing. Woody passed it to her.

Kayden took it from Cassie and sculled it. 'Easy mate,' he said to Woody. 'She's not used to this stuff they make up here.'

'If she's going to be one of us we have to initiate her. She may not even react to it,' he grumbled.

Cassie patted Woody's arm. 'Maybe one to every three of yours and we'll see how I go.'

Woody grinned. 'Atta girl, Cass. You've just fought with us and we want to share this experience with you.'

Kayden leant over towards her. 'You're a good sport, honey. I promise we won't let anything happen to you if this stuff affects you and decide to let your hair down, okay?'

Cassie nodded and grinned. 'In that case, if I like it, line them up, Woody.' She decided to throw caution to the wind. *If I die tomorrow, I'll leave this world knowing that I had the best day ever.* She smiled at her thoughts. *Jeez, I even think differently up here.*

Zoren turned up just as dinner was being announced. His overpowering appearance almost made time stand still for her as he glided in.

'Does he have wings?' Cassie whispered to Woody and he laughed.

'Yes, but not when in this form.'

'Wow, he is so over-the-top gorgeous,' she gushed and giggled.

Kayden took her drink. 'That's it for you, princess.' He grinned and shook his finger at her. 'Behave or you'll have me all jealous and there is no way to kick an angel's butt,' he whispered teasingly.

Talk about an archangel! He was the epiphany of one, perfect in every way. He was tall, with large shoulders, a thin waist, blond hair, long blond lashes and fair, flawless skin. His pale blue eyes were to die for: intense, faultless and fascinating.

He went around to the sisters, taking their hands and kissing them. Then coming around to Cassie, he took her hand and with no will of her own, she stood up to face him. He took both her hands and kissed them, whispering in a language she had never heard before.

His thoughts ran through her. *You are truly a gift from the gods. Welcome to our kingdom in the heavens, Goddess of Harmony.*

As he spoke, there was an air around him that drew her in by the musical tone in his voice. It was spellbinding and a feeling of bliss wrapped around her, relaxing her and making her feel enlightened. It was as if there was no one else around them: just him and her alone, floating inside a light in space. Cassie answered his questions with honesty, her mind unable to hold anything back. When he finished speaking to her she could hear everyone in the room again and she looked at Kayden, confused.

He talked to my mind, she said to Kayden and under the angel's spell her voice was only a thought as well.

He does that, honey, but your response to everything he asked was perfect. It's okay; no one else heard other than me. He captured you with his magic and talked telepathically to you as I am now. Your secrets are safe with us.

Cassie grinned shyly back up at Zoren, his smile back was charming as he pulled her out of the trance she was in. The air suddenly filling with music that floated around them. She closed her eyes, listening to the delicate melody. He was so enchanting she wondered how long she had been with him. For hours? Maybe she had. Time seemed to have no consequence at this moment. The music finished and Cassie opened her eyes. As he kissed her hands again, it broke the spell he held over her. She shook her head and giggled. 'You are *eno toh legna*, Zoren.'

He glanced over at Kayden with a curious look.

'She called you "one hot angel" but don't let it go to your head. She's taken, man,' he said, standing up and waiting for Zoren to release his woman.

Zoren smiled. 'And you, my fair lady are one *roirepus elamef, a sseddog ni yreve yaw,* and it is an honour to have you think so highly of me.'

Cassie started giggling while sliding one of her hands from his. Showing respect, she curtseyed. 'Thank you, kind sir.'

'What did he say to her, K?' Jason asked.

'He said she was a superior female, a goddess in every way.'

Zoren bowed and then placed her hand in Kayden's. 'Delightful.' He smiled at Kayden as he went around to the other side of the table between Adora and Dyna where the sisters had laid a place for him.

Kayden seated Cassie as well, bending over to her and talking quietly. 'You have earned his respect for what you were able to achieve in battle and Zoren is beholden to you. Now just try to relax, let your guard down a little and enjoy the rest of your night, honey. Let them see the woman who I have fallen so helplessly in love with.'

Still a little shaky from being held by an angel, she nodded and drank down the shot of starstarter handed her from the table.

During dinner Zoren went out of his way to include Cassie in the conversation and made her feel very welcome in their world. He was very sweet and not overpowering at all now he wasn't using his powers on her. She found it easy with him this way and after a few more Moonjuice's that she found very refreshing, he was just one of the guys and that's when the party really started to liven up. The meal was certainly unusual: Cassie had her first real taste of star food that she made her lightheaded and had to put aside. Indulged instead in that golden liquid they called Moonjuice.

As the night progressed into dawn, they all became louder and when the craziness escalated and they just started laughing at anything stupid, Kayden made a move letting them know it was time for them to leave.

The sisters tried to get them to stay but Cassie felt it was more the single men they directed the invitation to. Woody was the spokesman and declined politely, saying they had to go home so they could bed the horses down. On the way out Cassie said that the sisters also wanted to bed something down but it wasn't horses, and those guys just wouldn't be in it. This made them laugh more.

Kayden gave her playful smack. 'Come here, woman,' he said, pulling her over to him and wrapping an arm around her. 'Bad cloud girl.' He hugged her, amused.

Zoren staggered out with them, his arms around Woody and Jason. Ethan and Conor staggered out too, arm-in-arm, still joking around. Cassie hadn't had many shots of starstarter but figured it must have been something strong to have the men in such a state. When they got to the horses, Jason, Conor and Ethan came over and gave her a group hug.

'You're a good mate,' Jason said.

'Great night, kiddo,' Ethan said.

'See you at home, cloud girl,' Conor hiccupped.

Conor and Ethan put their arms back around Jason. 'Come on, mate, you better let her go before the boss makes us pay on the trip home.'

Jason agreed and let her go.

Kayden was talking to Zoren so once the boys left her side, Kayden moved closer to reclaim his woman. Woody nudged him off.

'Finish your chat, she's fine,' he said, sliding his arm over Cassie's shoulders and leaning up against his horse with her. Cassie leant into him and started to relax again. If there was one thing she had learned so far about Woody it was that he had a calming control over her that always made her feel at ease.

'It was a good night, hey Woodsta?' she said, still a little giggly.

'You held your own tonight, Cass. You did us proud.'

'Woodsta, I think I'm going to pass out,' she said as she slipped out of his arms like a slithering snake. She felt herself being lifted into arms before she hit the ground. 'Damn, you're quick and what's in that juice? Thanks Woo—' she slurred before passing out.

Chapter Thirteen
Family Friends

I t was midday before Cassie dragged herself out of bed. The men were still asleep everywhere: on couches, chairs and the floor. She stood at the sink, sculling her second glass of water and trying to focus on how she had made it home when Kayden came in from outside.

He was as bright as a button. 'Morning, sunshine! How's the head?'

'Morning! Um, fine … hey, how did I get home?' she asked.

'You passed out. Are you feeling okay?'

'Fine, I think, just a bit fuzzy on the details. I didn't do anything stupid, did I?'

Woody and Jason woke first and rolled over, amused at their conversation. They threw cushions at Ethan and Conor, making them sit up and look around to see what was going on before flopping back down when they realised it was just their mates annoying them.

Woody leaned on his elbow. 'No, you just told Zoren he needed to smarten up and not send us into any more traps,' he sniggered.

Jason joined in 'Yeah, we loved it. Someone needed to have a shot at him about it.'

Ethan stretched. 'And you told the sisters they need to visit a stylist for their hair.'

Cassie went a deep shade of pink and put her hand to mouth, covering her awed expression. 'I did … really? My God, that's so terribly rude.'

Conor sat back up, joining in on the conversation. 'And you told us all you loved us heaps of times, didn't she, guys?'

Shocked at her behaviour, Cassie glanced over at Kayden. He didn't seem concerned at all. 'You were charming and delightful. Nobody took offence to your jest.'

'The sisters … did they seem offended at my remark?' she asked, frowning at her lack of tactlessness.

'No not really. They were more shocked when you asked them which one of us was their favourite and wouldn't give up until they 'fessed up,' Kayden said, amused.

All the boys started laughing, pushing and poking each other, ribbing each other for the sisters' choices. Adora naturally picked Woody; Kewana couldn't decide between Jason and Ethan and finally said she'd take both. Dyna the youngest, picked Conor.

Conor came into the kitchen to get a glass of water. 'But of course we were only their second choice. Your boyfriend was first pick and now he is off the market we get his leftovers,' he said, taking big gulps of water. 'Damn boss could have had any one of them and he wants our girl,' he joked, kissing her on the top of the head as he walked past.

Kayden came around the other side of the bench to Cassie and held her gently. 'It was all in fun and my men weren't much better. They had the sisters quite embarrassed with their jokes and I don't know if Zoren will get over being rubbished the way he was. I might have to put restraints on the lot of you next trip,' he said, looking around and acting serious which made them all start laughing again.

Then the stories came out about what they had all said, making Cassie feel a lot better about the little bit of stirring she'd done.

Chapter Fourteen

Break Through

C assie loved her mornings now. She felt contented with who she was and for the first time in her life she thanked the heavens every day for bringing her to the Cloud Riders and most of all to Kayden.

It was early dawn and the paddocks this morning were green and lush after the rain they had received over the past few days. Cassie had been playing with Starburst and commented to Kayden how, as if by magic, her horse had grown up overnight. 'He looks nearly as big as Zoltan.'

'Yes, he's magical just like his dad.'

'I never really thought about who fathered him. I thought horses just did it with whomever they pleased.' She was intrigued that Zoltan was the father.

'Zoltan will only breed with one mare here and no other horse dares encroach on his territory.'

'Wow, he is like his owner then,' Cassie kidded him playfully.

He grinned and took a long look at Starburst, running his hands over his back and down his legs. 'Yes, I guess he is.' He snatched her up in his arms. 'He and I have found our soul mates and boy, let any other male try to move in on our females and look out,' he chuckled, teasing her back. He brushed her lips with his. 'And yes, he is grown up enough. So your little magic playmate is ready to be broken in for you. I've just summoned the team. They'll meet us back at the house.'

'What?' She tried to keep her surprise in check. 'Am I allowed to ride on my own?'

'Truthfully, sweetheart, I've fought against it entirely for selfish reasons. Been outranked by Zoren though. He wants you on your own horse so I can get back to leading the team. He reckons we won't see your full potential until I let you fly free, so to speak. As your leader, I agree but as your man I love the feeling of you against me and will so miss this sassy body stirring me up during the trip,' he chuckled, slapping her backside playfully. 'Now, go get your new ride so we can take him back with us.'

Cassie felt an excited rush. 'I promise we won't let you down,' she said as she ran down to the water's edge to grab him. Clutching his mane as they walked back up to Kayden she looked radiantly happy. 'Starburst here is very smart and combined with my powers we're going to make a good team.'

Kayden laughed. 'Alright, you don't have to convince me but you do have to convince Woody. He's the one with the special gift that can help you develop powers so you can use them without anger. You'll need to prove to him that you can summon up your powers without using anger to make them strong. Okay?'

The guys had already arrived by the time they returned. Cassie found them in the kitchen cooking breakfast and it smelt delicious. Cassie had a shower before joining them at the table. By then it was packed full of bacon, eggs, sausages, tomatoes, mushrooms, hash browns and the largest slabs of toast she had ever seen—catering slices, she was told. She had missed the gang and sat down, talking and digging in before Kayden finally joined them. He came out with his shirt off, looking all manly and yummy as he pulled out a chair next to her.

'Eb llits ym traeh er'uoy a kunh,' she said quietly and he laughed.

Ethan laughed as well and she looked at him suspiciously. 'Can't fool us anymore with that lingo, girl. I've been practicing.'

He looked at Jason and he nodded as if they were conferring. 'Be still, my heart you're a hunk.' He leaned over the table. 'That's what she said, hey boss?'

Kayden punched his fist. 'We can't have any secrets with you lot of quick-arse whiz kids around.'

Cassie decided to outsmart whiz boy. 'Tcelletni ruoy revo hpmuirt ot yaw a dnif lliw I.'

It took Ethan longer this time and then he chuckled. 'Ah … a reverse flip. "I will find a way to triumph over your intellect." Very clever, cloud girl but not clever enough.'

'Okay, I give in. Beaten fair and square.'

He looked chuffed, the rotten sod, she thought as she piled more food on her plate. She decided she'd better up her game and find other ways to beat their clever minds. A challenge! The thrill egged her on. God, was she becoming them now she was linked to them?

'Your games are fun, cloud girl but don't make it so easy next time.' Ethan sat down, grinning as a damn cat would just after eating a mouse and by the looks on the others' faces she knew they had been helping him.

'Ah, now I get it. This is my payback for calling him radar.' She swept her eyes around at all of them. 'Ganging up on the new girl, are we?' she giggled. Catching her eye, Kayden gave her a big grin as well. 'No … tell me they didn't get you involved.'

Kayden burst out laughing and hugged her. 'Sorry, sweetheart but you did wipe the floor with us all playing cards. We men have to stick together when our pride has been dented and you are such a delightful competitor.'

'Fair enough, boys, this is game on.' She started laughing. 'You are all going down for this.'

Jason kissed the top of her head and sat beside her. After putting the rest of the plates of food in the middle of the table, Woody looked at him, screwing his lips up in a smirk, 'Scoot over man, this is my seat. Moving to the chair opposite Jason attempted a protest only to be shutdown quickly.

Woody put his hand up. 'Not negotiable, Jason. Don't even try.'

Ignoring the show of pecking order, Jason passed around the bacon and they all chatted as if nothing was out of the ordinary. *He has clearly let them know it is Kayden, me and him, and then the others.* After cleaning up Cassie joined the men and stood up on the fence with them watching Jason and Ethan break in Starburst. Cassie however was still curious about Woody and jumped down, following Kayden into the stables to discuss it.

'How come the guys don't backchat Woody?'

'I wondered if you'd pick up on that,' Kayden smirked. 'I guess I should have explained it earlier but I've been overloading you with so much to get you ready for the next trip I didn't want to confuse you with whom to take orders from.' Kayden leaned against the stable door and rubbed his brow: the little habit she'd noticed he had when he was stalling for time while he worked out how to say something. 'I'll try and explain this the best I can. As a team, we power up and share the power between us, always distributing it evenly. I assess each task and only draw from each of them the power required. Drawing too much too quickly can drain our supplies.'

'You mean like I did when I overused mine.'

He nodded. 'Exactly. If we did that and were attacked on our way home or something else came up, we would be helpless. Therefore we share. Now, to answer your question regarding Woody: he is my second in command and is the only other one on my team who can draw power as I do, only he is even more gifted in this area than I am.'

'Woody is like me, isn't he?'

Kayden nodded. 'Very much so. The way you just knew how much power to pull from Zoltan and me before your final strike on our last mission Woody can do the same, only he can use any vessel. Whereas you draw only from the light, he can also draw from the darkness, only it is dangerous and unpredictable and can't be controlled. Innocent souls disappear within that cloud of murky malice. That's why I was so tough on you out there. A Cloud Rider is saintly, a gift from God and whatever the cost, we must survive for the better of all humanity. My only other option out there would have been to allow Woody to draw from the most powerful source known, evil.'

'Wow. So he's like the coolest sorcerer ever, but a good one.'

He nodded. 'Yet, while he is my right-hand man, you and he are equal and he was letting the boys know that. Try not to judge him too harshly for what he did in there. He meant no disrespect. It is a great honour to have Woody sit by you as an equal. In my time I have rarely seen him do this.'

Cassie was stunned. 'That's quite an honour then. I keep forgetting you men have come from an ancient era and many of the rules of old still apply.'

He grinned and moved from the wall he leant against, going over to her. Cassie felt his massive arms go round her and leaned into him as she listened to his voice that had gone husky and sexy. 'That's why I hate sharing you, sweetheart. The wait for someone like you to come into my life has taken forever and then some. That being said, I have to stop being so possessive and give Woody the time he needs to show you how to use your powers correctly. We both know your family has squashed your ability to draw on your gift naturally so I believe a session or two with him will sort it out in no time.'

* * * *

Woody came in a little bit later, embarrassed that he had to interrupt them. They had been mucking around in the hay and he found them in a passionate embrace.

'Oops! Just wondered if you had found the bridle yet.' He coughed, amused.

Kayden stood up, pulling Cassie up with him and brushing her off. 'We were just discussing you.'

A slight grin etched the corners of Woody's mouth.

'My girl here needs to start practising to use her powers without being coaxed. Maybe while we're breaking in her horse you two could take off and get a bit of practising in.'

Woody wasted no time putting his hand out to Cassie. He had been asking for time to help her for weeks, only Kayden was being impossible about sharing her for even an hour or two. He wondered what had changed his mind. 'At last, K man, you've come to your senses. Come on Cassie before he changes his mind.'

She slipped her hand onto his outstretched arm and Kayden winked good-naturedly at his woman as Woody dragged her out. 'I promise to have her back in a couple of hours,' he said, yelling over his shoulder while opening the car door for Cassie to get in. Within minutes they were thrashing through the bush on a red-dirt track, dust blowing around them in a cloud. They drove up onto one of the hills before they stopped for a look. Cassie followed Woody to a spot where the view was spectacular. They sat on an old tree stump overlooking flat land that went for miles. The red earth was habitat to snakes, scorpions and many other smaller insects and bugs that she watched scatter, not only to hide from the sound of their voices but to protect themselves from the scorching sun. Some small lizards ran under grey and black boulders that were shaded by green ferns that gracefully sprouted from black stumps. Large ant mounds stood meters high, dominant over shrubs and bushes. Dried twigs from trees that had weathered too many storms were strewn around, adding to the amazing sight of this outback land now called home. The old tree they sat under had branches that stretched out far beyond them, showing the years it had graced the earth. Everything here was fascinating to her.

Woody gave her a minute to relax and enjoy Mother Nature's vast landscape. Then he turned to her with a slight hint of apology in his eyes for having to disturb her peace. She could tell he was reading her every emotion. 'For me to get to the bottom of this, Cassie I need to know a bit about your power. What age did you notice it and what did your parents do to stop you using it? You can skip over bits you prefer not to relive although all of it will be relevant. Are you okay to talk to me about it?'

'I would prefer never to have to discuss my parents for the rest of time. However, if this is the only way I'm going to learn to use my powers on my own so I can take Starburst on the next trip, I'll try to recall a little of it for you.' She coughed and fidgeted. 'The first experience that comes to mind was at the age of six. I was in the garden playing when a man, one of Dad's friends, came and picked me up and sat me on his lap. He touched me in a weird way that confused me at first and then scared me. His hands were scratchy as he held me far too tightly and I started to cry and threw up my hand to stop him. Next thing I know, I'm flat on my backside. I'd thrown him across the lawn and broken his arm. I was terrified that I had hurt the man and Dad gave me a hell of a spanking, even though I tried to tell him what happened.' Cassie took a deep breath as she shuddered and shook the thought from her mind. She grabbed a stick from the ground and dug into the red dirt, making patterns as she recalled the next time she upset her parents. There were too many times.

'After that, the magic just seemed to happen whenever I put my mind to it. I knew it was bad to use it, but I was just a kid and spent far too much time on my own. My parents freaked out if they caught me so that's when I started to use them secretly. Mainly just to move things around my room—you know, just playing—except I was caught often and was severely punished time. At ten years old I was sick of being locked up with no outdoor activities: Not even allowed to go swimming in our pool. That's when it went to far. Frustrated and angry I eventually broke the lock on the door, going out into the garden where I played. The trouble over that little slip was not worth it as they barred me from roaming the house, ever, even when no one was around. That was when it really was hard to handle. It's just when you get older you understand more and it's hard to deal with the fact your parents don't want you around them at all.'

'So what actual age did you stop using your powers? Was it around ten years old?'

'Yes, pretty much. I'd stopped using my powers altogether by eleven, thinking they might even trust me again one day but they never did. Then it all went pear-shaped and I ended up here. I'd been locked up for so many years by the time they tossed me out that I had even lost the sensation of how grass felt beneath my feet.'

'Pear-shaped, what do you mean?'

Cassie threw away the stick she'd been playing with and sighed. 'Mum and Dad went away on business and while they were gone the nanny threw a pool party. She said to stay in my room or she'd tell my folks that I organised it. She was very kind to me but she did have a mean side so I did as instructed. The music was loud so I only glanced out my window for a minute to see what a party looked like and a boy saw me and waved. I ducked away from the window but he must have been inquisitive and came and found me. The stupid nanny left the door unlocked and he barged in. With beer on his breath, he made a grab for me, wanting a kiss. As he forced himself on me he said I wouldn't have been spying on him if I did not want some of him. I had no experience with boys and tried to explain that I was just looking, but not at anything in particular. He swore and got angry, then came at me again but before he even reached me I had smashed him through the bedroom door. The nanny heard the crash and the boy was taken to hospital suffering a concussion and whiplash. He had to wear a neck brace.'

Tears ran down her face as she recalled this story. It had struck deep; it had been the final straw and the last time she ever saw home. She knew she was a bad person but she had started to confess her sins to Woody now and like her tears, they just kept pouring out, so she let them. 'Mum and Dad were furious when they found out what I'd done to that poor boy. They had to pay the parents a huge sum to keep it quiet and then I heard them fighting and Dad was saying I was evil and I was too dangerous to keep around any longer. He said I would kill them in their sleep given half a chance and he wanted me gone. I cried myself to sleep that night and when I woke I'd been blindfolded and crammed into a box. That's when I busted out and found that I was somewhere between Perth and Mt Newman. Checking my watch, I'd lost two days so assumed I must have travelled for that amount of time. I swore to myself that if I survived I'd never use my powers again. Well, that was until Jason …' Cassie stopped, realising she'd gone too far and had said enough.

'What happened with Jason? You have to tell me everything, Cassie. Holding on to all this hurt's not going to heal what you've been through.'

More tears sprung into her eyes. 'It's a secret and if I tell, you might get angry.'

'Cassie, he didn't.' He seemed to guess, his voice almost a

whisper.

She shook her head. 'No, he didn't get a chance to go too far. I threw him against the wall and nearly put him through it. That's how Kayden guessed about my powers.'

'K was there? Blatzing hell, Cassie. The rotten bastards. How can you stand being around them?'

'Woody, let me explain. They had only seen me all dirty and thought I was a plant to infiltrate your group. I'd been locked in that box for over two days and then was caught in a dust storm. I smelt bad and was covered in red dirt from head to foot. The kidnappers had been rough when transporting me so on top of that I was all bruised from banging around in that stupid container. He just thought … it was a mistake and he has apologised heaps.'

Woody sat very quietly and she could tell he was fighting back anger.

Cassie burst into tears, stood and walked away, hiding her face so he couldn't see her face screwed up with emotion. How embarrassing this all was. *Why did I tell him so much? Shit, shit, shit!* She was annoyed with herself.

Woody was at her side in seconds, pulling her in for a hug. 'Stop running, Cassie and face this mess with me. It's the only way to get through it,' he growled at her and she cried more. He sat back down on the log, cuddling her until she calmed down. He handed her a hanky to wipe her face. 'That is the last time you ever cry because you think something is your fault, Cassie,' he said softly. 'None of this was your fault and you have to start believing that. I wasn't angry for one particular thing—I was mad at all of them. The dirty old man that needed castrating, not just a broken arm, your stupid uneducated parents and the nanny who should have been the one packed in a box. And yes, Jason for not knowing what a treasure you were,' he said, kissing her forehead. 'You have been treated appallingly for most of your life and it is remarkable you have stayed so sweet and kind. You've had every reason to go off the rails and maybe even use your talent for evil, just to get what you wanted. Instead you stayed the course and kept love in your heart. So from this day forward there will be no more blaming yourself, Cassie Wyatt,' he said, holding her shoulders and looking deeply into her eyes. 'No more, Cassie. It stops here now.'

'But if I didn't have this power my life would have been so different.'

'Yes, that is true. However you have powers and they led you to us and we are all so glad they did.'

She smiled weakly. 'Me too.'

'You were a gifted child, Cassie that's all. Your parents were idiots and should have asked for help from others like yourself. Instead they tried to slap it out of you and kept you imprisoned in your bedroom. Their actions were criminal and I can't believe you had nobody around you to let you know how truly clever you are or how your talent, later in life, would be used for something as incredible as we do now. Cassie, you are now involved in an organisation whose primary job is to save the world, sometimes weekly. You are one of the most important souls in the universe.' He lifted her hands. 'These are the hands of a very exceptional and powerful woman: a gift from the gods. You will find that in time, others will bow down to you for the lives you save. Never let me hear you say anything is your fault again.'

Cassie felt his sincerity and it gave her confidence that she got it all wrong. 'Is that what you had, someone who understood?'

He grinned. 'My whole life I was being prepared for greatness. My grandma always told me that a power like mine was not given to just anyone. I was selected from millions to one day do something that would be beyond any of my wildest dreams. I just wish she were still around to see how great my life is now. You too have been selected from millions to carry a gift that is so incredibly special and I want you to feel as happy as I do, Cassie but until we can open up all the wounds of the past and then heal them, the future will stay foggy for you. Come, walk with me, we'll have a bit of a stretch,' he said, pulling her to her feet. Taking her arm, he put it through his like the old-time gentleman she felt he was. 'When you were in your room and used to move things around, did you have to be angry to do that?'

'No, I just did it for something to do.'

'And you say you were around eleven years old when you stopped practicing.'

'About then. I just felt really upset that everyone hated me so I stopped experimenting.'

They had come to another big tree that was lovely and shady, with a mat of grass beneath it. Woody stopped and pulled Cassie down. She giggled at his quick movement. He laughed with her, saying it was all part of his plan to clear her head. He asked her to trust him; by now Cassie found trusting this sweet man very easy.

'On your back, woman,' he joked as he laid her down onto the grass.

They rested quietly on the soft ground. Woody leaned on his elbow, watching her. Finally when he began to speak, the soft of his voice made her feel dizzy. She closed her eyes as she concentrated on the words he spoke, already knowing he was using strong magic to calm her.

'Cassie, I have to see what this session has uncovered and need you to work with me. Open your eyes, sweetie and look directly up towards the sky through the trees and tell me what you see.'

'Nothing. Mainly just leaves are in the way,' she answered, looking from the leaves back to him.

He smiled. 'Relax your mind and look again. Move the leaves out of the way and feel the sun on your face.'

Cassie frowned, looking again. She thought about how nice it would be to have a little sun on her skin. She closed her eyes again and could almost feel the heat. She blinked against the blinding light. Her eyes popped open and she wanted that image in front of her, so using the determination of that thought, she parted the leaves slightly, feeling a little of the sunshine. Excited that her old gift was returning with ease, she moved the whole branch. The rays shone down and the sun was so strong it stunned her. A little blinded by the light and shocked that she had accomplished her task, she flipped the branch back.

She sat up, astounded, staring at Woody. 'I did that, hey? I wasn't just imagining it?'

He grinned. 'Yes, you did it. Now lie back down, I haven't finished with you yet.'

Cassie lay back down but was breathing heavily, still thrilled with her efforts. Woody could feel her emotions drum through him and stroked her head gently to relax her. 'This time I want you to look up at the sky and seek out the joy of the sun. How nice it would be for both of us. Try to softly float us both out into the sunlight. Lay us where we can both relax and enjoy it together.'

She closed her eyes as she imagined the sun. Her face twitched with the effort of moving them into the warmth. This time when she snapped her eyes open the shade covered them like a dark cloud and she used everything she had to take them from within it. As if in a dream, both of their bodies lifted and floated gracefully as if they were held together on a feather-down bed, light and comfortable. She relaxed, feeling the air flowing under her. Then there was the sensation of slowing and settling when the earth met their bodies again. The ground was warm and the bright glare made her squint. She looked into Woody's kind green eyes. It was only when his red locks caught her attention, glistening in the sunshine, that she realised she had definitely completed her task. She ginned and he smiled back.

'You have exceeded all my expectations, little one. No more for today. Just relax now and enjoy the sun that you have just worked so hard to get us into.' He bent and kissed her forehead before closing her eyes by placing his hand over them. As if by magic she felt herself going into a world of peace as she drifted off to sleep. When she woke, he was still watching her and grinned. 'Feel better now?'

Cassie nodded. 'How did you do that? I feel like I've just had my batteries recharged; that I could get up and run home.'

'I have a little magic up my sleeve that I keep for very special angels when they need a little healing. I made you experience some terrible memories that have now been dissolved, not removed. They are just in a place now where they won't harm you anymore.' He stood up, put out his hand and helped her up off the ground. 'We'll need a few more sessions, Cassie, are you okay with that?' he asked.

She nodded and laughed as he ran with her down the hill to the car. When they stopped at the bottom, she was still giggling as she breathed heavily from the quick jog. 'What was all that about?'

'I filled you with magic. Running should tame it down. The effects can be tricky sometimes but I'll be around you for the next few hours. Don't worry, you're in good hands.'

He opened the car door for her before getting in himself. Another courteous gesture that made her grin at his sweetness. As if in a hurry, he switched on the ignition and kicked life into the motor. Within seconds the vehicle was sliding slightly before it bumped roughly along the exposed track. 'Sorry I rushed you, sweetie but it took me long enough to get this session with you. Be blowed if I want to piss off your man on the first one.'

Kayden was waiting with a big smile when they pulled up. Cassie ran and jumped into his arms. He swung her around. 'Hi, beautiful.' Putting her down, he tucked her under his arm and leant against the car so he could talk to Woody. 'How did she do?'

Woody pushed his hair back and crossed his arms. 'Better than I expected for her first time. Broke through a couple of layers. However there's a way to go before I get her relaxed enough to use her gifts naturally. She's been through a lot, K. It's not going to happen overnight.'

Kayden nodded. 'I thought as much.' He gave her a quick glance of concern and then hid it with a smile. 'You're in good hands, sweetheart. If anyone can break through your wall of pain it will be this big lug. In the meantime, your horse is ready to go. Do you want to come and have a look?'

They went over to the enclosure where Jason and Ethan were still with Starburst. There was another man there wearing a brimmed hat. He looked like a real farmer and stood talking to Conor. Cassie couldn't help thinking how similar their physics were.

'Tremaine, this is Cassie. Cass, this is my brother Tremaine,' Conor introduced them.

Tremaine took his hat off and shook her hand. Cassie wasn't surprised to hear they were related although he did have hair, even though it was very short and dark. His nose was also flatter and wider and his lips were thinner. He smiled and that was when she saw Conor in him: his eyes shone golden-brown and he had the same cheek structure when his face lit up.

'Hi, Cassie. Me bro ain't shut up about you so it's damned nice to finally put a face there to your name. I look after them there horses for me man K when he needs me. Today but I'm just here to observe. Stoked to have been able see how this little one stacks up. They tell me he's your ride now.'

'Yes, Starburst stole my heart the second I saw him, shaking and wobbling around and trying to stand up,' she giggled, remembering. She walked closer to Tremaine as they both turned towards Starburst. 'Fascinating how quickly he found his legs and then walked around like a real pro. Jeez, and we call ourselves the smarter race.'

He laughed and nudged Conor. 'Yeah okay, she's all that and cute as a button and she's right. Those darn horses of yours are way more intelligent than a man like me's ever seen.'

Conor slapped his back. 'Just keep that on the down low, bro, we don't want no one stealing any of them.'

'Gotcha, bro. Anyways I have to get back to me farm there, boy. Can't go dilly-dallying here all day with a bunch of misfit cowboys. Bad for me image.' He tipped his hat to Cassie. 'Ma'am, nice to finally meet you. If you get sick of these hard heads, call over for dinner one night. Let me show you what a real home-cooked meal tastes like. You can bring the K man too if you have to bring 'im.' He grinned cheeky-like at Kayden before looking back at Cassie. 'Just stirring up your man there. Offer is there though. You're both welcome for sure.'

Kayden put his arm around her. 'We'd love to, Tremaine. I'll give you a ring.'

Conor pulled Tremaine's hat off him playfully. 'Hey, what about the rest of us, bro?'

Tremaine snatched his hat back off him, laughing. 'I told your young lady, a real home-cooked meal. Me ovens not big enough to put the whole dang cow in to feed you lot,' he said, getting on his horse. He tipped his hat. 'Ma'am, K.' He trotted off down the path.

After he left, Conor continued grumbling about Tremaine trying to steal his girl with a roast. Kayden reminded him Cassie was really his girl, which made him grumble more. They all laughed when he stomped off, saying he was going to cook her a better home-cooked dinner, not like his dopey brother would make.

'Now the dramatics are over,' Ethan said, still smiling. He opened the gate for Cassie to join them. 'Shall we?' He gestured for her to follow him inside the pen. She jumped down off the fence and went through the gate. Jason slid easily off her horse and stood beside Starburst, waiting for her. Cassie went over to her horse and patted his stressed features.

'What've they done to you, handsome?' She clucked over him as she ran her hand down his legs and over his back the way she had seen Kayden do many times to the horses. She could feel he was sweaty and a little shaken but other than that he seemed to settle at her touch. She stood in front of him, patting the softness of his nose and watching his eyes. 'Got anything left?' she asked him and he got a wild look in his eyes like the one he had when he wanted her to chase him. She laughed and shook her head. 'Not to play! To take me for a ride, silly,' she grinned.

He nodded and snorted. With Jason's help she put her foot in the stirrup and swung herself up on him. She leant over near his ear. 'You're a big boy to get up on. We might have to practice that.' She chuckled. 'Now be gentle, boy, I've never ridden by myself before so this is new to both of us.'

Ethan led Starburst around slowly at first while Cassie settled into the trotting pace.

'Just feel him beneath you, Cass. It'll help you relax into him and him with you.' She closed her eyes and could feel his rhythm and his strength. He was gorgeous and as if he could feel her too, he started to trot, then almost to glide. Cassie opened her eyes and realised they were both enjoying each other so much that they were actually off the ground. He never even needed wings. He flew using his own magic combined with hers. They eased back onto the ground and came to a stop.

Cassie looked around. There was total silence. The men had shocked expressions. 'He's a little miracle. He knows how to tap into my power.' She patted him, very proud of her clever horse. 'You won't even need those wings, will you, boy?'

Kayden came through the gate. 'I knew I had to save him for a reason. He wanted to be with you all along,' he said, lifting her off him. 'That was surreal, very clever.'

'He's a dream to ride but I think he's had enough for one day.'

Ethan agreed and took Starburst to clean him up and give him a well-deserved drink and a feed.

After a long, hot shower, Cassie ambled out into the kitchen. Conor was stirring gravy and still looking glum. She could smell the aroma of a well-cooked dinner filling the air. Slipping her arm around Conor's waist, she hated the vibe of rejection he was feeling from his brother. He put his arm over her shoulder, still stirring the pan.

'Want me to go sort him out for stirring you up or go give him a little zap, knocking him right off that horse of his, flat on his butt?'

Conor chuckled. 'It's okay, Cassie. He just knows you're special to me and is trying to push my buttons to make me angry enough to talk to him. I get it really. He has to work his butt off and all he sees me do is party and get with the girls. He's told me he knows something big is going on and it frustrates him that I keep it hidden.'

'You know I would never go hang with him without you. When Kayden makes a day, I'll get him to tell just you, okay? The three of us will sneak off and go eat his dinner and then I'll help you beat him at cards. Then if you still feel unhappy I'll just have to make good on that threat and zap his hiney anyway. How's that sound?'

He grinned and hugged her. 'Why do you care?'

'Woody told me how you guys feel me now we're connected. You know, about that hum that makes you want to be near me.'

He nodded and looked surprised that Woody had told her.

'Well, times that by five and you will feel what is inside me. So if you're sad, then I'm feeling sad too, me boy.' She grinned. 'Bet you all didn't know that. It started as soon as we ate our first meal together.'

'Same.'

Cassie nudged into him. 'Hey, but it is our little secret, okay? No way do I want my man getting himself all worked up that I can feel you all too.'

'You didn't even tell Woody.' He chuckled, looking a lot happier that only he knew her secret.

She shook her head. 'Now give me another one of those hugs and go take a shower while I dish up. Goddamn, you can cook,' she giggled, sniffing the air as he took off for a shower.

Kayden caught the tail end of the conversation Cassie had with Conor. He couldn't remember a time when the men looked so completely happy and so at ease with one another. They had gone from a confident five to a feeling of oneness. The magic of Cassie was a gift to them all.

CHAPTER FIFTEEN

My Prince

It was a stinking hot evening and that night after dinner they all cooled off in the lake at the back of the property. Afterwards Woody and Jason built a fire for them to dry off. Cassie cuddled up to Kayden, worn out from her session with Woody and glad for the warmth as the nights seemed to get chilly of late. It had been one of those fabulous days, one of the ones you slide into your memory bank to retrieve on a bad day. By the sound of some of the stories now being told, there were going to be a few of those. Her man's body was warm and the eyes she was trying so hard to keep open, shut with a thud. Almost overcome with sleep, she listened as the stories of other missions changed to the new threat in the galaxy. She smiled, imagining them waiting for her to conk out before bringing up something they thought might make her worry and in turn, hinder their fun together. She was sure they could smell her fear and she so wanted to change all that, to toughen up and become more confident and gutsy. Hopefully that would stop them treading on eggshells around her.

In her fog, their voices still made sense and she could almost feel the evil that breathed down their necks. This man's name was Aldebaran and this dark wizard had a friend, a tyrant called Conom. Both were powerful rulers and both were determined to take over the constellation of Orion's Belt. Both were hell-bent on destroying anyone who dared to stand in their way. As she listened to them work out a game plan to stop the feud and bring reconciliation, sleep overcame her. She felt safe enough with those around her to drift into a dreamy world of darkness and peace.

Eyes blurry from too deep a sleep, Cassie was surprised when she woke to find they had camped out all night. A sudden jolt of excitement gripped her: she had never slept outdoors before. It was nice to wake up and see all her friends still hanging out, even if they were asleep. The boys were lying on sleeping bags around the fire. They must have been in a deep sleep as they were breathing heavier than they did when they rested before a mission. Then she saw the empty carottles of starstarters they had brought back from the last mission and understood their comatose states.

Kayden still had her securely in his arms and her movement woke him up.

'Sorry, I didn't mean to disturb you,' she whispered as she rolled around to face him. His eyes were dreamy and loving and he started kissing her gently around her neck and then her face until he found her lips, groaning as his feelings overwhelmed him.

'Shh, you'll wake the others,' she giggled.

He put his head up and saw they were not in bed. 'Crap!'

'Shh,' she chuckled again.

He stood and pulled Cassie to her feet, taking her around to the other side of the truck. He leant up against it and pulled her into him again, covering her lips with his hot mouth while his tongue explored the sensitive and sensual parts of her mouth. 'I could eat you all up, baby, you taste so delicious,' he groaned.

'Later, bad boy, you have to go check the horses first.'

His eyes roamed over her and he grinned with a naughty, boyish look.

'Kayden, behave.' She slapped his arm playfully

He stepped away from her and put his hands up, smiling. 'Okay, but I'm coming back to get you, my lovely and sending this riff-raff home. I have something very special in mind for you today and you'll want it to be private.'

'Wow, the mind boggles.' Cassie did a little wiggle and twirl for him, lifting the edge of her T-shirt up to stir him before skipping off laughing.

Kayden pounced on her like a lion and snatched her up in his arms, growling deeply into her ear while nuzzling her hair. 'You're so wicked, woman. Now behave until I get back or look out,' he said, putting her down.

Jason lifted his head up, rubbing his eyes. 'Hang on, K,' he said pulling on his boots as he watched Kayden head for the truck. 'I want to come and check on Starburst, make sure yesterday hasn't rattled his chain.'

Kayden nodded, waiting.

Woody also stirred and jumped up refreshed, showing no side effects of all the alcohol he would have consumed. He threw some more wood on the fire poking at it with a stick. Ethan and Conor both just groaned at the noise, rolled over and went back to sleep.

The morning was crisp with the fragrance of fresh redwood in the air. It felt so peaceful just listening to the crackle of the flames as they bit into the dry wood. Cassie plonked down next to Woody, who put a friendly arm around her. 'Feel like working with me for half an hour while it's quiet?'

She didn't refuse. She felt like he had lifted a great weight off her in the last session and looked forward to learning more about her own abilities. What he had her doing already had amazed and excited her

He smiled at her enthusiasm. 'Just want to check your concentration after yesterday, see if you held it.'

'No probs, I am all yours.'

'Okay, cutie. I need you to be serious for me. Imagine we're on the other side of the lake and take us there—no dunking me in that water.'

Cassie looked over to the other side and then closed her eyes and concentrated. The temptation to drop him in that water was just too strong and she stopped and shook her head. 'You really shouldn't have put that thought in my head. I can't get past it.'

'Cassie.' He sounded firm, no nonsense.

'Boy, no guessing who woke up on the wrong side of the bed this morning,' she mumbled and closed her eyes again. She felt him with her as she visualised the other side of the lake. It was only after she felt them moving did her eyes open, allowing the magic of the moment to flow through them as they gently floated towards the opposite embankment. The sensation although strange left her empowered, determined and focused as she concentrated on Woody's arm around her so she could keep them moving. The spot she had chosen to set them down was coming closer as the thought popped back in her head about dunking him. It was just too strong and she started to let go of her new found gift when she heard him whisper in a grumpy voice, 'Cassandra.'

Something frightened her. It was what he called her. She shook violently as she fought to regain control. Once they sat back on solid ground, tears stung her eyes. Her breathing was uncontrollable and she was beginning to panic. She struggled to get up but Woody kept a firm grip on her. 'Woody, let me go or I'm warning you, I will make you!' she fumed at him.

'Shh … work with me, talk to me,' he said sweetly and kissed her head. 'Tell me what you're feeling.'

'Angry!' she snapped.

'What memories did it just bring back?'

Frustration and uncertainty weakened her mood. 'My mother was the only one who ever called me Cassandra. I never once saw fear in her eyes and yet she never once stuck up for me. I was her child, her daughter. Woody, why?'

'Maybe she knew where you inherited your powers from, Cassie. Maybe she was special also and kept it a secret so she could live a normal life. She would have been exposed herself if she pandered to you. You must have got it from one of your parents.'

Cassie breathed out a big sigh of relief. Could that have been it? she thought. 'I never thought about it like that. She may have struggled and suffered for years. I know how hard it was for me to hide away my natural abilities. She must have gone through hell trying to hide as well. I always thought I was just a freak. Hereditary never came to mind.'

'It still doesn't excuse her behaviour toward you, Cassie. You should forgive her. It will help you heal but never feel sorry for her. She made her choice and it made her a terribly selfish and dangerous guardian to you. You deserved so much better.'

Cassie felt calmer. She was blown away by how smart and caring Woody was. 'You always make me feel like I'm so worthy.'

He squeezed her gently. 'You, my dear Cassandra, are the most precious gift that anyone could ever dream of.'

She searched his face and almost smiled. 'It didn't cut me when you said it that time.'

'Because your name is beautiful and when you hear it I want you to remember it the way it was meant to sound.' He stood up, pulling her to her feet with him. 'No more today. Kayden's just returned and is looking for us.'

They walked back around the other side of the lake. Kayden did seem anxious. 'We've been summoned,' he revealed to them while searching Cassie's face. Without thinking, he tucked her hair behind her ears as if he was looking for something, maybe trying to read her mind through her facial expressions. 'How is she, Woody? Will she be okay to ride on her own? It's a renegade star this time. I'll need to be hands-free to help you. Zoren wants it extinguished.'

Cassie spun around and eyed Woody, remembering Kayden had told her it was Woody she must convince. 'Woody, please. I won't muck around, I promise. You're teaching me. I get it now.'

He crossed his arms, looking up at the sky, the muscle in the side of his neck twitching as he thought about his answer.

'Please. I promise I won't even smile unless you tell me to.'

He bit his lip and she knew he was trying not to grin at the pleading look she was giving him. 'Don't let me regret it, Cassie. You have to do everything you're told without even thinking about it. If you have any crazy thoughts at all, Starburst will feel it and you could endanger both your lives. Do I make myself perfectly clear? Not a twitch unless you're instructed to.'

'Perfectly clear, not a twitch. Thanks, Woodsta. Starburst is going to be so excited when I tell him.' She let out a yahoo and hugged Kayden, excited.

Before following the men down to the satellite room beneath the barn, Cassie stopped quickly to tell Starburst. He seemed to understand and then gave her crazy look.

'You're excited, hey boy.' She felt just as keyed up as he was. Giving him one last pat, she went below to join the others to be briefed.

They were standing overlooking an oval table in the centre of the room when she joined them. The middle of it was lit up with the portion of the sky they were going to. Kayden was just finishing off the measurements and even the floor was lit up under their feet with a red line, mainly through the zodiacs.

'How do you come up with the exact coordinates?' Cassie asked, curious.

Kayden glanced up, glad Cassie was interested in that side of it. 'In astronomy, constellations are measured from a line called the ecliptic celestial equator, which is the path that the sun crosses the sky over the course of a year. The moon and the planets also lie within that ecliptic.' She followed his hand along what she was sure was the ring he spoke of. He pointed it out for her. 'This ecliptic ring is what is used to work out the exact location of the constellation or in this case where the rogue star has been detected. By using longitude and latitude measurements it gives us the exact point we need to intercept the target.'

Kayden lifted his head from the table that was his map system to the stars. As he spoke, his voice was articulate. He looked comfortable and confident as he began briefing them while projecting the info from his laptop onto the huge wall-to-floor screen. Cassie imagined he would have made an excellent speaker, maybe even a president, if this job hadn't come about.

He ran his long, strong fingers though his silky strands of hair and she watched as he unconsciously pushed it back off his face: a trait of his that was so endearing.

'Aldebaran, as you all know is renowned for his wild nights and joyful events,' Kayden continued with a smirk, putting it as delicately as he could for Cassie's benefit.

The men nodded in agreement.

He glanced over and spoke to Cassie, catching her up on what the others would already know. 'Mulu, ruler of the Crux, better known as the Southern Cross constellation, has three sons and four daughters. The Cross family and Aldebaran's new pal Conom are among the selected friends who have enjoyed many a social evening partying with Aldebaran on his home world.' He turned back to the group, addressing them all again. 'One of Mulu's daughters fell in love with the womaniser Conom. He knew how she felt and even though he felt nothing, he bedded the virgin. Then before the night was through, he went back to the party and that very same night bedded sister number two.'

'Do you lot know this Conom?' Cassie asked, thinking about her first time and how devastated the poor woman must have felt. 'I'd like the chance to zap the womaniser on behalf of that poor girl.'

Woody cut in, chuckling. 'None of us have ever met Conom so his character is only on hearsay. We have intel that he's a gambler and spends a lot of time on earth when not on his home world playing war games and causing trouble. Even sends his people to our meetings to do his dirty work, never showing up to anything he's invited to. He's very choosy whom he takes up with and we're not on his pal list. Zoren's the only one who knows his true identity.'

Kayden nodded. 'Yes, Zoren believes Conom is guilty as charged. He has a terrible attitude towards females. Apparently, he laughed at both women when they confronted him flipping them off as being ridiculously childish and jealous. Zoren said when his team questioned Conom he denied it was his fault and said that neither was very satisfying. He joked, saying he gave them what they wanted and lived up to his side of the bargain. The three brothers are furious he treated their sisters so poorly and forced Mulu into a corner, insisting he make a choice. Mulu has since severed the friendship with Aldebaran, now standing by his sons. They are refusing to have anything further to do with Aldebaran until he sends his new friend Conom packing. Which will never happen.'

'What did Aldebaran do? Did he try at all to mend the rift?' Woody leaned against the bench, crossing his arms.

Kayden chewed his lip. 'I'm hearing you, man. Those two have been mates since even before our time. Apparently, Aldebaran couldn't believe his once loyal companion Mulu and his children could turn their backs on him so easily when it had nothing to do with him. So he has wiped them off his Christmas list so to speak and washed his hands of the lot of them.'

'So, don't tell me, the sons have linked up with his enemy Orion. And Orion is offering them hunting privileges on his land in return for loyalty,' Woody cut in.

'You've got it in one. Orion heard of the squabble and befriended the brothers immediately as a tactical advantage. He gave them his sympathy with an offer that was obviously too good to refuse. Now, as you can guess, the boys accepted, blinded by whatever was on the table as an offer. Now to rub salt into the wound they have deliberately become allies, prepared to take up arms against Aldebaran to protect their new friend Orion.' Kayden switched on another screen, showing them the location where they would be going. 'Anyway, the sons have put Aldebaran's back to the wall. He and Conom have reacted unfavourably and have now put in place a plan to wipe the Cross family from existence.'

'Can't you threaten to put out their stars if they refuse to stop?' Cassie asked.

Kayden shook his head. 'The wizard is pulling his power from the dark side and our efforts to get even near his home world have been useless. He has a protection up that is impenetrable by good. All we can do until Zoren finds a way around it is to stop his assault.'

Woody let out a huff. 'Why they thought they could go up against Aldebaran has me beat. Orion needs a kick in the pants for involving them.'

Kayden agreed, turning back to the laptop and punching in new coordinates.

Woody played with his jaw in thought. 'Yes, and I for one would definitely be willing to hand out such a punishment.'

There were a few snickers and whispered comments from Conor, Jase and Ethan who were already laying bets down in Woody's favour.

Kayden put up his hand for quiet. 'Okay, settle down, men. The last thing I need is a price on any of your heads after Orion regains consciousness.'

Woody still had a gleam of amusement but kept quiet as Kayden moved everyone's attention onto the screen on the opposite wall. The rolling images focused on the far side of the galaxy. Kayden pointed out the rogue star that was on its way to the Southern Cross.

'This is the star that Aldebaran and Conom have now deployed to seek out and destroy the whole of the Southern Cross constellation. They aim to wipe out the entire Cross family. The star is at the end of its existence and its ruler is on a suicide mission, wanting to go down with his ship so to speak.' Being Cassie's first real mission riding solo, Kayden wanted her to understand the dangers. 'This particular star will not be easy to control or even destroy. It's an eruptive binary explosive star. Abbreviated name is RSCVN. When ready to expire it sends out flares and shrapnel at massive speeds until it blows up. Due to the problems in the past, Zoren has requested you personally be on guard for anything we might miss.'

Cassie got how unpredictable the situation could become yet with her and Starburst's magic combined she felt confident they would handle their part in the mission. Kayden ended the session by closing down the computers.

Back inside the house, they all lay around resting although it wasn't easy. There was a lot of anticipation and speculation because they were coming to grips with a new rider. Cassie would have her own horse so it was becoming a drawn-out topic of concern. When Kayden felt the topic was done to death, Cassie could feel him calming them and knew it wouldn't be long before they would all be put into a restful sleep so they could recharge, giving them all an extra boost in power for the mission ahead.

When he woke them, the sun was setting in the sky. Refreshed and feeling like she could take on whatever was thrown at her, Cassie walked outside with the guys to drink her coffee and watch Zoltan lead out the horses. They trotted in formation and then stood in a perfectly spaced row before them. They almost kneeled on one knee as they bowed their heads to show their loyalty. Even Starburst did it and she thought he looked particularly cute doing so.

The men bridled their horses and jumped up. Kayden gave Cassie a magical golden bridle for her ride and waited to help her.

Once she put the bridle on Starburst he transformed into the most glorious of all. As with the other horses, the pearl-beaded armour covered him entirely. His white wings, although massive, looked so much softer, maybe due to his young age. The outstanding feature was the saddle. She would be sitting on a golden saddle while the others sat on black ones. Also while the other horses had coloured beads identifying them as individuals, Starburst had blended-gold beading that swirled around his body. His normally dark tail and mane changed to pure white and he had golden beads marking a crown across his head. He looked magnificent.

'My prince,' Cassie curtsied, and it made him snort and nod his head at her as if he agreed.

Kayden lifted her on to Starburst and Cassie transformed differently this time. She wore white leather pants tucked into knee-high boots with gold markings and a very high heel. The soft golden top to the outfit looked more like a seductively cut corset the way it laced at the front, showing a little more cleavage than she was used to. Golden bracelets wrapped around her upper arm and the clip that held her hair up felt to her like the shape of a horse. It had star shapes that dropped from delicate chains and Kayden could barely contain his amusement at her show of discomfort as she eyed herself.

'You have nothing to be shy about, my love. It is how the women dress up there. Although now I've seen it on you I believe it was designed with you in mind.' He grinned. 'You're both going to give the stars quite a surprise when you turn up today. If you don't stop that renegade star in his tracks, I'll be amazed.'

As they reached the portal in the paddock, Cassie felt totally at ease as she leaned down to give her horse some encouragement. 'You are going to so love this,' she whispered to Starburst as they entered the clouds. Her mind felt at peace as she let the flow of colourful patterns mesmerise her and as soon as she calmed, she felt Starburst settle down too. Woody was right—he was so in tune with her she would have to take control and keep him unruffled on his first trip.

While inside the cloud, the green, yellow and blue lights that formed the shape of a star blended together until the portal appeared, gradually increasing in size. This time however, the colours seemed to melt into each other, getting brighter as if they were iridescent paints swirling together until the portal was big enough for them to glide through.

Kayden's thoughts entered her tranquil state. *We'll come out in a minute and the horses will fly us up to another cloud called a noctilucent cloud which is around thirty-five miles long and fifty-six kilometres high. The cloud acts as a slingshot and will give us the height and speed we need to reach the Southern Cross.*

As they came out of the fourth dimension, they flew along until they reached a very thin, almost transparent cloud that shimmered gold, pink and purple. The coloured lighting jutted across their path in fine bursts, lengthways this time. They veered upwards so high that Cassie closed her eyes, only peeking as they neared the top. Once there, she opened her eyes to a blue lightning bolt. It shot across ahead of them, opening in the middle like a stretched rubber band that became another portal that slung-shot them straight through. The boosted speed that the cloud gave them was so intense everything was almost a blur. Then *presto*, they were up in the stars where the atmosphere was clean and clear and the view as always, spectacular.

Cassie patted Starburst as he stretched his wings out for the first time and flew on Zoltan's command. 'That was fun, hey, boy?'

He made a little snorting sound and shot her a little magic burst, showing her how much he had loved it. Like her, this was where he belonged, in the heavens with his dad.

From up here, the stars closest to her looked like glowing bubbles in all shapes and sizes. It amazed Cassie how silent it was. There were no sounds except the gentle flapping of the horses' wings and the slight disturbance they made that moved so gently around her that it felt like soft silk against her skin.

The Crux constellation Cassie knew as the Southern Cross was now remarkably right in front of her. As they came closer preparing to land, you could see the surface of the largest star, Alpha-Crucis. The superior design of their home was unusual to say the least. The huge estate below spread across kilometres of ground and the massive home was built in the shape of a cross, the extraordinary creation symbolising the constellation. They slid off their horses and chatted while Kayden went to speak with the Cross brothers.

Beneath Cassie's feet, she noticed the surface was flat and smooth—actually, she was sure it was metres and metres of slate flooring. Now, looking up at the home from this angle, it towered high above her. Large, smooth slate blocks shaped the walls which were covered by a black roof with what looked like pure-gold guttering that matched the window frames, balconies and doors. Beautiful lighting surrounding the luxurious-looking home and in one area in particular, it gave you the impression there was a well-designed waterfall and river surrounding the castle—this finished it off perfectly. Without the gold and special lighting effects surrounding the home, it may have been all doom and gloom. The critters on this planet looked like dark green, soft mops that cleaned and added a shine to the surface as they moved, seeing the path ahead with eyes that stuck out on long feelers.

Centaurs—half man, half horse—guarded the outer perimeter of the castle and as the team dismounted, more Centaurs came from a bunker underground, surrounding them but keeping a reasonable distance. The Crux constellation was at the foot of the centaurs' constellation so even though the centaurs were wild and unpredictable in nature, they did protect their own and this included their close neighbours, the Cross family.

Kayden came back with two of the Cross brothers. As they shook hand with Jason and Woody, she could tell the four of them were old friends by the way they joked with each other. Both men had very dark complexions with jet-black hair that was cut short. They were both big boys but still looked small against the team. Their only freakish attribute was the colour of their eyes. They were a bright purple, hidden behind long purple lashes. The taller one stood with his arms crossed most of the time and Cassie felt his eyes on her. He seemed to absorb her as if he could read her every thought.

Before they left they insisted that Kayden bring his team back for drinks later on, saying their father and other brother would be very disappointed to have missed them. Kayden accepted the offer graciously. Apparently the father and son were off somewhere taking the sisters to safety. Kayden never said where; he covered it by telling Cassie that the least she knew the better, in case the enemy captured her. Cassie knew the rest of the team would already have understood that, so appreciated knowing why he was being so secretive.

Waiting for the renegade star gave Cassie too much time to think. She was getting a little nervous. They had all been moved into position. Starburst and Cassie were a distance away ready to obliterate any outer crust that might fly off the star. Waiting, Cassie looked around her. 'Jeez, this is one big-arse sky up here,' she said quietly to Starburst.

As the ball of light came into view, Kayden had his team of men moved around it, getting into position. However, from where she sat there seemed to be something wrong. Kayden spun quickly to clear out the way of a lightning bolt and then Woody only just ducked in time to miss a burst of flame that darted out at him.

It's unstable men; the star's ready to blow. How like Aldebaran, the sneaky bastard to target us again for standing in his way. If it blows here it'll do a lot of damage to nearby constellations. Cassie, you're on. I need you to give the star a good shove. Thirty degrees north from where it is now and however far you can push it.

Cassie glanced up at the location he just gave her and could see it was clear of anything that shone. It was just black space. She calmed herself the way Woody had taught her and imagined the star and the empty space far above them. She popped her eyes open and with her mind, not even using hands, she shoved the star with all her might. She watched as it moved but she also felt heat and panicked that it was about to blow. Needing more power, she threw up both of her hands, putting a driving force behind it. The strike was so hard the star shot out of the atmosphere they were in, the boys hot on its trail. Even with her superior eyesight up here, they were soon out of her sight. She patted Starburst and told him he was a clever boy for helping her with that extra bit of power she needed. Cassie was told to stay put so that's exactly what she was going to do. And yet sitting so quietly, nerves got the better of her and she worried if they were alright as she couldn't even hear Kayden anymore.

Should I stay or should I go see if they're okay? The thought ran around in her head. *What if they're hurt or worse?* 'Damn, Starburst, this waiting sucks,' she bitched. 'If we go and they're fine, we'll be in trouble. Then they'll most likely never trust us again.' She kept patting Starburst, trying to make a decision. 'We'll show them we can be trusted, won't we, boy? Let's just sit tight a bit longer,' Cassie said as they sat and waited. And waited. And waited.

CHAPTER SIXTEEN

Aldebaran's Shock Surprise

C onom yelled at him angrily through the headset. 'Aldebaran, don't you dare. You'll hurt her. She's just a young lass,' Aldebaran had been watching from his home world via satellite and Conom had only just tuned in. He hadn't seen what the little witch had done. He hadn't seen the female of the group use her powers to shove their weapon out into the harmless realm of deep space. Aldebaran was so enraged he couldn't even get out what she was capable of. He was just about to knock the bitch off her horse for foiling his plan to destroy the Cross family when Conom forced him to stop. The fire in him to hurt something was raw and he had to battle to control it.

'Well, where the bloody hell did they find their new witch? I thought our crack team had executed their entire list of possible people who could have become future Cloud Riders. If we don't get rid of the damned pests we'll never get rid of Orion and I've had just about as much of him as I can take, Conom.'

'Aldebaran, I don't mind the slaughter of any man that gets in our way but I'll have no part of hurting this one. She seems to be a very young immortal, maybe just evolved, and can be controlled. Zoom in and get a look at her. Maybe she's from up here and we can deal with the family, frighten them into pulling her out of the team.'

Aldebaran turned the focus on her face. She was sitting quietly now, waiting for the others to return. He zoomed in on her face and felt a flood of emotion flow through him, an emotion he had not felt for years. He had followed this child through her entire life only getting rare glimpses of her from time to time when she went outside in the garden. Why she wasn't like other children and did not play outside daily was beyond him. It never even gave him time to snatch her up which is what he would have done given the chance. Her powers would have been so much more advanced if he had been able to get his hands on her for even just a short time. She certainly wouldn't be on the side of Zoren's sickening bunch of do-gooders.

He swore loudly and kicked over a stool in his way. 'I won't kill her just yet, Conom but whether you like it or not I'm taking her now. And she'll damned well come to me even if I have to bloody drug her, the traitorous little bitch. I'll show her which side of the fence she should be playing on and she will damned well listen. Not like her wretch of a mother.'

Conom was quiet for a minute and Aldebaran thought he must have gone. That was until he heard his very quiet and controlled voice come over the radio. 'I can sense you know this female well, Aldebaran but I'm warning you, buddy, I'll not stand by and let you murder one so young when she has caused no damage other than delay the inevitable. Just send another, Ald. Be very careful how you handle this. I'll be watching so make sure she's returned unharmed.'

'Just great. You can screw with their minds and treat them all like whores and yet with this one you suddenly grow a damned conscience. I really don't get you, Conom. Why is this one different?'

'Look at her. So faithful, waiting patiently, not even a movement. She's like a little doll. Please tell me if that ain't a quality worth saving. Play nice, Ald.'

Aldebaran threw the headset off him and chucked it up against the wall. 'Get me my potion book, now!' he yelled angrily at the servant standing by the door. He was furious Conom was going to make him return her. Aldebaran rubbed his hand through his hair in frustration. He was preparing to give them all a nasty bloody shock. 'She will come to me,' he growled so loudly that the walls shook with the intensity of his voice. Aldebaran's hands were shaking and he knew he had to calm down. He would scare the crap out of her, projecting the emotional energy within him.

Chapter Seventeen

Cassandra and Evil Merge

All Cassie could hear now was the gentle, light swoosh of Starburst's wings as they gently moved to keep them in position. She finally heard Kayden's voice as just a whisper. He must have been a long way out still and as he spoke, his words became clearer and she now recognised he was shrieking an order.

Cassie, look out behind you! Get out of there!

She swung around just as black veiling covered her, making everything dark. With great courage she calmed herself, imagining it off her but to no avail. Even striking it with her hand and trying to blow it off did nothing. It was as if it were a black nothingness, except she knew it was something supernatural, more powerful than the magic she possessed. Cassie and Starburst were being transported and she didn't have a clue where. The best she could hope for was that the others were following.

She was unable to even hear Kayden anymore so the unexplained cover must have blocked him out as well. Starburst and Cassie finally came to a stop. As visibility came back to her she found they were in the middle of a huge room. It was obviously a castle and the realisation that the wizard had just kidnapped them frightened the bejesus out of her. Big strong men twice her size with strange heads and big bones showing through their faces pointed weapons at her. She put her hands up to push the ugly boneheads away and again nothing happened. Her mouth was dry from fear as she panicked, not knowing what she could do to protect her and her horse.

It was then she heard a laugh: a sarcastic, I-have-you-right-where-I-want-you laugh. 'Your powers are useless here, so don't bother.'

Cassie looked around for the man behind the laugh but it seemed to flow all around her.

'I've been waiting many years for you to come home to me, Cassandra.'

She spotted movement and swung her head in the direction of the staircase. There, coming down them was a big man in his early thirties with an amused look in his eyes. His clothes were of the finest quality and the smoker's jacket he wore, he tossed aside as he walked towards her. He had lots of hair around his face and his beard hung down, unruly yet trimmed neatly on the sides. A wizard with a goatee. It almost made her smile. Now closer, she wondered if she knew him. How did he know her? He looked familiar and yet not.

'You've grown up a stunner, Cassandra. No doubt your friends will be frantic with the loss of such beauty.'

'You seem familiar with me. Nevertheless I'm not sure I've had the pleasure,' she smiled, trying to be polite and friendly so he didn't wipe her from existence. She figured if she played nice, maybe he'd let her live until at least help arrived.

'Let me clear up the misunderstanding, Cassandra. My name is Aldebaran. I'm your father.' If that was not shock enough, he continued. 'Your mother was my woman until she ran off with a wealthy human, a con-man. By the shocked look on your face I can see Mummy dear never told you who you are. I'm sorry to say the father you grew up with and thought was your dad, was not biologically so.' His attention was on Cassie's expressions, watching it change with her thoughts that she had not yet revealed. Even though she tried to come up with a clever retort, nothing seemed appropriate. 'Your mother, Alexis, she is well?' Not waiting for an answer and realising she needed time to let it soak in, he waved his hand and the guards put down their weapons. He walked over to her. 'Dismount, child so I can get a better look at you.'

Closing her mouth that was still open in shock, she slid off and stood leaning closely against Starburst, ever so glad he was there with her. At least he was real. This conversation was not. Maybe it was a joke the wizard was playing to rattle her. Okay, she thought. I'll play along with this psycho wizard if it keeps him from slitting my throat.

Finally finding her voice, she gave a slight cough before speaking. 'My mother is someone I care little about. You would have to go ask her yourself,' she said, glaring at the man who seemed delusional enough to believe that he was her father.

He threw his head back and roared with laughter. 'She always was a piece of work. It sounds like nothing's changed. She even has her own daughter hating her.' He stared at her intensely, looking for an emotion from her but she was a closed book since he had mentioned her mother. He wondered what had conspired between them to cause so much hostility.

'Hate is a bit mild where she is concerned.'

'I am glad then that it is she who has driven you back to me. Now you are here I want you to quit this nonsense of fighting against me and come home, Cassandra. You belong here with me and it is about time your ancestry was honoured.' He stopped and looked her up and down. Making a quick movement too fast for her to pull away from, he took her hands, turning them as if he was studying them. 'I always wondered if you would take after your old man. These hands are weapons of mass destruction. It looks like you are a real chip off the old block. A very powerful gift you have there, daughter of mine,' he said, letting her go and adding an edge to his voice that was grating to Cassie. 'You probably think you're very clever foiling my plans against the Cross family.'

Cassie glared at him angrily. This little game had gone on long enough. It was bad enough that he was calling her his daughter but comparing her to him was the last straw. 'My friends will be looking for me and I don't need to tell you what they will do to your star if they find it is you who has kidnapped me, never mind held me against my will.' She stood with her chin jutted out, hands on her hips, eyes dark and dangerous as she spoke.

He shook his head. 'You have my temper as well I see,' he smiled. 'You don't need to fret, Cassandra. I'm going to send you back to your friends but first I want an hour of your time to get to know you just a little. Come and have a drink. You must be thirsty—you've been out there a long time.' He put out his arm which she took, glad he wasn't kidnapping her and was going to send her home.

For my freedom, I can be nice for an hour.

'What's your poison?'

'Moonjuice would be nice.'

He had his servant pour them both a goblet full. If she had to stay here she needed something to give her courage. He sat her down near him at the end of the table so he could chat. 'You're the prettiest little thing I've seen in many years. You must take after my side because although your mother had attributes, one of her finest was not her good looks.'

Cassie thought his voice sounded far away as if he was trying to remember every detail of her. *Surely he is dreaming. Or maybe I am.* Yet watching his eyes turn a magical blue as thoughts of his past flashed before him she somehow knew he wasn't lying. Yet she still refused to believe him, even though his eyes were the exact blue that was reflected back at her whenever she glanced in a mirror.

'How did you know it was me?' Cassie asked, needing more from this strange man. He seemed so comfortable around her as if they'd been together like this for years.

He turned to face her directly again, his eyes instantly reverting back to the dark indigo or black they had been before.

Those eyes! Could mine have been able to change like that if I had become as evil as him?

'I've been watching you all your life, my dear child. As soon as the close-up shot of you came through and I saw you, I knew who you were. You have changed very little since I saw you last. You have your father's eyes and that, my dear girl, you cannot hide from me.'

'You must be some kind of genius to be able to see from such a distance. I just wish I could have taken after you, Pops. Then I could have seen you coming and run,' she mocked.

Aldebaran put his head back, laughing again making her smile. 'See, I knew you would have some of my sense of humour. Tell me then, young Cassandra, why did you join up with those thugs?'

She looked at him, wondering what to say and decided the truth was best because if he were that good he would know if she lied anyway. 'I'm in love with one of them. I was lost and had the spirit knocked out of me when they found me dirty and battered. They dusted me off, took me in, gave me time to heal and have given me a home. For the first time in my miserable existence I am actually very happy.'

Aldebaran moved her hair and searched her face as if he was able to read her every thought.

How is he doing that?

'Yes, I believe you are telling me the truth as you do look very healthy and happy. That is all a father can ask for his child. However, none of this will change a thing.' He looked away and breathed deeply, taking a big gulp of his drink. 'Regardless of you being my daughter, we are on opposite sides. You do know I won't give up my quest to rule this entire quadrant of stars and we will be coming up against each other more frequently. That's why I brought you here: to warn you that I have many tricks up my sleeve and you are no match for me, young one. When you realise this is where you belong, Cassandra, I will be waiting for you with open arms. Until then stay alert or you could get hurt or worse. You may be my daughter but to go up against me is ludicrous. May I make a suggestion? Go back and dump your friends and come home to be here, by my side as it should be.' His mood changed as he slammed his goblet on the table and glared at her. 'Or stay the hell home next time.' He glanced over at the Moonjuice she hadn't touched and calmed down. 'The least you can do is to have one drink with your father, Cassandra,' he said soothingly, snapping out of his irritable mood. 'You would make your old man very happy, sweetheart.'

Not at all scared by his mood swing, Cassie drank it down. 'Maybe it is you who should stay the hell at home, Pop,' she said with a sly look and a cheeky grin.

He roared with laughter again. 'You're a chip off the old block, I can see that.' He seemed happy now and stood up, walking her back to Starburst. 'All is fair in love and war. I guess until we meet again then, daughter of mine.' He lifted her onto the horse.

She felt darkness start to cover her again and she watched Aldebaran's eyes as they almost went black. They were unpredictable, as if he didn't want to let her leave. Maybe she had misread it; nevertheless there was that look. Maybe he was thinking twice about fighting against her. She could only hope so. His magic was very strong. His eyes softened just for a minute and out of reflex Cassie blew him a kiss, grinning sweetly as he disappeared from her sight, his eyes sparkling with a smile in appreciation of her response.

Wow, so that's my dad. He wasn't so scary and she had rather liked him when he wasn't annoying her with his demanding, come-home-now-daughter attitude. Then again it may have all been a trick. *Maybe he's not my father.* But deep down that didn't ring true either; he was someone alright. She felt it. So many thoughts ran through her head as she travelled back to where he had kidnapped her. She hoped the boys were still waiting. When she stopped, the black veiling came off and Conor jumped as Cassie appeared in between him and Woody. Kayden looked relieved and immediately ordered his men to move in close where they put a protective force around her while they travelled back down to the Cross brothers' home world.

As soon as Starburst's hooves hit the ground, Kayden lifted Cassie off the horse, hugging her. His arms trembled as he held her. She tried to tell him she was okay but he wasn't listening. He was so stressed he didn't seem to be hearing her.

'Please, Kayden listen to me. I was fine. I was with my dad, my real one. The enemy … he is my father. I'm sure he is not lying.' She finally got the words out in between kisses.

He finally registered what she was saying and pulled away from her. 'Aldebaran is your father?'

'That's what he claims. However under all that facial hair I couldn't really tell except for the eyes: they were familiar. He took me to warn me to stay home and keep out of the battle.'

'And what did you tell him?' Kayden asked, letting her go and backing away to listen.

'I threw the same words back at him.'

By this stage, Kayden was gazing through her as if she were a stranger. He was frowning and dropped his hand, not holding on to her at all anymore so she quickly told him everything that they had discussed, trying to ease his mind. Kayden continued to slowly back away from Cassie. He acted as if she was an alien, not really believing anything she was telling him. He even scoffed at her when she said she wasn't sure if he was really her father. It was almost as if she had been keeping a deep, dark secret that maybe only now, thinking he had caught her out, she had revealed.

Woody, Conor, Ethan and Jason were also acting weird and had the same expressions of disbelief on their faces.

'I … I'm not sure. None of us having known her long enough … maybe …' Woody stumbled with his words as he looked from the guys back to Cassie.

'What, so you all think this was just a setup? That I knew about him and he has planted me in your group to expose you? Well if that's how you want it, fine, but just remember I made a new life for myself. You came and got me, remember. I can't believe you all would think that,' she said, beginning to get ruffled at their reaction to her news that the wizard was possibly her dad.

'This doesn't look good, K,' Jason said, frowning. 'She didn't even have a birth certificate, no passport, nothing. We organised all new papers for her and really only had her word on who she really is. Data fed into a computer could have easily been forged to make her story legitimate. Maybe her so-called family overseas aren't real. We should have checked more thoroughly.'

The Cross boys came out in the middle of their dispute. Seeing the men rattled for the first time ever and knowing it had something to do with Cassie, they broke it up by offering the men a drink. As if she was a poison they couldn't wait to get away from, they followed the Cross brothers, turning their backs on Cassie and not even gesturing for her to follow. Cassie figured a little time on their own to discuss it privately was all they needed. Then they would come to their senses and apologise. She stayed with Starburst and waited. She doubted if any of them even noticed or cared that she was still outside on her own.

This is ridiculous. How can they believe me to be a spy?

After a very long time, the tall Cross boy came out, handing her a drink. 'Sometimes saving your friends' can be a thankless job, hey?' He sat with her.

'It's okay, I've been treated like this all my life and there's no reason for it to stop now.'

'Your friends think you're untrustworthy but you see, I read minds and know that isn't true. Is there something I can do to help?'

Cassie gulped the drink down and passed back the empty glass. 'Thanks, but like my dad said, what am I doing hanging out with thugs? You know, now I'm not sure either. Sorry to sound ungrateful but only I can fix this,' she said, standing up and noticing he looked a little dejected. 'Hey, thanks for the drink and the offer of support but if you don't mind I'd prefer to be by myself for a while. Honestly, I'm fine. Go back with the others and enjoy the night.'

He stood and left without an argument and Cassie was thankful for that. She watched him go back inside, feeling sad that the others all thought of her as treacherous. She patted Starburst. 'Do you know the way home, boy?'

He nodded and stomped his hoof on the ground.

Sticking her foot in the stirrup, she settled into the saddle and relaxed so he could find his way home. As they flew, Cassie felt as if she didn't care anymore. She had tried to live a new life and thought she had finally found friends but she had not. *What a joke my life is.* She could only hope that sometime in the future she might find a little heaven to make up for all the hurt that life had thrown at her so far.

CHAPTER EiGHTEEN

Aldebaran's Plan Thwarted

Aldebaran heard Conom call out. 'Ald, where are you, old man? I know you're here so you might as well come out and face me.'

'Piss off, Conom. I'm not in the mood,' Aldebaran grumbled at him as he tossed down his second full glass of ale. 'I tried to do it politely but now she's gone back to earth and it's all your fault.'

Conom stood watching him with a smirk. 'She's a bit young for you, don't you think?'

He threw the glass angrily at the wall. 'She's my bloody daughter. Get your mind out of the gutter.'

Conom walked over to the bar and poured them both another drink, handing one to Aldebaran before slouching into the chair near him. 'You did the right thing letting her go, mate. She would never have forgiven you if you'd tricked her with one of your potions.'

Aldebaran took a drink and frowned. 'I did trick her but it backfired. The stupid horse took her home instead of back to me. She's going to be so pissed off when it wears off and they all realise what I tried to do. I think I've just blown my one and only chance with her. Damn it, Conom, if you hadn't threatened me then maybe—'

'You still would have done exactly what you did. You're her father and were desperate. If she really is your daughter she will forgive you, old man.'

Conom passed him a cigar, striking a match so he could light it.

Aldebaran knew he was right. He would have tried anything.

'She's a real beauty, Conom. Never in my wildest dreams would I have thought the skinny little rake she was with pigtails and such a tiny frame would grow into such a lovely looking woman. She even has my warped sense of humour and she's not scared of me at all.'

Conom knew when not to talk and he just shut up and listened. Aldebaran never thought he would like someone's company as much as he did Conom's. He read Aldebaran like a book and was easy to be around, even when he would prefer to be by himself.

He drew hard on the cigar and sighed. 'She's in love with the leader. Tells me they all make her happy. Said something strange though, reckons she was lost and had the spirit knocked out of her when they found her dirty and battered. I swear if that mother of hers has been cruel to my child she will regret the day she ever took to my bed.'

'You sound like you still have a hard on for her, old man.' Conom threw the inappropriate suggestion at him with jest and it made him smile, bringing back many memories.

'Yes, she was all that and even more. I've bedded up to four women at a time and still they don't satisfy me as that witch did. She was not much of a looker but you don't look at the chimney while you're stoking the fire. No, my need was not to admire. My uses for her were pure evil and she was wild and one of my most cherished toys,' he said and made them both roar with laughter, bringing Aldebaran out of his mood.

Chapter Nineteen

Kayden's Near Loss

'L et's make a move, Kayden.' Woody stood up, steadying himself with the table. *Shit! Talk about overdoing it.* 'It's late and the horses need tending to.' He slurred a little.

'Is the traitor still out there? I'm not in the mood for any more lies,' Kayden said, not looking forward to dealing with the woman who had secretly withheld who she was. Worse though was the way she sneakily wormed her way into his world and now blatantly threw his love back at him by lying.

'Old man Cross told me she's long gone.' Woody staggered, pulling him up. 'Come on. She's with her dad now and good riddance to the lying bitch.'

'You're right. We can't stay here forever soaking in our stupidity. I can't believe I was so sucked in. All I know is she better keep right away from me from now on. If I get my hands around her bloody throat I'll squeeze the life out of her.'

Jason came around the other side of Kayden, helping Woody steady him as he walked. 'Maybe we should go and put out the wizards star that she's on and then she's on her own with no one. I tell you now if I had my time over, I would have not only hit her with the damned car but reversed back over her again. Sorry, boss but she's a no-good, lying, bitch. I should have stuck to my first impression of her. She's a spy all right—did us all over. All that crap about how happy she was with us. She faked it all.'

'That's enough Jason! I've had talking about her already. If I hear her name mentioned again, even whispered around me, I'll go crazy, I'm so livid.' Kayden kicked a chair that was in his way, then tried to calm down enough to say goodbye to the Cross family. He did manage a slurred thank you for their hospitality and an incoherent apology. He hoped they hadn't spoilt the night by brooding about the traitor Cassie. They had tried hard not to talk about it unless they were not being listened to, but he was sure the younger son knew what they were saying as he kept throwing Kayden angry looks. He tried to tell Kayden he was under some sort of influence. Yeah right, he thought angrily.

They mounted their horses and Kayden could hardly wait to get back home and think straight. The dark cloud hanging over him felt like a monkey on his back, mocking him at every turn. He wasn't even feeling upset about never seeing her again. Just so Goddamned, bloody angry with her.

They hit the clouds and like magic his mind cleared. He felt bile rise to his throat as he realised just what he'd been doing: thinking and saying spiteful, insulting crap about his Cassie all night. His neck cracked as he spun around quickly, viewing the rest of his men. They too had snapped out of it and were feeling the wave of guilt and ill feeling that had hit him.

'What have we just done?' was all he could say to them before he threw up. He was shaking with revulsion at how he had treated his princess. What had happened? Confused, his hands gripped hard against his aching head, glad that Zoltan knew the way home because he was too beside himself with disgust at his behaviour to even think about the trip. Pain gripped at his insides as he groaned. He felt like the biggest bastard ever.

It was dead quiet, not a sound. He looked around to see if the men were still with him. Woody looked worse than he felt. Kayden dropped back and rode in between Woody and Jason. *We must have been under a spell, surely,* he relayed.

Woody nodded but was having trouble even thinking. His eyes were glued in front of him.

What if she never comes home? Aldebaran has powers we have no idea how to fight. She thinks we hate her. How will we ever get her back if he keeps the spell on her? She'll never believe anything we say. 'God,' Kayden groaned out load, breaking the no-talking rule.

Woody finally found his voice. 'We should have guessed he would do something underhanded. He's the most goddamned evil lord in the whole galaxy. We should have come straight back home instead of thinking about a bloody good time. On top of what bastards we all feel, Zoren will be furious we've lost her. Magic or no magic, it will never be a good enough excuse for any of this mess.'

'Jeez, what were we thinking?' Jason frowned. 'We know how little and helpless she is compared to all of us. With all our strengths and powers we must have looked so frightening to her when we were attacking her about the story she was trying to tell us.'

'How could we have been so cruel?' Conor said and then cursed in a different language.

Kayden shuddered at the thought of five big blokes twice the size of her, all glaring down in disbelief, nothing but anger and contempt on their faces. He moved back in front of them, not wanting to picture any more of their fears in his head as well as his own.

They reached the ranch and walked their horses into the stables and a huge sigh of relief came from within them as they spotted Starburst. Kayden looked up, thanking the heavens above, while Starburst shook his head at them with disgust in his eyes. Kayden didn't care how he looked at him, he had never been so happy to see him. It meant Cassie was still here on earth.

He dropped Zoltan's reins and left his horse where it stood. With his heart just about in his throat he ran into the house, praying she was inside even though there were no lights glowing through any of the windows to say someone was there. The bedroom door was closed and he knew that he'd left it open. He was hoping against all odds she hadn't packed her stuff in a backpack and shot through. He opened it slowly. He could hear her light little breaths and his legs shook at the emotions running though him. He wanted to wake her and beg her forgiveness but feared he would scare her, having made her so angry she might accidentally blow him into a million pieces.

She's here, men. I don't care where you bed down tonight but I am going to go hold my woman and hope when she wakes she forgives me.

Before he even finished sending the message to them, Woody was at his side. 'Are you sure she's in there? It's so dark, I can't see a thing,' he whispered, peering in too.

Kayden nodded. 'I can hear her breathing. Listen: so sweet and melodious. Thank God.'

Woody nodded. 'Yes, I can hear it now too. That potion must have made her too sleepy to run. Even our whisperings aren't disturbing her even a little. The guys and I will bunk in the barn for the night. None of us are dealing with this real well. Wake us when she gets up, okay?'

Kayden nodded. He closed the door nervously and walked over to the bed. He slipped out of his clothes and slid in carefully next to her, trying not to wake her. She was like a magnet and rolled into him as soon as she felt him. He tried to stop shaking as he pulled her into him. *God, she feels so good to hold.* He prayed she would forgive him and stay in his arms like this forever. He lay there thinking about the first time he had held her. She had been on the side of the road, covered from head to toe in red dust, her face screwed up, holding back sobs of pain. Yet he felt her relax at his touch before she had opened up her gorgeous eyes for him. He was so shaken he had trouble breathing. Even picking her up to put her on the truck, her delicate little frame had just seemed to gently mould into his as if he'd been holding her all his life. He remembered getting really plastered with Jase to stop himself from going out into the barn and holding her during the night. In the light of the morning, Jason had finally convinced him that she was another plant and they should get rid of her before she worked her evil into him any further.

Kayden cleaned her up a bit before he took her home. He dragged her outside roughly, hosing the crap off her, angry she still had such an effect on him. Then he had deliberately watched her undress to see how confident she was, waiting for the so-called spy to throw herself at him further. He was shocked she was so shy. She went bright red as she removed her wet things, knowing he was watching her, so red in fact, her whole body seemed to take on the crimson shade. It was then that he had spotted her nasty bruises and the look she gave him was so wounding he had to get away from her. His stomach had turned that night for being so cruel, hosing her and leaving her in the barn like an animal. This night and then, were the only two times in his entire life he ever remembered feeling that sick. He pulled himself together, showered, and with every intention of taking her back where he found her, had marched out to the shed. Kayden had listened to Jason and knew he was right, she had to go. Seeing her curled up on the hay his whole body and mind weakened with the sweet look on her face. As he picked her up, he knew she was different and took her into his home and his heart, all in the same night.

Cassie moved in his arms and it shocked him back to reality. His mind had been going over every detail of their time together. He noticed when he joined her in bed that she was naked and his heart bounded heavily, holding her bareness against him, knowing this might be for the last time if he couldn't convince her he was sorry. There was no way he could sleep either because if he nodded off for just a few minutes and she woke, she might slip away in the night. He shook his head lightly, forcing himself to stop feeling so drugged by her nearness.

He stopped reminiscing and looked outside the window, watching as the sun touched the glass, the glare making him blink. Any other time he would be up now, tending to the horses, but this morning the whole universe could go to hell and he would still just lie here and wait. *Yes, I will wait even though all the tough-man act is threatening to cave and reduce me to a sobbing, blubbering, bloody mess if she rejects me.* At the thought he started to shake uncontrollably at the mistake he had made in not bringing her straight back here.

Chapter Twenty

Mending Hearts

Cassie had put Starburst in the stable and given him water, hay and a big kiss for bringing her home. She had gone inside and looked around, feeling too exhausted to even think straight. After a shower she walked into the bedroom with a towel wrapped around her. Even as her mind growled at her to get changed and be on her way, the bed was just too enticing. Just a couple of hours won't hurt, she thought as she threw the towel aside and slipped under the cool sheets. She would easily be gone by the time they made it back, knowing what time they normally arrived home.

She lay for a few minutes, contemplating what she was going to do with herself now. Yawning, she rolled onto her side, too tired to even think straight. Whatever Aldebaran gave her to drink had totally mucked with her head and without another thought she drifted off to sleep. She hadn't even felt Kayden come into bed. Yet now awake, she could feel she was all wrapped up in his arms. She tried to wiggle out and not disturb him but he only held her tighter, not letting her get up. He was awake and shaking but not talking. Is it his shaking that woke me? Is he angry? she thought, but couldn't tell.

'Please don't leave me.' His voice broke the silence. He was so upset that Cassie was gob-smacked.

'I don't understand. You don't trust me, why would you want me to stay? You're hardly making any sense. If we have no trust, our love is a lie.'

He lent over, his face full of sorrow. 'I do trust you, Cassie. I don't know what came over me. I was so scared when you disappeared. I knew the wizard had you and that he might do something to you and even knowing all that, I still couldn't help the dark feelings that came over me when you came back to us. It was as if I was under some kind of spell. It wasn't until we moved into the clouds that our minds cleared. I promise we're not like that—none of us are. We're all so shaken up for what we did to you. Please stay, Cassie and give us a chance to make it up to you. I love you and the boys all adore you. This is all crazy. We know you,' he said and allowed a sob to escape as he buried his face into her hair, kissing it.

Cassie breathed out all the nasty thoughts she had and sighed with understanding. 'I get it now. I told Aldebaran I was in love with you so he must have used some black magic on me to break us up. Now I know why he desperately wanted me to have that drink, a potion to repel you and make me look untrustworthy. With nowhere else to go he most likely thought I'd call him, knowing full well you would have all disowned me. That sneaky son of a bitch! Well, it backfired because he didn't count on Starburst being smart enough to know his way home on his own.'

'It had to be that,' Kayden was agreeing. 'I would never dream of treating you so appallingly. I'm so ashamed. You have no idea what a blessing it was when I came home and found you in bed. It was such a relief that you hadn't run a mile from me, from us.'

'I too was under the drug. Calm but just so tired. Hardly able to stay awake or think straight. The potion was obviously meant to keep me in a dreamy state of mind so I'd go to him as if it were nothing. It is only because Starburst is so clever I am here now. You know, he may have just saved us from being on opposite sides. That old man of mine, if he really is of course, has a bloody lot to answer for next time we meet. I won't be falling for any more of his potions either,' she said, now understanding what had gone down and feeling ticked off with Pops.

Kayden was still very emotional as he spoke. 'I've been lying here most of the night, not game to sleep in case you woke up and left before I had a chance to beg you to stay. Please say you forgive me, Cassie. I'm so very sorry.'

'I'm sorry too, Kayden but I do have to go.' And then she smiled. 'But only to go to the little girl's room and then I'll be right back,' she said, teasing him a little.

He knew she was trying to joke and lighten the moment and he tried giving her a smile before he rolled off her. But she could feel his emotions as he watched her walk to the door and knew he was still devastated about the whole situation.

When Cassie slipped back into the bedroom, he had his arm across his eyes, still miserable for what he had put her through. It was hardly fair for him to take all the responsibility; Aldebaran also had a lot to answer for. She eased into him very gently and he put his arms back around her as she tried to find the words to heal the moment. 'Next time a big black blanket attacks me, can you at least get me back to the clouds before you stop and talk to me?' she squeezed herself closer to him. 'Also, maybe not talk to me until the next morning just in case.' She kissed him around his neck. 'Because there is so much more we can do to pass the time away while we're waiting for the spell to break,' she whispered, kissing his lips.

His arms wrapped around her affectionately as he deepened the kiss, his love for her sending warm pulses through her body, luring her into his magical world. Cassie smiled, knowing that not even a wizard could break up a love like theirs forever.

After she caught her breath and Kayden had fallen into a restful sleep, she left him to nap and headed for the kitchen. If the others were feeling like him, they would also need some of her forgiveness. The best way she knew to show them that was to cook some yummy food for when they surfaced. Within no time at all, hot sausage rolls, cheese scones, and chocolate muffins were being pulled from the oven and the third batch of pancakes had been flipped from the pan. While she worked she thought about all the happy times they had together and mixed all that love into what she made. She was just flipping the last pancake and putting the last batch of scones in the oven, when Kayden came out. He came over, more confident and so much happier now.

'That smells so good,' he said, kissing her neck. Cuddling in behind her, he looked over her shoulder. 'Looks and smells delicious, honey. If this aroma doesn't wake the men up, nothing will. You're one of them now you know and they're not happy with how this trip went down. They slept out in the shed. They wanted to be here when you woke up so they could say sorry too.'

'Well, I kinda figured they wouldn't be far away if they were feeling as bad as you were. You think this should cheer them up a bit?'

Just as she finished saying it, the door flew open and they bounded in.

'While you lot chat, I'm just going to have a quick shower,' he said, kissing her cheek and ducking past a worried Woody who was heading straight for her.

'I feel rotten, Cassie,' he said, looking like he had barely slept.

She put down the tea towel and put her arms out for a hug. 'I thought my cooking would bring you to me.'

Jason came over and made it a group hug. 'We were all such mongrels to you and yet here you are, cooking up a storm and making all our favourite foods. Does this mean we're forgiven?' he said, kissing her all over the side of her face and making her giggle.

Then Conor and Ethan came in, joining the fun and making her giggle even more as they struggled to be the ones closest to her. They were all laughing and feeling better by the time Woody snatched Cassie up in his arms and pulled her from them. His warm smile and sweet face was all she needed to see to know that was how they all felt. There was a connection that none of them could deny. What one of them felt, they all did.

Once the others behaved, he put her back down so she could flip the pancakes still in the pan. 'Cassie, you know that even though Aldebaran is your father and may not harm you, we have to be mindful he is capable of these types of dirty tricks aimed at breaking us up.'

Cassie flipped the pancakes out onto the dish. 'We were all

pretty gullible, Woodsta, allowing Pops to have his way with us, me included. But we shouldn't let our work and the magic world up there interfere with our private time together down here. We have to become stronger than this and trust it will be okay the morning after each mission or the wizard has won.'

Woody agreed, brushing a little bit of flour gently off Cassie's cheek and smiling. She turned and pulled the last batch of scones out of the oven, asking Jason and Ethan if they wanted to start organising the coffees while she set the table. Kayden and Woody helped her while Conor poured out juices for everyone. At the table, Cassie watched the guys eating and chatting and as the food hit their empty stomachs she could see them not only sounding happier but looking so much better too. She grinned inwardly, knowing she had stronger magic than her father did. She had the most powerful weapon in the universe. It was called love, and she baked it into all the food that was enjoyed, right down to the last crumb.

* * * *

It was late in the afternoon when Cassie finally asked some of the bigger questions they had all kept ducking like the plague. Did they have girlfriends or wives waiting at home for them, or maybe kids?

Jason was making them a coffee. 'Hell no. And hell no, definitely no kids. You have to be kidding. When we're not here annoying Kayden, the rest of us live on the farm next door. That's how we get here so quick. To ensure we had plenty of room to play with our boys' toys, we brought adjacent properties. We were all going to live here with the boss, build onto this house. Only Kayden was always so damned grumpy with us living under his feet that we decided to expand the house next door. Give him space and give us sanity.'

'My Kayden.' Cassie nudged him and made him grin. 'He's a pussy cat.'

Jason eyed her. 'Do you recall the first day we met you? Well, that was him twenty-four, seven. You have worked a miracle, girl.'

Kayden threw a towel at him. 'And you can't tell me she hasn't changed you guys?' he stirred him back. 'I can't remember you guys ever wanting to spend this much time around any woman.'

Conor nearly choked on his drink. 'Yeah true, but tell me how many of them will get out of the bathroom long enough to let us enjoy them. Makeup, hair, clothes, salons and dreary shopping drive me nuts. Cassie gets up and cooks us the best breakfast ever, never fusses over her appearance and yet scrubs up a treat and knows how to enjoy the day. She's just like one of the boys.'

'Not to me,' Kayden said, running his hand down her arm and putting goose bumps over her.

Woody laughed. 'Come on, mate, quit that or you'll have us all looking up an old flame for the night.'

Cassie sat up straight, an idea popping into her thoughts. 'Great idea! Let's have a party at your house. Invite your girls, your friends and have a bit of fun. I reckon we deserve it. Music, dancing and alcohol. Plus, I'd love to see where you live.'

The men looked at each other with the cheekiest grins.

'Hell yes, we're all in. What do you say, K?' Woody threw an arm around Jason, waiting for his answer.

'I know where I'd sooner be.' Kayden pulled Cassie closer to him. 'Nevertheless, if it's fun you need, sweetheart then let's go have some.'

The guys scrambled for the car. Jason turned before he jumped in. 'We'll organise everything, boss. Be at our house around six, okay?'

Kayden nodded.

Woody eyed him suspiciously. 'We can pick her up if you change your mind and don't feel like coming.'

'I said I'd be there, now nick off.'

Woody laughed loudly as he sat in the driver's seat and kicking the engine into life, he skidded off along the dirt driveway.

'At last, we're alone.'

'See? That was my plan,' Cassie giggled.

'Is that right? You're just lucky they didn't drag us over there to help.' Kayden watched Cassie quietly for a moment with an inquisitive expression. 'Okay, spit it out. What are you thinking?'

'What they said before about me not fussing.' She angled her head slightly.

'You seemed confused. Didn't your mother or a minder tell you what was going to happen to someone with powers like yours when you come of age?'

'I know now from talking to Woody that my mother should have told me a lot of things but never did. All I do know is what I have read in books. When I ran from you and went to Perth I had my twentieth birthday. It was then overnight that everything changed for me. Not only the superficial changes as you see me now, like never having to shave or cut my hair. Normal female bodily functions ceased leading me to believe I may never be able to have a child. Then there were the personality changes due to the strange dreams and daytime flashes of another world, the one you have now shown me. I felt smarter, wised up about all sorts of stuff. At first my thought was that it was a reaction to being so stressed and I thought I'd go back to normal with time. Except I already knew from talking to other females at the Casino that I was different. Not that it worried me too much as I've been a special case all my life. Going to a doctor was out. I guess I just didn't want to end up a lab rat, being experimented on. Then what if they figured out about my powers? You can see why I just decided to hide it. I'm sorry, Kayden, I should have told you about the baby thing. You know, the not having kids thing. But I thought in time maybe I'd be enough for you.'

He looked at her seriously. 'Honey, I know already that having children for our kind is almost impossible. You are more than enough, so never question that but that's not what worries me about all this. I can't believe your mother could be so heartless. Cassie, how old do you think I am?'

She searched his face, suddenly realising what she had already assumed: that the boys were immortal like the others up in the universe above. Woody especially was a real old style gentleman, although she wasn't yet entirely convinced this could happen to earth dwellers.

'You look maybe early to mid-twenties. You and your men all

look around the same age. It's hard to say because you all act so grownup, as if you're a lot older than even that. I had given it thought, that you might be immortal like the rulers and gods up in the galaxy.'

Running his hand down her arm soothingly, he breathed out, sounding relieved. 'You have such insight, Cassie. I'm quite sure it's another of your powers that is only just beginning to develop. The men and I have been twenty for many years. Just like you, we had a growth spurt after our twentieth birthday where we developed into men almost overnight. You see, I know how weird that feels to go to bed wearing a man's size eight shoes and waking up needing size fourteen or bigger in most cases. Then the universe downloads a whole lot of information that your brain has no idea how to process at first. That's why your powers are still developing. It all takes time but believe me when I tell you, as soon as the time comes for you to use these powers, they will just flow out of you comfortably. None of us will ever age from this point on, honey because of our importance to the universe.'

'So we won't wake up one day and just age into old people once the universe is done with us like in the movies? Our bodies will not drop all our flesh and end up skeletons or maybe dust?'

He smiled. 'You've been watching far too many vampire movies.' He laughed, turning to her this time with sincerity. 'I can't believe you've gone your whole life with absolutely no guardians to care for you or teach you what to expect. It is the normal way with any of us. We are born with a carer to ensure we develop as intended.' He shook his head. 'Like us, you will live forever, Cassie. We are immortals: a gift from the heavens to keep the balance between good and evil. Only a selected few are born with powers like ours. Some of us were born to fight evil and some to fight the light. It keeps the balance within our galaxies. With your terrible upbringing I really believe that you were ignored for a reason, that you were destined for evil. Yet through all the misery, you kept your heart pure and never gave up. That alone shows me how strong and trustworthy you will always be.'

Tears ran down her face. She had fought and fought hard, many times wanting to give up and destroy every single person who was hurting her but to hurt them back she would be no better than they were. Then she would have never been here, right now, where she was the happiest she had ever thought possible and with a man who loved her, even if she might not be able to give him a family. *Hang on. Can immortals have babies, I wonder?* Pulling out of Kayden's calming embrace, she had to ask. 'So can immortals ever have children? I mean I was born from one, right?' She felt a little more hopeful.

'Yes, it's possible but rare. If immortals could breed without difficulty, the world would be full of us. It's easier for an immortal male to father a child with a mortal female but it does not mean the child will automatically be born immortal. That too, is rare and depends on whether the gods permit it. They decide how many of us are required each century and for it to happen here on earth is a rarity. You see, you are born with a mission in mind. To want to fight or destroy, as I said, good and evil is the mix. To do what we do, it's imperative to have your roots here, to grow up and love this planet so you have the passion to want to protect it; to be prepared to die for it.'

Cassie considered what he said. She may not have had the passion and upbringing they had but she knew she would fight to the death to save Kayden and his men. And in return, by keeping them safe, she would keep all those they swore to protect alive.

Chapter Twenty-One

Party Hour

When Kayden and Cassie arrived at the party it was in full swing. The boys had started to worry that Kayden had changed his mind. They said they were just about ready to come kidnap their cloud girl. It was sweet they even missed her with the women that were obviously flirting and flaunting themselves around them. Cassie counted about a dozen girls and a few extra men, including Conor's brother Tremaine.

From the little Kayden had divulged on the way over, she knew that the guests were apparently from around the area and always looked forward to a get together. They were used to the boys organising things at the last minute and said they would never miss one of their crazy nights.

Jason took Cassie on a tour through the two-story home. You could get lost in the rooms alone. The boys' rooms had their own ensuites, couches, TVs and stereo surround sound systems. Their beds were the biggest she had ever seen, all with canopies, plush quilts and pillows, similar to the style she had grown up with. Yet standing here admiring the furnishing was about as far as it went. She would sooner be happy with Kayden in his quaint two-bedroom home than have all the riches in the world. The bottom floor consisted of a sitting room, an ultra-modern kitchen, a dining room with a twelve-seated oval table and a massive theatre room. This led her out through large sliding doors to the entertaining area where pretty party lights grabbed her attention. The deck she stood on was lit up with hundreds of colourful fairy lights that cast cheerful vibrant shades over the guests chatting beneath them. She grinned, watching a few partygoers dancing and mucking around to one of her favourite tunes. Outside near the pool, two men she had never seen before stood at the BBQ cooking dinner, Conor and Tremaine watching on. Tremaine introduced the men to her as his two ranch hands, Rick and Steve. She chatted for a while before wandering off to fill her glass with more punch. The lights in the garden must have been on timer and lit up the yard, highlighting a large swimming pool with tropical plants. The palms framing the glistening clear water relaxed her immediately. The gazebo further down the backyard was also lit up with tiny bud lights and it made her smile. These boys had entirely too much time on their hands. It looked great.

Woody joined her, introducing her to his friend, Ella. She was tall, extremely well dressed in designer clothes, and her makeup and hair were perfect. She looked like she had just come out of a shoot for *Vogue*. She spoke down to Cassie with a fake smile and her eyes were cold. Yet when she looked back at Woody she glowed, and her eyes sparkled. *How fake?* Cassie couldn't help but sum her up in two words. It was very clear she had issues with the amount of time Woody was spending with the team. *Or more likely it's just me in particular.*

Kayden watched Cassie's reaction to her. Coming over, he put his arm around his girlfriend protectively. 'Ella, nice to see you again. I see you've met my Cassie.'

Ella ignored his comment about her. 'Kayden, you seem to have been keeping Woody very busy lately. I trust you've worked it out so I can steal him away for a few days. Our family will be holidaying at Cable Beach Resort in Broome and would like him to join us so they can get to know him a little better.'

Kayden stole a look at Woody and it wasn't a happy one.

Woody put his hands up in a submissive gesture while grinning. 'Sorry, mate, she only sprung it on me tonight too. I knew nothing about it.'

Kayden's reaction might have seemed polite to those who didn't know him but by the pressure Cassie felt as his grip tightened as he controlled himself, she knew better.

'Woody has commitments, Ella; he knows a few days are simply out of the question. The resort is a little too far for him to get back quickly if I need him home. In saying that, I'm sure you and he will try and work out a compromise.'

Ella touched Kayden on the arm. 'I'm sure you could manage for a couple of days without him, Kaydie darling. It would be easier if I knew what you two do over there. I could send you some paid help to replace him.' She spoke sweetly.

Kayden smiled politely, taking her hand off his arm and patting it before letting her go. 'You know it's not something I care to discuss, Ella. Good try though.'

She glared at Cassie. 'I bet your playmate knows,' she said in annoyance and waved her hand in a huffy, dismissive gesture. 'Have your little secrets,' she said, walking off irritably.

Woody was embarrassed. 'Sorry she's in a bit of a mood tonight. A few drinks and she'll settle down.'

'Don't apologise for her, Woody. It's exactly that feistiness that appeals to you, right. Well, in the bedroom anyway.'

'Cassie,' he said, laughing. He got that she was kidding with him but wow, she had it right.

Kayden was laughing too as Jason came to join them, wanting to know what was so funny. When Kayden told him, he laughed so loud Cassie thought he was going to bring everyone over.

'I've scratched my head for months trying to work out what the hell he sees in her and goddamn it if Cassie hasn't found the answer within five minutes of meeting her,' Jason remarked.

Woody was still grinning and put his arm around Cassie. 'You're too aware for your own good, young lady. Now, I better go find my livewire and cheer her up or I'll be sleeping alone tonight.' He winked and followed Ella inside.

Jason brought Cassie and Kayden a couple of goblets. 'Moonjuice?'

'Figured it was better for us than the punch their all getting into. They went and sat in the gazebo while she heard stories about the cold-hearted Ella. Ethan brought his new girlfriend over to meet Cassie and joined in. After a while she noticed Jason didn't have a woman in tow, hanging off him like the others did.

'Your girlfriend was unable to come tonight?'

'My type of female doesn't frequent nice parties like this,' he laughed. 'I prefer the fun without the commitment. These girls here all know the drill. If I want someone, I'll choose one at the end of the night. Or not.' He watched to see if it shocked Cassie. She smiled, realising what he meant.

'Then you should have brought a couple of your ladies of the night to this party. It might have been fun to see Ella's face, seeing as they dress just as she does,' she joked.

Kayden took her goblet, teasingly. 'That's enough for you, young lady. Woody wouldn't be impressed if he heard you put his Ella into their category.'

Jason passed Cassie his. 'It's okay, Cassie. You can drink mine. I'm loving you tonight, girl.' He kept laughing.

Conor and Ethan saw them having fun and wandered over with their women who had latched themselves to them. They were very sweet and glowed when given attention; nevertheless they didn't seem that interested. The two females were good friends and chatted for a while between themselves, then went to the powder room together. Jason threw an arm around them both and walked with them inside, reappearing back outside again within minutes, holding another Carottle of Moonjuice. When he returned, he squeezed back next to Cassie, finding her far more entertaining than anyone else there tonight.

'What did I miss?' he smiled, filling up their goblets again.

Cassie laughed at his fun attitude. 'I was just wondering why we had a party when we're all out here together under the gazebo on our own again.'

Jason pinched her cheek gently. 'Because we would sooner just be with you, silly.'

Conor and Ethan toasted Jason, confirming he was right.

'But why agree to the girls and this?' she gestured to the guests.

'For you, so you didn't feel overpowered by us blokes,' Conor said, grinning. 'It must be hard for you only having guys around you all the time.'

'And here I was worried about the opposite, thinking you must miss not having a woman around.' She rolled her eyes.

'We have one: our new little sister,' Jason grinned. 'When we need a woman in that way, we just disappear. You'll get used to us.'

'So, Woody must need a woman in that way because he hasn't come back. Is that what you mean?' she asked earnestly and they all burst out laughing.

'I think she's got it,' Kayden said as he refilled his goblet.

A funky song came on so Jason and Cassie started singing it together and jumping around dancing. When it finished, she plonked down next to Kayden, laughing. 'I think this juice has a different effect on me here on earth. You better drink mine if you want me to last the night,' she said, handing him her goblet.

Kayden was enjoying her as much as the men were and never did take that liquescent of hers. They continued partying and playing cards until the wee hours of the morning. Cassie's concentration was trashed she was so tired, but she and Jason were close to even so neither of them were considering giving in. The other players crowded around them and became more boisterous when the game kept going. They had two hands left when Woody came downstairs to see what the racket was all about. Seemingly annoyed with the state she was in, he growled at Kayden for allowing the game to go on, enticing Cassie to have so much of the juice.

'One more hand, Woodsta, then we stop. I have to win,' Cassie was slumped on her elbow not looking to well.

Jason tried to explain to Woody that the bet was for Cassie to give them all a back massage, insisting that she had to stay for them to win this hand. They were hardly making sense and kept making Cassie laugh. Woody took the drink off her, sculling it himself and replacing it with a coffee. She took a sip of the strong brew and the room started to swim, so that was it for her. 'I'm out, guys. Can't spin and play at the same time,' she moaned.

Getting up was more difficult. Slithering down the pillar, she grabbed Woody, who only just caught her. 'She's bloody paro. Who's been spiking her drinks?' He turned his head and seen they had been mixing spirits with it.

The guy that made them 'fessed up. 'We were just trying to help your boys, man,' he said, and Jason and Ethan tried to high-five each other, missing hands completely.

'That's real mature, Jason,' Woody said. 'Kayden, get up and look after your woman.' Kayden stood up and came over to help with Cassie. He was a goner as well. Jason and Ethan both passed out on the table leaving Conor to help sort out Cassie and Kayden.

He put his arm around Kayden. 'I'll take the boss, you grab the girl,' he slurred at Woody.

'We'll take them up to the guest room,' Conor suggested and Woody nodded.

Conor and Kayden staggered up in front of them and as Cassie neared the top of the stairs, she felt suddenly ill.

'I think I'm going to throw up, Woodsta.'

'Shytzer, Cassie. You sure?'

'Yep!'

He grunted and made a detour to the bathroom. When he came back for her, she had just started splashing her face and gargling with mouthwash. Even that made her dry retch. He frowned, seeing the shape she was in and suggested a walk.

'No! You have your girlfriend here. Don't be silly. I'll be fine.' Standing up with some scrap of dignity left, she tried to make it to the door but Woody caught her again as she stumbled. 'I'm fine, Woodsta. Your dream date is waiting. Just take me to Kayden.'

'You're too far gone to go to sleep yet. Damn those guys! Jeez, I leave any of them for five minutes and they are up to no good.'

'They're incorrigible but I love 'em,' she slurred.

'Well, your boyfriend's no better. He should have been watching you.'

'Woodsta, he's my boyfriend but he doesn't own me. I have to learn for myself. Go play nice with your friend. I'm fine really,' she mumbled, thinking he understood.

'You don't need to learn how to become a bloody alcoholic, Cassie. None of us expects you to drink like this. You only need just enough to get happy and then you have to learn to stop, tell them no!'

She nodded as he walked her down the stairs and out the front door. They walked for a very long time down a path before turning back. She was starting to walk better and her head wasn't nearly as fuzzy.

'Thanks, Woodsta. You're a real sweetie,' she said without the slur. It felt good to feel a little normal again.

He stopped and lifted her head to the moonlight. 'Wow, not only are you looking better but I could actually understand all you said that time. What possessed you to drink so much, Cassie? You must have known what they were up to. Didn't you taste the difference.'

'I did, but needed it tonight.'

'Cassie talk to me, what's this all about.'

She sucked in a gulp of air, thinking about this afternoon. 'Kayden explained to me today that I'm different from other girls. You know, immortal like you guys. Your girlfriend Ella; she looked at me as if I was a freak and I felt like one. I'll never again be normal like she is. Against her, I felt so insignificant, plain and inadequate. I was angry with myself for feeling like that so when I noticed they were adding liquor I kept drinking to make me forget. I'm no princess anymore, Woodsta. I used to have the prettiest clothes, shoes and makeup. Once I could have stood next to someone like Ella and felt an equal. I'm so sorry, I don't mean to hang it on your friend but it just made me remember and I feel so stupid now I've sobered up.' Cassie watched the change in his expression. 'You're disappointed in me, aren't you?'

'Cassie, I'm not disappointed. I just didn't know you missed the dressing up bit. You never seem to worry and I never thought it might be a part of who you are. I never gave it consideration that there might be a part of your life that you did enjoy and miss. At the casino

I remember now how perfect you looked with your uniform on and not a hair out of place. Sometimes boys can be so insensitive.' He ran a hand through his hair, pausing to find the right words. 'Sweetie, we have more money than you can poke a stick at and you only have to ask us and you can have anything you want. You shouldn't ever be made to feel inferior to anyone. I'll organise our designer to pay you a visit. Cass, you are our family now, the little sister we never had. Now I know how, can you please let us spoil you just a little in return for the joy you give us?'

She pulled him down and kissed his cheek. 'You are all so terribly sweet and that was just selfish of me to want more. Then again, if you're offering, maybe a couple of nice girlie dresses to wear to your parties would be more than enough and really appreciated. But I would like to work the cost of them off somehow. You know, maybe teach you how to play cards or something,' she stirred.

He laughed and gave her a hug. 'Whatever makes you happy, Cass. But it's not necessary.'

'Yes, I know but I want to and I promise I've learned my lesson about the alcohol and won't be so stupid next time.' They walked back to the house, arm-in-arm. She looked up to Woody like the brother she never had and felt closer to him at this moment than she had ever thought possible. It was as if they had formed an unspoken bond. It was nice to have such a good mate who saw her at her worst yet still cared.

He took her to Kayden and pulled back the covers while she got in. He kissed her head as he covered her up.

Kayden felt her and holding her gently, cuddling in. 'I missed you, sweetheart,' he whispered.

Cassie looked back up at Woody. 'Sweet dreams, Cassie.' He grinned caringly as he went out and closed the door. She felt so much better and happier now and went to sleep dreaming about pretty clothes.

* * * *

Next day while having breakfast, Cassie looked outside at the weather. It was a lovely sunny day and not one to sit around, Cassie took Kayden's hand and dragged him outside. Grinning, she pointed to the trail bikes in the shed. 'Never been on one. Feel like some fun?'

Kayden shook his head as his men joined them, inquisitive to see what she had spotted that was so urgent.

'Unless you sooky la-la's want to stay home and play nursemaid to your hangovers,' she stirred them

They were all bright-eyed and itching to be out there. She could see it on their faces.

'Well, I'm in. What about you lot?' Kayden asked hearing no answer. They had already started pulling them out, arguing about who was going to take which one. As the dirt bikes roared into life, Cassie started to shake with nerves and excitement.

'You okay, sweetheart?' Kayden asked as he cuddled her.

'Just nervous-excited.'

They went for miles. The bush kept changing from thick trees and scrub to just a few sparse bushes. The only thing that didn't change was the red dirt that flew up around them. They found some sand dunes and that was the best fun of all. The fine red dust puffed around them in a cloud, making visibility difficult but not once did it deter the riders. They slipped and slid their bikes up and down the mounds, barely missing each other. Cassie squealed and laughed, enjoying every bit with the skylarking daredevils.

Arriving home, the majority of the dirt was hosed off. The rest of it washed off as they threw each other into the pool. Afterwards, they sipped non-alcoholic cocktails and chatted while the bubbles in the spa did their job. There was a real bond of friendship forming. Cassie was becoming a part of them all, feeling them as they did her.

Later, lounging on the deck, Cassie asked Woody what he was still doing here. 'Aren't you meant to be on your way to Cable Beach Resort with Ella?' The minute she said it she wished she could have retracted it. The mood of the group changed as soon as the words left her mouth. Everyone stopped eating and looked at Woody.

Kayden frowned. 'Actually I hadn't given it any further thought as I would have laid a bet this was just another one of Ella's ploys to pull us apart, man. Are you really going to see this nonsense through?' Kayden asked with a serious, boss-like tone.

Jason could not help himself. 'What, you're not serious? You're really going to take off? What happens if we get a call out? Jeez, Woody mate, Ella hates us. Get involved with her kind and you can kiss what you do with us goodbye.'

'Shut up, Jason,' Woody growled. 'You don't know what you're talking about.'

Kayden intervened. 'Woody, it is your life and we can't stop you if you choose another path except Jason is right! I saw the look she gave Cassie last night: utter contempt. I won't have her around upsetting our balance.'

'So you're the only one who can have a girl fulltime. That's so much BS, Kayden.'

'There are girlfriends and then there other types of girlfriends who just want you as a possession. She has so much power over you already, what do you think will happen when she has you reeled in, hook, line and sinker?'

Woody's knuckles where white with anger.

Cassie started this argument and was determined to try and turn it around to give Woody a chance to see the real Ella. 'Woodsta, her world is far different from your sweet self. You are tall and handsome. The stereotype, women like her go for; however not as an equal but as a pet by her side. She'll make you so excited to be with her that you won't see the clouds for the stars until it is too late. Once she has you, the sex will turn off. Next thing you'll just mope around her waiting to do anything she asks to get back what you once had. After she has taken away your confidence and spirit, she will then take on a lover and it will destroy every bit of manhood you had left. I've seen this happen firsthand with my own sweet mother. I know you don't want to hear this but you, my handsome friend, are far too good for a woman like her. You're too close and wrapped up to tame Ella, to make her fall fully in love with you and accept you for all you are.' Cassie sighed, feeling his sadness but also his need. 'The only way it would be different is if she saw what you really did. A woman like her needs to feel you are above her, yet your laws prevent her ever being told what you do. On the other hand, let's say you did choose another path to be with her. I don't know how you can make her proud of you while working say, in her daddy's business when he's still the boss and you're just the employee.'

He had his head down.

'Woody.' Jason made him look up at him. 'There is only one way to find out if she's the real deal, man. Go, but with your eyes open this time. Turn off the gushy damned sex for a couple of days and just be with her. Talk to her, have fun and see if she is really what you want. You have to work out, bro if she means more to you than all us. Find out for all our sakes because she's an absolute pain to be around lately.'

'He's right, Woody,' Kayden said. 'She's even started to piss me off the way she's demanding to know more. Try as I do, I don't trust her and you have to have been around long enough to see through an act. You deal with that every time we travel through the portal. All I will add is that if you go and I call, then you'd better be back here double time or don't bother coming back at all. I'll know you've made your bed and best of luck to you.' He had an irritable tone to his voice.

Woody stood up, just as angry, ready to give Kayden a mouthful and then snapped his mouth closed and stomped back into the house to throw some clothes in an overnight bag and left.

None of the guys attempted to follow him in or buck up at what Kayden had said. She could feel they were just as disappointed in Woody as Kayden was although the look Kayden flung at them, daring any of them to support their friend, was enough to shut anyone up. He would have told them to go with him being in the mood he was in, and they knew it.

Tension was thick in the air. Even so, Cassie refused to let Ella spoil a day that had been one of her best days ever. The trail bikes had been an absolute blast. She jumped up. 'Come on, guys, do we really need Woody to have fun? Let's go play some cards and get drunk, seeing as the big guy's not here to growl at us tonight.'

She tugged at Kayden until he stood up and let her drag him inside. The boys followed, even though their hearts weren't in it. Cassie didn't care; she was determined to take their minds off it one way or another.

Conor went to the cellar and found a bottle of starstarter. This was poured out while the hands where dealt. Only this time, Cassie let them win, acting like a ditsy blond girl. They started having fun with her daft behaviour and even though they knew she was letting them win, they needed silliness to cheer them up. She started to get very tipsy, only this time she slowed right down like Woody had told her to, keeping her head in the game. It was hard though because of the fun she was having.

'Let's play strip poker,' she giggled, thinking that that would make it even more fun. *Now, I'll start winning*. She grinned mischievously to herself knowing the thoughts of Woody still gnawed away at them and the men just needed some entertainment. *Hell, we all do*. She had to think of something totally mind-blowing to stop them thinking for just a while.

Kayden held her face in his hands. 'You are so very cheeky, honey. We will play your game, only because it's our turn to amuse you for a while,' he laughed, knowing she wouldn't lose a scrap of clothing herself if she started to play for real.

Cassie picked up the cards and shuffled. 'Okay, here's the deal. The loser takes a piece of clothing off. Once you get down to the jocks, you nominate someone else to strip. That way it will keep us half decent,' she said as she dealt the first hand.

What came next was a real surprise and very, very sneaky. The men all conspired against her and Conor lost every hand and started nominating her.

'Kayden he's cheating!' she winged, and giggled as she removed her top.

He just smiled but in his eyes she could tell he was enjoying himself far too much to stop the game just yet. He was so naughty but she had started it and even though it had backfired, she was enjoying flirting with him and watching the fun he was having. Conor lost again and they started clapping for her to remove her skirt.

'This is so not fair,' she laughed. 'You guys are in so much trouble after this game's over. You know I'll get you back.'

Jason roared, laughing at her. 'It will be well worth it, girl. Now get your gear off,' he said teasingly.

She stood and turned up the music, slowly dancing as she unzipped her skirt. She let it drop before seductively sitting on Kayden's lap and hugging him.

He lifted her in his arms as he stood up. 'Show's over, boys.' He started heading with her to the stairs. 'Come, my lovely, the fun is only just beginning.'

'You are so right about that, boss,' Jason said as the three of them sprung at them, snatching her out of his arms and running outside to jump in the pool with her. Kayden had no choice but to give in and jump in to save her. They wrestled and struggled until they were spent and sobered up somewhat. She could see they were a lot happier again now and over the Woody thing. It was time she relaxed and just enjoyed their company again. They lay in the pool for a long time talking until Kayden saw Cassie yawn and shiver. 'That's it for us, guys, I'm taking my princess to bed.' He heard no argument this time. The boys were just as tired as they were.

It was way past midnight when Cassie finally dried off her hair and flopped into bed. Kayden eased her over to his warm body and cuddled her. 'Thanks for tonight. We really needed you, sweetheart. You came through for all of us.' He rubbed her head gently, soothing her into a deep sleep as he worried silently what he would do if Woody really didn't return.

CHAPTER TWENTY-TWO

Missing in Action

Zoren had another mission for the Cloud Riders. Even though none of them had received word from Woody yet, Kayden was hopeful he would have sorted it out by now and used his telepathy to let him know it was time to come home. The rest of the men were at the house, busy in the kitchen by the time Kayden and Cassie returned from the paddocks. They only needed to bring a couple of horses as Starburst and Zoltan were already in the stables. It had only been yesterday that Kayden and Cassie had gone together for a ride up in the hills and had a picnic.

While Jason helped Kayden unload, Cassie went in to help Ethan and Conor. They were making omelettes although once Cassie arrived they nagged her to make scones as well. They chatted while she mixed up the dough and cut it into shapes. Before Kayden and Jason returned, they were in the oven, baking away. It had only been a couple of days since she had seen them, yet she had missed their humour. Meals were always so much more fun with their kidding and jokes.

After breakfast, they went down to the satellite room under the stables. Kayden explained the mission to them while punching in coordinates and working out the best route to get there. He nodded at Cassie. 'Sorry, honey. It's your father again.'

She shrugged. 'Who's Pops gunning for this time?'

'Well, apparently Aldebaran and Conom made a direct strike

on Orion, sending in a few hundred soldiers. Aldebaran lost most of the soldiers sent into the battle—nothing he wasn't expecting. He was merely trying to find out what defences Orion had in place. Orion's two faithful dogs that rule the Canis Major and Canis Minor constellations, concerned about their master, joined forces and sent out a Z-Andromedae. The weapon was aimed at destroying Aldebaran's home world.' Kayden paused, facing Cassie. 'A Z-Andromedae is composed of a red giant star and a hot blue star. It is enveloped in a cloud of gas and dust that give out nova-like outbursts. The mix of two stars with its poisonous gas and flares nearly destroyed your dad's home.'

'Nearly?' she asked. 'Jeez, how come we weren't called?'

'Zoren had tracked it, sending another team, as it all happened immediately after the attack. Zoren's team never made it in time so Aldebaran had to summon all his wizardry powers, destroying the threat himself and losing many more lives before he could clear the poisonous gasses from the atmosphere around his home world.'

'So he's not a happy-chappie with Zoren either?' Cassie questioned.

'That's putting it mildly. He's sworn to make Zoren pay for the lives lost and has taken out a contract on the dogs. There is a bounty hunter on his way to capture them, dead or alive.' He glanced at Jason. 'The bounty hunter is our old mate, SX Arietis.' Bringing his attention back to Cassie, he continued. 'We have warned Arietis before about his greed for a quick buck. His star rotates at high speeds and is quick—damned cunningly fast. Without Woody it will be tough going catching him; however, I have every confidence we can still take him. Just in case we have a problem, Cassie, we'll need you to be ready as back-up. We may need you to shove him out into the universe as you did last time as a delay tactic while I try and reason with him.'

She nodded and he went back to his navigational charts to show them the coordinates of Arietis and where they would intercept him.

He addressed them all. 'I'd prefer not to tell Zoren about Woody until we find out for sure if he's going to be leaving us permanently.

On the other hand, if we get into any trouble up there without him then the decision will be out of his hands and Woody will be replaced immediately on our return.' Quickly switching off the screen, he leaned against the bench to talk. 'I want you to all understand: if he chooses to continue down this path with Ella, I'll not accept a half-hearted effort. I understand you're all great mates but it'd be no different if it were any one of you. I have no compassion for disloyalty and anyone who deliberately jeopardises the defence of our planet is not welcome on my team. We've all been down this path many times over the years. I have constantly reiterated that there is no reason why you men can't have girlfriends, even wives. However, they will never be included in our secrets or be allowed to interfere with you when I need you. The problem I see with Ella is that because none of you get on with her, it's going to make it impossible for her to live with you. On the other hand, I can't have Woody living so far away that he can't make it when I call. Nothing about this relationship is acceptable. If I have to make the call, I'll expect you all to cope with it and move on. Do I have your support on this issue?'

They all stood up straight, as you would imagine soldiers to act and saluted him. 'Yes sir,' they said in unison. They had all been together a long time and to see them daily, you could forget the military background they had all had in order to be in the elite group they now belonged to. Cassie felt so out of her depth when they did things like this.

Kayden saluted. 'At ease, men,' he said and he turned to her. 'Cassie, do I have your support? You may talk freely.'

'I have faith in Woody and believe he'll work through this. If he is so spellbound that all this,' she gestured around the room, 'and what we do here is not powerful enough to break him out of her clutches, I will understand your decision.'

He nodded. 'We have a bit more time before we go and believe Woody may still turn up. Let us go and unwind a bit. It could be a long night. Dismissed,' he said formally, as he always did.

It was very quiet as they sat around waiting. None of them felt much like discussing their thoughts because they were on a subject

Kayden was not prepared to hear or discuss with his men. Maybe with her later, yes, but she knew it wouldn't be in front of them. He was chosen because Zoren would know he was capable of making the hard calls and his tone was letting them all know he was going to do just that.

Kayden sat back on the couch with his arm around Cassie's shoulders, his eyes closed. Using his gift, he made them all rest and assisted them to escape from their thoughts for a while. Kayden put them into a sleepy trance: it was similar to an abyss: not dreaming, just a nothingness from which they woke feeling refreshed and alert.

She woke with a start when Kayden stirred. 'Sorry, sweetheart.' His voice was calm and Cassie was glad he had woken in a better mood. Jason shook Conor and Ethan awake and they all had a coffee before Kayden summoned the horses. Woody's horse didn't come out, making them feel a little lost without their friend.

Cassie rubbed Starburst on the nose and hugged him. 'We have to work hard tonight, boy. We're one short, okay?' Cassie instructed her horse before placing the golden bridle over his head, watching him transform. It still fascinated her.

Sitting on Starburst, Cassie followed Kayden as he paced before he finally came up to her. She lovingly touched his face. He wasn't happy Woody had let him down.

'He wouldn't have deliberately not turned up, something must have happened. Give him the benefit of the doubt and maybe leave him a note so he can follow.'

She watched as he walked inside and scribbled on some paper, leaving it on his bridle. He seemed happier now and jumped up on his horse, leading them out into the paddock.

Cassie for one, was pleased to get into the clouds. The mysterious and enchanting colours swirled and mingled before her, taking her mind off the Woody saga. They jumped from cloud to cloud until they moved through the final portal. Flying out of the fourth dimension they arrived at the stars that were being targeted.

As the horses landed the team on the constellation Canis Major, Cassie had to hold back a smile that threatened to expose her thoughts. The two dogs, Major and Minor said that they had smelt them coming and she put her head down and coughed to hide a giggle. They had the body and head of a dog but stood up on their hind legs and talked like humans. When they walked, they dropped down on four legs although they stood up again to speak. Talk about being in a *Scooby Doo* movie. This was fantastic.

Kayden went over by a bunch of trees that had no leaves to discuss what was going to happen. Major seemed concerned and let out a gruff bark at one stage. Kayden was probably telling them he was one Cloud Rider short.

Jason slid Cassie off the horse to have a stretch and stood with his arm around her shoulders. He was taking Woody's place within the group. She was comforted they also included her, considering there were many dogs around them, none of which looked very friendly towards her.

Jason was still very quiet and when Ethan and Conor came to stand with him she asked if they were all okay.

'We just don't like how Woody has just up and deserted us.' Conor spoke freely now without Kayden around.

'He's always been the sensible one, guiding us in our love lives and now he's doing what he's always frowned on us for doing,' Ethan grumbled.

'Ethan, some people in that position can be quite ruthless. I've studied up on this characteristic trying to work out my very own mother. They don't just pull you in with sex; it is so much more. Like the way they wrap themselves around you, smile sweetly and smell. They apparently wear a different perfume every night until they find the one that drives you crazy. They watch what clothes you prefer them in. Anything that repels you they delete from their wardrobe until all that is around you are the yummy things you can't resist.'

'He's always attracted women like that and usually tires of them and moves on. But evil Ella is such a strong personality she has started to control him,' Conor put in.

Jason agreed. 'What I don't get is he adores you, Cassie, yet his choice is the total opposite.'

'Don't give up on your friend. This is hard for him too. Can you imagine the hell he is putting himself through, bending backwards and doing what he can to please her but also missing you all like crazy? He would have received Kayden's call and is probably frantic about now because he can't get to us in time. That's the biggest lesson he has to learn. As Kayden said, she will always make it hard for him to respond and he knows now he has to choose.'

'I wish we were as confident as you are, Cassie,' Ethan said, a bit glum.

'It could be anyone of you in that situation. It would make no difference I would hold the same hopes for you. It would be a sad day for any of us if our chain gets broken.' She gave them an evil little look. 'And if this doesn't work by playing nice, I'll just have to go scratch the witch's eyes out and zap her so hard she never even tries to look back,' she giggled.

They all started to laugh and Jason squeezed her, feeling in a better mood already. 'You're good for us, Cass.'

Kayden came back, his face expressionless and his eyes more focused and darker than she had ever seen them. 'They're not happy Woody's not with us and that we have replaced him with a woman. Sorry, honey but the bitches in their packs are the weakest sex. They only use their females for breeding, not fighting. They're going to call on Orion to step in if we can't stop Arietis. This could blow up into a full-scale attack. What worries me more is that Aldebaran can at any time blanket Cassie and take her out of the picture so she can't help us fight. We men will have to be alert so we can warn her to get out of the way. Cassie, this time if I say move, don't even look behind you, spin in a downwards spiral and get out of there,' he said, putting her back on the horse. From his hands she could feel tiny sparks of concern that gave her body small anxious shocks where he touched. She knew he wanted to rip her off Starburst right then and there and take her with him on Zoltan but she also knew he needed to be hands-free to help his men.

* * * *

SX Arietis was in sight as Kayden pulled them up and positioned the horses where they waited patiently for instructions. Starburst and Cassie were to remain where they were until needed. She was the back-up to shoot him out into orbit if he passed by the others. The four of them shot off after Arietis to intercept him and to Cassie it looked as if he put a burst of power on and took off like the speed of lightning. If it were Kayden's plan to talk to him, it seemed unlikely he was going to hang around long enough to listen. The Cloud Riders were travelling so fast now they seemed to blur into the spinning star. She heard Kayden talking to Arietis, trying desperately to make him stop and discuss it. Kayden had called to Cassie to get ready on his command in order to push him out of harm's way. He moved in closer and just as her hands went up to push him out into the atmosphere where he could cause no danger, the star pulled up suddenly. It slowly moved towards her, stopping so close she could see a figure watching her from a control tower.

Kayden instructed them to land on Arietis's star. However, they were ordered to stay on the horses and to ready themselves for an assault in case it was a trick. Arietis was waiting for them outside with his many guards when the horses landed on the surface.

'Ahearn, lord of the horses,' he smiled at Kayden. 'You have recruited a new soldier and what a perfect vision. I couldn't help but stop to admire her just for a minute. Has she a name?'

His eyes were fixed on Cassie, so Kayden glanced over, nodding for her to answer him.

'My name is Cassandra Wyatt.'

He walked over to her in a trance-like state, took her hand and kissed it. 'Your beauty dazzles me, Miss Wyatt.'

'Funny. You shouldn't be so kind and flattering considering I was just about to send you to the never land.'

He laughed heartily and made her smile. She liked his laugh, even if he was a bad boy. Then his face became serious again. 'Perfection has always got an evil side. I wouldn't have expected less and yet even so, you have stopped me in my tracks. I am a man, after all and to meet such beauty is humbling. Thus I will allow your sarcasm towards me.'

Kayden wasn't giving her any instructions, therefore she figured he wanted to play this out and see what happened. Cassie pulled an innocent girlie look and grinned. 'I meant no harm by my comment. All is fair in love and war though, is it not?'

He laughed again while intensely watching her face, his eyes alert and strangely interesting. 'Ahern my man, can I walk with Miss Wyatt for a bit?' he asked without even looking away from her.

'Keep your guards from her, Ari, or else. And no bloody tricks.'

He helped her from the horse, introduced himself and asked her to just call him Ari. He put out his arm and she took it politely, not even a little scared of him. It seemed the only vibes she was getting from him were curious ones. If he attempted anything silly, she knew she could protect herself as he had not taken her powers, and yet she felt it would not be necessary as there was a feeling of peace for just these few moments, while he satisfied his need to know her better.

'You are almost angelic. Are you sure you are human?' he asked.

'I'm sure my persona is not why you've stopped in your attack. Granted my magical form may be a big part of that but there is something more pressing on your mind.'

'You're very perceptive. Ahearn has chosen his new member well. I've heard you are Aldebaran's daughter and yet you fight against him. Is that wise? I'd hate to see someone as mesmerising as you have a short-lived life. Your father is very powerful.'

'The old wizard may think he's my father but that is yet to be proven. If I'm a chip off the old block he may just need to rethink what I may actually be capable of.' She tempered up a little, thinking about Pops and what he did to her on the last trip.

He stopped walking. 'You're a tough little thing. Maybe I need not have bothered to stop and warn you after all.' He sounded amused.

She giggled to lighten the moment. 'However, it was very thoughtful of you so, now answer my question. Why would someone as caring as you want to hurt the Scooby Doo brothers?'

He roared laughing. 'I have seen that cartoon. Very funny. And now to answer you: it is all about the money, angel girl. Nothing personal.' He turned and walked back with her. 'Well, it is time we got back to me running and you trying to stop me.'

'Or you could call it off and end this peacefully.'

He stopped again. 'Are you trying to use your beauty as a bargaining tool?' he said, raising his eyebrows.

'No, not at all but if you don't ask, you don't get. I thought it was worth a try,' she gave him an amused expression that lit her eyes up further.

When they reached the team, Kayden was standing calm and unrattled.

'Your soldier is proposing I end this peacefully. I stand to lose a lot of money, Ahearn, so I propose an offer. I get to spend a few hours with your new soldier and I'll leave the dogs to someone else. This is a one-off offer and non-negotiable. I also promise she will be treated with the utmost respect and delivered back to you unharmed.'

'Good try, Arietis but she is taken and I doubt if I could trust you for a second, never mind a few hours. If you call this attack off, Aldebaran will just send another in your place so why should we waste our time with you?'

Arietis eyed Cassie. 'If you don't ask, you don't get,' he said with a smirk.

She giggled. 'Nice throwback,' she said as he helped her back on Starburst.

'To spend a bit of time with such beauty would have been worth the bounty but so be it.'

Cassie reached out to steady him as he suddenly staggered and clutched at his stomach. Then for some unknown reason he buckled over in pain.

'Ahern, get her the hell out of here,' he growled. 'Aldebaran has felt me weaken and is trying to work through me. I'll hold him back. Go!' he said louder.

Kayden had them off the star in seconds. Looking down, Cassie saw Arietis double over again and groan in pain. She wondered what Pops was doing to him and what his next move would be now that Art had helped them get away. Kayden was giving Cassie instructions so she had to ignore Arietis and concentrate on what he was telling her.

You'll be safe in our circle, so stay in the middle of us. Men, it's coming, so concentrate and link with me now. He sent the urgent response to them.

An electric blue light wrapped around each of them and as Kayden yelled, it was as if it stretched out, joining them all as one. The black, cloud-like blanket came for Cassie. She practically ducked, it came so close but as it hit the blue glow from the Cloud Riders it just seemed to dissolve against the barrier they projected around her.

We've foiled Aldebaran's attempt to grab Cassie from us and it'll take him some time to work out how we did it. She should be fine while we go get our boy. He's powering up, getting ready to run, so watch him, men, he's using massive amounts of flame to take off full speed. Cool your body temperatures so the heat doesn't penetrate your skin.

Cassie, stay put. When Arietis slingshots back towards the dogs, shove him as hard as you can up and out into the galaxy. Then I want you to stay and protect the two stars, Canis Major and Canis Minor. I wouldn't put it past Aldebaran to deploy another bounty hunter, knowing Arietis has just lost his heart to his daughter. He winked and shook his head. *You're really shaking things up a bit, my beauty.*

'But this isn't real,' she motioned at her angelic glow and attire. 'Maybe I should invite him home for coffee to see the real me who trudges around in T-shirts and gumboots.'

You underestimate yourself, sweetheart. To me, you look like you do right now all the time.

She couldn't help grinning at his sweetness. *Gee, it feels good to be loved even if his love is obviously blind.* She chuckled to herself as she turned to see what their renegade star was up to.

As soon as she swung around, Arietis took off at lightning speed. She closed her eyes, imagining him high up in the universe somewhere. Throwing out her hands towards him with a power that just kept getting stronger, she watched as her magic shot Arietis out into space, the Cloud Riders hot on his tail, moving so fast their silhouettes shimmered out of focus. Now that they were out of sight, she kept watch. She knew Pops would have something else up his sleeve and she wanted to be ready.

Just as expected, Cassie felt a roar and the sky seemed to shake. The team had spent many hours explaining all the different stars to her. That's why she could now easily identify that this was an unpredictable Dwarf nova, ready to explode any minute. Pops must have been furious and driven to the extreme to have risked exposing himself to Zoren like this. He would surely pay for such an attack on so many of the constellations at once.

A closer inspection, confirmed her thought, that it was a Su Ursae Majoris star. It was already sending out bursts of flames from the explosions on the surface. If it exploded now, the outer layer could blow away at many thousands of kilometres an hour, destroying the targeted dog constellations as well as damaging many others. *What is he thinking, being so dramatic?* He sure had one hell of a temper.

As it neared, Cassie closed her eyes and imagined sending it in the opposite direction that she had thrown the Arietis star. The team had enough to deal with as it was. She felt Starburst sending a shot of energy to help her and throwing her arms up, she shoved it hard and fast towards a safe location where it could cause no damage. However, before it was far enough away, it started to explode. Pieces broke away, scattering in all directions as it shot up into outer space heading for many of the constellations that surrounded her.

All Cassie could do was to keep the dangerous missiles that they had become, from causing any damage, quickly and precisely blasting them into harmless puffs of dust. She nearly missed a piece that got awfully close to the Gemini star but managed to destroy it just before it hit. The core went out of control, spun and turned as it exploded again, heading straight for Canis Major. Snatching it up with her mind, Cassie threw it back out into black space of nothingness where it should have gone in the first place. The impact had so much force in it that this time it was dead in the water, no harm to anyone.

With the stars now safe, she sat on guard again when a shocking pain shot through her. She buckled for a second before the pain released her. Checking herself out, she found no wounds. What in the hell was that? she thought, still stretching out her arm, checking out the area the pain was coming from.

She could hear Kayden. He was yelling an order to save Conor. He and his horse were hit and he'd been thrown from his horse on impact. *He's falling towards you.*

She swung her eyes above her head, seeing him coming towards her at a hell of a speed. She closed her eyes and put him on a cloud, slowing his fall and gently lowering him onto Starburst with her. He was hurt badly, blood oozing out of a wound. Something else was not right either. As she slid him gently in front of her, he groaned as his body leant back against hers.

'Sorry,' she said, holding him firmly so he didn't fall off.

His horse was still flying but in a bad state as well. Kayden had the reins, bringing it back to him. In between groans, Conor was telling her they had tried to extinguish the star without Woody but not having the dynamics of five, the star unexpectedly spun out of control and sideswiped him.

Kayden commanded the horses to land on the Canis Major star so he could do a patch-up job on Conor and Conor's horse. Even though damaged, Arietis had not been disabled and still posed as a threat. This left Kayden no choice but to put Cassie in harm's way for her to keep watch for him when they landed, while he attended to the injured team members.

Major and Minor were there waiting as they landed and were jumping around, excited. They barked out to Kayden what she had done with the Dwarf nova star. They had watched it all and were so impressed with Cassie's power that they hadn't noticed Kayden had a soldier in trouble. Up until then, Kayden was unaware another was sent. The look of gratitude made Cassie's effort worthwhile and overwhelmed her. Major and Minor jumped around Starburst until she was lifted from the horse and then both slobbered all over her face, licking her and rolling on the ground playing. They were gentle but she was not expecting they would be goofy like real dogs when they got excited. One minute she was being growled, licked and woofed at; the next, she was in Kayden's arms.

'Enough … sit!' he commanded and they both stopped, grinning, all goofy and happy-like with their tongues hanging out. They made her giggle but the happiness they shared with her was short-lived when Conor moaned again. Kayden put Cassie down, told the dogs to behave and went back to his patient.

Jason and Ethan had laid Conor down on the ground so Kayden could get a good look at him, inspecting him for broken bones and internal damage. His shoulder and arm had taken the brunt of the hit, leaving a nasty gash on his shoulder and a broken arm. He had three broken ribs and already the bruise on his chest was swollen, black and nasty-looking. Kayden then checked Conor's horse. The armour had prevented lacerations; however, it didn't stop the horse from receiving massive internal injuries.

Kayden took off his belt, giving it to Conor. 'Bite down on the leather, man, this is going to hurt. That arm will start to heal before we get home if I don't reset it.'

Jason and Ethan held Conor down as Kayden readjusted his bone so it joined again. Conor screamed and cursed Woody before passing out. Cassie must have looked white as a ghost because the doggies called for Kayden and he grabbed her as she started to fall.

'His pain went right through me,' she shuddered in shock.

'We're all linked now, sweetheart,' he said soothingly. 'We all felt it. The thing is, the Cloud Riders' power enables us to heal very quickly. If I leave it until we get home, it will set crooked and I will only have to break it all over again. It is far better to do it now. You okay for me to go back to him? Do you still have your wits about you?'

Now it was clear in her mind how it all worked, she could deal with the pain and weirdness a bit better. 'Yep, I have this, trust me.' She glanced down as he started to stitch up Conor shoulder. Even though she had her eyes scanning the heavens and not watching, she felt every thread he pulled through him. She shuddered at how this connection with the team had a good side but also the worst side possible.

Jeez! Toughen up, princess. It's not as if it's actually happening to you!

The two dogs came and stood each side as if comforting her. A sound above made them all look up. The dogs barked. Quickly picking Cassie up and putting her back on Starburst before she had even thought of it, Kayden was yelling at them to hurry. It was nearly on them. The dogs were barking frantically. She closed her eyes and was summoning up a visual and opening her eyes to slam her power at the target when all of a sudden it stopped dead. She had all the power and needed to release it, so instead she threw the energy force up into space where it wouldn't hurt anyone.

Kayden was surprised at Cassie's reaction not to blast the mongrel out of the sky for what he'd done to one of his team members. Still, it was her call, as he hadn't had time to think straight either while attending to his wounded soldier. The star was so close now they could see Arietis wipe his forehead and grin cheekily as he realised how close he'd come to being blasted. Art saluted Cassie and then left, travelling at a massive speed in the other direction. 'He's given up and just came to let us know.' She sighed and slid back off Starburst. 'Christ, what a night. I just about killed him.' She flopped down next to Kayden who put his hand on her shoulder, squeezing it lightly before going back to stitching up Conor.

Cassie sat quietly beside him, exhausted, chewing over their situation. That last effort had not only frightened the bejesus out of her but had also drained the last of her energy. Conor groaned and she instinctively ran her hand through his hair, trying to ease his pain while putting into perspective, what they had just all gone through. *This is so serious!* The true effects of the situation now weighed heavily on her mind. Not having a fifth member was a real issue and for the first time she finally understood Kayden's anger with Woody.

As she continued to contemplate what she could do to give Conor, Kayden and Woody more time, a crazy idea came to her. They had to get Conor home and she'd run out of power, meaning they were vulnerable against a further attack. If Aldebaran sent out another weapon, it could mean all their lives.

'I can only think of one thing that'll give you time, Kayden. Conor needs to heal and if we're called out in the next twenty-four hours, you'll only have three boys.'

'I know what you're thinking, sweetheart. I can feel your thoughts ticking over but you don't have to sacrifice yourself. If you go to Aldebaran, how can we trust he won't hold you captive or worse? I know he's your father but I don't trust the man. I'll work something out. None of us wants you to risk so much. You may never being able to return or worst, this time, it could be your life.'

'Kayden, my powers are weak and in the event of another onslaught, I'm powerless to help until I eat and rest. The only other alternative is to draw from the dark side, but Woody isn't here to help us so if Aldebaran really is my dad, I have to trust he'll do right by me. I'll get us the twenty-four hour reprieve even if I have to stay there and make him give it. He ain't seen stubborn yet, trust me.'

'Yes, my love and you can certainly be that,' he smiled, stirring her.

'Kayden honestly, until this moment I had no idea the seriousness of only having four and you know what? I'm one of the Cloud Riders now too. Just because we're in a relationship doesn't mean I stand idly by and not put my life on the line for my team as they would for me. This is the only way and you know it. So let me go do my job. Okay, boss?' She reassured him, knowing she was their only hope.

Kayden took a while to decide as he nervously rubbed his hands through his hair. She could feel him thinking a heap of thoughts, yet none better than the one she had just come up with.

'Hell, I've got nothing.' He had to agree with her. 'Will you be alright on your own?'

'I think so. I'm fairly sure Starburst knows the way back there. He seems to have a memory like mine. Just try to remember that when I get home, no matter what spell he puts on me, I'm not a traitor. I'm just me, the one who loves you, okay?'

Chapter Twenty-Three
Reprieve for Cassie

The armed guards surrounded Cassie as Starburst landed on the home world of Aldebaran. The largest of the guards lifted her off the horse and with a tight grip, marched her into the castle. The big doors opened to a huge room full of more frightening-looking characters who she assumed were members of his council. It was like a modern-day knights of the round table, only it was real, with big video screens and the buzzing of reports from different sources. Many were reporting on the action that was happening out on the battlefield her group had just fought on.

Aldebaran sat on a throne and looked really annoyed when the guard pulled her inside. He put his hand up, hushing the group. Then he made another gesture and all the monitors went dead so she was unable to see what his next move was going to be. With the room so quiet, all eyes were now focused on the person who had caused the shutdown.

For the first time, Cassie figured this was probably not one of her brightest ideas but she was not about to show them how scared she really was. The guard dropped his grip and she rubbed her arm, still feeling pain from his tight hold.

She glared up at him. 'Take it easy, big fella! Long hair and boobs normally means *girl*. That means, handle with care or else,' she stated firmly. Looking back at Aldebaran, she hid her fear and uncertainty, breaking into a sweet smile. 'Hi Pops! Just thought I'd stop in for a quick visit. You can tell your rough boys that I'm not here to hurt their sovereign,' she said, still rubbing the sting out of her arm. She then realised she was still probably feeling Conor's pain from his broken limb.

You could barely see the whites of her father's eyes, they were so dark, and his irritable expression showed her he did not approve with the intrusion. 'I'm not impressed with your antics out there, young lady!'

Hands on her hips, she motioned to the cameras. 'I wasn't very pleased with yours either, Father dear,' she said right back at him, holding her head up high and not letting him offend her.

Her comment must have amused him as he gave a slight smirk and there was a tiny glint to his eyes. 'So, why are you here? Let me guess. To beg for my leniency! I notice you have yourselves in a bit of a mess out there. Bloody shame. If I strike now with you here, I'll rid myself of your pathetic group forever.'

'Father, if I am a chip off the old block you would know I enjoy a good altercation, so hell no! Do I need or want your leniency? Hell no! Twice! I'm here to ask you to stand down for twenty-four hours. We have family issues that need attending to and not just what you can see out there now.'

He stood, his chest heaving from an intake of air. His face reddened with anger and his eyes were now almost pits, as if they'd disappeared and only evil remained. 'And what do I get out of this so-called stand down? What could you possibly offer to make it worth my while, to stop me from ridding myself of the damned Cloud Riders? Look around you, girl! There is nothing you could give me that I don't already have or need.' His voice was thunderous and threatening.

Cassie walked up to him, trying not to fall down like a lump of lard and disappear into the cracks of the floor. *Goddamn it! He's my dad, what's the worst that could happen?* She recalled how much she had suffered by the hands of her cruel stepfather and yet Aldebaran was making him seem like a pussycat. Even so, she placed one foot in front of the other having no intentions of letting her team down by showing weakness.

The guards went to stop her but he gestured for them to leave her alone. The closer she got, the more of his rage was apparent by the way the ground below her shook. The vibration scared the life out of her but she didn't waver or show any expression. Putting out her hand—she hoped like hell it would stop shaking for just a minute—she found one last smile. 'What do I have to offer you, Pops? I offer you a one-off chance to get to know your own child. I offer me—for twenty-four hours. Would that be worth anything at all to you?'

As if the touch of her hand had put him in a trance, all of a sudden the floor stopped shaking and the atmosphere calmed. Her hand felt small and delicate in his big paw. That alone made her aware of just how overpowering and strong he was. She was suddenly very aware that even though she was petite and fragile, she had just as much power: the kind you only find in a father's love for a child. All of a sudden he wasn't scary anymore.

'You're asking me for a twenty-four hour reprieve,' he almost whispered as his eyes softened and she saw blue sparks explode in them.

She nodded.

He searched her face and stood watching her for what seemed like hours—although she knew it was only a moment—before his face broke into a smile. 'Deal!'

Cassie had just made a pact with the devil and she knew he would try every trick he had to spin her around and ruin the relationship she had with her man and the rest of the team. Truly this was going to test her loyalty to the ones she had come to love.

He turned, not letting her hand go and addressed the many he had working for him. 'I'm suspending all military physical attacks and we are standing down for the rest of the day. I expect you all to reconvene here at 1900 hours tomorrow. Those of you staying the night, drinks and food will be served shortly. General Gatwick will now be in charge and will make sure all your needs are met. Appreciate your patience, enjoy the evening.' Lifting her hand, he placed it over his arm and patted it. 'When was the last time you ate,

Daughter-mine?' he asked as he guided her into another room: the dining room she had been in on her last visit.

'Um … breakfast yesterday,' she answered him. And not until then did she realise that they had fought all through the night and it was now the evening of the next day. No wonder she was bombed out and weary. Suddenly now aware of why Kayden always made them have such a big breakfast and a rest before heading off. 'It's tough work sparring with you, Pops. Time seems to have just slipped away. You really need to learn to stop for a lunch break.' She broke out into a chuckle and he laughed with her.

'I'll keep that in mind next time you are blowing up all my fire power.'

'Yes! I can just see that now. "Oh sweetheart, it's your lunch break. Oops sorry! I accidentally let a meteor go before I called it. Oh well, we didn't need that star after all, hey, Daughter-mine?" ' she joked again and made him laugh more.

'You must be thirsty as well,' he said, seating her at the big dining table.

'Last time you offered me drink it was a potion that repelled my friends. Are you intending to play nice this time, Pops? No games. What do you say?'

He showed his hands. 'Nothing sinister this time. Just me being your father, I promise.' Laughing, he put his arm around her and gave her a little fatherly squeeze.

It feels nice.

Servants came out with the evening meal. She tried a couple of things and then just pushed the food around her plate as they talked. He could see she wasn't interested in the food or ambrosia and asked her what drink she preferred.

'Same as last time,' she grinned. 'Starburst, straight up, no ice.'

'Make that two,' he said to the servant, not even raising an eyebrow. He eyed her. 'Just how I like it. You know, you might be more like your old man than you care to admit, Cassandra.'

As she sipped it down, she felt it warm her inside and she held the empty glass to the servant. 'Just bring the bottle, buddy,' she said with a cheeky look, smiling at Aldebaran and still trying to get a reaction. *Aren't fathers meant to be all funny about their kids drinking alcohol?*

'If I'd known you were this much fun, maybe I'd have come and captured you years ago.' He baffled her again with his wit instead of sniping.

'Your ex, my dear, so-called mother, would have loved it if you'd have kidnapped me. The bitch would have enjoyed her life so much better with me gone,' she let on, a bit more sombrely than she had meant to and sculling another drink.

'Why? Didn't Mummy dear get you that pony you always wanted?' he said a little sarcastically and with a jealous edge.

She made a face and shook her head. 'You have no idea what you left me to endure. I should hate you for leaving me with them.' She was annoyed that he was making fun of her. Then, not sure why, her anger boiled over, making her blab to Daddy-o just what a hard life she did have. She finished with the kidnapping saga and realised he had gone totally silent and the colour had drained from his face.

Aldebaran took a minute to process what he'd just learned. 'She didn't want you, yet she wouldn't let me have you either? Why did she feel she had to punish us both?'

'Maybe she wasn't really happy and blamed you,' she said in a sarcastic tone.

'Cassandra, stop it,' he growled. 'Your bitterness towards me won't help what's been done. I'm sorry for what happened to you but if we're ever to get past these trust issues you have to let it go.'

Tears stung her eyes—she'd never had a real father. He was talking to her as if he was and now she felt upset that she had hurt him. *Jeez, I am so damned confused with all this newness of emotion.* 'I'm sorry,' she apologised. 'I've had a bad couple of days and shouldn't be taking it out on you.' She poured another drink and passed him one. 'You're right, I probably just wanted to hurt you and it was childish and uncalled-for.'

'At least I know you can be honest with me,' he said.

Wiping away her tears, she eyed him. 'Our very first father-daughter fight,' she said with a little smile.

'Yes! We're both very stubborn,' he grinned.

She sipped of her drink. 'Even though it was in poor taste to throw all that family history at you, somehow I feel lots better for telling someone.'

He patted her hand. 'Because I'm your father, Cassandra and deep down you know that, you should know too that you can come to me about anything. I want to know everything about you.' He smiled warmly. 'So, tell me what do you and your friends do in your spare time?'

She ran her fingers around the glass and down the stem of it while thinking. 'Let me see. The property is massive and there is a great lake, so we swim and sleep out under the stars. They have off-road vehicles, the trail bikes we take up into the mountain range and spend hours on the sand dunes. The four-wheel drives are mainly used for hunting, a sport I have come to enjoy immensely. Oh and the boys throw lots of parties and BBQs where we normally end up pretty pickled and play cards. They figure if I'm under the weather they have a better chance of beating me. Like that's ever going to happen. Not!'

He seemed amused. 'Are you any good?'

'Pop, I reckon even if you were to use your magic I would still come up trumps,' she laughed, sitting back in the chair and looking cocky as hell. She could see he saw the challenge and wasn't about to let his own kid show him up. This would be fun and knowing he would probably be a bit of a gambler, she was going to enjoy a little family rivalry.

'Then let's see if you take after your old man,' he said, shaking his head and looking pleased that she wanted to play a game with him. It was a bit of healthy competition that he looked forward to, especially with her looking so smug. *Yes, I will enjoy this too!*

The table now cleared and a new deck of cards shuffled, both were eager to let the games begin. Wit and cunning showed on their faces as both wanted to come out the winner. Father against daughter: maybe it wasn't on the battlefield but it might as well have been.

Neither was to be merciful. The first hand went in Cassie's favour and Aldebaran tried hard to hide his irritation that his daughter might be more of a challenge than he had thought. He hated to lose and she was causing him real grief of late.

'Okay, Cassandra, game on!' He rolled his head as she dealt the next hand.

'Sorry, Pops but I'm good. You can give up now if you want,' she stirred.

'Just deal, cheeky one. I still have a few tricks left.'

As the night went on, Cassie kept beating him and as she dealt the cards she told him of the bets they made, in particular the one where they played strip poker.

'Lucky you're getting smashed on the Moonjuice your giving us, because at least I can tell you anything and you won't be quick enough to catch me and discipline me in your state.' She slurred a little.

'Don't bet on it, young lady! I still have some wits about me. Winning at cards proves nothing, just that you cheat a lot,' he laughed at her.

'Cheat, you say!' She jumped up, grabbed his arm and a card fell out.

He grabbed her and tickled her, making her fall clumsily on his lap. She looked at him seriously for a minute. *He feels like home.* She wrapped her arms around his neck. He was limp at first and then cuddled her back. Spent and too dizzy from the drink to move, she put her head on his shoulder and fell asleep.

In the morning she found herself in a strange bed, fully clothed and under the covers. The curtains were closed so the room was in darkness. She had no clue what time it was but knew she had been sleeping a long time. Jumping out of bed with a spring in her step from having such a great night she went into the en suite and showered. Walking out of her room, she looked over the railing and called out. 'Hi down there, is anyone around?' A servant walked out from below. 'Can I get you something, miss?' he asked.

'Coffee would be nice and can you tell me where they put my

horse?'

'Yes ma'am. Coffee is on its way and your horse is in the stables to the left of the front door. I'll take you as soon as you're ready.'

'Ready!' she giggled. 'I'll take the coffee to go.'

She checked her image in the wall-to-wall mirrored tiles at the end of the corridor. Her outfit, even though slept in, had magically refitted itself to her after the shower with not one crease. Her face and hair were the same, perfectly replenished as well. A happy glow reflected back as the image was that of someone who had maybe just stepped out of a beauty parlour.

'Amazing,' she giggled, touching her reflection in the mirror before skipping down the flight of steps, feeling like Cinderella going to a ball. *Magic! How lucky I feel. This new world is so cool: an absolute dream.*

She chatted to the servant (whose name was Lamar, she discovered), while sipping her coffee as she was directed out towards her horse. Lamar had worked in the castle for twenty-two years. Cassie was pleased to think that if her pop could keep his staff for that long he mustn't be so bad after all.

Arriving at the stables, Cassie found Starburst looking well rested but restless. She took him outside for a run and a bit of fun with her before putting him back in his stall. After getting him a fresh bucket of water, she filled his feeder with some grain from the stockpile in the loft as well as leaving a decent pile of hay to munch on while he waited for her.

'We'll be here for a bit longer, Starburst,' she told him. 'But tonight after dinner you can take me home. Okay?'

He nodded and snorted so she took that as a yes.

Skipping back into the house, Cassie felt like a great weight had fallen from her. Talking to her father about her mother last night had purged many ill feelings. And now knowing Starburst was looked after, she could enjoy the rest of the day. She was starting to believe that her father wasn't that bad after all and was looking forward to spending the day with him.

On re-entering the castle, the servant Lamar took her straight into the dining room where Aldebaran sat reading a book. It looked like he had only just woken up. His hair was a little ruffled and his eyes had dark rings as if he'd had very little sleep. She guessed it had been a bit of a shock with her just turning up and no doubt it would have interrupted his sleep. Unlike him, she always slept well and drinking never gave her a hangover so she was glad for that.

'Can't you handle it like you used to in the old days, Pops? Hope I don't inherit those genes.' She stirred him as she sat down and poured a juice.

He looked over his novel. 'Someone woke up in good humour this morning.'

She looked carefully at him to judge his mood. The last thing she wanted was to put him in a grumpy frame of mind and have it spoil the day. Then she remembered that this was the old way that she used to think. She had to stop worrying that he would turn on her like her other parents did. As Woody said, they were not like normal people. They were cruel and spiteful. Yet it was strange because although she knew her dad was both, there had been no sign of that towards her. She had to give him a chance to prove he was different, worthy of a daughter's love.

She reached out for a pastry. 'We've all day together, Pops,' she said, drinking down some juice. 'So, tell me what do you and your friends do in your spare time?' Throwing his words back at him in a playful way she said, 'Don't tell me you only play war games. Surely there must be some fun things to do on these stars?'

He put his book down and sipped his coffee. 'Aquarius has a huge water park with tunnels and slides if that interests you. Aqua is the ruler of the zodiac known to you on earth as the water sign. She's a good friend of mine and I'm sure she wouldn't mind a visit.'

'Beats sitting around here all day watching you read a book,' she joked again and liked that he seemed to be enjoying her fun side and taking her comments as they were intended.

He shook his head. She was so much like him that it amazed him. 'You're so cheeky, young lady. I'll take you on one condition. You eat something. And I just hope you can find a pair of bathers upstairs that'll fit you.' Looking at her shape he said, 'It's been a while since I had someone so petite visit me.'

She looked down at her outfit. 'What sort of magical world is this? Surely if this outfit can mysteriously not get wrinkled, if I strip off near water shouldn't bathers just appear on me?' she asked, raising her eyebrow, uncertain but hopeful.

'You're a fascinating woman, Cassandra. That logic is quite kooky yet possible. Take a pair from upstairs just in case.'

Lamar served her a plate of eggs and bacon. 'Normal food!' she said as she ate heartily for the first time since breakfast two days before.

He smiled. 'I took note of your indifference to our food last night. I thought you might appreciate some earth food.'

'Thanks, Pops,' she said, digging her toast into the runny eggs.

After both had eaten, Cassie ran upstairs and found a pair of bathers and a towel. When she went to join Aldebaran downstairs, he was talking quietly to one of his guards making her frown as she walked towards him.

'You're not breaking your promise to me and playing war games behind my back are you, Pop?' she asked, feeling a little flutter of worry begin to grip her stomach.

He gently took her chin in his hand. 'Don't frown. I promised you, Cassandra and I'm not about to spoil our time together. I just need my home protected while I'm gone.'

The second he put his arm across her shoulder, a bright light surrounded them, the room they were in shimmering out of focus. Amazed with this form of travel Cassie was in awe when the view changed and suddenly realised he had transported them both to the Aquarius constellation in what seemed like an instant.

'Cool trick,' she said, looking around at the castle before them and to the left, the water wonderland. The sparkling water glittered and shone as the sunlight touched it. A woman came out with a warm smile. Cassie figured she must have been Aqua. 'I wasn't expecting you today, Ald darling. Who's your friend?'

She stunned Cassie with her beauty. She had long, curly, dark hair and a perfect figure. She wore a white mini-dress with a gold sash that highlighted her waistline. Her ankles, wrists and hair glittered with diamonds that sparkled like the water. She had a sort of childlike sweetness yet if she was friends with her dad, Cassie knew that she would hardly be naïve or innocent, truth be told.

Aqua hugged Aldebaran maybe a little longer than normal, leading Cassie to believe they were a lot more than friends and Pops had been holding out on her. Aqua stayed hanging off his arm while her dad introduced them.

'This is Cassandra, my daughter. She paid me a visit, yet after only a few hours finds me boring. So bringing her here for some fun in your water park gives me the opportunity to catch up with you as well, my lovely.'

Cassie smiled and shook hands with her. 'Hi Aqua, nice to finally meet one of the twelve zodiacs. Coming from earth, I would never have dreamed the water sign would actually have such a magnificent setup. We all just thought you were a statue holding a water jug. I'm amazed at how magnificent all this is.'

'Yes, we only give earth visions of what we want them to believe. This will be our little secret, okay?'

'Sure. As if anyone would believe all this. I'd be labelled crazy and locked up in a padded cell if I divulged anything I did.'

Aldebaran laughed. 'Your secret is safe with Cassie. She's one of the Cloud Riders.'

'Ald, my God! You two are mortal enemies—how can you be associating with each other? Zoren will have a fit.'

'It's alright, Aqua, she came to me. He knows. We have both agreed to stand down for twenty-four hours while her team sort out some personal business. It's mutual and benefits both of us. This is the first opportunity we've ever had to get to know one another a little better.'

'Then when she goes back, your plans, Ald, have they changed?'

'This changes nothing for either of us. It'll be business as usual again tomorrow.'

Cassie chuckled. 'Yes, I'll be back out there giving Pop hell again and he'll be throwing whatever he can back at me. He will lose of course! But I'll let him try.'

'Cheeky monkey.' He grinned good-humouredly. 'See what I have to put up with? She's a cocky little thing who needs to learn a lesson. I am so looking forward to her leaving.' He laughed with her.

'Bring it on, Pops!'

He grabbed her, not even waiting for her to change and threw her in the water. Drenched, she came up still laughing. She swallowed a mouthful of water and nearly choked but kept giggling.

'See? Even choking doesn't work with her. She's like a cat with nine lives.'

Even Aqua was getting into it now and was smiling at them both. She could see they definitely were father and daughter. She was happy that Ald had the chance to meet her even if they were rivals.

Cassie looked under her top and saw a gold bikini top had magically appeared. She took off her outfit and threw it at her dad. 'You wet it, you can hang it up to dry,' she chuckled.

Aqua bent down, picked Cassie's top and pants up and draped them over a chair. 'You go have some fun, Ald. I'll organise some lunch for you both.'

'That would be lovely of you, sweet one.' Aldebaran kissed her hand tenderly, making Aqua blush and giggle before she left him to have some private time with his daughter.

Cassie pulled herself out, ready to dive back in, when she saw her dad just standing there watching. 'Come on, old man. Let's see if you can keep up with your kid.'

He smirked, threw off his shirt and flew after her, catching her on his way and throwing them both in the water. 'Give you old man crap, you little stirrer?' he laughed.

They spent half the morning going up and down the slides. Her favourite was the tunnel. It went very dark and you could feel weird things touching you as you went through. It made you quiver with horror before being flung high up in the air. They dragged themselves out, laughing and exhausted.

Wrapping towels around themselves, they sat in the lounges by the pool with Aqua while servants brought out savouries and ice-cold drinks. These they enjoyed while chatting about how much fun they'd been having. Aqua seemed to have a thing for her father and constantly touched his arm or hand as she talked. He seemed to enjoy her constant flirting and was kicking back, relaxing and having a good time. Cassie hated to break up the fun he was having but she knew she would be going soon and wanted a bit of alone time with him before she headed off.

Aqua asked if they could stay for dinner but Aldebaran saw the look on Cassie's face and declined, saying that he had just a few more hours left with her so he wanted to head off. He slipped his arm around Cassie and she was not prepared for her father's powers. Her clothes appeared on her, dry and pressed. Her hair was again dry and her makeup felt freshly applied.

Aqua grinned. 'Your father's great to have around the morning after,' she said. 'He does have a way with making a girl not only look good, but feel good.'

Cassie put her hand up. 'Far too much information!' she giggled, looking up at her dad.

Aqua and her father both shared a look of tenderness before Aqua disappeared from their sight.

It only took an instant to get back, therefore Cassie felt she had time to pay Starburst a quick visit to make sure he was alright. Going inside the castle, she noticed her father had organised a drink for them both. She was happy that he wanted to just sit back and chat to her. He was making her feel very comfortable and welcome.

'You seem very connected to that horse,' Aldebaran commented.

Cassie took a sip of drink, recalling the first time she saw him. 'I watched him being born and it was the first time I'd ever seen anything give birth. When he came out, he was an unsteady skinny little thing that could barely stand. He wobbled and made me laugh as he tried so hard to stay on his feet. He was beautiful.'

'You missed a lot, didn't you, Cassandra? Like today.'

She smiled. 'Yes but yesterday is gone and from now on I intend to make everyday count and experience all the things I've only read about. What we did today, to visit a water park was high on my to-do list. So thanks, Pops. It was crazy fun and I loved it.'

She got up and walked around the big study they'd been sitting in. She couldn't help but admire the books he had crammed onto the selves. There were even moving ladders to get to the paperbacks way up on the top shelf. It amused her he would need them with all his magic. He could have just summoned one to him.

Before she left, Aldebaran made a toast to his daughter. Cassie went to have a drink and then stopped to think about it before swapping their drinks and taking a sip of his. He gave her a quizzical look. 'Swapped them just in case you send me home and everyone hates me again. You know that was a pretty dirty trick.'

He smiled; his eyes glowed with a crafty flicker. 'A father will do what a father must do to be able to spend time with his little girl. You forgave me though or you wouldn't have come back, no matter what the reason.'

'I have no need to carry a grudge. Unlike my pops, I can forgive and forget.' Darkness filled his eyes and she knew it was silly to spoil the day with one of her flyaway comments that were not called for. 'Sorry, that wasn't only rude but none of my business. If you allow me to pull my foot from my mouth I would like to retract that silly comment. I really would prefer not to bring business into our time together and spoil the lovely day we've just spent together. All too soon we'll back on opposite sides and I don't want to think about that just now either.'

She felt his mood lift instantly. 'Thanks, Cassandra, I appreciate you apologising. It's one of your many traits I find adorable. To tell you the truth I never want politics to deter you from visiting me. I'm stubborn and change is not easy for me nowadays. At this time I can only see it causing us both heartache. Instead I would prefer you to visit because you just enjoy your old man's company.' He held out his hand for her to accept this or not.

There was no way Cassie wanted to even think of him as anything more than her cool dad who had given her his time freely without an explanation as to why she had requested it. She ignored his hand, instead wrapping her arms around his neck and hugging him. This time he automatically hugged her back. 'You would have made a pretty good dad. Thank you for showing me that,' she said, meaning it.

He growled in a playful way. 'I could eat you up, you're so sweet,' he chuckled, making little chomping noises around her ear and making her laugh happily.

Walking out to the horse, Cassie was sad to be leaving. She had enjoyed getting to know her real father and hoped one day, to visit again.

He held her for a long time, silently searching her face like he was looking for something. When a tear ran down her face at the sadness she felt at having to leave him, he smiled with utter joy. 'I knew you loved me too,' he said, pleased. 'Come and visit me again as soon as Kayden allows it. I'll understand if it won't be for a while. After all, we are enemies and you have been in the rival's camp, which in war times is frowned upon. But I had the best time, Cassandra. Thanks for making an old man very happy,' he said, helping her up on the horse.

With tears in her eyes, she blew him a kiss as Starburst flew off and headed for home.

Chapter Twenty-Four
Second Chance

Starburst landed them in the paddock and trotted back to the horse stables. The slow trip back to Kayden's farmhouse had given her time to try and calm down a little. Even the magical cloud with its colourful lighting did little to ease her mind. Since leaving the comfort of her father's home the worries of what she was coming home to washed over her to a point where she was on the edge of bursting into tears.

Was Conor better? Had Pop put a spell on her that would make Kayden distrust her again? What about Woody? Would he be there waiting or be replaced by a stranger?

Starburst trotted the last few yards to the barn. Kayden heard them and was out of the door in a flash. He lifted her off and held her while their emotions stabilised. He had missed her terribly and she had not only missed him but now missed her dad.

After Starburst had been tended to they went inside and had coffee and a chat. As Cassie sipped it, she told Kayden all that had happened since she'd last seen him, starting with the massive room where Aldebaran played his war games with his officers to the wonderful time she had with her father on Aquarius. She broke down and tears ran down her face. 'You know, he really is my father and he loves me. Because of that I was unable to approach the subject of the war going on up there. It just didn't seem appropriate to bring it up. I hope I haven't let you down.'

'You haven't let anyone down. I wouldn't have expected you to be negotiating at this early stage. It has taken the men years to learn the correct techniques. You could've really ticked him off and made it worse, so you've done well. And as for him keeping his side of the bargain, we've not been summoned by Zoren yet so your dad kept his promise. He didn't attack while you were with him.'

Pleased her father didn't lie to her, she then focused on the other of her worries. 'Is Woody back and how's our Conor?'

He shook his head and looked at her a bit forlornly. 'I'll be replacing Woody. He deserted us, Cassie! He forced me to keep a secret from Zoren—who is not going to be impressed when he finds out. He could have indirectly killed Conor with his thoughtlessness. Also to stop Aldebaran from attacking anyone while Conor was healing, it put you in a most compromising and dangerous position. Admittedly it turned out okay with your father—but it could have been disastrous. I was imagining all sorts of scenarios. Most of all I hoped you would get home safely or we would have had to find a way to go in there forcibly to extract you. Not counting the constant worry I've been under having to leave you up there. It was crazy of me to even consider that mission with only four of us. I've already stood Woody down and I'll be telling him tonight that he's no longer a part of the team.'

Cassie put her cup on the table. 'So you haven't told Zoren yet?'

He shook his head. She felt relief flood through her, knowing that there was still hope for Woody if she could get Kayden to discuss it further.

'But it turned out alright, didn't it?'

Drinking the rest of his coffee, he picked up both their cups and put them in the sink. He wished they didn't have to have this conversation. She obviously didn't understand how Woody's actions could have compromised the whole mission. He knew she wouldn't let the topic drop and he'd missed her so much he really would sooner be holding her and loving her than getting into something he had already made a decision on. 'Yes, it turned out alright. Aldebaran actually acted as a father should. He kept his word and you are back.

But Cassie, you know it could have ended badly, very badly. I have a big responsibility up there and if things go wrong I'm the one held responsible. Earth is in danger every time they go to war. The human race is too important to have a member of my team putting themselves first.'

Cassie wasn't going to give up. His argument was solid but his team was also important. Replacing a member at this stage, with her only a learner, scared her more than even the thought of what her father could do. He'd left a door open and she took advantage of it. 'Kayden, what would have happened if, when you had fallen in love with me, I was the one with no powers? How would you have concealed your secret from me? You knew I was starting to work it out for myself and I knew there was something very weird going on. Would you have been able to walk away from me?'

He put his head down and clamped his hands together. 'I've given that a lot of thought and I don't know the answer.'

She touched his face and he looked up. 'Would you have trusted me enough to tell me?' she asked. 'Because I know that I would've taken this secret to the grave. I loved you that much. I was away from you for three months and never thought I would ever see you again and yet I didn't tell a soul—even after I knew.'

Kayden stared into her eyes. She knew he was working through what she'd just said so she continued. 'Maybe in certain cases, like Woody's, the partners could be taken into their confidence. That is, if it is serious and he loves her like you love me. What is the worst that could happen? She blabs! Yet who would believe her? Such a wild story! In Ella's case we could justify it by saying it is the ranting of a spoilt little rich girl who is trying to seek revenge. The tale is so wild no normal person would ever believe it.'

'It's a big call, Cassie. The other guys don't like her and neither do you so how can she fit in with us?'

'I thought about that. I know Woody wouldn't want her around all the time because he does like his freedom and she's a jetsetter. If she understands what his big connection is with us, she may settle and not be so jealous and bitchy back at us, maybe preferring instead to just pop in when she's in town. She'll understand his commitment to the bigger picture and knowing her kind, I can guarantee she will actually feel quite proud of him.'

'If you're wrong we could end up with a situation,' he said, concerned.

'So, we all disappear for a while, live somewhere else. It doesn't have to be here. Rent these two farms out for a while as you do when your neighbours start to notice you not getting old. When it dies down or she dies, we move back.' She grinned a little deviously. 'When Ella gets old, Woody will want her less and less. We're a family forever! She'll only be a thorn in our side for maybe ten or thirty years, tops. But I can guarantee she'll do one of two things. She'll stick around, as I said, until she gets old and he dumps her nasty self. Or she will be married in the next twelve months to someone she can own. She will always keep Woody as her lover which is all he really is asking for anyway.'

'You make a lot of sense. Being so angry with him has stopped me looking at it with any sort of perspective.' He smiled, kissed her cheek and stood up. 'Woody and the boys are waiting for me to discuss the issue but until you returned, I wasn't able to face it. Feel up to a little visit with them tonight? It's time we all discussed it like grownups. It would be better as a group decision; changing the rules on partners will affect all their relationships from now on.'

Cassie ducked in and had a quick shower to freshen up before going out into the barn to get Kayden. He wanted to check on Starburst. As she entered the barn she could tell by Kayden's grin as he talked to Starburst telepathically that he was pleased they had kept him in good condition.

* * * *

It was getting late when they arrived at the boys' home. They were all out the back, lazing around on the outdoor lounges, not even slightly looking like they were ready to retire for the night. Cassie knew how they felt as she herself wouldn't be able to sleep until the Woody problem was sorted.

Woody was sitting on one of the deckchairs with his elbows on his knees and his head and shoulders bent. He looked miserable, waiting to hear his fate and who his replacement was going to be. Cassie could tell they had all been discussing it and Kayden's visit would be just a formality.

Cassie went around and gave them all a kiss and a warm greeting. Her bright chatter cheered them up—except for Woody— he just sat quietly looking like he didn't belong with them anymore. Jason asked Kayden and Cassie if they wanted a tea or coffee. Cassie really needed more than just a hot beverage, asking for a nip of spirits to be added. All the men went inside to give Cassie some time alone with Woody. She knew secretly they would be hoping she'd be able to fix the mess that Woody left in his wake. It was obvious how upset he was as his body trembled when she went over to him and put her hand on his shoulder.

'I've really stuffed up this time, Cass. Sorry kiddo—maybe you better go and not stand with the enemy,' he choked emotionally.

'I missed you, Woodsta. And you're not my enemy—never will be.'

'Don't be nice to me, Cassie. I don't deserve it.'

'Woody, stop it. Just because you made an error in judgement doesn't mean your friends will desert you. We all muck up and unless you're a robot and programmed to be perfect, this will not be the last for any of us.' She patted his shoulder friendly-like as the others came out and she moved back to where she had been sitting.

Kayden looked serious as he walked out to the others. Woody sat nervously, waiting for the final blow to his shattered life.

'I wanted us all together to discuss the issue regarding Woody and the whole girlfriend situation that I thought I had put to rest. It's been brought to my attention tonight that I may have been a little hasty with my decision.' He gave a slight nod towards Cassie and they exchanged a knowing glance. 'Cassie feels that if any of you do fall in love and want to reveal our secret world then you should be able to do just that. She herself is living proof that she knew all about us yet lived in Perth for months and never breathed a word, even after we had broken up. Why? Because she could be trusted! Her love for me, for us, even though squashed, stopped her from giving any of us away. She would never have done that. With that in mind, the ruling on secrecy that we put in place when we all formed as a group needs to be revised. Maybe other women can be trusted too. You see, guys, this isn't all just about Woody.' He paused. 'It affects you all. If any one of you falls in love from now on, you should be allowed to use your own discretion as to how much is revealed. As Cassie said, if the love turns bitter and they mouth-off about what we do, it's their word against ours and we can always just pick up and leave for a few decades until those people are no longer around and come back as we always do.'

They all nodded in agreement.

'Woody, I want you to feel free to tell Ella whatever you need to. If Ella knows, Cassie feels she will stop being a spiteful to the rest of the group and will never again selfishly prevent you from preforming your duties. I hope she's right, Woody. I was ready to replace you mate, I was so angry at you. Piss me off like that again and even Cassie won't save you next time, I don't care how attached she feels to you. Is that understood?'

Woody straightened and nodded in agreement, unable to believe what he was hearing—that he had been given a second chance. He still looked gutted but at least he was sitting upright now and not stooping anymore.

'Okay, enough said. You're back in and so is your woman. Woody, hear me and hear me good! There are no more chances. What I just put Conor and Cassie through was uncalled for. They both paid a high price for your desertion and I won't let it happen again.'

Woody put his head down and collected himself. When his gaze came up to meet Kayden's it was full of remorse. 'I never thought this would happen to me: that I would fall for someone so hard that it would make me end up betraying you all. It's something I'll have to live with now. A hard lesson learned and I thank you all for giving me the opportunity to continue with my relationship with her, but I have already broken it off with Ella. Regardless of how this would have ended here tonight, I can't see it working. Changing the ruling on this makes no difference to my decision that this should be over.' Woody sat back in the chair, looking a bit more comfortable about talking to them about her. 'When I went away with her I realised that for me it was more than likely only about the sex. Her world was so different to mine and didn't interest me. Her friends were stuck-up and they all bitched about each other so much that I went on a bender. When I received your message that we had a mission on, I had no way of getting back. You see, I couldn't drive as I had written myself off to put up with them. Ella couldn't drive me because she had gone out with her girlfriends. She wasn't answering her phone, not even the texts I sent her. Neither could any of the guys I was with as they were all as smashed as I was. I went to sleep it off, only by the time I finally made it back here it was too late. I knew you guys would be possibly on your way home and that I was in trouble. I am committed, Kayden, more than ever. I can't believe I stuffed up so badly and nearly lost everything that I've ever truly loved. I apologise, not just to you, but to all of the team for being an idiot and I hope you can all forgive me.'

Conor patted him on the back. 'It's okay, mate, I forgive you. But if you ever do it again I'm going to put my size twelve right were the sun don't shine and my frigging broken arm will feel like a mosquito bite compared to how you're going to feel,' he teased. 'Mongrel!'

Woody gave him a man hug. 'Thanks, man! Glad you're okay.' He then knelt in front of Cassie. 'I'm so sorry, Cass. We've all been worried sick about you. Did your father give you a hard time?'

'I'm far too tired to tell you about it tonight but just like you I had to say goodbye to someone who would prevent me doing my job if I became too involved.' She touched his cheek caringly before rolling her shoulders and breathing in deeply. She really felt bombed. 'And most likely the same as you, there is only so much stress a person can take in one day,' she said, exhausted.

'Yes, you look tuckered out. We'll talk tomorrow.' Woody watched her, worrying that she'd really overdone it and took on board that it was all his doing.

Kayden moved over and put a protective arm around his woman. 'Well, that's it for me too, boys. It's been a long day for all of us. We'll sleep here so we can get an early start in the morning. We need some bonding time so discuss it between yourselves and let me know in the morning where you want to go. Goodnight all!' He waved over his shoulder, leaving them flabbergasted as to how Cassie could have worked that miracle on their boss. Cassie smiled as the sound of whooping and hollering sounded out behind them. Woody was back, her dad hadn't put a spell on her, and she was in her man's arms.

Chapter Twenty-Five
Surrounded by Beauty

The sun shone brightly through the window as Jason pulled the curtains back. 'Come on, you two, you're sleeping the day away!'

Kayden was all wrapped around Cassie. Loosening his grip and stretching, he asked if the horses had been checked.

'They're fine. Woody went down to the paddock before he went to bed early this morning.'

Cassie groaned and cuddled back into her man. 'Then why do I have to get up?'

'We all want to take you somewhere special today,' he grinned. 'It's a bit of a drive so we need to leave shortly.'

Cassie smiled. 'Sounds like a reason to get up then.' She sat up, stretching.

Kayden threw a shirt at Jason. 'Nick off and let the two of us get ready then,' he joked with him.

Jason gestured to the coffees beside the bed. 'Drink up and get a wiggle on then,' he said, throwing the shirt back at Kayden. In high spirits, he left them to it.

An hour later, they piled into Conor's black Hummer that seated all six comfortably. Together they travelled along the Great Northern Highway and turned into Karijini National Park. Woody drove while Jason and Ethan acted as the tour guides. The brothers' double act was quite entertaining. 'It is the second largest national park in Western

Australia and one of the most spectacular sights in the Pilbara. It has gorges, crystal-clear rock pools, waterfalls and the best scenery you will see anywhere.'

They gave a vivid description, stopping suddenly as they reached the Oxley Lookout. The view making them all catch their breath, Cassie seeing firsthand the most stunning view ever. Below was the junction of four gorges: the Red, Aeano, Joffre and Hancock. She greatly admired the tremendous forces of nature that must have torn the earth apart, leaving such beauty in its wake.

Further into the ranges, they pulled up in the car park of Fortesque Falls. Here they had to walk down a steep trail leading to the waterfall. Down the path, the foliage increased in density. The tropical plant life was a lovely contrast against the iron ore-rich walls, in shades of deep purple to earth reds. Finally the pathway opened up to a breathtaking sight of spring-fed pools beneath the stunning Fortesque Falls.

It looked so inviting that Cassie kicked off her shoes and tossing her dress aside, dove into the cool, clean water. She enjoyed the fresh feel against her skin and the taste of spring water on her lips. On coming up for air, waves of water exploded all around her as the boys bombarded her. Boys will be boys, she thought, giggling.

After the dip, they walked up another path and turned right to the fern pools about ten minutes away. Here they could only admire the perfect bush setting: so green and lush around sparkling pools. They all sat and soaked in the beauty of nature at its most healthy, relaxing in the sun, deep within their own thoughts.

Woody was the first to speak. 'What was it like spending time with your dad? Is he as wicked as they say?'

She nudged him. 'How did you know that was who I was thinking about?'

'Just a guess,' he said, looking out at the kids playing under the waterfall. He too would have been thinking of Ella. They both had a lot to work through; maybe they could help each other.

She turned to him, crossing her legs. 'In so many ways he was just a dad and nothing more, a parent who showed his daughter what it would have been like to have had a real father. I felt special and loved.'

'So, then the princess felt sad to leave even though she knew he was really just a mean old tyrant who was to be her enemy.'

Cassie looked up at Kayden who was sitting on a rock near them and frowned. 'It was so hard. I've never had a parent love me before and it really tugged at my heartstrings to have to leave,' she sighed and dropped her shoulders, feeling the real worry.

Kayden stood up and pulled her to her feet. 'Cassie I'm so proud of you for what you did for us but seeing your father again will make you confused. Know that I have to take that decision out of your hands. As your boss I have to insist that for the time being you should steer clear of Aldebaran. You need time to get over him. You have to get your head back into the game. There's a major war going on up there and we need you to be thinking clearly. Okay?'

She knew he was right but she hated him for saying it. 'Dad said you'd keep me away from him and believe it or not, he does understand why. That being said, I do need time to sort out my feelings for him. He really threw me a curveball, being so sweet and kind when I was expecting an angry wizard to cast a spell on me or something along those lines. To fight against him is going to be tough if I soften too much towards him.'

Kayden hugged her for her bravery. She was obviously having a hard time with it, more than he had thought. The guy must have really done a number on her because she was usually good at picking up on bad karma and Kayden knew he was one of the worst.

Cassie suddenly felt overwhelmed with the heartbreak of losing another parent. She started to shake and cried for a very long time. She cried for a father who could have been her saviour as a child and for a life that would never be because he could not be the father she now needed him to be. She had let him love her and she had returned it without question. Now home, reality hit and she to let it go as nothing good would ever come of their strong bond while they fought on opposite sides.

When she finally calmed down she felt better, as if all the sadness had finally run out with her tears. Cheering up, she realised that she had brought everyone down and decided to cheer the team back up. All of a sudden, she put a big grin on her face and giggling, she wriggled from Kayden's arms and ran full pelt into the spring.

Woody reached her first. 'You're crazy, girl. You had us all worried sick,' he chuckled.

'I'm better now. As if I'm going to let my personal life totally spoil our trip! I want to remember it as being fun.'

He shook his head, grinning. 'You asked for it then.' With that, he lifted her up, tossing her high into the air. The others had joined them and she caused some frenzy as they all fought to catch her.

The sun was high up in the sky by the time they headed back to the car park. They were all still fooling around and Cassie stirred Ethan up so badly that he and Jason grabbed her. While Jason held her down, Ethan wrote in a black marker on her stomach, 'Bad Girl'. When they let her up, she lifted her shirt to have a look and to proudly show off his artwork. He had written it in calligraphy and it actually looked quite cool.

'I'm not washing this off, you know.' She danced around, admiring it. 'Actually, that gives me an idea. Seeing I'm a part of the team now I should be initiated into it. Let's go to a tattoo shop so I can get the Cloud Riders emblem you all have on your arms.'

Kayden reached for her and grabbed her around the waist. 'You're such a little rebel. The guys can't do anything to upset you, can they?' He looked over at Ethan. 'Now, what have you started?'

'She'd look sexy with tats,' Ethan laughed.

Kayden punched him in the arm and then gave Cassie a very seductive look. 'I know.'

'Then we can go straight there on the way home? I saw a tattooist on the way here,' she nagged.

'I guess it won't hurt to at least take you there to have a look. It might frighten the hell out of you and make you change your mind.'

She nudged Ethan, seeing as he was the one she had been stirring all the way back from the waterfall. 'What do you think?'

He grinned. 'Might be worth seeing you in pain. Might just shut you up for a bit.'

Kayden bent down and talked quietly. 'If you really want this, you know I won't stop you. However, I must warn you that I'm very partial to a woman with a tattoo. Therefore, don't go holding me responsible for my actions if you look too hot. Are we clear, gorgeous?'

She hugged him, laughing. 'Promises, promises!'

'Well it looks like we have a date with our tattooist,' he grinned. *My woman got me all excited, we're going now. Stuff the food. Get your selves in the car.* He grabbed the keys and moved her quickly over to the car. *If you lot aren't in and doors closed by the time I've buckled her in, you lot can walk home.* He chuckled to himself as he relayed the message to the men only.

'You do know after the needles stop jabbing it smarts like a burn,' Ethan warned as he jumped in the Hummer. The boss wasn't going to give her a chance to change her mind. He was keyed up and that meant leaving the horror stories for the rest of them to tell so as to maybe put her off.

'Shh,' she said, putting her hand to his lips. 'I don't want to know. I want the team symbol. End of story. No scaring me or the lot of you can wait outside.'

'I'm not waiting outside, Cassie. Those stirrers can though. I want to see it happen so don't think for one minute that you're going to spoil my fun. No damned way!' Kayden grumbled, amusing her.

'We all want to see!' Woody added.

She shook her finger at them. 'You're all bitches and sadists. Okay, but you have to behave.'

'Promise,' they agreed, hitting each other.

'Like she's dumb enough to think we'll shut our traps,' Jason joked.

Pulling up at the tattooist, Cassie was a bit nervous but she put her mind at rest knowing that it would be over in an hour, after which she would be walking out of the shop with the Cloud Rider marking.

Marco the tattooist was a good friend of Kayden's and had done most of their tats; therefore he knew she was in good hands. The guys pulled up chairs to watch, making jokes and taking bets on how long it would be before the poor guy was zapped into the shop next door when he hurt her. He was a funny character and she liked him. When he finally asked her where she wanted it, there was no other choice. Kayden had already decided it would look better below her belly button, close to her right hip but smaller and more feminine. Kayden seemed very pleased with that spot and shook his head at any other suggestion. 'My girl, my spot!' He refused to listen. Cassie didn't care, just so long as it was on her somewhere. So she lay back and Marco started the artwork.

It was a little over two hours by the time he switched off the gun and the damned needles stopped striking her skin. It wasn't something she would ever want to do again, especially in such a tender spot. Ethan was right: it now just felt like a bad case of sunburn but she would heal quickly and admiring it in the mirror, she was happy with the result.

Without warning she started to feel a bit light-headed and Kayden caught her, snatching her gently up in his arms. 'You alright, gorgeous?'

'Your princess is sore and sick of being tough.' She dropped her lip. 'I think I need spoiling now.' She gave a girlie smile and his eyes melted. She could tell he loved that she had dropped the hard-core act and needed him.

Arriving back at the farm to drop the guys off, she felt tender and not very sociable. All she wanted was for Kayden to take her home so that she could just feel miserable and sore all by herself. However, they had other plans. The guys knew what she would be feeling and were refusing to let her be miserable. They propped her on their couch with pillows and told her to sit still while they organised cinema food and a movie. They fed her hot dogs and ice cream while watching a chick flick. How they had one in the house was beyond her. She had thought she would have to watch a rerun of *Seinfeld* or a gory man movie. She cheered up that they had gone to such an effort.

Dawn was beginning to throw light across the sky when she

woke the next morning. They'd made her sleep all night on the couch to prevent her from rolling over in her sleep, hurting herself. What she hadn't realised was that they had all crashed there on the floor around her. Aw, that is so sweet, she thought, looking around the room at everyone sleeping. She found Kayden wrapped up in a sleeping bag right beside the couch. She sat up and groaned with the tenderness.

Kayden sat up. 'Are you alright, honey?' he said a bit groggily.

'Sorry I woke you. I am okay, just moved too quickly,' she whispered.

'You don't have to whisper,' Woody said. 'We're like doting parents waking at your every murmur. Boy, you talk a lot in your sleep.' He chuckled and she heard little sniggers from around the room.

'Shut up! What did I say?'

They all laughed.

'You were growling most of the night at Marco, calling him everything,' Jason stirred.

Kayden chuckled. 'Enough, guys. You didn't move all night, honey, they're just being stirrers.'

She threw back her covers. 'Well, if it's okay by my doting dads, I have to make a trip to the bathroom,' she giggled with them.

Kayden helped her to stand up and it pulled a bit on the tattoo. She groaned. 'Next time I get a dumb idea like this, remind me not to.'

'And that would stop you?' Kayden asked, still fussing over her.

The boys were all sitting up now, watching. They had her going—now it was their turn. She walked a little bent over and complained a bit. Then looking back at their concerned faces she stood up straight and smiled. 'Gotcha!' she giggled as she went up the stairs.

She heard them all laughing. Woody just shook his head. 'Little bitch! She had us all going for a minute. I'm going to slap her backside when she comes back down.'

Kayden got all defensive, 'Like hell you will! No one touches her sexy toosh but me.'

Later that day, Kayden checked her tattoo and took off the bandage and they all came over for a look.

'She's like us, now,' Jason said. 'Heals fast now she's linked with our team magic.'

Cassie grinned, happily looking down at it. 'It does look cute though, hey?'

'Just wait until I have you on your own and I'll show you cute you are,' Kayden whispered in her ear before getting up to help with dinner. The BBQ smelt delicious and Cassie lay back, relaxing and sipping her cocktail while she waited. As the evening stars glittered in the sky, she wondered what mischief her father was conjuring up. He'd be bored now that she was gone and would no doubt be up to no good.

Woody came and sat next to her, looking up at what she was studying.

'Do you miss her?' Cassie asked, turning her head towards him.

'A little, but she's no good for me.'

'You know why I asked that, don't you?'

'You want to forget where you left a piece of your heart too?' Woody said, understanding where she was coming from.

Cassie nodded. 'I find it strange that evil can walk both sides— be rotten to the core but also be almost perfect. We that love them can see both sides and yet choose to ignore the evil, preferring to only acknowledge the perfection. They have such an advantage on us. They see us as a challenge, using our kind hearts to get what they want. It's hard to get over their perfect side, isn't it?'

'You have it down pat, Cass. We're players for their amusement and if we dare end it, the rejection drives them insane. They have calculated our every move, not putting a foot wrong. It kills them to think we have worked them out. I've not heard the last of my Ella, or you of your father. They view it as a game, one that they lost and will continue to play until they win us back or become bored with it.'

'Tell me, Woodsta, how are we to say no when we see them next in all their perfection, smiling at us like butter wouldn't melt in their mouths?'

'We replace them with a real friend, one who understands because they're going through the same thing.'

'I'm not alone in this, am I?'

'Not while we have each other.'

They formed a pact that night that they would drop what they were doing if the other needed them. Cassie was happy she had found a friend like Woody.

After dinner, they sat around until late, talking. They told Cassie that if she rested one more night to make sure she was over the tattoo, they would go somewhere fun the next day if there was no call-out when the horses were checked in the morning. A movie played, although she only watched half of it. She was too excited and tried to guess where they would take her the next day. Being locked up most of her life had made her want to experience anything that was going.

* * * *

In the morning she slipped down next to Kayden on the floor and his arms automatically wrapped around her, pulling the cover over them. He kissed her, losing grip on reality as he remembered her tattoo. If the others weren't in the room he would have made good his threat to her for looking so sexy now with a tat. *Damn the men, using this as a team thing and talking me into staying an extra night.* He wanted to get up and kick them all awake for being sneaky mongrels and stopping him from having fun. Bastards!

He moved from her sexy comfort and stretched, sitting up. 'Feel like coming with me to check the horses?' he whispered with cunning on his mind.

She nodded and he stood, taking her hand and quickly pulling her to her feet. Stepping over sleeping bodies, they worked their way out the room. Woody was the only one who stirred. Kayden told him when the others woke to get ready and pick them up from his house. He had other plans in the meantime and left, grinning happily.

A couple of hours later, they were back in the Hummer and heading off on a new adventure. The day was just starting to warm up as they set off and it was only then that Kayden told her they were going to spend the night on an island where the beach was to die for. Cassie was excited as she had never seen a beach before, never mind swum in salt water. They tried to tell her how bad it tasted and she laughed, not believing them, thinking they were just having a bit of fun with her as they usually did when she didn't have the experience to know better.

They went through a little town called Onslow to get to Beadon Point, where she had her first real look at the sea. It was tinged green in the shallow areas, changing to shades of light blue that blended into indigo blue as it got deeper. Looking at the horizon, the colours seemed to join up with the sky, only broken by a few wispy clouds. From the boat ramp they went a further twenty-two kilometres offshore to the Mackerel Islands, which are comprised of ten islands. They stopped at Thevenard Island: a lovely holiday destination with chalets that ran along the beachfront. These, as she found out, were where they would be staying.

Jason and Conor threw their gear into a couple of the chalets and they quickly changed and met down by the shore. The guys were taking Cassie on her very first snorkelling experience and couldn't wait to see her reaction to salt water in her mouth. The beach felt soft under her feet and the sensation of it squishing between her toes she found quite unsettling. Kayden thought her reaction to it was funny and cracked up laughing.

The rotten sod. She looked up the beach to where there were girls running out of their cabin and into the water. Her mind went into overdrive. This was her chance to get a little alone time with her man. To even out the odds a little she decided to plan a way they could be together, even if she was being a wee bit sneaky with it. *But when up against five scheming team members, I am learning to beat them at their own game.*

'I'll be back in a minute,' she said, heading towards the girls.

When she made it to them, given the challenge she had walking on sand for the first time, she started chatting to them, asking their names, where they were from and if they wanted to join her and her friends for a bit of snorkelling.

'What! Those hunks? You're telling us none of them have a girlfriend?' They seemed gob-smacked and excited. The younger one, Sonia, stayed calm, being the spokesperson for the others.

Cassie pointed out Kayden. 'All except that one,' she warned them. 'He's all mine.'

As Cassie thought, they were here for a good time as well and were more than happy to join her group for a bit of fun. They followed her as she headed back down the beach to join the menfolk.

She had a cheeky grin as she came back with the girls, telling the boys they wanted to join them. The guys just smirked at Cassie, knowing exactly what she was up to. They would deal with her later but for now none of them were going to knock back five beautiful beach bunnies. They happily paired off with the women to show them the ropes, seeing they had never snorkelled before either.

Kayden nudged Cassie as they waded out into the water. 'Very sneaky, Cassie. I just hope you don't intend to fob me off to one of them as well.'

'You even look at one of them and you are toast, buddy,' she chuckled. 'If any of them even get within cooee of you, sweet-cheeks, you know I have powers and I will use them,' she added as her hazel eyes turned green.

Kayden grabbed her, amused by her jealousy. 'I believe you would at that, my little feisty one.'

Never having swum under water before, the women all had to be shown. A couple of the girls acted ditzy playing the helpless damsels for extra attention. Damned if it wasn't working! Cassie watched as the men pandered to their every whim. They were actually enjoying themselves immensely.

Cassie stuck her head underwater to wet her face and hair before putting on her mask and came up spluttering and disgusted. 'Yuk! That tastes like over-salted water. What the hell's this crappy taste?' She spat and couldn't stop laughing. The waves started throwing her about and felt irritated and cranky with the pounding they gave her. 'You can have this! I'm getting out.'

Everyone was cracking up laughing at her so much that they

could hardly hold their own footing. She stomped back up the beach with Kayden on her tail. Snatching her up in his arms, he carried her back. 'You ain't going anywhere, missy. We want to laugh at you so get back in the water so we can have some fun.'

Once she became desensitised to the motion of the waves and the unusual feeling of looking under the water with goggles on, she had a blast. In the meantime, the guys got to have a good laugh before taking off ahead of her with one of the women in tow. Kayden nearly drowned, he laughed so hard.

'You wait, you bastards. I'll get you back. Just wait and see,' she warned through tears of hysteria.

All the pretty coral and the colours of the fish were extraordinary. Cassie had only ever seen them in books and was fascinated by how defined the colours were. *There's no way to appreciate it fully until you see it with your own eyes.* She was amazed.

Kayden kept trying to get Cassie away from the group but the guys were on the ball and kept following him, just to annoy him. Cassie didn't notice what was going on around her as she was too interested in snorkelling. She found some little crabs under a rock and over further she spotted a group of fish that looked like they were wearing evening dresses, their fins were so delicate and long.

Finally dragging her out, Kayden took the opportunity, while the men were playing a game of beach volleyball against the girls, to disappear with her for a few hours. It was late afternoon when they finally came out of their chalet. The beachfront was empty so they strolled along the edge of the water while waiting for dinner. They passed a table set up ready for the nightly meal and a chef who had just started to cook on the BBQ. It smelt delicious. They thought a short walk would keep them amused while they waited and were surprised to come across Jason.

'He's with Sonia McMasters,' Cassie whispered. 'He normally goes for the tall attractive women. She's hardly his type at all. I'm shocked.'

They'd been kissing and Sonia seemed a bit embarrassed that they had been sprung. She was so shy compared to her brazen friends. Jason had once told Cassie what type of woman he preferred yet this young girl was no rough diamond, so it had Cassie stumped as to what he saw in her. She was quite a plain-Jane, even if she was quite sweet.

Hand in hand they walked back together, the aroma of the food wafting up the beach making the four of them look forward to a nice meal. When they arrived at the table, the others started to surface from their chalets as well with their choice of woman on their arms, all except for Woody. He walked out with two of them, making Cassie smile, knowing he would need at least two to replace his evil Ella.

They'd all been drinking, except Jason. Cassie was sure he'd not even had a drop and wondered what Sonia had that the others didn't. Eyeing her again for a minute, she couldn't see it. Shaking her head, she grinned. *Sun must have got to him and mucked with his senses.*

The meal was superb and later they sat on the beach drinking shots of tequila, watching the stairway to the moon. Kayden explained it only happened at a certain time of the year when there's a full moon. 'As it rises over the water at low tide, it creates the effect of stairs, giving the illusion that they reach as high as the moon.' Cassie thought it was awesome.

Afterwards, he pulled Cassie up and took her for a private stroll. Out of sight, they decided to have a private skinny-dip together. They left their clothes on the beach, swimming out and frolicking in the night with the waves lapping and rolling around them.

'I've really enjoyed today, gorgeous. Thanks for making me feel so special,' he said, kissing her. Cassie melted in his arms. Being naked and kissed in water, she felt so sexy and wished they had more time. She doubted she would forget today for a very long time. All the new experiences and the laughs they had still made her smile or squirm with the remembered joy.

As they returned and rounded the cape, they spotted the rest of the team sitting on the beach on their own. She felt for the surprise that she kept for them in her pocket.

'What happened?' Kayden asked once they reached them.

'Did the girls get sick of you dorks all at once?' Cassie joked.

'No, they're fine. We've just had enough and told them we needed time with our sister,' Jason said, sounding a little flat.

'Yeah, there's only so much girl stuff we can put up with,' Conor said. 'They were getting on my nerves.'

'You can say that again,' Ethan grumbled. 'Just one more stupid question and I would have exploded.'

Cassie started to laugh although she stopped when they all looked deadly serious. 'Sorry, but you guys are unreal. Five women, all available and you're sick of them already. Jeez, the poor girls have literally thrown themselves at you all day. I don't get it.'

'You just hit the nail on the head, Cass, thrown themselves at us. Where's the chase or the thrill?' Conor grouched.

Cassie could see they all needed cheering up although she had no idea why. *Spoilt ratbags. They should be kissing my feet. They should be so grateful.* She grinned to herself. They were so going to cop it, the unappreciative sods. She went behind Woody and Jason, who sat together and knelt down, putting her arms around them. They let out a sigh and relaxed with her touch. Even though she knew it was a Cloud Rider's bond she was amazed how much power she had over them and it excited her just as much as it did them.

As they depended on each other, they now also depended on her. Only, being a female, it was shaking them up a bit. Maybe it was a protective thing that a man naturally feels towards a woman. Whatever it was, she felt it in them, mixed with the need to be with her too. She grinned mischievously to herself. She had a game and now seemed the perfect time to play it. She knew it would rattle them further but the ungrateful sods deserved it. Afterwards, she was sure they'd be glad to hand her back to Kayden to get some peace for a while.

'Well I guess we better cheer you all up then. I have a new game that starts off boring, but you'll love the ending. Do you want to play it?'

'Go for it, Cass,' Woody said and she felt his mood lift already in anticipation of what she was going to get up to.

She made them all sit together. They only had their swimmers on and no tops so this was going to be easy-peasy to play, she decided.

'Now, we're going to start off with a guessing game and it may sound dumb at first so have patience.' She started with Woody first and wrote on his back with her finger. He had to guess what the word was.

'Jam boy,' he said. 'What does that mean?'

She pushed him from behind, smiling. 'You have strawberry hair and are so very sweet.'

Woody smiled and sighed. 'Jason, check my back. Did she scribble on it?'

He looked. 'Nope, you're good.'

'I know she's up to no good,' he said. 'But I'll play her dumb frigging game.'

She went to Conor, slipped out the texta from her pocket, wrote 'Bad Boy' and he guessed it. On Jason, she wrote 'Evil Boy' and on Ethan, 'Wicked Boy'. Then back to Woody, she wrote 'Devil Boy' and stood back, admiring her work. She ran off down the beach laughing.

They all looked at each other's backs and when they finished laughing at each other's names, they took off after her. 'You are so dead, cloud girl!' they called after her, hitting each other for being so dumb and letting her do it, while laughing and running after her. Kayden watched her pull the texta out and tried to warn her and then just shook his head and grinned, knowing she was really going to cop it this time.

Woody reached her first and had her under his arm, dragging her back. 'Take it off and we might go lenient on you.'

'I can't, I haven't bought the remover with me. Wait until the girlies see you tomorrow. I doubt if they will be falling all over devil boy now.' She kept giggling.

'You little ratbag, I can't think of anything bad enough to punish you with just yet but give me a minute,' he was saying as he brought her back to the others. 'What have you guys decided?' he asked. 'She reckons she can't take it off. She didn't bring anything to get the stuff off.'

'Cassie,' Jason said. 'That was a dirty trick. At least we did it where you couldn't see it.'

'Well, you said the girls were annoying you. I've just put repellent on you. I was trying to help, evil boy.' She kept cracking up laughing. 'The chicky-babes are going to love this: a story about dumb-shits who let their sister scribble all over them. It will be laughed about for years.' She kept making fun of them.

'I say we drown her first, then feed her to the beach bugs and bury her under the sand,' Woody was saying with revenge in his tone.

'I say we draw all over her so she looks just as bad,' Jason said.

Cassie realised she was really in for it and tried to wiggle and get loose from Woody's grip.

'I vote we stop her from going anywhere near Kayden so she can't have any fun with the opposite sex either,' Ethan said wickedly.

'And I think she should be made to give us all a back massage after we get this scribble off,' Conor said, smiling like his was the best punishment.

'It's decided then,' Woody said and lay her wiggling on the ground. 'The punishment is what we all said.' He grinned roguishly. 'Well, maybe not drown her but all else stays.'

Woody, Jason and Conor held her down so Ethan could grab the texta out of her pocket and begin drawing on her.

'Cassie,' Ethan said playfully. 'The more you wiggle, the worse the writing will look. Keep still.' He was laughing as the other three stopped her from moving.

When they'd finished her front, they rolled her over and did her back. She grabbed a handful of sand and when they stood her up, she dropped it down Woody's pants.

'Little shytzer,' he said laughing. 'She just threw sand down my bloody pants. You're in so much trouble now, girl.'

He picked her up and they all went into the water after them. She had only used a water marker and it came off as they mucked around in the water. Kayden tried to rescue her at one stage but they all attacked him and he gave up and let the games continue.

Woody was the first to realise that the texta was coming off and smiled, shaking his head. 'You are so not getting away with it because it's coming off. You're still going to pay for making us freak out,' he grumbled and threw her up in the air, over to Jason.

When they sat back on the beach, they buried her in the sand. There was no way she could move so she just had to wait until they were bored without her and pulled her out. 'That's no fun,' Jason said as he dug her out. 'She can't talk or laugh when the sand's packed around her. Forget that stupid game.'

As soon as she was free, she ran to Kayden and just as she nearly got to him, Woody snatched hold of her and sat her back between him and Jason.

'But that's not fair,' she whinged. 'That punishment was only if you couldn't be with the girls. It should be nullified now the scribble's all gone.'

'So does that mean you're sorry for what you did to your friends?' Woody said. 'Are you actually going to say sorry, Cassie and give in?' he asked.

'When hell freezes over maybe,' she said defiantly.

He put his arm around her. 'I thought as much. Now, you still have one more penalty facing you, and that is the back massage. This time you'll be watched, young lady, so no more drawing!'

Jason came back with beers. 'We need a drink first. Cassie's worn me out.'

Now I have to watch them all clink their bottles together and the rotten sods all drink to that. This is hardly over yet. She sat planning.

Woody felt her thinking. 'I wouldn't, Cassie. If you ever want to be back in your man's arms again, behave!' he said firmly.

She glanced over at Kayden and he was lying back comfortably against a log that had been washed up onto the beach, having a drink. He seemed amused that she didn't give in and was waiting for her to act up again. He looked so inviting with the glow of the moonlight reflecting on his skin that she no longer wanted to play with the boys. She wanted to play with her man. She sighed, knowing she was just prolonging the inevitable. 'Okay, who's first for their massage?' she asked, giving in.

Woody was the last one and when she finished she bent down to his ear. 'Sorry, handsome. Forgive me,' she whispered and kissed his cheek.

He rolled over and sat up, giving her a hug. 'You can make me so frustrated and cranky, yet say four little words and I'm sucked in. I do but I'm not the only one you rattled tonight.'

She went over and knelt behind the others one at a time, whispering a message just for them before kissing them on the cheek as well. Ethan started laughing. 'You must really want to be with the boss to have given in. Go on, I'll let you off.' He grinned and the others nodded.

She collapsed into Kayden's arms, worn out. She needed to toughen up to be as strong as the guys but she knew Kayden would always be her safe haven.

The night was still young for the night owls so a game of cards was organised.

And me? Well, I need a drink, so agreed.

Chapter Twenty-Six

Just Too Hard

During the evening Cassie laid on the couch for some shut-eye. She had enjoyed her day and fell asleep listening to the guys joke and hang it on each other as they continued the card game. Dawn came and the light shone on her face, waking her. Getting up, she looked about for Kayden. Not finding him inside, she wandered outside, thinking he might already be up and had gone for a morning dip.

When she finally found him he was lying out on the beach and right there was every girl's nightmare. A woman, although fully dressed, was wrapped in her man's arms. Her whole body started to tremble as she went to confront him.

He woke, looked up at her and turned to look at the girl in his arms. 'No, Cassie, it's not what you think. I don't know how she ended up here. I must have thought it was you.'

She shook her head in disbelief, unable to control her shaking any longer and she turned and ran out of sight to where she could calm down.

She heard Woody calling out to her as he headed towards her but she put her hand up angrily. He stopped, seeing by look in her eyes she would possibly inflict pain on anyone that came near her or attempted to stop her at that moment. She was so filled with anger!

He had no choice but to let her be until she had calmed down. She heard Woody and Kayden arguing. The chick jumped up, laughing as if it were a big joke. Cassie was so livid about her attitude that she had to really restrain herself from turning and zapping the stupid bitch. She needed to be on her own and didn't feel up to an argument or lies. In a total trance, she turned her back on them all and the situation that she had no idea how to deal with.

Trudging through the scrub, she ended up at the wharf where a boat was getting ready to leave. The captain was on the deck smoking a pipe and when she asked if he would give her a lift to the mainland, he was very obliging. Most likely he felt sorry for her as she was still shaking uncontrollably and as white as a sheet. As the boat pulled away from the dock, she could see Kayden and the team arguing on the beach.

She watched, not really taking it in until her legs crumbled under her and she sat right where she was until they reached land. She was still numb and apart from the shakes, she told herself that she would get through this deceit.

She hiked back home and walked the long path up to the house. Inside it was cold and uninviting. Walking straight back out again, she decided she might be able to think better if she was with Starburst. Any comfort, other than human, was what she thought she needed. To her disappointment, when she reached the paddock, Tremaine was still there checking on the horses. *I'm in no mood for him either!* She sighed, changed her mind and detoured around him.

As she walked, her mind went into overdrive. Her past fears of not being worthy of her untrustworthy family and friends all jumbled around in her mind, mixed with the present. She had nowhere to go that she could think of. In her state of mind, she just couldn't think past putting one foot in front of the other. She was unable to comprehend why Kayden would want another girl in his arms. She thought about their time together, reliving every minute and trying to find a break in the connection somewhere that she should have noticed.

Is it the boys? Is he jealous? Does he want to get back at me for mucking around with them last night? Or is his love all just a con to have me join his team? Her mind went round and round until it felt like it was going to explode.

She finally realised where she was and stumbled around in the brush before finding the lake. She couldn't get rid of the thought of another woman wrapped in her man's arms. As she thought it, a stab of pain folded her over and she screamed with the severity of it. She rolled up in a ball, trying to stop the pains that gripped her stomach. She felt delirious and was burning up with a fever. She rolled around with beads of sweat pouring off her face.

She had just been bitten by something and she realised that it must have been poisonous due to her reaction. She tried to get up a few times but kept passing out, the pain getting worse, until she felt a little nudge and opened her eyes to Starburst.

'Go get help!' she told him, rolling over and groaning. He must have felt she was upset to have come so far to find her.

* * * *

Coherent at last, she was glad when she woke and had been found. Kayden was in the chair next to her and she looked away, still angry with him. The nurse came in, confirming what she had already figured out, that a poisonous spider or snake had bitten her. She still had drips in her arm and complained about it while the nurse removed the thermometer from her mouth.

As Cassie expected, the nurse only took the thermometer from her before leaving. Now they were on their own again, Cassie shook even more, knowing she had to deal with what had happened.

Kayden looked irritably at her, stopping her fear and turning it to anger.

'Why are you here, Kayden? Shouldn't you be with your new girlfriend?' she snarled.

She could feel him suck in his breath and she waited for what seemed like ages before he let it out. 'I can't believe you would think I would do that to you, Cassie. Obviously, our relationship isn't that strong after all. I've just come to let you know that I give up. You win. I am sick of you running every time something goes wrong. I'm sorry that silly little tart came and cuddled up to me but maybe you might try to understand a little of what I go through every time you kiss or hug one of the guys. It always has to be all about you or nothing. From now on, I'm your boss and that is it. The boys are happy for you to stay with them. If you wish to stay on as a member of the team, you're welcome to but I don't want you to come home.'

She glared at him with hatred. 'Good! You're just as painful. I'm sick of having to try to make you and your damned buddies happy. I'll not be staying, so don't flatter yourself that you're worth waiting around for. Get out and don't let the door hit you on your way out, you dirty rotten two timer!' she added furiously.

After they released her from hospital the next day, she had no idea what she was going to do or what the day would bring. Woody stood waiting for her as she came out the front entrance. He took her arm and as much as she wished she could tell him where to go, she didn't know where she was and needed him to drop her off somewhere that would lead her anywhere but back to Kayden's.

'Just drop me off on the highway, Woody. I'll hike back to Perth and try to pick up where I left off. I was a fool to come back here and think that someone would …' she ran out of bother. She was so over people not loving her the way she did them. She just wanted to give up.

'Cassie, I have told you before, to find happiness you have to stop running. To stay is to fight for what you believe in. Stop being afraid and look your fears in the face. Stay the course. You know Kayden wouldn't have done that to you and he's not just angry with you at the moment. He is angry with us all but he'll work through it. Come home with me, with us, where you belong. We are your family now and we want you with us.'

Tears streamed down her face. 'Family! How can you say I'm family when I keep hurting everyone?'

'Because we understand. We boys adore you!'

'I'm just finding it hard because all I can see is her in his arms and it makes me want to just run and run and run until I'm too tired to see the damned image!'

'Then we'll do it together, around the property and out along the main road, every day. You're not alone anymore, Cass. We'll be your rock until you become one. How about it? Tell me what you have to lose. The road to Perth is just outside our front gate and if at any time you really don't want to be with us anymore, I'll take you myself.'

Chapter Twenty-Seven

Months to Heal

It had been four months since she'd moved in with the boys. Woody had been right. They were her world now and she loved being the centre of theirs. At last she had found the family that she always wanted. Kayden had stopped moping around and over the past few weeks had began to join them again, his personality surprising them all. He was jovial, funny and a joy to have around. Cassie didn't love him anymore, he was just a boss and that suited her fine. Woody had become her friend and love, she adored the ground he walked on. He had seen her through so much and his friendship was beyond anything she had ever had. She could sit for hours and listen to him and most days they would just talk until dawn.

They had kissed a few times but she had not been able to go much further than that and she knew it worried him. She just needed a bit more time and he seemed to understand. Once they were in the kitchen and Kayden had walked in on him kissing her but he had just walked out again, not saying anything or showing any reaction. She knew he was over her too.

They continued to have wild parties and the house was always full of chicks and booze. It was an exciting time for Cassie. She was young and it was fun to cut loose, especially after the exhilaration of their missions. Her father was still causing trouble and Woody was always there for her if she saw him at a distance and it upset her.

Woody hardly talked about Ella anymore except when she rang

him. Then he would be straight out to tell Cassie all about it. They were pretty well inseparable.

The morning after one of their wild parties, Kayden sent Woody and Jason on a reconnaissance mission. The mess from the party they had the night before was left for Ethan, Conor and Cassie to clean up. Well, that really just left Cassie; the other two were still entertaining two of the girls from the party in their rooms. She decided it was probably her turn to clean up anyway. Rolling up her sleeves, she went around the backyard, picking up empty bottles, cigarette butts and food scraps left over from a food fight.

Kayden came over and asked where Ethan and Conor were. After telling him they were busy with some chicks, she told him he could go up and see them if he wanted. He said he did not feel right disturbing them and had only come around to see if they wanted to go to the races with him. Seeing they were busy, he asked if she wanted to take off for a couple of hours to fill in the day instead.

They had been talking nicely again now, so she guessed it would be okay. After all, he was just her boss now.

There were horse races at Wittenoom and even though she was his second choice, she was glad to do something other than clean up on her own. They laid bets on the horses while Cassie sipped on an ice cola. It made the heat of the day more bearable. She had a lovely time and on the way home he asked her many questions about Woody and made her laugh a lot about stories of old. 'Now you're sleeping with Woody you would know that anyway,' he said at one stage.

It came out of left field and she stared at him for a moment. 'Woody's not like that. We aren't … I haven't …' She turned and stared out the window, not knowing what to actually say.

'Sorry if you thought I was prying. I didn't mean to put you on the spot. I just assumed you two were an item that was all,' he said, sounding innocent enough.

Cassie turned to him and grinned. 'That's alright, I overreacted. It's complicated,' she said and just changed the subject.

After he took her home, he stayed and helped her finish cleaning up. The boys surfaced every now and then to see if Cassie was alright and then went back to their rooms. They had a swim after they finished cleaning and then opened a bottle of Moonjuice, sipping it in the warm spa. The bubbles and the drink relaxed her after what seemed like a long day.

'You know I never touched that girl, don't you?' he asked, trying to smooth over their past.

'Yes, I believe you now because you have no reason to lie anymore. Maybe even then.' She was being honest because he was.

'Then why did you leave?' he asked. 'I know it's all in the past but I just needed to ask.'

'It took a long time for Woody to help me work through that. At the time I just kept seeing her in your arms and couldn't get past it. I guess we both had issues. Sometimes two people are just not meant to be.' She lay back.

'You must really love Woody. He's been a good friend to you and you've never run from him,' he said quietly.

'I do love him dearly. He's my best friend in the whole world and if I ever get the urge to run, he has brainwashed me to come get him. He runs with me until I have nothing left. I've never had so much devotion,' she said.

'Then what's stopped you from committing yourself to him?'

She sat up angrily. 'It's really none of your business, Kayden. I shouldn't have said anything. I have my reasons, just leave it at that!'

He moved towards her with a look in his eyes that she had not seen for many months and she backed away.

'Don't you dare!' She flashed an angry look at him but he ignored her and slipped his arms around her. His lips came down hard against hers. He didn't let her go until she stopped struggling. It was her body that finally gave her away, melting into him as her arms wrapped around his neck. He'd stirred up something she had buried deep inside. He pulled away, leaving her breathless. He watched her as she tried to pull herself together.

'You're still in love with me, Cassie. You can't lie to me.'

She tried to get out of his grip. 'No! No, I don't, I love Woody now.'

His mouth came back down on hers, kissing her so gently and lovingly that it nearly broke her heart. Tears streamed down her face.

'What are you doing to me?' she cried when he let her go. 'You will only hurt me again! You threw me away. Woody has stuck the pieces back together and now I have to be his. I can't be disloyal to such love.'

'Cassie, you don't have to tell me how much I hurt you. I've lived with it every day and every night for months. I really thought you would be better off without me. I honestly wanted you to find happiness but I am still terribly and unconditionally in love with you too. I can't be the good guy any more. I'm the evil boy come to steal you back any way I can and I don't care if Woody beats the crap out of me—or you tell me to go—I'm here to get my woman back if she'll have me. I don't want you back just as my lover, Cassie. I want to marry you and be with you always. Will you marry me, Cassie? Now, today? We'll drive somewhere and find a priest. Please make me the happiest man in the world and say yes.'

She put her head in her hands and sighed. 'I thought you didn't love me, Kayden. I've led Woody to believe he and I have a chance by letting him kiss me. I'm so confused.'

He came back over to her. Just his touch sent electrifying sensations through her. 'We love each other, Cassie. We always have and always will. I'm going to go and let you work out how you want this to go down. But I'll not take no for an answer! I'm not letting go this time and if you're unable to tell Woody then I will. It's better he gets hurt now rather than later when he's taken you to his bed. You have nothing to give him because you know you will always keep yourself only for me.'

He kissed her again. Her heart just about thumped out of her chest and her body wrapped around him, feeling every curve that she had missed so terribly. She groaned.

'I love you. Come home, baby,' he whispered. He let her go and got out of the spa.

CASSANDRA

* * * *

It was late when Woody and Jason arrived back. Cassie was still up, tortured by what had happened. She tried to act normal but what was normal? She was falling apart with guilt and old feelings. Jason took his leave and Woody came over to where she sat and put his arm around her. 'What's up, Cass, did you miss me?' he joked, trying to break down the barrier he felt around her.

She looked affectionately at her best friend and wondered how she could ever break his heart and live afterwards. 'Kayden came over today.'

'He'd better not have upset you! No wonder the bastard was in such a good mood. What did he say?' he asked angrily.

'He came to get the boys to go to the horse races but they were busy with their girls so I went.'

'You what?' He stood up, angry. 'He hates the horse races. I knew there had to be a reason why he started to sleaze back over here. He wants you back, doesn't he?' He paced.

'I told him I loved you and was committed to our relationship but ...'

He grabbed her by the shoulders and taking one look into her eyes, he knew. 'He bloody kissed you, that sneaky son of a bitch!' He was pacing again. 'I'm going over there to knock some sense into him. He sent us off so he could be alone with you. That lying, cheating mongrel!'

Jason came out. 'What's going on, mate? What's all the yelling about?'

Woody was furious. 'We put her back together and she just gets happy again and his frigging highness comes over and tries to steal her back. Bloody kissed her as well! Of all the dirty tricks, he sent us off so he could spend the day with her.'

Jason shook his head. 'You knew it would happen, Woody. We all tried to tell you a love like theirs would find its way back. I guessed it tonight when I saw that sparkle back in her eyes that has been missing for months.'

'Thanks for the bloody support, mate!' Woody growled angrily. He went over and swinging Cassie up in his arms carried her inside and up the stairs to his room.

'Don't do anything you'll regret, Woody!' Jason warned. 'Let it go, for all our sakes.'

Woody laid her gently on the bed and lay beside her as they had done many times before. He looked at her for a long time and then rolled away, lying on his back and putting his arm over his eyes. She cuddled up to him, feeling his pain, while tears ran down her face for the hurt he was feeling. He felt her quiver with silent sobs and he cuddled her until she stopped.

'I love you both,' Cassie sobbed. 'I'm sorry. He tricked me. I thought I'd buried all those feelings. You're my most favourite person in the whole world and I can't bear the thought of never talking to you again. Your friendship is so deeply set inside me. You're the voice in my head and I can't believe this is happening to you—to us.'

He kissed her gently as he had done so many times but he became more urgent and she let him, hoping he could change her mind. But as he started to take off her clothes, she froze. He flung himself back on the bed.

'I'm sorry, try again. I'll control it. Make me love you instead,' Cassie begged him. She kissed him again but he went cold.

'Your love for him is deep in your soul. You can only give me some of your heart and it's not enough for me. I have to move on and find someone who loves me. The only way that is ever going to happen is to make a clean break.'

'But I do love you. Please don't take your love away from me. I'll never see him again, I promise. Stay with me, Woody. I choose you,' she sobbed as she begged him.

'You're breaking my heart, princess. But I'm not the one you want and I can't see how I can ever get over you if I try to stay your friend while watching you with him. It doesn't work that way and you know it.'

She leaned on her elbow, watching him. 'Can't we still be the same? What has to change? I've always kissed and cuddled you from the first day I met you. I've loved you since the first time I laid eyes on you. I thought you were so handsome, you blew me away. We've bonded like no other friends could; our friendship is strong enough to last many lifetimes. I'm willing to give up Kayden for that friendship. Doesn't that mean anything to you? I'll still see you every day and we can still have our alone time together. Please don't run from me. You told me not to run and I stayed for you. Can we not work through this together? Let's spend a couple of days on our own, just to talk.'

He pulled her into him. 'I can't think straight,' he said. 'Just let me hold you and sleep for a few hours and I'll see how I feel when I wake up.'

She cuddled into him, not ever wanting to let him go and cried herself silently to sleep. 'I love you,' she whispered to him but he never spoke for the rest of the night.

In the morning they were still in each other's arms and when she looked at him, he smiled at her. 'I've been watching you sleep,' he said, running his hand caringly over her face. 'We are two of a kind, you know and it only just dawned on me. Cass, it's not just you holding back. There's someone I too have been holding onto and if I've learnt anything from you it is that true love never dies. I think it is time we both sat up and took a good look around us. We've both needed each other so much that we built ourselves a fortress and hid inside. Somehow we forgot the fact that there was a world out there and that we were really just a brother and sister leaning on each other until we found our wings.' He sat up. 'It's time we let each other spread those wings and find true love. I was watching you before you woke, trying to imagine the love you had with Kayden and my mind went straight to Ella. She never gave up on me but I've hidden under the protection of your umbrella, maybe just like you and Kayden. I never gave her time to adjust and learn. I never trusted her. But you know, I think it's time we trusted someone other than ourselves. I was wrong, Cassie. We will always be together. I want to share with you the lows and highs in my life like I always have and hope you'll still do the same.'

She smiled and cried at the same time at his happy revelation.

He wasn't going to leave her. *We will always be just how we have always been, best friends.*

When they went downstairs, Jason could see they had worked it out. Woody told him he was taking her home and then he was going to visit a friend. He added that they shouldn't expect him until the following day.

Cassie kissed Jason. 'Thanks for being the best friend ever to both of us.'

As Woody dropped her off, Cassie kissed him and wished him luck. 'Go get your girl,' she said as he grinned sweetly at her.

Chapter Twenty-Eight
Angel Gift of Mine

Kayden heard a car and went out, ready to face the music. He had kissed Cassie and begged her to come home and he knew Woody was there to take revenge on his dirty-arse tactics. 'Hell, I even sent him off on a bogus mission to get him out of the way. I can just imagine how this is going to go down with his temper. Nevertheless, she is mine and he had better just start getting used to it. I found her, you bastard!' he muttered as he watched the car approach. 'She's mine … mine!'

The nights he had agonised over the image of her asleep in Woody's arms—not his—twisted his guts even now. *He can smack my frigging head in if it makes him feel better but at the end of this day, I swear she will be mine again.*

The car pulled up a little way away from him and Kayden watched, confused as Cassie kissed Woody while saying something to him. They were smiling at each other. *What the hell! Don't tell me she hasn't told him yet. Jeez, Cass, he has to know! If you're coming home to me I won't be giving you back, ever! She's my girlfriend, woman-thief. That's right; I'm doing the thieving this time. Man, it feels good. Bastard! Stop kissing my woman.*

He stood, wondering how, if she had told him, he could hold and kiss her with so much tenderness and walk away with a smile, knowing he had lost her. *I knew she was an angel but she must be a gift from above if she's able to break up with someone so amicably. God hear me now, if she is coming back to me, I promise never to let my foolishness ever hurt one of your angels again. Please give me a chance to show you I'm worthy of such a gift.*

Woody turned the car around, his face giving nothing away. As the dust shot out from beneath the tires, Cassie stood in front of him, just as he had found her that very first day, red dirt floating all around her. The powdery residue lightly settled onto her hair and her delicate, cream-coloured skin. She had the most adorable look on her face: so shy, so innocent. All that time and she hadn't changed a bit. She was pure and sweet. *God, I love her.* His eyes filled up, knowing without her having to say a word that she had come home to him.

Kayden wrapped her up in his arms. Just the feel of her body against his broke his hardcore act and a very unmanly sob broke from his lips as he found hers. Her love poured into him with the magic she was capable of. It was like an explosion of dynamite bouncing off every wall inside his body.

She was waking him up from a long sleep and every part of his love dissolved back into her. For so long now he had not even been able to hold another woman and God knows he'd tried, just to get through the loneliness. But they were not her, he thought as he intensified the kiss and moaned from the pure pleasure she was able to give him.

Had she felt this good before? Yes she did, you goon, you didn't appreciate just what you had. He cursed himself. *Jeez, I can't shut my mind off.* He was so excited, yet he knew that they had to talk. Yet as they walked inside together, feeling as he did about her, he doubted either of them would be discussing anything rationale for a while. He shuddered as the tingle of the thought of making love to her made him urgently find her lips again.

Later that afternoon, Kayden knelt down and proposed for real, putting the biggest Goddamned diamond that he could find on her finger. *So that every bastard in the universe knows she's mine!*

Not giving her a chance to get away this time, he called a local priest to come out the next afternoon and marry them. He asked if there was anyone special she wanted as a witness. *Hell—today she can ask for the moon and stars!* And she did. She asked for Aldebaran.

Jason offered to take the message which she handwrote so that her father would know it was from her—no tricks.

* * * *

Hi Pops,

I'm getting hitched tomorrow and would love you to be there. Nothing fancy, just with the friends you see me with. I would love to see Aqua again too if you wanted to bring her.

Love,

Your daughter, Cassandra xx

Chapter Twenty-Nine
Mr & Mrs Kayden Hunter

On Jason's return, he and Kayden put their heads together to organise the wedding. All Cassie knew was that Jason had talked Kayden into holding the wedding at the boys' home next door. With the gorgeous outdoor paradise set around the gazebo, she had to agree it would be perfect. She wasn't allowed to worry about anything so while they huddled over the kitchen table she took a nice hot bath. She had so missed Kayden's bath, his shower, his bathroom, his bedroom, his house, him! Well, everything.

She could barely wipe the smile from her face, Kayden was making her feel so happy. The only other thing that would make her day complete would be if Woody and her father turned up. Even so, she refused to let their absence spoil her day. She was marrying the man of her dreams and nothing could pull her down from the blissful cloud she was on.

Kayden had pre-organised everything from Cassie's dress to the flowers and the wedding cake. He'd been planning it for weeks, waiting until he had it all organised before he came for her. Cassie was amazed at how patient he must have been, planning all this behind their backs and coming to visit, acting like nothing was happening. Seeing her with Woody must have been hard, yet he never showed it. He said she was worth waiting for and he wanted everything just perfect this time before he made his move.

'How did you know I still loved you?' she asked. 'Even I didn't know.'

'The second night I visited I saw Woody kiss you in the kitchen, remember? And you looked up from his kiss, towards me, like you had just kissed your best friend or brother. I just about grabbed you there on the spot, I was so excited. You see, I know what your face looks like after you're kissed by the man of your dreams and I realised right then and there that I was still that man and it was not too late. I went home and planned carefully how I would steal you away and make you mine forever.'

The next morning, their wedding day, they checked the horses before joining Jason at their place. Conor and Ethan had just finished cooking breakfast on the BBQ so they were just in time to enjoy a relaxing meal before they got lost in the day.

The house was already buzzing with hired hands bustling around with fine china and flowers. In fact, she'd never seen so many flowers. Kayden had been secretly working with a wedding planner who knew exactly what he wanted and had it all organised, just waiting for his okay to go ahead.

Cassie had thought Kayden was joking when he said he wanted to marry her straight away. She hardly believed anything could be organised so quickly. However, as he said, money could move mountains.

Today, he moved that mountain.

Hair stylists, nail technicians, makeup artists and the dress designer all fussed over her until she stood elegantly dressed and made up, standing in front of a full-length mirror. The luxurious, white-satin gown she wore was covered with super-soft see-through material and as she moved slightly, it glistened in soft pastel shades like the colours she saw when going into the clouds. The dress was off the shoulder: a snug fit to the hip line and then slightly flared and trailing out behind her. It was the prettiest, softest wedding dress she could have ever dreamed of being married in. It made her feel sexy and even more grown up. The image of a very elegant woman was reflected back at her.

Her hair was up with just a few curls twisted here and there to soften the look. There was no veil. *Thank goodness.* It would have so spoilt the look. Instead she wore a delicate tiara of diamonds that picked up the glimmer of the beading in the pretty gown. She had thought that the only way she would ever look so beautiful was by way of the magic horse but today she felt like a flower that had just bloomed and for once she really felt like a true princess. She had come from royalty and for once in her life she accepted her rightful place in the world: a princess on her way to marry her prince.

The wedding planner came to collect her, walking her down the stairs and out onto the patio.

The pool fence and tables had massive white flower arrangements tied together with soft bows that reflected the same pastels as her dress. The pool itself was covered in floating stars with candles, representing the skies they travelled in and the gazebo was stunning with the laser lighting forming the shapes that they saw before moving through the portal. Her man had thought about everything and the attention to detail was exquisite.

She felt every face turn as she stood viewing the enchanting décor. She noticed that not only family was here but that all their party friends had turned up as well. The guests went dead quiet as Cassie appeared before them. The only sound was the tweeting of birds and the flutter of their wings in the trees. She could see Kayden waiting in the gazebo and she finally grinned, the sight of him settling her nerves.

Her handsome man wore black pants with a satin white shirt under a white jacket. He looked stunning while calmly waiting for her.

Feeling more relaxed she glanced around, seeing her father intently watching her. Cassie had dreamed of this day, to be married and have her father walk her down the aisle. Well, maybe it wasn't exactly an aisle but to have him share her special day was more than she could have ever dreamed and she shed a tear of happiness as she held out her hand to him.

He patted Aqua's hand that he held and let her go to be with his daughter. He smiled so affectionately when he reached for her that she knew their love for each other was real too. She knew he was going to be there for her regardless of their battles in the sky.

He kissed her cheek. 'You look even more beautiful in your own world, Cassandra. Thank you for inviting me. I think you know how much it means to me to be here, don't you?' He was tenderly holding her hand.

She gave him a quick hug. 'I really wanted you to be here, Pops. I love you,' she whispered before letting him go.

Her eyes watered and he smiled. 'Don't you go spoiling your beautiful face with tears today. If I don't see anything but smiles I'll have to steal you from them and take you home with me where I will endeavour to make you smile for the rest of your life,' he chuckled.

She giggled at him and his humour before slipping her hand through the arm that he offered her. He pulled her closer to him.

'You're not nervous too are you, Pops?'

He turned and let her see the love he felt in those big dark eyes. 'I have dared to dream since you were born, that you would want me by your side on your special day. I'm in seventh heaven, honey.'

He kissed her hand and they walked along the glistening path covered in fairy dust that led to the man she wanted to spend forever with. As they walked, Cassie's eyes drifted to Woody, her special friend that stood with Ella, his caring smile showing how happy he was for her.

She stopped and hugged him on the way past. 'You look beautiful, sis,' he said and she smiled, so happy they were okay again.

Letting him go, she faced Kayden, amazed when Aldebaran put out his hand and shook Kayden's as he wished him every happiness for the future with his daughter. They were polite, which was all Cassie could ask for.

She had never seen Kayden in a suit and he took her breath away. He was so handsome. She noticed that the tie and hanky in his jacket pocket matched her dress. The wedding planner hadn't missed a thing to make them look just perfect together.

Saying their vows was a most enlightening moment. Kayden was so sweet and loving that it brought tears to Cassie's eyes. How lucky she felt today, marrying such an adorable and genuine man.

When the priest announced them man and wife and said that he could kiss the bride, he pulled her back into his arms and gave her the biggest smooch. As he pulled away he smiled. *Stuff the buffet! I want to eat you,* he said telepathically to her and they both busted up laughing. She slapped him playfully. Nobody but the Cloud Riders knew what he had said and Cassie could hear them cracking up laughing.

'You'll keep,' she grinned.

They faced the crowd and she pinched his backside. Woody saw what she did and had to stifle a laugh with a cough. Kayden couldn't stop grinning, thinking he was so funny.

With the vows taken and snapshots for the family album out of the way, the DJ started playing songs, marking the beginning of the reception. After the wedding waltz, Cassie had a dance with Woody so they could catch up.

'So you married the girlfriend-stealing mongrel,' he smiled.

She nodded. 'So you're back with the bitch from hell. Is she drinking wine or a saucer of milk?' she chuckled.

'Touché! We hate each other's partners. Let's just admit it and call a truce.'

'Anyway, have you told I'm-so-gorgeous-my-love-puffs-don't-smell about us yet?'

'Ella knows everything,' he said, trying to be serious. 'The anger she once had is gone and yes I finally have her respect. Unlike you, she treats her man with a delicate tongue.'

'Get lost, Woody.' She pushed him playfully. 'I'll give you a delicate tongue. Go find your licker then and leave me the hell alone so I can go seduce my damned husband.' She chuckled and he walked off laughing so loud he attracted everyone's attention.

Cassie was glad she and Woody were back to normal and nothing had changed between them. Later that day she eventually spoke to Ella and even though they would never be great friends they were putting the past behind them for Woody's sake. Ella even told Cassie how stunning she looked and Cassie knew that that was a big compliment, coming from her.

Aldebaran and Aqua had to leave early, but not before they enjoyed some of the reception. Cassie hung off him as they laughed and joked together about the fun they had during their visit to Aquarius. Aqua seemed to enjoy the reception as well, even getting Kayden up to dance while Aldebaran held his daughter lovingly and danced her gracefully around the floor. Before leaving, Aldebaran asked Kayden where he was taking his daughter for their honeymoon but Kayden said they were unable to go anywhere in case they were summoned to stop an attack.

Then you could have knocked her over with a feather: Aldebaran gave them a wedding gift far beyond anything money could buy. He not only promised to cease all attacks but said he would also peacefully handle anything else that came up for one whole week. This was so that Kayden could take Daddy's little girl anywhere in the universe that she wanted to go. Kayden was blown away as they shook hands on it.

Aqua suggested they spend a couple of days at the end of the week on Aquarium, neutral ground. She thought the four of them could kick back, have some fun and it would give Cassie and her father a chance to have a bit of time together again. Kayden didn't seem to think that would be interfering with the order of things if they were on a neutral star. Aldebaran was ecstatic at Aqua's suggestion; wrapt when Kayden accepted.

As Cassie and Kayden waved them goodbye, Kayden surprised Cassie further by telling her how much her dad's personality was similar to hers in so many ways and that it was hard not to like the guy, making her happy he felt that way.

'So, my Mrs Hunter,' he turned to her. 'We have five days to go wherever your heart desires. Tell me, my gorgeous wife, where you would like to go on your honeymoon?'

'You'll probably think I'm crazy for even thinking this but it's probably been centuries since you or any of the guys have had a full week away anywhere. Let's use this opportunity for us all to take a break.'

'Whatever you think, gorgeous. Just so long as we're together, I don't care who's around me. I'll just see what the men want to do.' Kayden telepathically spoke to his team. His ability to leave one or more of his team or the horses from his telepathic thoughts allowed him to speak to his men and leave Cassie from the conversation.

Cassie's gone off the rails and wants you block-heads to come on our honeymoon. You can come if you nick off whenever I want to ravish her and I don't want you to touch her, kiss her or even look at her or you'll be put on the next plane home. She's mine now and I'm not bloody sharing anymore. Tell her what I just said and you're dead! Just get yourselves packed and get your selves on to the plane in an hour or you're not coming.

Cassie heard cheers and yahoos coming from around the backyard. She had no idea what Kayden had just said but it obviously sounded like they had agreed. They took only seconds to gather around them.

Kayden slung his arm around Cassie protectively as they both moved in to hear where they were going. 'It will have to be somewhere here in Australia just in case something goes wrong and Aldebaran reneges on his deal he made with me. Seeing there will be none of us here to answer Zoren's call we'd better make sure we're no more than a six-hour plane ride away.' He smiled down at Cassie. 'The where is up to my new wife. Just name it, gorgeous and we're there.'

'I don't know,' she grinned, looking around at them all. 'It's your country. I'm sure each one of you has somewhere fun you want to visit.'

Woody stood with his arm around Jason. 'Well, the guys and I have always wanted to go back to the theme parks on the Gold Coast in Queensland. We had a blast years ago when we were there. Maybe we could stay in Surfers Paradise and check out a nightclub. In the morning, while the ladies shop us men can hit the surf.'

Ethan butted in. 'What about a road trip down to Margaret River to visit the wineries?' Conor agreed with him.

Jason was just about jumping out of his skin by the time his turn came around. 'I vote for Sydney all the way. Staying at the Cross, gambling, and doing as many ladies as we can. I want some bloody fun for a change.'

Kayden put his hand up as they all started arguing over whose pick they would choose. 'Okay, guys, we only have five days. However, if we leave now it gives us six nights. How about two nights in Surfers Paradise, two nights in Sydney and two in Margaret River. That way, you, my gorgeous bride, get to see a tiny bit of Australia. And the rest of you get a taste of where you've been nagging me to let you visit for a very long time now.'

'What about you?' Cassie asked Kayden a bit apprehensively. 'I'm sure you'll have somewhere in mind as well.'

'I got the girl,' he smiled. With that, Kayden told them they only had moments to get ready. 'Guys, come on. If we want to be on a plane by late this afternoon you had better get moving. We have reservations to be made, gear to pack, guests to say goodbye to and Tremaine needs to be okay with minding the horses while we're gone. If you want your girlfriends to come, tell them that what they can't find upstairs in the wardrobe, we'll buy for them. No time for anyone to be racing home first. I want us out of here in an hour.'

Woody dropped his arm from around Jason and took off with the others. Cassie smiled as she watched them jumping around, hugging each other.

'This is going to be the best honeymoon and holiday ever,' she said happily to Kayden once they were on their own again.

He agreed. 'That it will be, my sweet and by the way, I saw you dancing and laughing with Woody before. You both seemed no different to the way you've always been. I'm glad there's no hard feelings.'

'He's a good mate. He's with Ella now and very happy.'

'And you, Mrs Hunter, are you happy?'

'Yes, Mr Hunter but it'll be some hours before I get to show you.'

'Bloody hell! A man does the right thing and gets married and his woman is already putting him on rations!'

'My very naughty tiger man, we haven't the time. You've only given us, well, half an hour now to get packed and on our way the airport. Behave!'

'No way dream girl, I've got time. Lean up against me for a second and it'll be all over. You look such a sexy hot minx. I'll take what I can get at this point. Don't tell me no!'

Cassie slapped his arm playfully. 'Quit it and go get ready. Tremaine needs to be informed and I have to pack.'

Kayden laughed with her before ducking off to organise a sitter for their horses. Cassie went upstairs, amused by her mad-dick husband, knowing life from now on was going to be a whole new ball game. Kayden was really coming out of his shell and Cassie loved the new him. She quickly changed and packed enough clothes for the trip, still chuckling every now and then at how much fun the day had been as it continued to consume her thoughts. Once ready, she went back outside to say goodbye to the guests. News of them leaving had all but cleared the place out. The wedding planner already had the staff cleaning and the evidence of a wedding was barely visible. By the time Cassie left with the guys to go pick up Kayden at his ranch, the house was spotlessly clean and all that was left was to lock up.

She glanced back before getting in the car. It might look like nothing had gone on in there today but in her mind the wonderful memories of her wedding day would always stay as fresh to her as they felt right now.

Chapter Thirty

United Amusement

She sat in the plane listening to Jason and Conor chat. They'd be touching down in Queensland around nine in the evening. It was roughly an hour's drive to the Gold Coast. They'd book into the hotel, dump their bags in the room and hit one of the nightspots. They'd planned it down to the last detail as they always did, once a course of action had been decided on. To ensure all this went down smoothly they had insisted Kayden change into a dark suit before he left his house.

Cassie didn't have to be told as she had already noticed the girls were still dressed in formal dresses so she changed into a light blue cocktail dress with matching shoes.

The hotel was in the centre of Surfers Paradise. Looking out over the balcony, Cassie could see the beach to the right. The reflection of the full moon over the water and sand was not allowing the couples any privacy tonight. Soft light illuminated over the waves allowing her to pick out silhouette figures still surfing. Along the beach, lovers strolled hand-in-hand while others sat together in the sand.

Below in the mall, she could hear music that attracted her attention and she looked to the festivities below. The many restaurants spilled seating out onto the footpath where people dined and she watched as others wandered around window-shopping. Buskers were singing on each corner and attracting small crowds of onlookers. She could only just hear their music over the pub band below.

Kayden joined her, soaking in the view as she had done. 'This is the real world, gorgeous. This is what we fight to protect.'

Everywhere they looked, lights gleamed and life and laughter surrounded them. 'I've never seen anything like it. It's beautiful and alive. I love it.'

'Me too! All the cities have their own characteristics and charm. But I have to admit this is one of my favourites.'

Cassie closed her eyes and took a deep breath. She could almost taste the sea, never mind smell it. That, mixed with the aroma from the kitchens below and the spirits and beer that were flowing, made her excited to go down there and experience every bit of it.

'We can stay here and enjoy it from our room if you prefer, gorgeous.' Kayden kissed her neck, running his hand down her spine. She opened her eyes to a cheeky grin.

'As tempting as that is, below us is the famous Cavil Avenue that is beckoning me with its restaurants, night clubs and the waft of food and fun.' She smiled. 'Do you mind?'

'Mind? I want to throw you down on the bed and love you to bits!' he joked with her. 'Really though I don't mind at all. I want to be the one to show you what the nightlife here is all about.' He slipped his arms around her waist and danced them inside.

'With you in it, it'll be perfect.' She smiled at his good mood as her attentive husband waltzed them out of the door to the elevator.

The streets were lit up and the joy of being on the other side of the country with no responsibilities was putting them all on such a high that they could scarcely wait to begin enjoying it. The nightclubs and pubs were in full swing. The sound of the music and the noise of hotted-up cars filled the air. Some slowed down, checking out the single girls who stood in groups, giggling and enjoying the attention.

They picked out a reasonable-looking nightclub and went in to check it out. This one was clean, had good music, attentive bar staff and was full of loud and obnoxious drunks. They figured they would fit in here just nicely. Pleased with their choice, they parked their butts on some stools by a tall round table.

Jason attracted a following as soon as they arrived. He was the only one without a woman and being tall and well built, coupled with his adorable blue eyes and shoulder-length blond hair, he had the girls swooning all over him. Unfortunately, Jason had no time for most women, only wishing to taste, not buy. He much preferred his call girls, saying it was better than having to put up with tears and tantrums when he tossed them aside in the morning light.

The evening rolled on and so did the drinks. Cassie was having a blast, dancing and enjoying herself with Kayden. Woody and Ella were right there beside them putting any grievances aside as they too let their hair down. Cassie had to admit that Ella and Woody did make a stunning couple. Conor and Ethan's girlfriends danced on their own during the night as the two boys hung out with Jason. They were true party animals and the girls had been around them long enough to know not to interfere with boy-time. They were both a couple of sweeties although she doubted they would have lasted as long as they had if they hadn't been so ditsy and non-confrontational.

When the boys were inebriated to the point of holding each other up, Kayden and Cassie walked them back to the hotel. Jason made a call on the way and when they walked into the foyer there was a lovely, classically dressed blond waiting for him. He dropped his arm from around Kayden, gave Cassie a kiss on the head goodnight before he casually headed for the woman and seductively called her name. She turned and he put his arm out to her as he walked her to the elevator. When the elevator stopped on their floor, he gave them the biggest grin as he walked her to his room. Cassie giggled at him and he turned, winked and closed his door.

'He's just so happy not to have to commit. He's a strange one,' Cassie commented.

Kayden picked her up, pretending to carry her over the threshold even though they weren't home. Lovingly gazing into her eyes he smiled. 'He will find you one day and it will blow his mind. Before I held you for the first time I was exactly like him. I never wanted a woman around for companionship. I always considered them obnoxious, annoying even and only good for one thing.' Sitting her on the bed, he bent down to take off her clothes. 'Then you came into my life like a whirlwind and shook me to the core. I couldn't get enough of you.' Unzipping her, he slipped off her dress. 'I remember the first time I held you,' he began to divulge, while hanging up her dress. 'I thought I was feeling an angel and right there, that minute, I never wanted to let you go.' Coming back to her, he pulled the comb from her hair, kissing her neck.

Cassie turned shyly. 'I didn't know I was your first love. I thought with your hunky body and face you would have lost yourself in love many times over considering your age. Pardon the pun, old man.'

Standing up, he removed his clothes. 'Only once, and I've just married her. Now come here and I'll show you old man. I'm going to kiss, lick and love you till dawn, gorgeous!'

She chuckled and jumped up on him so quickly that he only just caught her, falling back on the bed with her, both laughing. Cassie quietened down first and moved his hand down so he could slip off her knickers. He suddenly went from being jovial and mucking around to a quivering mess. She knew he'd wanted her since their wedding vows. All he whispered out next was her name before he claimed her lips and his hot sweet passion swept them both away. He drew a lust from her that she never knew before. He was attentive and loving, leaving no part of her unloved. Cassie wondered if every couple experienced such a sense of throwing caution to the wind on their wedding night. Nothing more to hide, just the raw need for each other that pushed the boundaries well beyond the limits to an experience she could never have imagined.

CHAPTER THIRTY-ONE

Unit Amusement
(Day One)

C assie could hear ringing. Shaking herself she grabbed
for the phone.

Hanging up, she rolled back into Kayden. 'It's just the guys giving us a wakeup call. They said they don't care if we're newlyweds or not, if we don't get ourselves downstairs in half an hour they're all coming up to drag us out.'

She groaned and kissed Kayden's sleepy face. She threw the sheet back and sprang happily out of bed, throwing herself under a hot shower.

Kayden begrudgingly joined her, still groggy and tired. 'You were a knockout last night, honey. I'm still getting chills,' he said quietly in her ear as his hands started to roam happily.

She giggled and slapped him playfully. 'The gang's going to be here knocking at our door any minute.' She slipped out from his arms and getting out, flicked off the hot tap, leaving only the cold-water running. He smiled while he scolded her for the way she tried to cool him off.

In the bedroom, Cassie sorted through her clothes, hanging up what needed to be hung. She thought how glad she was that Woody had kept his promise about buying her designer clothes. When she had moved in with him, he'd organised a dressmaker. He had spent hours with her, going over magazines and picking out outfits that would suit her. He always appreciated her making an effort to look nice. But today she was spending it with her man and wanted his full attention so a little mischief outfit was required.

Pulling on a short, box-pleated skirt and a halter-top she smiled at the look on Kayden's face as he came out of the shower.

'That's very cruel, honey. I can't believe the way I am feeling! You're going to tease me all day in that cute little number.'

She went up on tiptoes and kissed his cheek. 'I want you with me all day. I'm using the clothes' power to make sure you don't leave my side for a minute.'

He laughed and snatched her into his arms. 'You don't need a skirt on to have power over me, my beautiful wife!'

Her evil plan backfired and the mini skirt was just too much for him. It was another hour or so before they finally made it down to the foyer where the others were all waiting.

Conor, Ethan and Jason had gone surfing after waking them up and the girls had gone out shopping. Ella and Woody only just joined them, making Cassie not feel so bad they may have held them up. She did make a little excuse saying they'd drifted back to sleep but she doubt if it washed, especially because Kayden couldn't wipe the smile from his face.

Just then the cars turned up and there was a mad rush to get into them, all of them now looking forward to spending as much time as they could at Sea World.

The fun park was amazing to walk into. Cassie wanted to touch and look at everything at once. They only just arrived in time to watch the dolphin show. The crowd cheered as the dolphins leaped high out of the crystal-clear water in unison, showing off their skills. The show escalated when two dolphins towed the keeper, who barefooted it around the perimeter.

'Can we go see them?' Cassie dragged them after it was over and once she had felt them for real, snatched the schedule up in her hands.

'To the sea lions!' She had the team all under her power so they could do nothing but follow her. They all knew it and even using all their powers combined couldn't break free from her magic so they could hit the rides.

Kayden felt them try to power up. *You know she doesn't know she's doing it and it's our little secret so let's keep it that way, okay? I want her using whatever she has, even unconsciously. It may come in handy to her later. Just suck it up and enjoy the ride.*

Unable to do anything else, they all sat quietly and watched the entertainment, astounded at how excited they became when Cassie did. She was getting more powerful and they all knew it; what had them stunned was what this was for. What was coming that only she was being given an extra boost for, and not them? The thought of her not being with them and working on her own stressed them out and yet she kept diverting their thoughts, keeping them as happy as she felt. They clapped and cheered as the sea lions counted with their flippers, nodding and shaking their heads when answering questions. The whole act was to find the golden ball and the sea lions made it funny. Cassie made it a very different experience and they left, glad they had watched it with her.

She didn't have to ask Jason and Ethan twice to feed the sharks so she could watch. When lowered into the underwater aquarium, they waved excitedly to their team who watched from the viewing room that was on the other side of the glass wall. Both boys were on tenterhooks as the sharks already smelt food and started passing close to them, their large noses butting up against the cage in a frenzy to get to them, not caring about the food but wanting the boys for dinner. The boys were annoyed that they were unable to use powers in front of so many onlookers, both wanting to punch the suckers just for fun.

The keeper gave Jason and Ethan a fish each to hold up so that the sharks could feed from them. A loud crack on the cage door sent chills down the spines of all the onlookers as the sharks smashed with full force into the cage door as they snatched the fish. They took off angrily and bit in, sending white fish flesh spewing around the cage, attracting other large sharks and causing a feeding frenzy. The fish suddenly became aggressive and for safety reasons, the cage lifted quickly as it was battered and butted up against, all the way to the surface. Jason and Ethan were positive Cassie had something to do with it to give them some excitement, but when confronted she just smiled and still on a high, dragged them off to the ski show. The cars and general skiers kept the boys happy while Cassie enjoyed the skit, clapping and laughing as the boat turned a car and drove up onto the beach. Afterwards the girls had photos taken with the male actors, leaning up against one of the lovely old vehicles. Not to be outdone, the guys took off their shirts and got photos taken with the female actresses and loved the attention they got, not only from the girls but from the crowd that clapped and cheered for more.

'Show offs,' Cassie grumbled as she linked arms with the girls and strode off, making the boys run to catch up.

When the men finally reached them, Kayden laughed, lifting Cassie up in his arms. 'Come here, little jealous one, no way are you going anywhere without me, ever again!'

She giggled and wrapped her arms around his neck. 'Promise?'

'You have my heart and my word,' he said, putting her down and grabbing her hand. 'Now, your punishment for running away?' He considered, his eyes darting around. 'To the rides with you, young lady!'

'Now that kind of punishment I'm going to love.' She grabbed his hand, dragging him to the fastest ride she could see. With that, the spell was broken. It was her time with Kayden and the rest of them now got it. She wanted them to enjoy and appreciate things they would otherwise have taken for granted. They were chuffed as they grabbed their partners and went to do their own thing; chuffed that she had wanted them with her that much, even if she had just dumped them for the boss. They took off in different directions, free, yet so very happy for the experience.

Back at Surfers Paradise the girls went fashion shopping while boys went down to the beach to catch some waves and do a bit of surfing. Kayden and Cassie hit the mall, preferring to enjoy the atmosphere that surrounded them. Two girls in skimpy gold two-piece outfits stopped to chat and they found out that they were the fabled Gold Coast meter maids. A silver statue moved and startled them, making both laugh as they saw it was just a man covered in silver paint.

Tables of patrons from restaurants filled the air with noisy chatter and laughter. Upwards, there were skyscrapers that towered around them like alien monsters protecting this little part of the world. As they strolled hand-in-hand taking it all in, Cassie had the feeling this would have to be one of Australia's happiest holiday destinations.

Chapter Thirty-Two

Unit Amusement
(Day Two)

The trip to another fun park left them exhausted and looking forward to a little time out before they had to leave for the airport.

Back at the motel, the gang were all going for a bite to eat but Cassie was far from feeling hungry. 'I want a nice soak in the spa and that's where I'm heading.' She grabbed a towel and kissed Kayden. 'Unless you're hungry too? I can relax later if you prefer something now.'

'Your idea sounds just perfect. We can eat later on tonight when we get to Sydney,' he said, following her out.

'Sounds good to us too!' Woody and Ella joined them, only they were more prepared, bringing down a couple of bottles of bubbly and some glasses. After pouring them all a drink, Woody sat back to relax in the spa with the rest of them.

Not being able to resist annoying Kayden and Woody, Jason came down as well and slipped in between Ella and Cassie. 'A thorn between two roses,' he said as he held up his glass for Woody to fill. 'As if I'm staying there with those giggling chicks,' he said. 'You're not getting rid of me that easy.'

Cassie giggled at him. 'We might as well enjoy you now because when we get to the Cross I doubt if we'll see you for dust.'

'You're on the money, honey but definitely not for your eyes or your ears, little sister. I can guarantee that K will keep you as far away from there tonight as he can get you. But hey, I still want to catch up with you guys tomorrow morning. Aren't we all going sightseeing?'

Cassie suddenly felt nervous for him if he was going to go to the Cross on his own. All the rest of them had partners so it looked as if he would be unaccompanied. 'Surely you aren't thinking about heading out by yourself in a wild place like Kings Cross?' she asked, alarmed that with all the stories they had told her, he would be game enough to go into the untamed jungle on his lonesome.

'Don't look so worried, Cass. The guys would never allow me to go and enjoy all the nightly spoils and booty on my own. No, Ethan and Conor need some time out from the girls, so they're feeding them now. When we touch down, us boys are going down to the Cross for a boys' night out. Woody's gone to the light, like Kayden, so my guess is you guys will probably hang out together.'

'Great plan, dimwit. What about their girls? I'm not frigging babysitting,' Woody drawled and rolled his eyes.

Jase laughed. 'No way! They've already planned to go to some male strip club they know of. So there, sweet, it's all organised.'

Woody grinned with a sly dog look on his face. 'Good! Because me and my man K are treating our women to a bit of indulgence and taking them to the revolving restaurant in the city before showing them a little of the nightlife from the comfort of a limo.'

'Are we?' Cassie hugged Kayden. 'Cool,' she sat back, happily thinking about what they were going to do and was wrapt that they weren't just going to be sitting in a motel room like she had thought was going to happen.

'No doubt about our Cassie, she's easy pleased. Why don't you come with us, K and let her go have a real treat? She'd have a blast at the strip joint with the girls,' Jason said, trying to stir Kayden up.

Kayden stiffened and Cassie could tell it made him annoyed that he'd even suggested it. Jason knew how easily led Cassie could be but not tonight. What Kayden had planned sounded just perfect to her.

'I can't answer for Kayden.' Cassie took another sip of her drink. 'But for me, there is no other man worth looking at after seeing my man naked,' she giggled. 'There are five men around me constantly with buff, fine-tuned bodies. Why would I then bother to go to some sleazy little hot spot? Looking at something that doesn't come close to you lot or to my hunky man?' she asked, closing her eyes. The image of her husband doing his own little strip tease couldn't stop her from grinning.

'I'm stunned! You've never complimented any of us before. I just had to take a second to see if you were being serious or having a lend of me!'

Cassie sighed lazily. 'Ella, tell him! Are they or are they not, all drop-dead honeys?' She grinned.

Ella took a minute. 'My Woody is my perfect vision, as yours is Kayden but yes the rest of the boys do look well above average on the who's-hot radar.' She smiled as Cassie clinked her glass together with hers.

Kayden grinned from ear to ear. 'Right back at you, beautiful! There's nothing at the Cross for me any longer either.'

Jason was still gob-smacked and sat quietly sipping from his glass. Cassie could see his mind going over something. 'Whatcha thinking, Jason?' she asked.

He emptied his glass and poured another. 'Remember when we were on the island and I was canoodling with that cutie? Well, she said exactly those words and that's why I dumped her. I thought she meant that any one of us would do. I really liked her too. Had feelings for her, straight up, enjoying her so much I even took it slow.' He looked at them and smiled. 'I know, not me at all. You know I still think about her every now and then. She really pressed the right buttons for me. I must have been crazy to let that one go. Too bad now though. I don't even know her name or where she comes from.'

Cassie thought about the one he was with that day. 'Which one? Do you mean the one with the girl-next-door look and hazel eyes?' she asked.

He nodded. 'That would be the one but I would hardly call her the girl next door. She was a real hottie.'

'Well hottie lives in Margaret River, our last stop, and her name by the way is Sonia McMasters.'

Jason slapped the water with excitement and drenched them accidentally. 'Your power to remember names! I forgot about that. We could look her up!' His grin spread over his entire face as he lay back and sculled his drink. 'Sonia ... that's right ... that was her name,' he said quietly to himself and the boys both grinned at each other.

'The boy's got it bad! Who would have guessed our man Jase would fall for a real woman?' Woody commented.

Jason smiled again. 'Little Sonia! The name just rolls off your tongue, don't it?' he said again and they all laughed at him going all gooey over a girl at long last.

'Is this going to spoil your fun tonight?' Cassie inquired.

'Hell no!' he said, sitting up so fast that he almost spilled his drink, making them laugh. 'My little Sonia may tell me to rack off yet so I better not go loaded,' he laughed.

Cassie slapped him. 'You're disgusting, Jason, stop it,' she giggled with him.

With the booze gone, they decided to get out of the spa and go have showers before heading off for the airport.

The flight was barely an hour's trip so it was exciting to be stepping off the plane and seeing a brand new city. Looking down from up in the plane, the city looked awesome with all the lights mapping out just how dense the population was, expanding out over the land for miles.

Kayden asked the driver to drop them off at a luxury hotel called The Observatory. Cassie followed Kayden and the porter up to The Observatory Suite, the most opulent and expensive of all the suites, luxury at its finest, the décor elegant and filled with charm.

Kayden put his arms around her. 'Living in a castle most of your life I thought you might like somewhere a little bit special to make you feel like a princess for a night.'

'You know you never have to be so lavish with your money to please me. Just so long as I lie next to you, I'm happy staying anywhere. However,' she spun around in a circle with her arms out. 'This is exquisite and definitely does make me feel so very, very special,' she said, stopping and hugging him.

'Special, is that all? I hoped I would get maybe great sex for being so thoughtful.'

'You, my husband, will get more than that if you do a little strip later to make up for me not going with the girls. I want to experience everything Sydney has to offer. That being said, I'd sooner it was you that showed me what I may be missing, not a stranger.'

'Strip? You don't have to ask me twice,' he laughed, grabbing her and sitting her on the bed. Turning up the music from the surround sound system, he began entertaining her, throwing his clothes aside and then attacking her. 'Now it's your turn, gorgeous and if you strip as quickly and as impatiently as I did to get to you, I'll have to smack you.'

She went to get up.

Just thinking about gently smacking her sexy toosh, he grabbed her. 'Stuff it, cutie, I'll take your clothes off for you!' he said impatiently, wanting her now.

She giggled and wiggled out of his grip, giving him a show that would make up for him staying at home with her too. That is, of course, if he had let her finish. He snatched her half-naked body up in his arms and carried her to the bed. 'My girl, yum! Come here so I can have some dessert before dinner,' he chuckled before kissing her into submission.

Later—much later—they met the others downstairs. Jason, Ethan and Conor had a look in their eyes spelling a night of pure hell-raising. The sweetie twins cabbed it to the strip club and their three mischievous team members left just after them.

As for us—well Kayden and Woody never do anything in halves. The longest limousine Cassie had ever seen pulled up for them. She stepped into something close to a nightclub on wheels, excited to get to the restaurant where they would be eating one thousand feet above the city and as the restaurant revolved, they had promised her a spectacular view.

The restaurant was known for its selection of freshly caught, delicious seafood and the meal lived up to her every expectation. Overindulged in explode-in-your-mouth sensations, Cassie declined dessert when handed the menu although when Kayden's dessert came out it looked so delicious that she weakened and let him feed her a spoonful. As he pulled the spoon away he kissed her mouth, sending her into a delightful spin. 'I didn't know desserts could be so dreamy to eat,' she grinned as he let her go.

When they left, she turned to take in just one more look out the glass walls. The restaurant was entertaining and as promised, the view, stunning. 'I just want to lock it in my memory to have always.'

Kayden slid his hand in hers and walked her out. 'It pales compared to you, my beauty,' he said sweetly.

Relaxed after seeing the Cross at night in the comfort and safety of the limo, they went back to the hotel to have a drink in the Martini Club. The room was unusual for a drinking lounge. With the waft of the rich leather and mahogany furniture mixed with the books that lined the shelving, reminded her of her father's library. Somehow, it was so comforting to feel a part of him with her tonight.

Kayden had only had a few sips of a Martini when they received a distressing call from Jason. The boys were in a situation and needed help. He never explained, just gave the address and hung up.

Arriving at the destination, they found only a big old green door. Standing against the door was a huge obese man who had a sumo wrestler look about him. After getting permission for them to go inside, they entered, going up the darkened stairs. Coming to another door, it opened into a games room. It was full of cigar smoke mixed with the odour of expensive leather. The lounges flanked a large round table that had huge comfortable leather chairs pushed up against it. Here a dark-haired man sat, his expression unreadable. Jason was in a chair over by the far corner, held by the shoulders by two oversized goons. One had scars and a patch on his eye, the other had so many piercings on his face and ears that Cassie was surprised he could even hold his head up straight.

Goddamn, they look bad arses.

Conor and Ethan both had men standing over them with weapons drawn. It looked like Jason had tried to stick up for the boys and was being subdued and kept away from them under tighter security.

It was obvious without asking that the guys had been playing cards and had become over-confident and lost, not having enough cash to cover their debt.

Woody crankily asked what they owed.

'Ten G,' the man sitting at the end of the table said with an accent. Maybe South African, Cassie thought as she eyed him, coming to the conclusion that he looked like a mean sucker and not one to be stuffed around. His eyes alone held a tone of impatience, showing them that even having to bother with this situation was an insult. He looked about two seconds from giving the order to take the lot of them down and with this firepower someone was bound to be shot or worse. His men looked very trigger happy, especially the one with the eye patch.

One of the armed men finished counting the money Woody and Kayden emptied from their wallets. 'Still five G short, Mono,' he said to the man at the end of the table.

The man they now knew as Mono sat eyeing Cassie with a steady gaze as if he was trying to work out if she was someone he knew. He looked a mean mother and yet he was from a world she knew so well. With his jewelled watch and gold chains, down to the expensive suit and brand of shoes that her stepfather used to wear, everything about him screamed money and worst of all, arrogance. He had dark hair, an olive complexion and eyes so black with annoyance that they were just glistening pits within sockets.

Kayden stepped closer to him and the guard beside him pointed guns at him. 'Look, man, we have the money. We can double it if you wait until the bank opens in the morning. Let's just calm down and I'm sure we can come to an arrangement. What do you say?' Kayden knew his boys were in trouble and was trying to defuse the situation.

Mono seemed calm on the outside but underlying anger was showing in his eyes. 'I won't be here in the morning. I've given them long enough to come up with what they owe me.' He summoned his guards to take it out of their hides and the guards moved toward them. Cassie could see this was not going to end nicely.

'Wait!' She put her hand up and sexily walked over to the table, lifting her tight skirt slightly so she could lean on it, looking Mono directly in the eye. The split was up to her thigh and her boobs spilled teasingly from her top, showing just a little lace from her low-cut bra. His eyes roved over her body without expression but certainly not with distaste.

'How about you and I play a real game of cards, sugar and if I win, my friends and I all walk out of here owing you zip,' she said with a rather sleazy drawl.

'And if I win?' He seemed slightly amused.

Cassie moved her hands gently off the table and ran them slowly over her hips and down her thighs, straightening her dress and talking quietly. 'Then all bets are off, we take you down and you walk out of here with nothing but a headache from being thrown against that back wall,' she said, smiling sweetly. She looked sideways at Kayden and he winked so she knew he was okay with it.

'And who, may I ask, out of you lot, will be tough enough to throw me against the wall?'

She walked a little closer, slowly, so as not to startle him and as she did she ran her finger on the table then put it in her mouth and sucked it sensually, closing her eyes as if she were enjoying more than just the finger. Seductively pulling it from her lips she opened her eyes and grinned. 'Um—that would be me,' she said again, so honey-smooth that it even surprised herself.

He threw his head back and laughed. It was a truly amused laugh so her plan to seduce him into a game felt inevitable. 'Because you amuse me I will play the best out of three hands,' he gestured to his guard who pulled out a chair for her. 'Drink?' he said, clicking his fingers to the bar person who practically ran to him to see what he wanted.

Cassie smiled back. 'Shot glass, rum, straight up,' she said.

He sat back in his chair and she was thinking that maybe the guys had better get ready for plan B. This one was a challenge and so far with his poker face she had been unable to read him. But she still had a few tricks up her sleeve to thaw out Mr Freeze. She pulled the clip out of her hair and shook the long locks out, letting the curls fall sexily around her shoulders. Still there was not an expression she could pick, yet as she shook her head slightly, there was a definite glint that flickered in his eyes. Gotcha, she thought as she searched his poker face for anything else.

He leaned back, watching her antics. 'This may be the conman getting conned. I'll be watching you, lady, so no tricks.'

'No sleeves,' she said, lifting her hands up. 'Are you telling me a little five-foot nothing female has you running scared?'

'Not at all. I'm amused that you'd think you would even be good enough to play against someone like me but it is your boys' funeral not mine if you lose.' He shuffled the cards.

'I would like to request a new unopened pack, not that I don't trust you but neither of us then have reason to believe the other has cheated.'

'Fine,' he said, annoyed again as he summoned a new pack that he quickly pulled the wrapper from. 'Any other requests before we start?' he asked sarcastically.

She sculled her drink and put the glass in front of him, at the same time gesturing for him to drink his. 'Yes, one last request. Keep them coming unless of course you're unable to handle a couple of drinks with your opponent.' She smiled, angel-like.

He looked at her for a minute and must have decided against what he was going to say and downed his drink, knocking on the table for two refills.

Cassie won the first hand, tossing another shot down and gestured for him to do the same. He was a bit moody and so she thought she would lull him into a false sense of security and let him beat her in the next round.

'Mono,' she smiled. 'You have an extremely pleasant accent, South African isn't it?' She tried to sweet-talk him.

'Shut the hell up. Your pleasantries won't get those impudent fools from getting what's coming to them,' he said, concentrating on his cards.

'And your sweet-sounding voice will not stop what is coming to you,' she said gulping down yet another, motioning for him to keep up. He drank and slammed the glass against the wall. It shattered as it hit the tiled floor, the sound breaking through the deadly quiet room.

She shook her head. 'Temper, Mono. I imagined you as a much better adversary than this.' Cassie motioned for another drink as he dealt out the last hand.

'You're far too beautiful to be so damn annoying,' he said and played his hand.

He then seemed in a better mood when he won the next round but on the final hand, after he flipped over his last card and she had beaten him, all his anger came back. He stood up, flinging his chair back. 'What is your name, young lady?' he asked.

She stood up, putting her hand out confidently to shake his hand. 'Cassie. That would be Mrs Cassie Hunter.'

He stood glaring at her for a minute and a strange look come over his face as he finally took her hand. 'Well then, Cassandra Hunter,' he said, becoming calm. 'It's been very interesting meeting you although I can't say I enjoyed it totally,' he said, kissing her hand and staring into her eyes, trying to soak her in as if not wanting to ever forget her. 'You and I will definitely be meeting again and when we do you must give me a chance to redeem my money,' he said, letting go of her hand. With an air of arrogance he swept out of the room, not even taking the time to glance at anyone else, his guards following closely behind him.

Jason, Conor and Ethan were up like a shot, fussing over Cassie. 'You were unreal,' Jason said, thanking her at the same time as the other two.

Kayden came in and snatching Cassie off them while he gave the boys an *I've warned you about touching my woman* look. Cassie gladly fell into his arms. Totally wiped out and wanting to get the hell out of there, she had to wait for Woody to finish growling at the guys. And boy, was he going to town on them.

'If Cassie hadn't bailed you numskulls out it would have been a blood bath and we may all have ended up either in hospital or dead! We don't need this sort of exposure and you know it!' He was yelling now.

The disciplining went on for a further few minutes with lots of cursing before they backed down and promised to behave. 'I don't even want to look at the idiots tonight,' Kayden growled. 'Guys take the winnings from the table and piss off out of my sight. We'll finish this in the morning.'

'No more bloody cards or else,' Woody yelled at them as they bolted out the door, laughing and giving Woody the birdie.

Woody and Kayden hid an amused expression as they turned away, both knowing if they were still single, they would have been right there with them, looking for more bloody mischief and running a-muck.

Ella was impressed on the way back to the hotel. 'Quite the little gambler,' she said to Woody as they talked between themselves, Woody telling Ella about Cassie's casino days.

Kayden was laying little kisses around Cassie's shoulders and whispering how sexy she had looked when she ran her finger along the table and licked it. 'I could have come over there and taken you right on that table it was such a turn on.'

She started to thaw out and giggle a little at his enjoyment.

Woody started to laugh. 'Cut it out, Kayden. Don't forget we're here too. Find a room!'

Kayden replaced her strap on her shoulder and sat up chuckling.

'I was trying so hard not to smile at her,' Woody remarked. 'She just about had the poor guy drooling. How he stopped himself from not bowing down and giving her his whole fortune at the end of it I'll never know. I have to admit you were extremely entertaining, Cassie.'

'Weren't you scared just a little?' Ella asked her. 'I just about jumped out of my skin when he slammed his glass into the wall.'

'You can't let them intimidate you. I've seen worse behaviour and was expecting it because he was really very good. The only way I could think to rattle him was by making him drink with me. I had the impression he was not use to being told what to do but would have seemed weak to you lot if he'd refused me. I'm just glad it was only three hands. His eyes were the only part of him I could get a reaction.

That was why I kept up the act to get something, anything, from him. He was a hard nut to crack I can tell you.'

'But you let him win one. I saw that look you get when you do it to us,' Woody eyed her.

'Yes, I had decided that was best as I could feel his anger from where I sat. And yet when I did the final count of the cards afterwards, he would have actually won that round fair and square. I think I met my match in cards tonight,' she admitted. 'He may have actually won fair and square if we had kept playing.'

Woody was thoughtful. 'Maybe a rematch would be fun to watch then.'

'That's not going to happen,' Kayden snapped abruptly, sliding his arm back around her and looking out the window. He stayed quiet the rest of the trip. They pulled up at the hotel and he said goodnight politely but moodily and took Cassie up to their room. She knew he was pissed off because he'd even knocked back a nightcap with Woody which has never happened.

Chapter Thirty-Three
Uncovering a Lie

Kayden was fuming inside. He was so sick to death of Woody and the guys encouraging Cassie to become someone she wasn't. Why couldn't they love her just the way she was? *'A rematch might be fun to watch,' that big mouth said, thinking it was funny. Just because she chose me, he wants to stuff it up for me. Let his bitch-wife act like a sex goddess and have every man in the room fall at her feet and see how he likes it! See how insecure he feels going out with the hottest hottie on the planet.*

He threw himself on the bed, punching the bloody pillow just to get rid of some of his frustration and wishing to God it was Mono's fat head. *Jeez, the control it took not to smash his smug mouth on the way out of that room.* If it wasn't for the gun cocked at his head, Kayden would have knocked that gloating look right off his face. *'You and I will definitely be meeting again and when we do, you must give me a chance to redeem my money.' Who in the hell does he think he is? And like he will ever get within two feet of Cassie ever again!* Pulling the pillow under his head, he lay watching his gorgeous wife, trying hard to calm himself before she came to him.

She lifted her dress over her head and hung it up; her delicate lace underwear barely covered the intended areas. He felt a tingle just looking at her. *She's damned perfect.* Every curve, every tantalizing move she made had him enchanted. *How can love hurt so badly yet feel so divine at the same time?* She fiddled and took her time, a habit when unsure how to approach him, or a subject. *Now I've gone and scared her! Good on you, Kayden. As if it is her fault that you're a jealous son of a bitch. She's just stopped us all from taking a bullet and you're angry, totally confusing her.*

'Cassie honey?' Kayden put his hand out for her to come to him.

She glanced around at him, her smile radiant. She giggled and started to dance seductively, giving a private showing just for him. *She's such a delicate little flower. Where that other Cassie came from I have no idea. My Cassie, who is here tonight with me is innocent, a little shy but the most adorable sweetheart, doing everything she can to make me feel like I'm the only man in the world she loves.*

'Are you angry with your princess?' she purred, crawling on the bed as a little kitten would flee if scared even a little.

He grinned, his mood changing immediately, just feeling the touch of her hand on his leg. 'No, not at you, sweetheart, just angry at myself for giving the go ahead for you to play. I should have known I'd get jealous,' he said, gently lifting her on top of him.

She had an unsure look on her face, maybe even a little sad. 'I never meant to upset you, Kayden. I was too busy concentrating on how to beat him to think about how it looked to you. I'm sorry you had to be put through that.'

She rolled off him and turned onto her side, watching.

Kayden wanted to talk to her. He wanted answers but decided to ease into it. 'You did well, honey, it's just me. When you're with me on your own, you're such an angel: naive and fragile. I feel like I need to cover you in cottonwool to protect you, to keep you safe. Then when I see you do things like you did tonight, and how you are with the guys sometimes, you don't seem like the same girl.'

She flopped on her back, looking up at the ceiling.

The last thing she needs is for me to be upsetting her after what she's just been through but Goddamn it I want answers. That act tonight was totally not her and if it was, then why was she so worn out? She should be bouncing off the ceiling and on such a high from winning! No, there is more to this little charade.

Cassie took a big breath and faced him. 'If you really want to know how much I need you, combine your power with mine and take a look. We're married now and I want no secrets between us.'

Kayden was stunned. *Is she really going to bare all? Surely there are secrets, especially between her and Woody that she prefers to keep secret. With her powers growing as they are there won't be any secrets she can hold back from me once I connect with her in this way.*

'Cassie, you don't have to, honey. I'm just being over-bossy and irritable. You're dead on your feet. Let's go to sleep and talk about it tomorrow when we're both not so tired.'

She wrapped her arms around his neck. Their joint power was letting him feel her every emotion. 'No, Kayden, now!' she said firmly. 'Put one of your clouds around us so you can see once and for all how I really feel about you.'

He nodded. 'You know I'll see everything, don't you, angel?'

'I know but if it makes you realise how much in love with you I am then it is worth it.'

Kayden nodded and closed his eyes, willing himself to her and covering them in a magical cloud. Her childhood flashed before him, giving him a glimpse of how scared and rejected she had felt. Being unloved by all that surrounded her impacted on him like a wave of pure heartbreak. He felt the stinging of her beatings and afterwards, when she would hide and fear for her life. He caught a picture of her as a child, trying to understand and always running and hiding from strangers, parents and not long ago, from him. The pictures burned into his mind. He quivered as the impact of her sadness, her uncertainty and then her joy and love for him rocked his body. The atmosphere cleared and he sighed deeply. The sharing of so much emotion unconsciously reduced him to tears that streamed down his face.

God! Can even ten lifetimes of joy ever make up for such acts of cruelty towards her? No wonder she thinks she doesn't deserve me or anything I offer her. What a lifetime of unnecessary turmoil!

Opening his eyes, he found her lips and kissed them gently. How he wished, while he was in there, that he could have taken all that horror from her and thrown it out into the universe so that she would never feel hurt again. Yet he knew it was a part of what made her the person she was today.

She was quite pale now and even though there were so many things he was aware of now he knew it was not the time to discuss them. What he did know was that she was still his fragile Cassie and she was still every bit the girl he fell in love with. She had just become more powerful, using her newfound gifts to get her through the tough act. No wonder she was so exhausted. She had nothing left after using so much magic. Then she'd come to him for strength and to draw from his power to rebuild hers. All that time he had thought she was just sick of playing and he was her boring safe harbour.

What a fool I've been, wasting months thinking she never loved me enough and yet all along, I was the one. All this is so that she can toughen up and be with me always, trying to mould herself into the person she thinks I need.

Emotionally unable to articulate the right words, he pulled her into his arms and laid her tired, power-depleted body on the bed. Slipping a pillow under her head and pulling the covers over them both, he just wanted her to rest. She cuddled into him, her body delicately wrapping around his.

'Are you angry now you know I'm not as tough as you thought and it's only magic that gets me through the hard stuff like tonight?' she asked sleepily.

He ran his hand gently up and down her back to relax her. 'Sweetie, I'm not mad but things are going to have to change a bit now that I know. What you did tonight to protect your teammates, your friends and me, were admirable. However to deliberately get the guys to play games with you to desensitise your fears is ludicrous. Games like that only makes me angry and does bugger-all when it comes to toughening you up. It's in your personality to be the way you are and that is who I happen to adore. Quit trying to be someone you're not and let us just love the woman you are.'

'What I want most of all now we're married is for you to help me because nothing I'm doing is working. I've tried so hard, Kayden and I'm done. What you do with me now, even if you take me out of the

Cloud Riders because you think I'm not strong enough in character, is up to you. I just want to be your wife and be the best one I can. Nothing is more important to me.'

Kayden lifted her chin and looked into her drowsy eyes as she battled to keep them open. 'You're not getting kicked out of anything. Right by my side is where I want you and I always have. And I promise that next time you play the heroine I will understand it is all an act and will be right there to catch you when you fall.' He smiled as she touched her lips on his and purred out a thank you. 'Sweet dreams, beautiful,' he whispered as her eyes dropped and sleep claimed her. As for him, it took many hours for him to calm down, unable to control his emotions at what he had uncovered. Cassie's hidden garden that she had taken him into had opened up to him her most precious secrets. He thought of all the nights he anguished over unnecessary issues and yet there it was, so easily staring him in the face: with everything she did, her desire was to try to please him. She lived for him, would die for him and he could clearly see, his woman was just so in love with him.

He watched her angelic features as she slept. The creamy flawless skin, cute button nose, perfectly shaped lips and long lashes swept across her slightly flushed cheeks that still glistened with tears she had shed with him. He kissed them gently, feeling the damp softness and she groaned ever so quietly in her sleep. He knew she felt him and the sides of her mouth quirked up in a little smile. 'You're my angel,' he whispered softly to her. 'All mine. You hear me? Mine,' he squeezed her softly, feeling so happy he could have thrown his hands up and jumped around like a madman. *God, I am so very, very much in love with this woman.*

CHAPTER THIRTY-FOUR

Unit Amusement
(Day Three)

Kayden had gone to see the boys while Cassie got ready for the day. She stood out on the balcony, viewing the city and getting it all straight in her head. She was still a little surprised at Kayden's reaction last night. It didn't matter to him that she was a sook and that she wasn't strong and tough like the other team members. To him she was just Cassie, his mate, his woman, his wife!

She felt on a bit of a high because she didn't have to put on an act anymore. She could just be herself now. No more pretending to be who she was not.

Kayden came up behind her. 'The cars are out front but Conor and Ethan didn't come home last night until a little while ago so the girls aren't happy. They need a minute.'

She smiled when she saw Kayden standing there, holding a wrapped box. 'I went down this morning and brought you a little gift to make you feel better. I was pretty hard on you last night and I hope you'll forgive me.' He looked down at the box. 'I hope you'll like it,' he grinned, pulling the lid off. 'Okay, you have to hold out your arm and close your eyes.'

He clasped a bracelet around her wrist. When she opened her eyes it was an exquisite bracelet with charms of stars, the moon, horses and a heart, each trinket having diamonds, rubies, amethysts or emeralds set into them. They hung delicately off a white gold chain and as she moved her arm, she swore they reminded her exactly of the beauty and array of colours from the sky above. 'It's just perfect. I love it.' She jumped into his arms, hugging him for his thoughtfulness. 'You're so going to have a monster on your hands if you don't stop being this good to me,' she kept grinning, blown away by his sweetness.

'My monster, though.' Cuddling her, he knew he was going to absolutely ruin her from now on and he didn't care if she turned into the most spoilt bitch he'd ever met. He'd love it.

Later, as they waited in the foyer, Conor and Ethan came in looking very submissive as the girls were still giving them a bit of a hard time. The trip into the city was relatively quiet but the mood improved as they all took in the sights along the way. They drove across the famous Sydney harbour bridge getting a good view of the Opera House before fighting their way through the massive twists of the freeways. Cars, buses and trucks muscled their way through the busy streets and on the sidewalk, shops of every kind spilled out. Colourful, fashion-conscious women and men filled the streets. Some gathered at the lights and when they turned green, rushed across, barely looking where they were going as they wrote messages on cell phones or listened to their favourite tunes.

The parks were flourishing and a floral array of blooms gave off fragrances that wafted into the car as they passed them. Cassie even got to see what they meant by road rage which was running rampant the further into the city streets they went. There was honking of horns, frustrated yelling out of car windows, even a fight over a car park. She was entertained both in the car and out on the streets. Once they hit the city she was amazed even more by the compacted beauty of its massively high buildings and their history within. The limo pulled up at the Pavilion where they had lunch. The restaurant, positioned on the edge of the Royal Botanic and Domain Gardens, was picturesque. Later enjoying a stroll in the luxuriant parklands where soft blooms highlighted the walkways and neatly carved bushes made the walk very pleasurable.

The next stop was the Art Gallery, just across the road from the restaurant. Cassie noticed that it featured many Australian, European and Asian artists. There were many she just didn't get.

The guide ignored her with an almost impatient huff as he continued the tour. 'Over this side we have the Australian landscape by John Glover who painted it on his property at Patterdale in 1835.'

Further on she tuned in again, becoming a little more interested.

'Here we have *The Arbour* by Emanuel Phillip Fox which was a lovely garden setting of a family enjoying the outdoors, set in the early Victorian era.' The guide moved them on. 'Last but not least is the Ned Kelly series by Sidney Robert Nolan who found painting the legendary character was a way of painting the Australian landscape in a completely new way.'

Cassie knew art would never be her thing; however, she left with an appreciation for the artists who had worked hard to create masterpieces that would last for many generations to come.

Leaving the gallery, they walked the couple of blocks to get to the Mint. It was located in the historic precinct of Macquarie Street and when they arrived the tour guide told them it was the oldest classically detailed building in Australia.

Cassie was bored looking around and hoped this would be over quickly. She loved to learn but couldn't for the life of her work out why anyone would be interested in gawking at money. 'Man,' she sighed, tapping her foot, impatient to get it underway.

She felt a pat on her shoulder as the guide, seeing her lack of interest, was motioning for her to follow while he continued to talk.

'In the earlier days, money was originally printed on a cotton-based paper that burnt easily when disposed of.' She heard him direct it at her.

Feeling guilty, Cassie made eye contact, grinned and followed the group as the funny little guide with glasses far too big for his head, continued.

'That all changed in the 1960s when Australia was hit by a major forger of the ten dollar note.' The guide nodded at her, looking pleased he had her attention. 'They then came up with the polymer note, now used Australia-wide, which is harder to print but deters criminals from copying them. The other advantage to the notes is that humidity and microbe activity doesn't deteriorate the polymer. It is twice the cost, however last four times longer.'

Okay now he had her attention. *This is kind of interesting.* 'Then if it is a plastic, how is it destroyed when it ages?' Cassie asked.

'Polymer does have its drawbacks, I admit. The black smoke when burnt causes air pollution. The mint gets around this by shredding the old damaged notes into tiny pieces and sending them off to a plastic recycling plant.'

The guide clicked his tongue that made a funny sound at the back of his throat. Cassie turned to hide her grin. The guide hadn't noticed his weird habit and thinking he had lost her attention again, raised his voice. This had Cassie going again and her infectious mood filtered through the group, making them all nudge each other as they too noticed the louder he got the more he made the weird sound.

'The disadvantage of the banknotes—*click click*—was that they found solvents and ultraviolet light—*click click*—deteriorates them but the advantage of it not being easy to forge well outweighs—*click click*—the few negative issues.'

Kayden held himself, shaking the man's hand and staying chatting for a minute while the rest of his team ditched him and split, chuckling and hitting each other as they made their way back to the cars.

Back at the motel, Kayden punished them for being a bad influence on his woman and told them all to get lost for a while. 'We'll catch up with you at the airport the next morning.' He let them know in no uncertain terms they would be on their own until then.

Cassie cuddled into Kayden. 'Yes it was all their fault, honey.'

He smiled lovingly. He was no push over and knew exactly who started it but it was a great excuse to get some time alone with his new wife. 'Sure, sweetheart!' He hugged her back, loving that she put up no protest and wanted to be with just him as well.

Chapter Thirty-Five
Unit Amusement
(Day Four)

They arrived at Margaret River just before lunch the next day in plenty of time for Cassie to organise a special someone to meet them at the local pub.

'Let's stretch our legs and walk,' Jason suggested. Cassie grinned, knowing if he knew what she had planned he'd have practically run there. However, the walk to the township was not as far as she thought and the lodge being nestled among towering Karri trees made the walk along the pathway, pleasurable.

* * * *

Seated and noticing that Jason was busy going over the lunchtime menu, Cassie excused herself when she saw Sonia McMasters arrive. She looked more grownup and stylish in the lilac fitted sundress she wore, than when Cassie first saw her on the beach. The thin straps of the dress over her tanned shoulders highlighted a small butterfly tattoo on the side of her neck. This was accentuated by her light-coloured hair that she had simply swept up into a braided pigtail. Her makeup was sparing, maybe just a bit of lip-gloss and eye makeup; her olive skin needed very little.

She spotted Cassie and pulled her sunglasses up on her head and with her three-inch heels she looked taller than Cassie remembered. Her outfit did her figure justice and combined with her overall appearance and stunning smile, she looked very eye-catching.

Cassie could now see how Jason had seen her. He had looked past the bikini and sea-drenched hair to the woman she now saw. *Men have such an unusual way of being able to see us women — so different from the way we view each other.* Cassie gave her a welcoming hug and they stood chatting as if they'd known each other for years. Cassie felt that it was refreshing to have a female-to-female conversation for a change. Oh sure, Ella had begun to thaw where Cassie was concerned, but Ella was not a girly-girl. Sonia on the other hand was the opposite and didn't stop for a breath and had Cassie giggling at her fun sense of humour. Walking to the table, Cassie noticed that Jason was so busy taking to Ethan about the pub grub he never noticed she had disappeared for a while. He had a little surprised expression as she introduced Sonia around the table and when Cassie got to Jason, she smiled and joked, 'I'm not sure if you'd remember Jason.' Jason grinned as he walked around to Sonia, took her hand, and after greeting her with a kiss on the cheek, he guided her over to sit with him, not once letting her hand go. It was kind of cute and yet so Jason, to be comfortable with a woman he barely knew. She giggled sweetly and Jason smiled so brightly that even Cassie's heart melted at the look he gave her.

They had a nice lunch although the sparks flying next to Cassie were hard to ignore. Jason was charming and entertaining and Sonia enjoyed every minute of him. They decided to go for a walk after lunch.

Turning, Jason winked at Kayden. 'Don't hold up the winery tour, guys, I'm busy.'

Kayden threw him the keys to the hire car. 'Better be there to pick us up at Driftwood Winery, Jase. The rest of the boys look like they've already started to settle in for the day and that's our last stop.'

'Jeez, K, can't you control your damned team for one day? I might have plans.'

'No! And you better not ditch us, buddy.'

Jase snatched the keys and flipping them all off, turned to Sonia. 'Come on, sweetness, we have better things to do than hang out with this riff raff.'

Kayden laughter had him take one last sideways glance, before hustling Sonia out.

'Payback's a bitch!' Woody grinned as Kayden kicked back in his chair, pleased with his plan to irritate Jason, now that he too had found someone he wanted to spend time with had worked.

* * * *

The rest of them drove to Sandalford Winery first. The boys went over the top and bought cases of the wines they liked, having them delivered direct to their ranch up north. Then they were off to Driftwood Winery and sitting up at the old comfortable bar, their journey ended for the day. The atmosphere was enchanting and the bar staff kept them entertained to a point where staying for dinner was just a given, seeing as none of them had any intentions of leaving just yet.

CHAPTER THIRTY-SIX
Designated Driver

A rriving at Driftwood Winery, Jason could hear the rowdy voices of the team as soon as he opened the car door for Sonia. *Man, I could get used to having this babe by my side.* He had nearly had to perform an operation to sever his lips from hers to bring her out for some dinner. He waited as she replaced the gloss he'd kept kissing off her mouth and he promised this time that he would leave her alone. *But hell, I lied.*

He pulled her back into his arms and leaning her up against the car, claimed her mouth just one more time. He pressed up against her, his hardness ready to explode at any moment. The little tease moved gently against him, making him groan and then she giggled. He slapped her backside playfully for stirring him up further but he loved whatever the hell she was doing to him. God! If she was going to feel as good down there as she did while he explored her mouth, there is no way he wanted to make it a quickie. *Hell, no!* He already wanted to spend the rest of his life just kissing her mouth, never mind thinking any further just yet.

He let her go and saw she was just as aroused as he was. Jason smiled at her lovely glowing face. 'I promise I'll leave you alone until after dinner. I have to do this with the team. We only have a couple of nights left of our holiday together and then I am all yours. Okay?'

She grinned all cheeky-like and wrapped her arm around his neck like a child you have just said no to who wants to change your mind. She felt so delightful that he moved her back against the car where he could control it. 'I want you too, sugar, you have no idea how badly I do, but not here and not like this, okay? You mean too much to me to treat you like that. Let me take you to dinner and do it right.'

She sighed and gave him the sweetest smile: the kind of melt-your-heart smile that you want to work for eternity to keep on the face of the angel giving it to you. She lifted her purse and taking out her lip-gloss, applied it perfectly while watching his face. He still had her firmly in his arms and melted into her as he watched her slide it delicately over her lips. 'God, you're so sexy, babe!' he groaned as he ached with desire. He closed his eyes for a minute, feeling her for the last time and then looking back down at her he took her hand, taking her into the winery. For the first time in a very long time, Jason was sober and walked into what he was normally the instigator of. Cassie and Kayden were singing a love song that was playing; Kayden had moved to get her up and waltz to it. They floated around the table, so much in love that there were emitting a magical glow around them. Jason looked to see if the waiters had noticed but they were too busy fussing over the others to even glance at them.

Conor and Ethan had dumped the girls again and were canoodling up to a couple of female guests who had joined their group. There were also a few males who had joined them and one had Ethan's girl up on the dance floor. *Knowing my brother the way I do though, it won't worry him one bit. He likes what he likes until he gets bored. Yep, and tonight he is bored of her and off after another.* Woody also had Ella on the dance floor and Jason had to admit she had really cooled her spiteful nature and tonight they actually looked happy together. Would she fit in? Well, only time would tell but to have the man happy? *Hell, I am willing to give her another go.*

She waved and Woody stopped dancing so they could come over to greet them. 'Sonia,' he smiled and greeted her with a hug as did Ella, making Sonia feel comfortable to be there.

The team noticed that they had arrived and his Sonia, taken from him, passed from one to the next, getting hugs and kisses from the team. *I know they're just making her feel welcome but man do I have a case of the green-eyed monster.* He wanted to just snatch her off them and have her back at his side so bad that he was clenching his fists.

Kayden came up and slapped him on the back. 'It's annoying, hey?'

Jason swung around at him and when he saw the understanding look, he took in a deep breath and calmed down, knowing this was what they had put Kayden though since he met Cassie.

He put his arm around Jason's shoulder. 'Come have a drink, J man. They'll let her come back to you quicker if they see it doesn't bother you.'

Jason shook his head and grinned. 'Ah shytzer. What the hell! I know you're right. I've done it to you enough.' He laughed and Kayden for once, laughed with him.

'I know, you were the worst and now I get to enjoy watching some score settling.'

Chapter Thirty-Seven

Unit Amusement
(Day Five)

Cassie wasn't sure when or how Kayden and she made it to their room but somehow they got into bed and woke up snuggled up to each other. After a hot shower, they felt reasonably good to go. They were being picked up at mid-morning by 'The Wines for Dudes tour' which would take them to three wineries, a brewery, a chocolate factory, a cheese factory and somewhere in the middle, lunch at the Voyager Estate.

Sonia had stayed the night with Jason and after joining them for coffee, he took her home so she could change and join them. He was always a happy little soul but this morning you couldn't wipe the perky happy grin from his face. He was a wee bit besotted!

This was Kayden and Cassie's last day with the team and they intended to enjoy it. Their plane flew out that night and that would get them home well after midnight where they would make their way up to Aquarius to spend the next two magical days together with Aqua and Aldebaran.

Jason had decided he would stay on a couple of extra days with Sonia and her parents.

Woody, Ethan, Conor and their girls were going to drive to Perth. There they were going to spend a couple of days at the casino so that the girls could do a bit of shopping. As Kayden said there was no reason for them all to rush back when they still had two more days.

The tour was a great finish to their holiday. Driving through the prettiest green paddocks with mostly black and white cows was a complete change to the brown and black cows up north. She wondered if these magnificent beasts were the producers of the wholesome milk, used in making the very tasty full range of Margaret River cheeses they had just eaten. The creamy or sharp explosions in her mouth as the samples hit her tastebuds made for an unusual and very pleasant experience. Bumping along the road, they came to the chocolate factory. Cassie was expecting a *Willy Wonka*-like experience and was only slightly disappointed until they had sat down, ordered coffee and the first delicious treat popped into her mouth. That was the end of her then! She was in seventh heaven. Conor and Ethan dipped their chocolates in their coffee and made a disgusting mess; however it gave them all a good laugh. Arming themselves with one of their flavoured ice creams and bags of the divine mouth-watering chocolates, they hopped back on the bus.

The tour finished way too quickly. Or did the day magically shorten? Cassie was sad when it was over as this was now when they all had to part ways.

Packed and ready to leave, they all stood around saying their goodbyes as they parted ways. Woody held her for a very long time before she left. They had an attachment none of the others would ever understand. 'See you in a couple of days, Cass,' he smiled. 'I miss you already,' he whispered before he let her go.

'Ditto,' she said, wiping the tears from her eyes.

Ella just hugged Cassie and chuckled. 'Honestly, you two! You would think you're not going to see each other for months!'

Woody wrapped his arms around both of them. 'My girls.' He kissed them both, chuckling.

Ella slapped him. 'You'll get "my girls" when I'm finished with you! Get out of here, she's our girl,' she joked with him, giving Cassie one last hug. 'Come back safe,' she said. 'He'll be impossible to live with if you don't.'

That, on its own finished off the day perfectly. *Ella and I have become friends.* Cassie was now looking forward to seeing her when she finished her holiday and felt a happy glow as they drove way.

It was late when they arrived home and exhausted from the trip, went straight to bed. Next morning Tremaine knocked on the door as they were having breakfast to let Kayden know he had just checked the horses and as requested, Zoltan and Starburst were in the barn. He was in a hurry to go milk the cows but told Kayden he would keep an eye on the horses until the boys came back from Perth.

Kayden gave him a thick envelope full of cash. He paid him very well to care for their prize horses and Cassie wondered if Tremaine ever questioned why. Even though he was Conor's brother, Tremaine would have no idea just how vitally important they really were.

CHAPTER THIRTY-EIGHT

Constellation Aquarius

Putting Cassie on the horse for the first time in months, Kayden's heart pounded. For such a long time it had been Woody helping her and at first he'd told himself he didn't give a damn and would trot off without waiting for them. Nevertheless, his heart ached. She was letting another do something that always gave him such pleasure.

To watch her transform was indescribable. If he said it nearly made him weep to see such beauty would be closer to the feeling. Not to do it was ten times worse and the pit of his stomach would twist with hatred for Woody. *Yet, how can I blame him when it is my fool fault for letting her go? My job! Mine at last and mine forever.* He picked up her hand and kissing it, put the reins into them like old times and smiled happily. Kayden felt a burst of power surge from his excitement at being with Cass again and doing a somersault, he flew through the air on a high and landed on Zoltan. He always disciplined the boys when they did that. *But hell, they're not here to see.*

They arrived on Aquarius at mid-morning. Kayden hadn't expected such a huge water park. It was many times bigger than any he had ever seen.

Aquarius had never had the need for the Cloud Riders; therefore this was Kayden's first visit. He grinned, realising now why she had never needed them. With Aqua being Aldebaran's girlfriend he'd never allow anything to happen to one of his friends, never mind his girlfriend. Aqua was very lucky that she had such power overseeing her world. Many others were not so lucky, especially the ones Aldebaran called his enemy.

Kayden took a deep breath and cleared out his thoughts, putting work aside. This was a honeymoon for Cassie and he wanted her to enjoy it. He had to see Aldebaran as her father and not his enemy for the time being. He had grown to trust Cassie's instincts and something told him she would work this out with him later when she was ready.

The servants took the horses and Kayden noticed that her father was now outside Aqua's castle waiting for them.

'Here goes then, good and evil under one roof. I must be in love,' he joked as he took her hand and they walked over to him.

Aqua was also standing with him and waved to Cass, looking excited. They were keeping good their promise to spend time with them there. As they neared, Cassie couldn't wait a second longer and let go of his hand to run to Aldebaran's arms like a child. With his arms outstretched, he snatched her up, swinging her around and laughing.

Kayden had to bite his lip with the reflected emotion she surged through to him. It is one of the many pleasures of being linked to her, Kayden thought as he watched their joy in seeing each other and wondered what her life would have been like if her father had been allowed access to her. It was endearing. And in that moment he wished to the heavens above that Aldebaran's eyes would be opened; that he would never destroy the love she offered so freely.

Cassie stood back next to Kayden, pointing out the slides in the park she most enjoyed. 'I'm sure Aqua has added some new ones,' she looked about. 'Watch this!' She slipped off her clothes, revealing a pair of blue bathers the same bright colour as her eyes. 'Pretty cool, hey? You try it.' She came over, helping him take off his top, she was so eager to get going.

Kayden grinned at her impatience. She already had his fly undone and as he slipped them down, she was right: black board shorts magically appeared.

'Whatever you're around, your clothes just seem to know. I've even noticed they change colour under certain conditions. Last time I was here the magic dressed me in a golden one piece,' she responded to his amazed look, pulling him by the hand to join her. The boys and he had removed their clothes before but only for a roll in the hay with a lassie. He guessed the magic must just know when they wanted them off completely or when they needed them replaced. Or was this another of Cassie's powers that she was passing on to them? *No doubt it is.*

'Come on, old man,' she called out to Aldebaran just before she dove in.

Kayden was still laughing when he hit the water. He couldn't believe she would call the most powerful man in the universe an old man. Her dad was on her heels and she was laughing as he came up holding her. Aldebaran winked at Kayden before throwing her high in the air towards him. She squealed with delight and hugged Kayden tightly as he caught her.

For the next few hours Kayden and Aldebaran were dragged around the circuit by Kayden's playful little kitten as she jumped from him to her father, keeping them both on their toes as they never quite knew which one she would throw herself at next. She trusted them both completely and Kayden began to trust her father with her as well. Who would believe a cranky and bad-tempered wizard unable to even converse with them on any level because he was generally so moody could be such a gentle soul? His love for her was so raw it was visible in every look, every movement. When he held her it was as if he held a delicate artefact, one that might break if held too tight. Yet he held her with a passion that no man would ever be able to pry her from his hands unless he let her go. She was right. He would have been a good father with every ounce of his being. That was what he was right now.

When they got out, Kayden held a towel for her and she came over for a cuddle, sitting on his lap while they talked to Aldebaran and Aqua. Kayden watched Aldebaran with Cassie chatting and laughing together. It was easy to see that he meant more to her than

Kayden had originally thought, and her, him. This was no game to him at all. Kayden would have picked that up in a minute. No—her dad was genuine, yet it was beyond him how in a couple of days he would put aside what was now so obvious—all this love—and take up arms against her, putting her in such danger.

Kayden figured all he could do was sit back and let it all unfold. He knew this girl-woman would never join her father and walk on the side of evil. He knew her too well. Therefore, in the end, this would be about what he would be prepared to lose his daughter or Orion's Belt, the section of the universe he and Conom fought to take over.

Aqua put on a lovely spread of delicious treats that Kayden knew were all Cassie's favourite foods and after they sat and enjoyed the afternoon, chatting and getting to know one another. It was Cassie who made the first move, getting up and stretching. Aldebaran suggested that Kayden take her for a rest before dinner. Aqua took them inside to show them where the guest room was.

The main room to her palace was dazzling to say the least. It was light and airy and glistened the same as the water outside. The walls were a pale blue and the floor was a highly polished white tile. On the tiles were large, sky-blue plush carpet squares where elegant white leather lounges and recliners had been placed, maybe to prevent scratching the high-gloss tiles.

The guest room was unique. The walls were the same blue as the rest of the rooms, only the roof was dark blue. Hundreds of tiny down lights lit up the ceiling depicting the many constellations in the sky. The luxuriously oversized bed had a star-shaped bed head and the veiling that surrounded it had little golden stars embroidered into the netting. Positioned under the bed was a massive star-shaped rug that you sank into so deep that it gave you the impression you were walking on a cloud. The furniture was pure white, including the leather two-seater that sat against royal blue drapes, drawn so you could see the water park from the private balcony.

They went to clean up in a light, marble-textured en suite that had silver and blue star taps and mirrors.

They cuddled on the bed. Cassie was totally in love with the room, saying what a nice person Aqua was and how comfortable she was making her feel. He ran his hand down her back until she dozed off. He wondered if his home was really enough for her but not once had she ever said she missed all the finery she grew up with. He was never one for material possessions and never had been but if she wanted more, he hoped that she knew he would give it to her. *Hell, I would give her the goddamned universe if it was mine to give.* He finally drifted off, letting the worries of what he had compared to her new friends in the sky drift away. He held all he needed in his arms. The rest, they could work out together after their honeymoon was over.

One of the maidens knocked, came in and woke them for dinner. They showered and made their way down. They both laughed as their clothes changed with the influence of the room. Cassie now wore a light-blue evening gown with silver stars embossed into the material. Even her silver heels had stars on them. Kayden's shirt was white with buttons the shape of stars. His dinner jacket had a hanky in the pocket that matched Cassie's dress. He was so glad the magic didn't give him bloody stars on his shoes! He doubted he would live that down if the guys ever heard about it.

They were ushered into the dining room where Kayden danced his delightful wife around as they waited for her father.

'Hi Pops.' Cassie made Kayden aware they weren't alone.

Aldebaran also looked refreshed so they assumed he and Aqua must have rested as well. He was so different in looks to Cassie and yet Kayden knew by just talking to him how alike they were. She was a blond-haired, blue-eyed beauty, delightfully petite with a scrumptious figure and yet still so fragile. He was a thickset bloke with a build more like a rugby player, as strong as an ox. His hair was dark and his eyes were so black they looked evil unless he looked at Cassie. It was then that they changed to an indigo blue with traces of the same sapphire shade she had in her eyes. Then and only then could he see any similarities. The love he carried for her was strong and any dumb fool could see that he absolutely adored her. The more Kayden saw them together, the harder he knew it was going to be for both of them on the battlefield. *Will I lose my only love, or will he?*

As they dined, Kayden and Cassie told stories of their holiday so far, enjoying the mood that the day had put them in, although unsure as they staggered up to bed how they could have ended up so inebriated, when they barely had anything to drink.

Aldebaran practically carried Cassie to the bedroom. She staggered and sang songs, telling her father he was good fun for an old boy. He laughed at her all the way up the stairs, not once taking offence to any of her kidding. In fact, he loved it. Aldebaran whispered goodnight to her as she closed her eyes and dropped off to sleep.

Chapter Thirty-Nine

Aldebaran takes Control

Before Aldebaran left the room, he looked back at them. Kayden was hugging his daughter so gently and she, with such love in her body language, cuddled into him. They were perfect for each other and he couldn't take one without the other, so both it would have to be. He needed to have more time with his daughter and he was determined he was going to have it.

Taking them up to bed, he had thought Kayden was going to pass out even before he made it to the bed. With all the booze mixed with the magic potion he had drunk, Aldebaran was surprised he'd even made it. He should've known Kayden wouldn't give in unless Cassie was in his arms. His love and protectiveness of her was admirable and because of that he had earned a father's respect and his daughter's hand. He had given it freely to him but to none of those other creeps he worked for. *Them, I still want out of the way! Permanently!*

Aqua had argued with him for days but he wouldn't give in. Tonight was the night.

'They'll wake up tomorrow in a trance and won't be leaving until I'm ready to let them go.'

He thought back to the night when Cassandra had first told him of her terrible childhood. He hadn't believed her at first. He was devastated that she would disrespect her mother, the woman he had loved like no other. Then he had looked into Cassie's eyes and deep down into her soul. He could see the tortured scars she carried, open wounds that still needed healing, scars only a father's love could really help heal. He hated his ex for the first time ever for what she'd allowed her husband to do to Cassandra—to him! He knew in that instant he would take revenge on the people who did this to her. *And my God, she will pay for lying to me and hurting my sweet, adorable daughter.*

Aldebaran went back downstairs to a very nervous old friend.

'Ald, they're under my care. When their friends come looking for them what do I say?' she asked.

'That they left and you haven't seen them since.' He rolled his shoulders, releasing some of the stress he was feeling. 'Tomorrow, I'll take them to my castle for dinner. Because they're under my control, they'll agree happily. I'd take them now but I'd prefer to keep them here just one more day in case something goes wrong and they come looking for Kayden earlier.'

'Why is she so important to you that you would risk having your star put out or your kingdom gone? This is insane,' she argued. 'Am I not enough, Ald? Please,' she sobbed, tears running down her cheeks.

He went over and held her, the look of sadness and fear stared back at him. 'You know how I feel about you, Aqua love, but she's my daughter. I just want a little while to get to know her, to have her close and love her the way she deserves to be loved by a father. I'm sorry if you don't understand that.'

'But to kidnap them, even for a day? She'll never forgive you and you'll spend the rest of your life regretting that you may have been able to freely see her more often.'

'Aqua, the last few months just watching her from afar has been killing me. I'm their enemy. She won't be allowed to come back to see me again after this visit and you know it, just like last time. Kayden is smart and I know he will make her break all ties with me when they get back to business. He really has no other choice. I would do the same. He's done this for her to make her wedding special, that's all. You only have to look at the guy with her to see he would give her the moon if it were his to give.' He sighed, went over and poured a nightcap. 'Aqua, don't fight me anymore on this. I'm tired and need you. Just give me the chance to get to know my little girl, please.'

Aldebaran felt worn out trying to convince her. If she fought any further, it would give him no other choice but to go up and take them now and she knew it. The ball was in her court. Aqua stood for a minute and he waited to see if she really did care for him. Did he have her loyalty as a friend? He was begging her and she knew it was not easy for him to have to ask for help. She walked over, slipped her arms around him and kissed him sweetly. He knew she had given in. He grabbed her and returned the love she deserved. *She's my woman and I'm glad she's chosen to stay that way.*

Before they retired, he went in to check on them to make sure they were okay and that the potion he had given them was not harming their fragile, earthy bodies.

In the morning they both came downstairs hand-in-hand. Aldebaran put his book down to say good morning. They both acted laid-back so he knew the spell had worked. From today they would get up every morning until he decided otherwise, with no other thought but to enjoy the day. Time would be of no interest to them and their old life, for now, was a foggy nothing. *They'll believe whatever I want them to.* This afternoon he'd be taking them home with him.

Feeling a twinge of guilt for deceiving them this way, he coughed and fidgeted but thankfully it was just a fleeting thought and was soon gone. He couldn't think of any other way to keep them a bit longer.

The only drawback was that Orion was still out there annoying the hell out of him and he would have to refrain from any kind of retaliation for the time being. Yes, he considered thoughtfully as he took a sip of coffee, to continue the war will only bring the Cloud Riders to my doorstep before I'm ready to give her up. Even though they wouldn't believe him at first, his performance that he would have to work on would make it look like he had nothing to do with their disappearance. *To convince them further I'll offer my services to search relentlessly.*

After hugging Cassandra before she sat down for breakfast, his heart was bursting with the sound of waking up to her chatter. *The years I've wondered how this would feel and now it is here. I've missed so much, but no more!* She was telling him how magical her room was and Aldebaran was glad Aqua had also assisted him with the decorating of her room in his home. In fact, since her first visit he'd made major renovations to the castle, hoping that one day she would visit again and maybe want to stay a while. He never dreamed that it would be so soon.

While they chatted together Aldebaran went over his plans, making sure he hadn't missed anything that would remind them of their past. He had even taken their horses to his home world and hidden them. He knew that if Kayden or Cassandra mounted the magical beasts the horses might be able to break the spell. He sighed, hoping he hadn't left anything out and frowned at the same time as Cassandra seemed uninterested in breakfast. He had noted she just drank a coffee and was instead itching to go out and have some fun instead. She was nagging at Aldebaran to hurry up with the breakfast thing so they could go back out to the water park and not waste the day.

He shook his head as he stood up. She was like an excited child and her eyes flashed and glistened playfully as she spoke. Kayden was no help: he just glowed with love and was ready to pick her up and run with her if Aldebaran didn't agree. He could see he was going to have his hands full trying to give her any kind of fatherly discipline. She playfully grabbed him with one hand and reaching out to Kayden with the other, kissed both on their cheeks. Her innocence always put a tingle through him as her lips touched his skin and yet she never once seemed to feel his evil, even from their first meeting.

Aqua joined them and all three were spellbound with Cassandra as she had them laughing and enjoying every minute of the park's wonderment. They had a light lunch and sat back in the chairs, chatting. It had been a couple of hours since lunch so Aldebaran took that opportunity to suggest to Kayden that they take Cassandra home to his house for a rest before dinner. He was relieved when he agreed without question.

Cassandra hugged Aqua like she was leaving an old friend and he could see Aqua was quite chuffed to have made such an impression on her. He put his arms around both of them and transported them to his home star.

He had arranged for a few guests to come over for dinner. Feeling so proud of his new family, he wanted his friends to meet Cassandra and her new husband. The castle was still being prepared and wishing to surprise them, he took them straight to their room for some time alone.

The dinner party was being held in the newly renovated ballroom and the designers were just finishing it off. Aqua had been a shining star in his planning as she helped him make his castle into somewhere a young lady would be happy to be. He waited downstairs for the happy couple to come down after sending the servants to wake them up. He knew they had barely slept much on their holiday so they'd still be playing catch up.

He heard Kayden's voice first and spun around to see him twirling her around and pulling her in for a quick kiss before heading down the stairs. Yes, magic was in the air tonight. Once they reached the bottom of the stairs he noticed their clothes had changed again. Tonight, Cassandra had on a gorgeous little cocktail dress that had layers to the skirt and spun out sweetly as Kayden twirled her around and danced with her to the music that was quietly wafting through the castle from the band in the ballroom. My friends are going to love them, he thought as he watched them. When they reached him he was surprised that Kayden swung her to him and he took her warm sweet hand in his and waltzed with her for a minute before sending her back to her man. Her eyes were alive and she smiled so angelically he wondered how he was ever going to set free an angel such as her.

At least that was a thought he needn't dwell on tonight but he knew only too well that if they weren't under a spell, tomorrow he would have to be saying goodbye. *And for the life of me I can't have that happen just yet.*

He took them both into the ballroom first and the precious expression that spread across Cassandra's face as it lit up made all the tiresome planning and renovating so worth it. The long dining table in the middle of the room was fully set with silver, crystal glasses and fine china. The six, twenty-piece candleholders were alight and arranged along the table. The flicker of the flames danced around the room, reflecting in the mirrored walls and picking up the colours in the crystal chandeliers overhead. The floor, instead of being slate, now resembled a highly polished dance floor and the band was set up on the new stage that he would now use often to bring in entertainment for Cassandra's amusement while she was his guest.

Big French doors took up one side of the room: these were now open and led out into the entertaining deck where you could view the twenty-metre pool, complete with waterfall and spa. It was all set in a tropical paradise that had green and blue spotlights strategically placed so they shone up on the lush vegetation and palm trees. He had enclosed the pool area to assist with the plant growth but tonight the auto roof was pulled back so they could view the real stars above. It was also the first time he had seen it lit up. He was impressed with the designers. They had excelled themselves and he would reward them well for the results.

'I don't remember the castle looking so enchanting, Pops. I barely remember what it looked like before but I'm sure I would have remembered this,' she grinned.

'After your last visit you loved the water at Aqua's so much I thought I might put in a pool for you when you visited me next. The ballroom was just Aqua's extra touch to give us all somewhere to dance when I throw my parties. I'm glad you approve.'

Lamar the butler came out to let Aldebaran know the guests were arriving. Not wanting to leave his friends unattended, he went to greet them, leaving his daughter and son-in-law to soak up and enjoy the new surrounds. He had only just finished introducing Cassandra and Kayden to the couples who had arrived early, when Conom arrived with his entourage. Aldebaran was excited for them to meet his closest friend. Conom looking surprised and a little amused when introduced to Cassandra. He took Aldebaran aside.

'I can't believe you, Ald! You have her under a spell,' he hissed.

Aldebaran shook his head as he stood. 'What do you mean?

Have you lost your mind man?' he growled, trying to act innocent.

'Ald, it just so happens I played cards with this little minx just a few days ago and she is very intelligent. And believe me she would have remembered me for what I put her through.' Conom looked annoyed that Aldebaran was hiding something.

Conom had caught him out so he dragged him away from prying ears. 'Okay maybe just a little one so I can have a few extra days with her. Can you blame me? I'm her father for Christ's sake. I just need a bit more time with her. Why is that so hard to understand? I've copped it for days from Aqua. Not you too!'

Conom shook his head and smiled. 'Okay, settle down, big guy. Yes, I understand but with this playful little soul you may be biting off more than you can chew. She's a bit of a handful.'

Aldebaran couldn't believe that Conom had already met his daughter. What were the odds she was talking about Conom when she told him about the card game she'd played in Sydney? 'I'm still getting my head around you being Mono. She told me about your game but I never connected the name. I can only imagine what it would have been like with you two at it. Neither of you would have liked to lose. And yes I agree she can be quite a handful and quite ruthless when it comes to winning.'

'Ald,' he said quietly. 'She came across as the hottest hottie I'd ever met and she was lucky I didn't kidnap her myself. I had a hard time not getting up and kissing that sexy mouth. I am sorry if that offends you but she was something else. I've been in lust with her ever since and yet looking at her now, butter wouldn't melt in her mouth. I find it hard to believe the two are the same girl.'

Aldebaran threw his head back and laughed. 'You keep your devious little hands off my daughter.'

Conom put his hands up in a submissive gesture. 'Hey man, well warned but you can't stop me having fun with her. She's a blast. What's big lug hubby like when he's not plotting against us?'

'The son-in-law I always dreamed for her. You'll like him, Conom, give him a chance. Okay?'

He patted him on the back. 'For you, I will try and that's all I can promise. But hey, good luck with the rest of it because I wouldn't want to be you when she wakes up from this spell.'

Aldebaran looked at him seriously. 'When this is all over and I send them home, Kayden will make her break all ties with me like last time, regardless of what I do here today. So I hope you're right, old friend and she does challenge me because it will be better than never hearing from her again.' He looked around and saw them both getting into the star starters. 'You'll have to excuse me. The kids are getting into it early and if I don't slow those two down you'll be seeing a lot more of the Cassandra you saw the other night.' Aldebaran grinned as he walked away.

Conom laughed. 'Bring it on, I say! This place could do with a bit of livening up.'

He is so much like me, just wanting excitement in his life. Aldebaran would normally agree with him but this was different. This was his daughter who had pushed his buttons and he could feel himself change the minute he looked into her eyes. He magically felt so much older and now wanted to be the best father he could be to her.

He went over and Kayden passed him a slammer. 'Come on, Dad, join us?' he asked, stirring Aldebaran and waiting for him to slam and raise his glass with them. Aldebaran was so shocked that he called him Dad that he slammed with them and drank it down. Cassandra put her glass down and passed him a Moonjuice and he sculled that as well.

'Go Pops,' she giggled. He shook his head and smiled. 'Now, you two, go mingle. You won't last the night at this rate,' he chastised them and watched as they laughed like two naughty kids and wandered off, chatting to the guests.

Aqua finally arrived with the twins Gem and Mini from the Gemini constellation. Conom was quite partial to both girls and unable to decide between them, generally left with both. Cassandra was excited to see a face she knew and walked around with Aqua and the twins as they went from guest to guest, mingling.

Meanwhile, Aldebaran noticed Kayden talking to Pollux and Caster, the rulers of two of the larger stars in the Gemini constellation, both bodyguards to the twins, Gem and Mini. They were safely engaged in a conversation with Kayden, discussing growing their Gemini group and the politics they faced in trying to bring new baby stars (undeveloped protostars) into their domains to grow and develop them within the guidance of their constellation. Kayden had lots of knowledge on this subject and Aldebaran could tell he was enjoying himself.

When it was time to sit down for dinner it was obvious that Conom was looking to finish off that card game but he was going to get her good and plastered first. During the meal he constantly filled Cassandra and Kayden's drinks. The three of them became quite noisy, joking and hanging it on each other. By the time the meal was over, Conom had them both in the palm of his hand as they took their party out by the pool.

When Aldebaran finally made it outside to them, Cassandra jumped up happily, slipping her arm through his. 'Hi Pops, we haven't seen you all night. Great party!'

He looked over at Conom who had a smug look, knowing he was checking up on him. Aldebaran glared at him to behave and just smiled at Cassandra. *This is what I want: her to be happy, and while she is, I see no reason to interfere.* 'Glad you're having a good time, sugar. Just came out to see if you needed anything.'

'No, we're good. Conom here is keeping us entertained with his travel adventures.'

Being called back inside, he left them to their fun. Not without his own tricks though, once inside he gestured for the band to play louder and it was not long before Kayden had Cassie up dancing. Sniggering at Conom and getting the finger from him, he sat back to watch as Kayden brought his new bride onto the floor. *I won this round.*

A more up-tempo number began to play and the two of them started to jive. Conom couldn't help himself. He sneakily invited Aqua onto the dance floor and then changed partners with Kayden to win round two.

Little twerp, grinning his arse off at me, Aldebaran thought as

Conom whipped Cassandra away, spinning her around and making her enjoy his attention. Everything was a game with Conom but he guessed if Kayden wasn't concerned about the attention Conom gave to Cassandra then he should stop being an over-protective dad and let them just enjoy the party. Aqua seemed to take pleasure in Kayden's company as well. Contented that at last the night had turned out well, he turned to get another drink and enjoy the rest of his evening.

At the end of the night when most of the guests had left, he found Cassandra, Kayden and Conom sitting around a table near the pool playing cards. Conom needed to play Cassandra and beat her to keep his pride intact and they had only just started. He decided to sit in.

'What's the bet, Cassie?' Conom asked. 'A win is no fun without a reward.'

'Well,' she said smiling. 'I haven't any money on me or any possessions worth betting against so what about the winner gets to throw the loser in the pool and they have to do ten laps before they can sit back at the table and play again?'

'Very innovative! But if you were to lose—which you will,' Conom grinned, 'It'll be a boring old game until you join us again.'

'Okay, what about the winner gets to choose a day's activity and the ones that lose have to go along with it, regardless?'

'That sounds more entertaining. You have yourself a deal!'

Cassie gave Kayden a questioning look and seeing he was fine with it, agreed with the terms.

At the end of the round, Conom and Cassandra were even. This was the final hand and the decider. Aldebaran had never known anyone to beat Conom and he could tell he was pissed off and trying to hide it. She stirred him up and rubbed it in every time she won. To his credit, Kayden did try to discipline her although he enjoyed her so much it was a half-hearted effort. It didn't matter what she did, he loved every minute of it. Aldebaran did too. He had waited a long time for Conom to meet his match and tonight he had.

He grinned, thinking of how much trouble Conom had gone to, getting her onside and then filling her with drink to ensure his win. He wondered if Conom would be beating her if she were sober. Conom insisted on a star starters before the last hand and Kayden grabbed the bottle, getting them lined up. This last drink would do Kayden in, Aldebaran thought until he saw Kayden wink at Cassandra. He realised that Kayden was still able to keep up and maybe they were playing the player.

This was going to be interesting, seeing if they let Conom win. If they did, it would be to enjoy his company for another day. His kids were playing Conom and all of a sudden he felt proud of them for being able to hold their own against a warlord like Conom. He had been worried all night that he was up to no good. Yet here they were; they had read him like a book and were having just as much fun back at him.

Cassandra touched Kayden's face, smiled and threw her hand in, letting Conom win.

Conom, finally pleased, stood up to leave. 'Well that's it for me. I'm calling it a night.' He stretched and downed the last of his drink on the table. 'I'll organise a day of pleasure. Well, it will be for me anyway, watching you guys squirm,' he grinned slyly.

He lifted Cassandra's hand and kissed it. 'Until then. It's been a pleasure, Cassie. Kayden.' He smiled, and nodded at Kayden next. Then he went inside and his entourage followed him as he left the castle.

Aldebaran picked up Cassie's cards she had thrown in. 'You let him win! Why?'

She shrugged. 'Well, technically we were the winners. Now we get to have some more fun with him another day.' She smiled, putting out her hand to Kayden.

'Are you ready to retire, beautiful?' he asked sweetly as she leaned into him.

'Excellent party, Pops. We're off to get some shuteye.'

'Sleep tight, Cassandra.'

This was getting very complicated and Aldebaran sat up with Aqua, trying to make sense of the way he was feeling. He was having second thoughts, unsure whether he could go through with his devious plan to keep them there against their will. He knew now how caring Kayden was with her and really, she was the happiest she'd ever been in her life. It was then that it suddenly dawned on him that in the end he would be the one to make her miserable when she found out he couldn't be trusted. Another parent disloyal to her!

His heart ached for the damage he might have caused with his selfishness.

He went up to their room and watched them sleep for a very long time. Then with a conscience ready to explode, he took the spell from them. He knew he had been wrong and that in the morning he was going to have to fess up and beg their forgiveness. In just two days they had taught him so much about family values and he hoped they would not turn their backs on him as they had on her mother.

Chapter Forty
Family Secrets

C assie woke up in Kayden's arms and tried to remember the night before. She had really tried one on at the party and wondered how they ended up in bed. Everything was a little fuzzy. She knew they had ended up at her father's and she looked around the room, admiring how much effort he had gone to making the place so nice for their holiday with him.

Kayden woke and said he felt a bit weird as well. 'I think we'd better dry out today,' he decided. 'We've just been drinking far too much, that's all.'

He suggested they go for a swim before breakfast to clear their heads. So as not to wake everyone they slipped downstairs quietly and out into the pool. The spa water was warm, inviting and felt like a bubbly hot bath. Lamar brought them coffee and as they sipped it they tried to remember how they ended up here when they were meant to be holidaying on Aquarius. Cassie was also amazed at all the renovations that had taken place since her last visit.

'He would have done all this for you, Cass. He knows how much you love the water.'

'Yes, I think he has.'

'We're meant to go home today, Cass but if you wanted to stay an extra couple of days to make your dad happy, seeing he's gone to so much trouble, then it's okay with me.'

'What about Zoren and work?'

'If there's any trouble, Woody will let us know. We have our horses so we can just meet up with them at the location where we're meant to be.'

Aldebaran finally came out, looking really worn out and waved to them.

'We better go see what's up.' Cassie grabbed a towel each for them to dry themselves off as they walked inside.

He was sitting having a coffee and staring into space. Aqua was beside him, holding his hand as if she was comforting him.

'Is everything okay, Pops?' Cassie asked. He put his head down. Caringly, Cassie went over and pulled up a chair next to him. 'What's happened? Tell me,' she said, reaching for his hand. He pulled it away.

He coughed as if words were choking him. 'What I'm about to tell you is going to make you hate me, Cassandra and God knows my intention was never to hurt you. I couldn't lie to you anymore.'

Kayden came and sat by her, putting his arm around her and bracing for bad news. If the bastard hurts her, I'm taking her away and never letting him see her again, Kayden thought angrily.

Aldebaran started from the beginning and when he finished telling them what he'd done, his eyes were red and his face was long and full of remorse. He gulped back his emotions and hung his head, disgusted with his little plan to kidnap them both.

Cassie stood up with tears stinging her eyes and walked outside. She needed a minute to cool off and discuss this with Kayden. She was too upset to think logically and needed him alone so they could discuss her bonehead of a father.

Kayden sat by the pool with her. 'Honey, we both knew what Aldebaran was capable of doing. But to confess when he didn't need to, has me a little rattled. In just two days, your love for him has made him turn a corner. He could have kept us here for months and we would have been none the wiser. Yes, his motives were selfish and he had to know I would never let him see you again. It was a crazy move and a big risk to take.'

Cassie calmed down and started to see the big picture. She

finally had a parent who loved her and now she was feeling a bit overwhelmed. Together they thrashed out all the logic in the world— why they should just leave— but their hearts were pulling them in another direction. He had gone to great expense to stop his fighting for them while they went on a honeymoon and was willing to stop any fighting while they were with him. Then there was the remodelling of his castle for Cassie so she would feel happier in these surroundings and his grief at hurting her was just so evident. They came to an agreement and walked back inside.

Kayden spoke for both. 'What you did was very underhanded and stupid to say the least, Aldebaran. If you had gone ahead with it, not only Cassie but I too would never have forgiven you. We trusted you. Your daughter trusted you. Yet you intended to throw that away like it is nothing to you?'

Aldebaran had his head down and was so upset that Cassie could feel the stress from where she stood. She wanted to go to him but Kayden held her firmly. He needed a dressing-down and knew she was too soft to do it.

Kayden continued. 'I just wish you'd understood the hardship your daughter has endured to get herself to this point. However, confessing to us has made us see our relationship might still be salvageable if you can promise me that such foolishness never enters your head again. I'll not have Cassie upset or hurt by you or anyone else! She has had enough hurt and if you want her in your life you have to stop this madness. She's not a toy or a game to play. She is your daughter and my wife. If you cannot promise to just love her and make that enough for you then we are leaving now.'

He met Kayden's eyes with sincerity. 'Don't go! Don't take my little girl away,' he pleaded.

Kayden looked at him, frowning. 'For the life of me I can't figure out what madness made you think I would never bring her to see you again. I would never upset her that way. I had asked her to give it time before she saw you again only because she was so distraught when she came home last time. She had bonded with you so strongly in just that short time that she sobbed deeply having to leave you. It has been her choice, due to you both fighting on opposite sides, to break ties with you, not mine. For goodness sake, Aldebaran, why didn't you just talk to me about it? From now on you damned well better!'

Aldebaran looked miserable. 'I thought you had only included me to make Cassandra happy on her wedding day and that you only brought her here because we kind of roped you into being here, not because you really wanted to.'

Kayden shook his head. 'I'm here not only for Cassie but because you were like her in so many ways. I wanted to get to know you better as a father-in-law. That was why I came. Just this morning we had been discussing staying on an extra couple of days because we were actually enjoying ourselves. This was meant to be a family vacation. What we do as Cloud Riders and those politics should never have entered into this, Aldebaran.'

'I know. And I feel a real idiot, Kayden. I didn't know you then but I have come to know you and that's why I couldn't go through with it. I can't believe I've blown everything because of my stupidity.'

'Before I take this any further I need you to be totally upfront with us. I need to know everything because we both now remember that Conom was the man Cassie played cards with to get our friends out of trouble. Is he just another setup, Aldebaran?'

'No.' He shook his head. 'Definitely not! Conom, as far as I can tell, really does like you both and just loves a challenge.'

Kayden believed him and let Cassie's hand go. It was her turn now to sort it out with her dad and show him what a family was all about and what it meant to be a part of one. Lies, cheating and deceit had to stop right here, right now. She ran her hand through her hair, another nervous trait she shared with her father. With a sweet grin she held out her hand to him. 'Maybe it's time we both threw self-doubt aside and replaced it with a little trust. And maybe somehow we may put the pieces of a life we should have had, back together.' She looked at her father and smiled.

He grinned back, knowing what she meant to him and willing to give anything a go just so long as he had her in his life. Aldebaran's eyes were misty with unshed happiness that Cassie was going to give him a second chance. He hugged her before moving over to Kayden and offering his hand apologetically. He had barely finished saying sorry when he pulled Kayden in for a group hug with them both.

It was much later that Aldebaran worked up the courage to ask if they would stay a couple more days. The more he drank the cockier he got and his nagging at Kayden finally worked. Kayden grinned, giving in and Pops was delighted. He squeezed them both and even called Kayden 'son'.

Kayden and Cassie excused themselves to give Kayden time to contact his team and let them know the change of plans and what he wanted them to do in the meantime. Kayden used Zoltan and his own power combined to send them a message telepathically, letting Woody know he was to continue in charge until he returned and to let him know the minute there was a problem. He asked Woody to get Tremaine to check Mother as she was nearly due to have another of Zoltan's foals. Kayden said the boys were just as good with the horses as Tremaine but Tremaine had delivered many calves and foals on his ranch and was better to have around Mother in her condition. Cassie always smiled when he call Zoltan's playmate 'Mother'. Kayden had explained that Zoltan would not service any other mare.

'Even Zoren has no answer for Zoltan's strange behaviour,' Kayden added.

'He's just in love with Mother then? That is so cute,' Cassie smiled.

Kayden confided that Zoltan only bred when there was a need for more horses. 'I have a feeling Zoren may have a need for another team in the future as we have plenty to replace ours if anything happens.'

'Are there more immortals living on earth?'

'To protect the earth you need to have an earth-bound connection—you know, be born here. I doubt we are the only ones here but if there are more they will be born in secret as our horses are and like us, something will happen to draw them to each other and eventually to us, just the way it has always been. Zoren has many teams looking after the universe and beyond.'

It was some hours later that Kayden finally found time to spend with his new wife. Aldebaran had got plastered and was sleeping it off downstairs. Kayden had outdone himself pleasing Cassie and she had enjoyed a hot shower before he even stirred. She grinned at the satisfied expression on his face as he groaned and rolled over, reaching out for her again.

'Hey, clean girl, come and let me get you dirty again.'

'You're pushing it, stud. Hit the shower and make it a cold one. Don't forget we promised to dine with Pops tonight. It's getting late so we better get a move on.'

'You're so not fun when you're at your father's house. I'm so going to make you pay for making me share you on our honeymoon. At least I can tell the boys to nick off and they do. I say that to your father and he'll probably turn me into a rodent or a toad, the old wizard,' he grumped as he turned on the hot water in the shower.

Standing under warm water, he was still grumbling when Cassie threw her towel aside and jumped in the shower with him.

'You're bloody ruined,' she giggled.

'Oh gorgeous honey pie, I'm so loving you again now,' he chuckled, snuggling into her.

When they finally made it downstairs, they found Aldebaran sitting in an armchair, reading and relaxing.

Cassie pulled the book from her father's hands. 'Hi Pops, miss me?' she smiled.

'Every second you're not with me,' he growled like a big bear and tickled her until she gave him the book back.

Kayden plonked himself into the chair near him and hearing him growling, grinned. 'So what's for dinner, Poppa bear, porridge?' he joked.

Aldebaran grabbed him. 'Call me Poppa bear?' he growled, ruffling Kayden's hair. 'And as for dinner, you have two choices. Conom invited us to have dinner with him tonight or if you prefer we can stay home and I can cook some porridge for you!' He grinned and shook his head.

Kayden was amused at his humour, giving it straight back at him. He wasn't a bad old dude after all and he was actually beginning to like the guy. 'Conom's invite sounds better than the gluggy crap you'd serve us up. Hell yeah, I'm in!'

Aldebaran smiled and directed attention to Cassie.

'Let's go then.' Cassie was excited. 'Come on, Pops, get up and do the transporting thingy you do. I'm starving,' she joked with him.

Aldebaran looked amused. 'Come here then,' he said, standing up. 'And there will be no stirring Conom up tonight playing cards and beating him again. He's happy he won. Let's just leave it at that so I don't have to put up with him bitching after you go home.'

With that they magically appeared on the Monoceros star. Kayden told Cassie it was the home of the mystical one-horned unicorn.

Conom was overjoyed to see them and showed them around his mansion. The entrance was like walking into an atrium. It had many floors. To get to each level there was a glass elevator or if you felt up to walking, a staircase of marble trimmed with gold which twisted charmingly between each floor. On the lower level he had a gym, sauna and spa rooms for treatments and massages. On the same level was a huge cinema room for movies, complete with popcorn machine and snack bar. The next three floors were like luxury apartments complete with en suites. Viewing the one he showed them, they noticed how the light-coloured walls and floors were a contrast to the red, green and gold furnishings. The elegant curtains opened up to ceiling-to-floor balconies that allowed one to sit out under the stars at night.

The ballroom and entertaining rooms were on the top floor and the roof was their last stop. It had a lap pool that seemed to just run off the roof. The illusion was amazing. The area was fitted out with a bar and sitting at it, miles up from the ground and under the stars like that, made Cassie feel as if she were having drinks in the clouds. It was so enchanting she just sat in awe for a while, sipping her cocktail.

Kayden and Conom were talking and Conom must have seen her far-away look and asked if everything was okay. Cassie shook her head. 'You star owners have far too much time on your hands. Your homes are so exquisite and over-the-top magical. I'm just a bit speechless.'

Conom laughed. 'You're thinking that what we have should be enough, right?'

She raised her eyebrow in a teasing manner. 'Well yes, I think you and my dad need to go find a good woman each, settle down, and start making little stars to share your fortunate life.'

'And forget about taking over more universe real-estate,' Conom added, still grinning at Cassie as he tactfully changed the subject, taking them down to dinner. The dining table was set with a lazy Susan in the middle that turned so they could share the different dishes that came out. Conom had organised Indian cuisine and they all over ate with the delicious dishes of curries and naan breads that came out. He was a good host and went to a lot of trouble making the night for them just perfect.

After dinner, no matter how much Aldebaran protested, the cards were brought out and a game had begun.

'So what stakes are we playing for tonight?' Cassie asked as she shuffled.

Conom grinned. 'You both still owe me a day out as it is. What say tonight we play for two days but somewhere on earth? Ald and I will come to you, though. We could possibly take off somewhere for a whole weekend: shooting, fishing, the works. What do you think?'

Kayden thought about it. 'Whoever wins gets to choose the destination.'

They agreed and the hands were played.

After an hour or so of playing and when he had only won a couple of games, Conom looked at Cassie with his dark eyes squinted and a look of being sucked in. 'You were holding back on me, girl. We need to make the stakes a little more even.' He nudged Kayden. 'What do you reckon, mate? Every time she wins she has to drink a shot. If the only way a man is going to beat her is when she's flat out drunk, then so be it.' He gestured to a servant to bring a carottle of Starshooter.

They both laughed and poured the drinks, Kayden enjoying it as much as Conom now.

'Gang up on the princess, is it? Okay I'm up for it. The guys do this to me all the time. But don't go all sooky la la on me if I still beat you both.'

They knuckle-crunched and passed Cassie her drink.

Time ticked away and so did her sense of judgement. She started to muck up the counts and giggle too much and she lost quite a bit. Everyone was happier now. They ended up kidding around and boisterous, the game became unpredictable. In the end, no one cared if they won or lost and Kayden decided to end the game when Cassie collapsed into his arms. He wasn't much better as he held her, slurring that they had better go to bed. Cassie felt herself being lifted and realised her father had picked her up. He carried her to one of the rooms and she could see Conom arm-in-arm with Kayden, staggering behind them. Cassie was giggling at them holding each other up.

Aldebaran put her on the bed. Cassie felt the room spin. 'Pops, I'm going to be sick,' she whined.

'Well, that'll teach you for always taking up a dare. I want you to stop being so easily influenced. You will end up an alcoholic, Cassandra,' he scolded.

Kayden chuckled at him scolding her. 'Yes, Cassie, stop being a naughty girl.'

Aldebaran growled. 'Kayden it's not funny! You both drink far too much and you have to start controlling it.'

'Okay, Poppa bear, point taken,' Kayden slurred.

Aldebaran went crook at Conom next. 'Conom help me with Cassandra. She's going to be ill. You helped get her in this state so you can sort it out while I get Kayden into bed.'

Chapter Fourty-One

Not my Finest Hour

Conom could tell that Ald was angry that he'd encouraged his kids to drink again. He had no idea how hooked on his damned daughter Conom was and if he did, Conom would be getting more than a cranky sneer right then.

Kayden had called out to Cassie as Ald had stomped off, carrying Cassie to bed. *Who would have guessed that a week after I nearly wiped out his team over a card game we'd become best bloody buddies?* He was a riot and too easy to like. *How we're going to be on opposing sides in a few days' time is beyond me.* He wanted to go home with these guys and party until they dropped. He wanted to hang with his girl and hear her laugh, watching her every expression and soaking her in until finally his eyes gave him some peace.

'Dad's pissed, hey?' Kayden slurred and then chuckled as they crashed into the wall.

'Yeah he's pissed, buddy but not as much as I'll be if we go through a wall. Concentrate on your walking. Your girl's in good hands,' Conom grumbled and then couldn't help but grin as Kayden gave him the thumbs up and a wink. Conom put Kayden's arm back around him. 'Let's give this another go. Ald will give me a hard time if I leave you to sleep here,' he said as Kayden started to slide down the wall.

'Okey-dokey, C-man,' Kayden said, making him grin more. How could he not like this dude? There was not a damned mean bone in his body. Even growling at him didn't ruffle him one iota.

In the bedroom, Cassie wasn't looking too hot. She'd just said she was going to be sick and Ald was growling at her, saying she was going to end up a drunk. She looked like she was going to cry but Kayden was quick, noticing her mood immediately and making a joke of it, telling her she was naughty. She looked over and grinned at him. Ald glanced around at Kayden and went off at him for not taking better care of her.

Jeez, he is in such a bloody bad mood. He's acting like a ... father. Wow, so that is what all this is about. My mate's gone all daddyfied on me. Hell, he's normally worse than I am. Now, look at him. Bloody hell, he's going for 'father of the year' for sure. Conom wanted to laugh and hang it on him but the mood in the room was far from amusing. *Cassie is sick, my man here is hardly standing and Ald looks ready to explode.* Then the words he was dreading, that she was going to be throw up.

What am I, frigging nurse Conom? He knew Ald wouldn't do the sick thing, even with his own kid. Vomit made him heave. *I wish she would just let go right here to piss him off. I would never let him live that down. All the crap he puts up with and does to others and yet the smell of puke brings the big man to his knees.*

Ald took Kayden while Conom whipped Cassie up in his arms and headed for the bathroom as her eyes began to roll back in her head. He left her on the floor with her head in the toilet bowl. *Thank goodness her hair has been braided and is all tied up. Washing sick out of hair is something even I refuse to do.*

He went over and splashed water over his own face to sober up a bit. How was he to look after her when he felt not much better? *Is it punishment?* His face looked back at him in the mirror. *Yes, I've brought all this on myself and need to suck it up.*

Cassie had flushed the loo for the third time and was curling up on the floor. Picking her up, he put her on the bed. She groaned again so it was back to the bathroom. This time he wasn't mucking around, she had nothing left to throw up so it was time for something more drastic. He turned on the shower and put her under. He could hear Kayden call out for his princess but he would have to wait or come and help. Ald, the mongrel had long gone, probably at the first sounds of her heaving. *The bloody weak mongrel. I'll get him good for this later.*

Cassie started to get some colour back in her face but her lips were turning blue and she was shaking. 'Time to come out, sweetie,' he said, wrapping a towel around her. The clothes she had on now were drenched. 'I'll hold the towel up but you have to take your wet gear off, sweetie or you'll catch a cold.' He leant her up against the shower wall and she grinned and started to slip down the wall. 'Whoa, steady there, little one.' He grabbed her just in time. 'It looks like we're going to have to become very familiar with each other or you will catch your death.'

She lifted up her arms so he could slip her dress over her head. Still holding her with one hand so she didn't end up on the floor, he grabbed the towelling robe and placed it around her the best he could while she giggled and went all jelly-like on him.

'Cass you're a hopeless drunk. How do you manage when I'm not around?'

'My best friend Woodsta cares for me. I love my best friend to bits. He growls at me more than you do though,' she chuckled, leaning into him.

'Okay, I have you decent so while I hold you, can you to wiggle out of your underwear,' he said, unclipping her bra. 'You can't sleep with anything wet on, sweetie. You will end up with pneumonia.'

After a struggle, she was free of clothing. Luckily her hair stayed dry; he was no good at the whole hair-drying thing. He pulled out the scrunchie and let her hair fall out, checking it was dry. Nope, she's good to go, he thought as he combed it through his fingers. *God, even her hair feels and smells divine.* She must have seen the look on his face and he flushed with embarrassment. She touched his face, her eyes glazed like she was somewhere else. *Maybe I remind her of someone else.*

'I miss my Woodsta,' she smiled. 'You're like my Woodsta, you know. Do you love me too?'

He picked her up. 'Yes, Cass, I'm afraid I love you too,' he said, thinking she wouldn't remember anything in the morning anyway so he might as well be honest. He walked her back over to the bed and pulled the covers back. After helping her in he pulled the covers over her. Kayden, out cold, felt for her and reached for her, pulling her into his arms. 'I missed you, sweetheart,' he said groggily, cuddling her.

'I missed you too, handsome,' she whispered.

Looking down at them Conom knew in that moment that he would make any sacrifice to have a love like that. How could it be that this was the only girl in the universe he had ever wanted that with? Fate was cruel and this was it at its finest. Never had he ever been so low in morals to even think of taking another man's wife. But here now with her, his morals were so screwed up.

He touched the softness of her cheek. 'Sweet dreams, Cass.'

CHAPTER FOURTY-TWO
The Big Dipper

D ad woke them up the next morning. 'Are you two sleepyheads ever going to get up?' he asked, sitting on the bed and passing them a coffee. Cassie checked she was decent and remembered she had woken in the middle of the night and put a nightie on. She stretched and sat up, taking the coffee from her father.

'If this is how you're going to wake us up every morning, Pops, you'll never get rid of me.' She joked with him and made him smile.

Kayden groaned and sat up, throwing pillows behind Cassie so she could lean back. He kissed her cheek. 'Morning, beautiful,' he said sweetly. Then glancing up at Aldebaran, he grinned. 'What time is it, Poppa bear?' Kayden joked.

'Midmorning and your porridge is lumpy and cold, you bastard,' he grumped back, making Cassie and Kayden crack up laughing. Aldebaran shook his head, amused. 'Okay, you two stirrers. I wanted to take you somewhere fun for the day but now you can both stay here and Conom and I will go on our own.' He laughed with them.

Cassie stopped mucking around. 'Really? Where're we going?'

'It's a surprise. Now get up. Breakfast is ready.'

After getting out of the shower, Cassie braided her hair back and her outfit changed to a pair of shorts and a girlie top that showed off her tattoo. While she slipped into the flats that her shoes had magically turned into, Kayden came out the shower, towel drying his hair and grinning at her.

'That looks pretty hot, honey,' he grinned.

'Maybe it's the way I did my hair. The magic just keeps mixing things up. Should I take it out?' she looked in the mirror, unsure now.

He grinned. 'I thought as much. It is your magic that's making all these changes. I think your subconscious actually knows what's coming up next and dresses accordingly. Don't stress, just go with the flow and don't you dare spoil my enjoyment by changing a single thing, you little hottie. Get here now!' He laughed as he chased her around the bed, joking and having fun with her.

Finally ready, they took the elevator to the bottom floor where they found the others eating breakfast. Conom looked up and nodded, his face pale, his eyes dark and tired-looking.

Aldebaran was reading as usual as he ate. Cassie put her arms around him and he smiled, looking up at her. 'You're looking a bit better now.'

'Sorry about last night, Pops. We'll try to behave a bit more today.'

'Somehow I don't think either of you will, but it is nice to hear you'll try.'

Cassie let him go. Grinning, she walked past Conom, ruffling his hair. 'Thanks for last night, ace. Hope I wasn't too much bother.'

He had a tired expression. 'You were no trouble, little one.'

She grinned back at his sweetness. 'Even so, thanks for being a good friend.' Sitting down next to Kayden she picked at a bit of fruit and some juice and waited patiently for them to finish eating so they could go do something. 'So Pops, give?' she finally asked, unable to wait any longer.

'How does a fun park sound?'

Cassie jumped up and pulled at him. 'Let's go then, we're wasting the day,' she nagged, going over and pulling Kayden and then Conom up. 'Come on, guys, get with the program. Pops is waiting.'

'Who's waiting?' Conom asked, a little annoyed.

'Did you have to tell her where we were taking her, Ald? I would have liked to at least finish my coffee first,' he grouched.

Cassie put her hands on her hips. 'Come on, ace, stop acting like a princess and toughen up,' she baited him.

'Why you little ...' he grabbed her under one arm and in seconds had his other arm around Kayden's shoulders and had transported them to the fun park. Aldebaran shimmered in straight after them, still laughing at how easily she could work up Conom.

'I think you've met your match there, Conom.'

'I'll give her princess! After what she drank last night it'd be my pleasure to watch her go green,' he said mischievously. 'You'll be begging us to go home after you've ridden the Big Dipper.' His ruthless expression didn't worry Cassie one little bit.

She ran over to her father for protection, pretending Conom scared her and laughing at how quickly he reacted. His mood is going to make today so much more fun, she thought.

'Being Daddy's little girl is not going to protect you today, young lady.' Conom put his arm around Kayden and whispered something. They both came over and kidnapped her from her father's arms.

'My own husband!' she laughed as they took an arm each. 'Traitor!' she added, stretching up and kissing his cheek, loving every minute of it.

Kayden told her they had landed on the Big Dipper constellation which is part of the Ursa Major Great Bear constellation. He and Conom took her through to the main entrance. She could now see that the Big Dipper was just a big fun park with heaps of rides and games to play.

To get to the rides, they had to pass by some of the Great Bear constellation and could see bears roaming in their natural habitat. She would have loved to have gone in for a closer look as they were quite magnificent to watch; however Conom was dragging her away.

'Come, inquisitive one, I'll bring you back another day.'

They stopped in front of a set of carts. 'Here we are,' Conom said with a little snigger in his tone. 'The longest ride in the universe: the Big Dipper. It starts here and curves around like a big snake, the speed whips you around and goes so fast it almost takes your breath away, it drops you so rapidly, so be ready,' Conom explained, putting her between Kayden and himself. 'Do you need a spew bag?' he joked.

'No, it's okay. I'll just use your lap.' She stirred him up.

'You dare!' He looked at her, shocked, and Kayden cracked up laughing.

'Don't worry, Conom, she's just having a lend of you. She's tougher than that.' He calmed him as they took off.

The ride was nothing like those at the fun parks she knew: it was way cooler. They dropped so fast it felt like their stomachs were in their throats and it corkscrewed around until their heads spun. With all the stars, you couldn't even focus on a horizon to steady yourself. They just looked out at the atmosphere. When they reached the whip-around they thought they were going to fly off the edge and each felt as though they would continue to travel out into space with no end. It was freaky and scary, exhilarating and fun.

When they pulled up it was Conom and Kayden who looked a bit green. After Cassie laughed heaps, she got back in with her father and went around one more time. He held her all the way around and when they reached the whip, both put their arms up and screamed really loudly and then laughed all the way back. When they stopped, her father gave her a big hug for including him by going around again, just with him.

Kayden raced over, grabbing her for the next ride. 'Come and have a look at this one,' he said, keyed up. 'It'll blow your mind, Cass.' He explained it. 'You have to sit on a rubber tube with handles. It shoots you through a tube and up high into space. You came down and land on a white puffy cloud that softens your fall. But it's like a trampoline that bounces you up and onto another four clouds before you stop. The whole time you spin and have to hold on or you end up in space and they have to come get you.'

'Cool, let's go,' she said as he took her hand and they ran over to it. Luckily they could fit four on the tube so this time they could all go on the ride together.

The first time Cassie's hand slipped off, her father grabbed her and held her until she steadied herself again. The second time, Kayden and Cassie were laughing so much they both let go, accidentally on purpose, so they had to be rescued. It was so much more fun floating, waiting for pick up. They copped a scolding from Aldebaran for deliberately doing it to see what would happen.

He is so cute the way he worries.

The park was closing so they only had time for one more ride. Kayden wanted to go on a star ride that spun you while dipping five ways before spinning high into the atmosphere and down fast like a top.

'You're used to chasing stars and catching them. This is right up your alley but for me, not so much.' She was unsure. 'However, I might not get up here for a holiday again for a while so will give it a go.'

Boy, was she sorry she'd agreed to go. By the time the ride finished she was dizzy and they had to hold her while she steadied herself. Conom transported her directly to the top deck, helping her onto the lounge by the pool.

'She looks pale, Kayden. Is she going to be alright?'

'I'll live.' She frowned at their fussing.

'She just needs a rest. Don't forget we had a late night as well. I'll take her for a sleep. She'll be fine.'

Kayden walked her back to the room, lying with her on the bed. She felt better in a horizontal position and brightening up, they talked about how much fun it had been. Conom knocked and asked if they were decent and came in with water and a tablet. He saw Cassie was starting to look better from just lying down and suggested they have a quiet one, maybe have a cinema night so Cassie could continue lying down on a recliner.

'It'll make your father think we're being responsible,' Kayden kidded.

Aldebaran stood at the doorway. 'I heard that, son. And it wouldn't hurt either of you to behave for one night.'

Conom and Aldebaran left to organise cinema food, arguing about just what Cassie would prefer and both acting like doting parents.

'They've taken a real shine to you, honey,' Kayden noted. 'I'm pretty sure neither of them has ever cared about anyone this much, ever. Maybe you're just what they needed to stop them worrying about what they want for a change, forcing them to think about someone else. Anything else.'

Conom knocked on the door and came in. 'You guys right to move yet?' he asked.

Kayden helped her to stand up. She wobbled a little as if she'd been drinking and giggled. 'Come here, my delicate little flower,' he said, lifting her into his arms.

'I can walk,' she tried to protest.

'You're as light as a feather, honey. You're no bother, really.'

'The joys of being married to a superhero,' Cassie shrugged, glancing at Conom. 'These powerful muscular brutes ended up with all the strength. It's not fair. The only gift I got is to knock things out the way and blow things up.' She poked fun at herself.

Conom looked fascinated. 'Powers?' he inquired.

Kayden reminded him of the first time they had met and of her threat if he was to hurt her friend.

He seemed surprised. 'I thought she was joking, you know. Acting the tough little minx.'

'No, that was definitely not a bluff. She could have put you through the wall,' Kayden chuckled. 'There might not be much of her but she sure packs a punch.'

'The only time I've seen her is when she's on the horse watching you guys. Ald told me she was gifted but never elaborated on what. He handles most of the battle plans. I just sign off on it. I'm on earth most days and miss a lot of the action up here. You see, once it gets out about her capabilities, it is her that will become the target. Really, K, it's not safe for her out there at all.'

Kayden stopped at the doors to the cinema. 'I try to keep her away from the danger as best I can but don't worry so much, Conom. She can take care of herself. Trust me.' He grinned and kissed her on the forehead. 'Hey, cloud girl.' He turned back to Conom. 'And not only that, she is surrounded by my men and they would never let any harm come to her either. Between the five of us we guard her with our lives. My men have a real bond with her. Not sure how it happened but I think it's her powers mixed with mine when I connected her to us as a group.'

'What do you mean, connected her? How?'

Kayden smiled. 'Top secret. But let's just say we all feel her even if she's not with us. We can tell she's happy and okay wherever she is.'

In the cinema Kayden sat her on the twin recliner and she watched as Conom and her father seemed to be having a heated argument. They both had strong personalities and Cassie shrugged, turning back to Kayden. 'Wonder what that's all about.'

Kayden had an idea but just smiled. 'I guess you're shaking them up. Let's not worry about them for now. You just worry about me and me and me.' He grinned.

She laughed at him and he was right. He was so much more fun to worry about as he whispered what he would prefer to be doing with her rather than sitting watching a repeat flick with these twits. He just never stopped with the humour and she loved it.

The food started to come out and it shut Kayden up while he pigged out on mini hotdogs, hamburgers, popcorn, ice-cream and lollies.

After the movie finished, Cassie stood up, feeling a bit better. She stretched. 'Anyone feel like a spa before we hit the sack?'

Aldebaran frowned.

'Okay, Pops, alcohol-free I promise. Just a nice relaxing spa and hot chocolate after.'

Kayden stretched. 'Sounds good to me. Conom, you in?'

He stood up. 'I'm in. You don't have to ask me twice to find a way to relax before bed.'

'I might call it a night, kids. I didn't sleep well last night,' Aldebaran said.

'Just us then,' Conom said, making a move.

Chapter Fourty-Three
Melter of Hearts

After the spa, they sat sipping hot chocolate and Conom asked when Kayden and Cassie would be leaving.

Kayden looked down at her. 'We really need to get back, probably tomorrow some time. I have many unique horses and they are in constant need of attention. And even though you and Ald have not been causing us grief, the rest of the constellations still need protecting and I've had a feeling all day that something is not right in the universe. I'm afraid it'll never end for us.' Kayden threw an arm over Cassie's shoulders. 'Sorry, honey. Are you okay if we leave tomorrow?'

Before she could answer, Conom sat up in his chair, looking anxious. 'Does Cass have to go? I don't like this at all, Kayden. I know you like her with you but I wish you'd reconsider and realise how much danger she's in out there.'

Kayden grinned. 'You guys are the ones causing the most danger for her at the minute, Conom. Call off the war and it will be easier for her.'

Conom leaned into the headrest, defeated. 'Ald is cross and that's why he retired early. He's angry I'm calling it off. Well, my part in it anyway. I'm afraid things have changed for me now that I know you both so well. It just feels all wrong.'

Kayden leaned back in his chair as if the wind had just been knocked from his sails. There were a couple of minutes of uncomfortable silence before anyone spoke. Kayden inhaled and breathed out with a whistling sound. 'Well, you certainly threw me. I never expected you to be able to give up so much. Aldebaran must have been quite shocked when you told him.'

'I think he was expecting it. After I took care of Cass last night we had words. We argued until it was nearly dawn this morning before we both stomped off to get some sleep.'

Kayden grinned. 'It looks like she's melted all our hearts in many different ways.'

Conom reached over and tickled her. 'Are you using powers on us, you little melter of hearts?' He laughed and released her.

'Yes, I have a machine and it sucks out all the mean stuff and I jump in there and take its place.' She joked with him.

Kayden stood up smiling, pulling her into his arms. 'Then for goodness sake give me that damned machine so you'll stop jumping in men's hearts or I'll end up with an army instead of a select group of loyal supporters.'

Conom laughed at Kayden's kidding. 'Well, it will be a long day with Ald if you are both leaving tomorrow so I'd better get some shuteye.'

He ruffled Cassie's hair with his hand as he walked past. 'Goodnight, stealer of hearts,' he grinned as he left them.

Morning came too soon and Zoltan sent Kayden a telepathic message from Zoren as he expected. After a quick breakfast they went back to the star Aldebaran to collect Starburst and Zoltan. Cassie noticed her father was overly quiet and not once during the morning could she even get a smile out of him, no matter how much she tried. His face was expressionless and when he thought she wasn't looking he had a constant frown.

This was the Aldebaran that she'd first met, having quiet, moody moments. She wondered if her father would come back to her to say goodbye. Had she already lost him to the battle of the stars? Was his mind on a strategy again, just waiting for her to leave? She just wished for one last time that she could have his big bear arms around her.

'I love you,' she said as they were about to mount the horses and leave. He never answered, just stood staring into space. She shook him. 'I know you love me, Pops, so you can act as tough as you want.'

He looked down, giving her a weak smile and lifted her up onto Starburst. 'Have a good trip home, Cassandra,' he said and stepped back.

Kayden said goodbye, and getting the horses into space, they left. Cassie was sad her father had ended their stay in one of his moods. He was angry Cassie had made such an impact on Conom. That he had gone cold on the war if it meant fighting her and not only that, they were leaving early after promising to spend the last day with him.

Kayden also commented that it could just be a parent thing. He said that some parents were like that when they had to say goodbye to their kids the first time. They had to act all tough and uncaring or else they might fall apart if they succumbed to their feelings.

Whatever the reason, they had to leave things the way they were until they had time to come back and work it out with him. He was part of her now and she wanted him in her life. She would definitely be sorting it out. She knew he loved her because she could feel it when he hugged her. He just needed time to catch up and realise what she already knew.

Chapter Fourty-Four
Hydra

As soon as they appeared in the paddock, Kayden summoned his team. The men received the message and were waiting at the house for their return. As soon as they trotted into the barn, Kayden knew there'd been a shift in their dynamics. Only Ethan and Conor came out to meet them. Jason and Woody were inside waiting, which was highly unusual. Once the horses were taken care of, Kayden followed them into the house. Jason and Woody both had their girls. Jason, the little surprise package, had proposed to Sonia and she was now part of their secret too. But they had kept the girls inside until Kayden had given permission for them to view the team in their magical form.

Business came first with Kayden so the men and their issues would have to wait. Jason and Woody left the girls to chat and have a drink while they followed Kayden and the rest of the team down to the satellite room. Kayden was in no mood after Aldebaran had upset Cassie. He felt sure in Aldebaran's state of mind, that he would be planning something to coincide with the mission they were now being sent on and wanted to be ready for anything he might throw at them while they were up there.

While Kayden worked on coordinates, Cassie filled her team mates in on their trip away. Even now Kayden felt blown away at the work she did up there and yet knew she really had no idea what she had accomplished.

Conom was a real threat to the universe and when they had first come out of the trance, he was almost the same man they had all met in Sydney. His features were hard, eyes black as coal, deep-set and, angry-looking, his body rigid and pumped, ready to battle with Kayden at any moment. How Cassie was able to see through that and not be frightened of him was beyond him. In fact it was so disturbing that he nearly brought her home, but she refused to leave because she couldn't see the way he saw the situation. She had laughed at the way he perceived the warlord and accused him of just being a little over-possessive.

Well, hell yes I was! He punched harder on the keyboard and the guys stopped talking and looked over. He took a deep breath and smiled to show them he was cool. He watched as they went back to their conversation.

In the end he'd caved in and given her a couple more days to see what she was capable of doing. Hour by hour he had watched as the most ferocious-looking character mellowed and in the end practically bowed at her feet, swearing his allegiance to her, to be in her life in whatever way she would have him, never taking up arms against her again.

The boys will go ape-shit when I tell them later, privately.

He tuned in on Cassie talking about her dad and even though he liked the guy when he was around Cassie, there was a side he saw before they left that he just did not want to cross. His adoration for Cassie could not be denied. Yet maybe it was because they were father and daughter that her power didn't work on him. She was wearing him down but had not won.

The fight in his eyes when we left showed me he is the strongest son of a bitch I have ever met and it is just going to take a bit more time for my stealer of hearts as Conom calls her to get her dad to lay down his sword against her as well.

Kayden switched on all the monitors and called for quiet. Woody as always stood with his arm around Cassie and Kayden was glad he now had Ella and would leave Cassie the hell alone. *Not that I'm jealous of course. Much!* He grinned. *She might be a stealer of hearts but her body and soul belong to me. And here with my men I'm not going to share her ever again. Well, not unless the bastards steal her. Then I'll just kill 'em.* He almost chuckled at his thoughts. He smiled at her, loving his little lady with all he had to give. He just wanted to get this out of the way so he could snatch her away from them and hold her possessively until it was time to leave.

She grinned up at him as she took a step away from the boys and giggled, making him laugh more. *The little bitch knows she's stirring me up and knows exactly what I'm thinking.* His men wanted to know what was so funny and he told them with an amused expression to mind their own Goddamned business.

'Well, its official,' Woody chuckled. 'The turncoat has dumped us for married life.'

Kayden laughed louder. 'You bet I have, so keep the hell away from my woman or I'll replace you all with robots.'

They all couldn't stop laughing. They had their boss back and loved it. Pulling himself together, he turned back to the screens. 'Okay, enough fooling around. Let's get this out the way.' He became serious and so did they.

'The long feuding between the constellations Corvus, Crater and Hydra has come to a head.' Cassie looked unsure of that particular feud. Kayden smiled at her, knowing she needed to know the full story to understand. 'This is for you, gorgeous one. The story goes that Apollo sent his raven called Corvus to get water in the god's cup called Crater but on the way the raven saw a fig tree and stayed on it until the fruit ripened. He then ate all the figs before returning with the water. When he did return, in one hand, the crow had water in the cup and in the other, a water snake called Hydra. He blamed the snake he carried for being so late. Apollo was furious and knew the raven was lying. As punishment he banished the raven into the sky with the snake, the cup of water and until this day the snake keeps water from the eternally thirsty raven. They now make up the constellation Hydra, Corvus and Crater.'

She nodded, liking these little stories from the sky.

'Anyway, the raven made friends with the ruler named Leon

from the zodiac Leo constellation. Leon and the raven have since joined forces, deploying a white dwarf Supernova to destroy Hydra. Corvus's strategy is for the nova to partly explode, just before it reaches Hydra, causing the outer casing to shoot away injuring the snake, leaving only the core. This will then hit the snake at full speed and with Hydra already weak from the smaller blasts, the snake will be disintegrated.'

Kayden opened up a wider image of the area and showed them a simulation. 'In theory, what they've planned sounds feasible. However, Zoren's team are pretty sure the explosion will be big enough to reach and destroy the constellation Pyxis as well.' They all watched as the simulation and recreation of the explosion did damage much more than Leo or Corvus had predicted. 'As you can see, we could have more than just one constellation in trouble out there.' The last position he charted was the location where they would need to be to prevent it from happening. 'By information received from Alpha base we must intercept here.' He showed the team. 'This is where we have to destroy the Supernova before the outer case explodes. Are there any questions?'

'We leave earlier than usual?' Woody leaned toward the last screen, reading the distance on the monitor.

Kayden nodded. 'Sorry. It won't leave you much time to say goodbye to your women and this being the first time, I would have liked them to feel a bit more comfortable about all this. Regardless, it is what it is. At least they have each other once you and Jase have gone.'

After further discussion on the line of attack and everyone was satisfied, he switched the equipment off and taking Cassie's hand in his, they headed back to the house to get organised.

Jason couldn't wait to show them Sonia's ring and said why they couldn't wait for them to get back before proposing. He described how Sonia's folks were not going to let her leave home and just go live with someone she hardly knew. He'd up and asked for her hand in marriage right then and there without another thought. He looked so happy holding her that Kayden couldn't help but feel pleased for the over-impulsive fool. *Shytzer, who am I to talk? Cassie did the same to me.* He smiled as he looked down at the remarkable lady in his arms with her angelic smile. *Yes, love sometimes finds us in the most unusual places.* He snapped out of his soppy, love-struck mood. He really needed to talk to someone and pulled Woody and Jase aside.

He told them how Cassie had befriended Conom to a point where he practically bowed down at her feet. Filling them in on all the details, he gave them the picture to see if he was being rational in his thinking. Could he have dealt with anything differently? More than anything he was looking for support, maybe even a little advice on how to proceed from this point onwards.

'Bloody hell,' Woody scoffed. 'He already had his tongue hanging out when they first met, I could tell. Now you say the man has laid down his arms for her?'

Kayden frowned. 'He's really taken to our girl. I nearly thought I would have to run with her. As we had all felt his rage, one could also feel his passion for her. I'm no fool and have to be mindful what this very powerful warlord would do if I was to take her away from him permanently at this stage.'

'What has Cassie said?' Woody inquired.

Kayden ran his hand through his hair. 'She only sees him as a friend, someone kind and gentle. She has no fear of him at all and doesn't see him at all the way we all do.' He sighed and leant back against the wall. 'I trust Cassie that she'll sort Conom out and break the spell or whatever it is she has over him when she's ready. I honestly believe the universe is using her as a key player in a game to tame these ruthless individuals. I can think of no other explanation.'

Woody swore and hoisted himself up onto the bench, thinking.

Jase seemed to be the only one of them who was not disturbed by any of it. 'Jeez, you two. The ones who should know her the most, you sure don't know crap!' Jase said, flooring both of them. 'Cassie has managed all of us with diplomacy and decorum. Each one of us has played a very special part in her life, after which she's rewarded us with such happiness that words can't describe. Kayden, you saved her and she gave you her body and soul. Woody, you cared for her like your own and she manipulated us all so that you could have your love, Ella. I was her friend whenever you two couldn't be and she gave me Sonia. This Conom is in her life now for a reason maybe yet to show itself. But when it does he will be loved and rewarded as she sees fit. We are her knights and the universe is her round table. Whatever it is that is drawing her to him we have to trust that just like us, she will sort him out and then leave him as happy as we are.'

Woody shook his head. 'I think the J man may just have something there, K. It's been staring us in the face all this time. How could we have missed it?' Woody slapped his forehead. 'Damn, if that does not beat all.'

'That it does, my man, that it does.' Kayden rubbed his chin, finally letting Jason's theory allow him the relief he needed to slot the weirdness of the situation into perspective.

Jase put his arm around Kayden. 'Anytime, K! Cassie and you are tight, man, never lose sight of that. All the rest of us are pawns in the game our princess plays. When she gave me Sonia she gave me a dream come true and that was when I worked it out. I knew then that she was not just a princess we saved but had to be a goddess to do what she does.'

'That, Jase, is exactly where my train of thought had gone and I was thinking I might be going crazy with such an idea. I so needed someone else to say it. Conom called her a stealer of hearts. I'm starting to think that maybe that is exactly what she is.'

Woody grinned. 'Yes that sounds like our Cassie girl. Suits her to the core.'

Jase rolled his eyes. 'God, no. Please, no disclosing what we've just discussed or we'll never hear the end of her jokes about us thinking it. I can imagine the aftermath of problems it would create and can just hear her now. "Excuse me, goddesses do not cook or clean" or "The goddess would like her coffee now". Kayden, this is between us forever. Cloud Riders code of secrecy! You have to promise.'

They all laughed again and attracted the girls who came over to them. 'What's all the laughing going on over here? We want in on the joke,' Sonia purred, leaning into Jase.

'Never going to happen, sweetie, boys' stuff. But you can come with me and show me how much you'll miss me while I'm gone,' he chuckled, dragging her to Cassie's old room. 'Later, men,' he said over his shoulder, smirking.

Ella was grinning up at Woody. 'Well, K, I have other pressing business with my woman. Wake us when it's time to leave,' he said, throwing an arm around Ella and taking her to the main bedroom.

Cassie was still chatting to Conor and Ethan, who where lying down on the sofas, so Kayden made himself comfortable next to his honey and smiled. *The boys will be just about ready to enjoy themselves about now. What a bugger I can't. No bedrooms left. Oh well.* A grin widened across his face as he closed his eyes. Night boys, he thought, and chuckled as he put them all to sleep. *Ah, to be the boss, revenge is so sweet.*

Chapter Forty-Five
Sweet Betrothed

When Kayden woke them up, the many harsh comments coming from the bedrooms were directed at Kayden. Cassie could feel his body trying to hold back fits of laughter.

'I can only guess what that was about.' Cassie nudged him. She turned around to face him and he had the biggest grin. 'Just having a bit of fun with the boys. Payback can be so pleasurable.'

'Coffee, cheeky one?' She was enjoying his lightened mood.

'Love one, sweetheart,' he smiled as she jumped up, quickly moving from him as he made a grab for her. She saw in his expression what he was about to do and ran off on him, giggling. 'Not so fast.' He chuckled as he reclaimed her, growling as her father had—as if he were a big old bear too. He made her laugh more.

In between his foolery, Cassie finally made everyone's drinks and they went out on the veranda to drink them and catch up with each other while waiting for Zoltan to lead the horses out.

Cassie turned to Ella, sensing she was a little hurt that Sonia was engaged before her. She had caught the look on Ella's face when Sonia showed Cassie her ring for the second time. Woody saw the look too and pulled her next to him. 'Come here, woman.' He smiled and winked at Cassie. 'I wanted to wait until you guys were here so you could be a part of my surprise,' he said as the horses trotted out of the barn at Kayden's command.

It was the first time the girls would be seeing the horses or their transformation. Cassie knew how dazzling a show it was going to be for them. They all placed their golden bridles on the horses and mounted them. The girls gasped at the transformation and when Kayden put Cassie onto Starburst, Sonia squealed and ran over to hold Cassie's hand.

'Sorry, I have to touch you. My God! You look like an angel,' she squealed again excitedly.

She turned to Jason who jumped down to give her a hug. 'You okay with this, sweetie?'

Sonia was crying and laughing, trying to take it all in. 'More than okay, babe.' She jumped up on him, throwing her arms around his neck and giving him heaps of kisses. Jase loved it, more than pleased with her enthusiasm.

Ella stood unmoving, watching Woody with undeniable love and pride. Woody dismounted and bent down in front of her on one knee. 'Honey, I have loved you from the first moment and I will never love another as I do you. Will you marry me, beautiful and be my wife, even if I do have to run off on you all the time like this?'

Tears rolled down Ella's face, never loving anyone the way she did the man who knelt before her. While they were apart, Ella had missed him terribly and knew for sure he was the one she wanted. Her heart was already his. She bent down eye-to-eye and kissed his lips. 'Yes, my love. I would want nothing more than to marry you and be your wife. As for you running off and looking like the biggest hunk in the universe? Not so happy I don't get to enjoy it like the tarts up there but I'm sure I'll get over it while going on a shopping spree with your money while you're gone.' Showing no emotion, making him laugh.

'What about kids? Can I keep you barefoot and pregnant in the kitchen? If I'm away, I want to know no man will look at you. A fat belly should do the trick,' he chuckled.

'Kids are fine, sweetie but the men are still going to think I'm the hottest thing on two legs because I am,' she stirred him.

'That's it! For a wedding gift I'm coming back with a chastity belt and locking you up until I get back.'

'Jealous bastard,' she slapped him playfully.

'Get fat before I get back or I'm not marring you. I'll find a way to keep them rich sods away from my sexy woman yet,' the fun-loving kidder said jokingly as he give her a big smooch before getting back on his horse. He looked down at Sonia, now holding Ella's hand. 'Go help your friend get fat or I'll never talk to you again.'

Both women laughed uncontrollably, as the team rode off. Woody was a funny bastard and Cassie was glad he felt it important to have them there to witnesses the proposal. She couldn't have been happier with both women.

The clouds were different today. The colours were soft and swirled together like soft ice cream. It was relaxing and there was something different about it as they slipped out and into the fourth dimension, landing on the Cirrus cloud which looked wispy and feathery. While they were in it, the cloud felt soft against Cassie's skin, almost as if tiny feathers were running gently along her arms and face.

The colours were white and silver with touches of gold. It was very pretty to be in but whipped you with incredible speed high into the portal of the next dimension where they came out into the solar system. The colourful planets and stars in the clear atmosphere sparkled and glittered as if she was in fairyland — if that even existed. *Yet, this is real so who knows?*

From the height they were at, she could now make out Pyxis the mariner's compass. They landed on Velorum, the controlling star that was ruled by Captain Rogers.

The captain came out to greet Kayden. He was an elderly man with a very long grey beard. He was wearing a typical captain's hat and lived in an old battle ship that was wedged in some sand and on an angle. The ship was quite a few meters from the shoreline, obvious that he had been ship wrecked for many years. He seemed a bright old chap, even though his face was badly lined with wrinkles from years of harsh weather on the seas, although his eyes seemed young, alert and friendly.

He had a couple of men with him who must have been under his command because he growled orders at them before he flicked his hand as if he was swatting a fly, dismissing his men and dragging smoke from the pipe that hung from his mouth. The men quickly disappeared back into the ship bringing out something and passing it to the captain. Turning it to show Kayden, Cassie could see it was a compass and she realised he was showing Kayden new coordinates and pointed above him to Argo Navis, the ship constellation. He seemed concerned about the damage to the sail if the attacking star reached them.

A Knight's Struggle

K ayden hadn't allowed the team to dismount. Time was of the essence and after talking to Captain Rogers, he wasn't sure if they could prevent the damage that the pending Supernova was now predicted to do, in its condition and current path it was on. This news wasn't what Kayden wanted to hear. Mounting Zoltan, he directed him to follow the new coordinates he had just been given.

He relayed his team the bad news by telepathy in case someone was listening in on their conversation. He knew most of them had the technology to do so and didn't want a bunch of rulers going off half-cocked, thinking they might have lost control of the situation.

Captain Rogers has had a report that a Comet has just passed by the deployed Supernova travelling around 30 000 miles an hour. The heat projecting from the Comet would have to be well over 3000 degrees Celsius. It's not only knocked our Supernova off course, but the massive heat injection has sped up the death star's expiry time, he relayed to the team. Kayden looked around and could hear it in the distance before it was even in sight. *Something's not right, guys. It sounds all wrong. It sounds unpredictable, so brace yourselves. Expect the unexpected. If it blows before we reach it, slip into clean up mode and get whatever Cassie misses. We can't let any of the iron shards reach the constellations.* He glanced over at Cassie and she looked as cool as a cucumber, already powering up. *It sounds ready to explode, Cassie so be careful and once you've tossed the thing to the coordinates I've given you, get the hell out of here and wait back over near the Pyxis constellation for us, okay?*

She opened her eyes and nodded. He could only just see her through the haze. She was glowing like the brightest star in the sky and when he called out, she threw her arms up towards the Supernova. At the same time, there was an explosion. Cassie was so busy concentrating on moving the Supernova, she never noticed it as it was not in her vision. Kayden spotted it and tensed.

Cassie! Break left! he ordered, at the same time instructing Zoltan to move Starburst for her if she was unable to do it quick enough. She hadn't seen the piece of the outer casing that had exploded from the nova but could see it now, hurtling towards her at the speed of thousands of kilometres an hour.

Cassie did as she'd been instructed. However, the shard still sliced her arm and the impact caused her power source to waver. She screamed out with pain as it bit through her skin and even though hurting, she still kept her concentration on the nova and tossed it out to the intended destination, the force of her reaction breaking the wound open that she thought had been sealed by the heat of the offending object.

Kayden sent the boys off after the Supernova.

Cassie, will you be okay for a few minutes? We have to get this.

She nodded, holding on to where the shrapnel had sliced into her and stopping the pain to a certain degree.

That's right, Cassie, keep pressure on it. Just give me five.

She gave him a signal to get going. He knew his little brave soldier would hold strong until she felt his arms around her and he shot off after the team. Zoltan picked up speed, taking control, enabling him to take a second to look back to check on her. The hot shard that sliced her should have cauterised the wound. He wondered if it must have cooled a bit before it hit her, unless she had overused her powers and opened it up, as she was bleeding profusely, blood floating in the nothingness around her. She had the most sensitive skin he had ever known and he felt for her as he watched her rip the string from her corset top. As she did a new one appeared making her smile, and him too, as she quickly wrapped it around her arm to try and control the bleeding. As he returned his vision to his men, he saw there were more steel chards flinging from the nova in all directions, and his horse carefully navigated around the danger. Worried they were in the thick of it he picked up speed to get free, his senses picking up before he heard the explosions around him. A quick glance back towards Cassie again, saw her using her other hand to blow them into powder before they could reach him or do any damage.

Cassie, no commander could be any more proud of you than I am right now, he communicated to her as she fought bravely. He reached the Supernova, the boys already positioned, as they waited for him to slide onto the northern tip. His second in command had linked the boys and Kayden felt the force of Woody's power connect to him, dragging from them the magical force that was needed. Kayden felt the pull of the energy field from deep within him as Woody took what he needed from their powers to put this one out quickly before it did any more damage. At the same time an explosion blasted on the south side where Jase was and a huge chunk hurtled off.

We have to persist in our quest to defuse the situation before we can clean it up or we'll end up with a bigger mess than we already have. Kayden commanded Woody to continue as they spun with the out-of-control Supernova. He worried Cassie was battling one-handed but knew they would be there to help her any minute now.

There was a loud gushing sound as the remains of the Supernova stopped dead in the sky, floating with no energy left to hurt a soul. Kayden put his men in a spin, the team rotating at cyclone speed around the dead missile, blasting the remains into translucent powder. The threat of the core alleviated, Kayden sent them out to clean up the remnants.

They were like mini-tornados, rotating so fast you could only see a blur of brightness crackling with lightning that destroyed anything they touched. They had become more powerful since Cassie had joined them, somehow tapping into her powers as well. The massive speed they travelled, picked up the iron shards and obliterated them on their way down to her. It was quite a picture to see them work.

We're coming now! Hang in there, Cassie.

It was then that Kayden spotted yet another chunk hurtling towards her with such speed none of them could stop. The damned Supernova had almost detonated before Kayden and his men could put it out. Fractured casings from it were what hurtled towards her from all directions.

She was battling other remnants and maybe due to the pain she was in, had not detected the largest of them all.

Cassie, break right! Kayden called down and even though she and her horse immediately did as he instructed, it was just too late. The shard was on top of her and even her hand was not quick enough to blast it. Her right arm was so badly damaged it was slowing her reaction time. She ducked and screamed as it sliced into her shoulder. Kayden swore, feeling the blood rush from his face as he saw the trouble she was in. He growled at his men to hurry. Stopping what he was doing, he made a beeline towards her. Being further from her than the rest, he was relying on at least Woody to reach her in time.

He yelled at her to break left this time but with two gashes now on that side, she wasn't as quick with her movements and she screamed as Starburst dropped left, making her weight shift and forcing her to hold on with her bad arm. Without warning, two shards collided, changing course and spun out of control heading right at her.

He could do nothing but call out for her to duck, and watch. Waiting for what seemed like ages, yet would have only been a millisecond in time, he saw the impact of the casing from a Supernova that threatened to take his wife and eternal love from him forever, snatching her from this universe and from his arms.

His body powered up as his fear took over, hurrying him towards her and hoping like hell one of them reached her in time, praying for more speed and a miracle.

Suddenly a shadow came over her and she was gone.

Chapter Fourty-Seven

Ophiuchus Constellation

L epius heard Covin call out. 'King Lepius, you're needed urgently,' He put his cigar and medical files down and went out to see what the racket was about. There was yelling coming from below in the hospital and Lepius knew that for his commanding officer Covin to be involved, there must be a medical emergency so he rushed out, grabbing his medical bag on the way.

Covin was annoyed. 'Conom's in the hospital with a girl and will only see you. He's so angry he's shaking and scaring the hell out of the little thing he's holding.'

Lepius transported them down and saw that one of his doctors was trying to reason with Conom but that he was, as Covin had already informed him, cranky as hell.

'I'll only have the physician Lepius touch her, so get the hell out of my face and go get him,' he growled loudly at the doctor.

Lepius could see he was holding a female who had blood dripping from her arm and shoulder. Conom was an old friend but not one who had an ounce of patience when it came to something he wanted. He was more powerful than any warlord he knew and Lepius wondered how this young one had him so wound up. They both had the same taste in women so it certainly couldn't be sexual, that was for sure! He had no relatives either, so what was causing him to act so freaked out?

Lepius saw the doctor look in his direction and Conom swung

around. 'Lepius, you have to help me. She's hurt,' he said, walking over to him. His whole body was shaking and his eyes held more fear than he had ever seen in them. He was in love with her but shook his head, not believing what he was seeing in his face. He was ready to crumble.

'It's fine, Conom. Come, let me take a look.' Lepius gestured and made Conom follow him into one of the operating theatres. He patted the table. 'Here,' he said, turning to get some sutures and a needle loaded with painkillers. He was in so much of a mood that Lepius decided to keep his questions to himself until later and just kept working quietly. Lepius watched as he laid her so carefully on the table and kissed her forehead.

'Lepius is the best there is, sweetie. He'll make you feel better in no time,' he said, holding her hand and still shaking.

She amazingly enough had no fear of him, just concern. 'Conom, you are sweet to save me but the others will be worried. Just let them know I'm safe, please,' she said so sweetly and quietly he almost had to strain to hear her.

Conom kissed her gently on the hand and nodded. 'Can I use the NAVcom?' he asked the doctor. His voice was irritated yet she still just smiled at him, unperturbed.

'Just through the door there,' he said.

Conom looked back at her, not wanting to leave and she smiled at him so beautifully, Lepius could almost see him melt. He walked out of the room, unable to do anything but what she wanted.

'You have him quite rattled, young lady. Do you have a name?' Lepius asked as he pulled up a chair next to her and examined the wounds, cleaning them up.

'Cassie,' she groaned out as he moved her. 'Mrs Cassie Hunter. I'm a Cloud Rider and found myself in a bit of bother extinguishing a Supernova that exploded as we were putting it out. Conom intervened and saved me from being totalled by a big portion of it. He's very angry with my boss at the minute, who happens to be my husband. So I have just asked him to at least let them know I'm okay.'

'Yes, I got that. Nevertheless, I would be very careful how

you handle this, Cassie Hunter. He is a very powerful man and is obviously much taken by you.'

Lepius watched her expression as she nodded. She already knew how he felt and even though this woman seemed young and vulnerable, there was insight and strength in her that even he could feel. There was a lot more to Cassie than his first impressions had told him and he realised she was no one's fool.

Lepius could barely hear what Conom said on the phone but the rumbling of his angry tone shook the walls as he spoke, so he assumed Conom hadn't patched anything up with whomever he spoke to.

Conom pulled up a chair, trying to compose his rage. With those dark pits for eyes, he would frighten the best of them and yet at the touch of her hand, his mood eased. 'Everything's fine,' he lied to her.

Lepius could tell she also knew he was being a little evasive but seemed happy her friends at least knew she was alive. 'Conom, my knight in shining armour. Thank you, my friend.' She smiled and his face softened under her gaze. She was playing a deadly game with a man she should not be mucking about with. Could she not see his temper? That alone should warn her about him. At least he had stopped shaking with anger now so Lepius at least felt better she was able to calm him.

He put the needle in her arm and one in her shoulder. He wished he could also jab one in Conom to calm the cranky bastard but thought better of it. He didn't feel like running at the minute. He sniggered and hoped they couldn't read minds. 'I just need a second to let that take effect, Conom. She's losing a lot of blood so with the pain easing she'll most likely go to sleep. So don't go freaking out. Just trust me that she'll be fine.'

With that, her eyes started to flutter and she closed them. 'Lepius, do something,' he growled, and started getting upset again.

'She's better being out to it. She'll feel no pain or sensations now while I stitch her,' he reassured Conom.

He moved restlessly, agitated, but let him stitch both wounds. You could have cut the silence with a knife. He watched her face and then looked back at what Lepius was doing. Seeing she felt nothing and that her breathing was steady, he settled down.

Bloody hell, he's like a damned time bomb, touchy as all hell. After he bandaged her up, he removed her bloodstained shirt and a new one just magically appeared. She must have been cold as this one had sleeves and a bit of white fur trimmed around it. Lepius jumped back when it happened. It was the first time he saw Conom smile.

'She rides the magical horse outside and it can feel she's cold. Her clothes change with the temperature and mood of the moment.'

'Well I'll be,' Lepius smiled. 'Never seen that before.'

Conom scooped her up in his arms and sat holding her so gently it amazed him. He could easily see he wouldn't hurt her in a fit, although he wondered if the ones he stole her from knew that.

'I think we both need a drink, man. Come back to the palace and I'll fix us one while we wait for her to come around. It's okay, she's not hurting, just sleeping.'

He stood up with her and Lepius transported them back to the palace. Covin was still outside the ward waiting and came back with them. Even though Conom was an old friend, Covin would trust no one around his king, especially one so twitchy. They both watched with interest as Conom carefully sat with her in the armchair and brushed the hair from her face.

'She's very beautiful, Conom,' Covin said. 'Not your type at all or am I missing something?'

Conom looked up and frowned. 'She's taken and very happy but he's a bloody idiot and does not deserve her.' He started to get angry again.

Lepius passed him a few stiff shots of whisky in a glass that he drank down in one quick gulp. He was sure it hardly even touched the sides. Conom passed him back the glass. 'Man, I needed that. Thanks, doc,' he said, sounding a little more human. 'She's a fast healer, doc. It'll only take a couple of days. I wonder if I could stay here with her just until she gets well. I need some time to work through some issues and need a safe haven to do so.'

Lepius knew it wasn't right what he was doing, but she looked no fool and it was better he were here with her where he could control any dangerous outcomes and at least give her some form of protection rather than send them to God knew where, then worry himself sick what he might do to her if she woke and wanted to go home. That was going to be an interesting scenario. Would he be so easily swayed by her demands then? The way he acted, he doubted if God himself could prise her from his hands in the emotional state he was in.

'Not a problem. I'll have a couple of the guest quarters upstairs made up for you both,' he said, already making up his mind that he would organise for her to have the room next to his. At least he would hear if Conom did get a bit frisky with her. He took Covin aside and explained his plan. Covin went out to organise it with the servants and Lepius watched as they hustled double-time up the stairs to get the rooms ready.

'Are you awake, princess?' he heard Conom ask.

Cassie opened her eyes, groaned, and seeing who had her, happily wiggled back into Conom like a helpless little kitten and went back to sleep. Conom grinned so elatedly when she cuddled back into him. He could not help but feel for the guy: in love with another man's wife and a damned Cloud Rider for God's sake. *Man, this isn't something I wanted tossed in my lap.* But here he was and so was she.

'She will most likely sleep now for the rest of the night. Why not go and lay her on the bed upstairs so she can stretch out and be more comfortable? That way you can come and join us for supper. You look beat,' Lepius suggested.

Conom sat looking at her for a long time as if he didn't want to put her down. Then with a sigh, knowing Lepius was right, he stood up. 'You're the doc and I guess you know better than me. I just don't want her scared when she wakes up.'

'If it makes you feel better I'll have a maid sit in her room. She can come and get you the minute she stirs and wakes.'

He nodded and followed Lepius up to the suite that had been made up for her. The chambermaid was still fussing when they arrived in the room so Lepius told her to stay. She pulled the covers back while Conom laid her on the bed and Lepius smiled as her outfit changed to silk pyjamas. Conom hardly even seem to notice he fussed so much making sure she didn't hurt herself if she moved around in her sleep. He lay her on her good side and put pillows along her back to prevent her rolling over. Then when he was happy, he pulled the covers over her and kissed her gently on the cheek. 'Sleep safe, sweetie,' he whispered and turned to face the maid. 'Even if she groans you must tell me so I can come up and get her comfortable again. Do not disobey me or I'll make the rest of your life miserable,' he warned in a low and dangerous voice.

All Lepius's staff were used to being threatened and yelled at so Conom didn't frighten her at all. The maid just curtseyed and promised to do as he asked before sitting in the chair next to the bed as instructed.

Chapter Forty-Eight
The Princess Kidnapped

Kayden was frantic. Cassie was in so much trouble and death was imminent if they did not get to her on time. He was freaking out as Cassie screamed and then ducked. He ordered his men to forget every other order and just grab Cassie. He could see that she had another slice across her shoulder as well and his guts twisted that she had been put in so much danger.

He'd had no idea that this nova was this far gone. Zoren's people were getting sloppy with their reporting and heads were going to roll this time. Where Cassie was concerned there could be no margin for error like this.

No more Mr Nice Guy, no bloody way.

He grimaced as he heard the men suck in their breaths, realising that a portion of it was going to slam directly into Cassie and her horse. Waiting for the impact seemed to take forever as their adrenalin kicked in and everything around them seemed to go into slow motion. Kayden used every ounce of power to speed up the horses to reach her and as his hands went to grab her a shadow fell over her and she and Starburst disappeared.

Unable to think past cleaning up the rest of the mess, they formed a star shape around the rest of the Supernova crust disintegrating what was left. They all sat, shocked at what had happened, glad she was safe but wondering if she was alright and mystified about where she had been taken. Kayden was sure Covin was responsible but it had happened so quickly that he couldn't be sure.

He instructed the horses to head for Aldebaran. As they landed the butler raced out. 'Quick! The Lord!' was all he said and scurried back inside, forcing them to dismount quickly and follow him. Inside they found the butler who was leaning over someone. 'Lord Aldebaran!' he was calling, trying to get a response.

The wall had been smashed so Kayden realised that Aldebaran had been slammed into it and was still unconscious on the floor. A nurse was now at his side, checking his vitals and waking him up. Kayden bent down beside him to listen to what he was trying to say.

'Conom, he sounded more angry than hurt! She was injured. I tried to stop him but he was too angry with you for letting her get harmed. I don't know where he's taken her.'

Kayden felt sick to the stomach already and it wasn't helping. 'Please calm yourself, Ald. Let the nurse check you out. Conom won't hurt her, she'll calm him.'

He looked pained. 'But he's in love with her.'

Kayden nodded. 'I know.'

'But I don't know what he'll do! He's so powerful, Kayden.'

'He won't hurt her. I've been watching. Give her time to sort it out.'

Aldebaran groaned as his head was being wrapped to stop the bleeding. 'How are you staying so calm?' he moaned again.

'I trust my wife,' he confided as he helped him up and to the armchair. 'Now, tell me everything that happened.'

He seemed a bit embarrassed. 'We couldn't help it, we were watching. Conom was angry enough when she had her arm cut the first time and I tried to switch off the communication then but he wouldn't have it and argued with me. Cassie was hit again and this time her shoulder was sliced. He just freaked out, swearing at both of us and saying neither of us deserves her. He said we were reckless for letting her do what she does. I had just about settled him when that last portion of nova headed for her. That's when he literally picked me up in a fury and flung me off him. I don't think he realised his own strength: so much mixed passion and protective concern. He damned near threw me through the stone wall, the mongrel bastard.'

'I'm grateful she's safe, Aldebaran and as much as I'm twisted with guilt for what I had to put Cassie through, our job is to prevent any damage to the stars when under attack. Cassie is a soldier and in battle as you are well aware, there are sometimes unavoidable injuries. She was coping and yes it was touch and go but hell or high water I would have made it to her in time.' He sighed. 'I'm damned annoyed at Conom for taking it upon himself to have such little faith in me that he felt it necessary to abduct my wife from the tyrant he thinks I am. He stood abruptly, putting all emotion aside. 'Sorry to leave you like this, Aldebaran but we have to get back to the mission and the mess it has become. Keep me informed with any news you find out about my wife.'

Aldebaran sat up, holding his head that was aching. 'She was hurt and I tried to let her be. I have to admit though, Kayden, I was terribly relieved when I came round just now and found she was alive, even if the traitorous bastard has taken her from us. He'll have her at a hospital somewhere. I'll make inquires while you're gone and try to find out where,' he offered.

Kayden thanked him and left with his team to finish what they had started. His men quietly followed him out and Kayden injected a feeling of calm through them and instructed them to keep their minds on the mission until it was completed. The last thing he needed was for them to freak out as well. He linked with the men and sent Cassie some healing once they all mounted their horses before heading off to Pyxis, after which he would make a quick stop at Hydra to assess any damage, before heading to Alpha site where he hoped Zoren's team had monitored it and had a fix on where Cassie had been taken.

They arrived at Pyxis and landed on the star Velorum, the home world of Captain Rogers. After greeting the Captain, they followed him inside his ship. The ship had been dug out underneath and he had built a mansion underground. The walls were of a sandy appearance, giving them an authentic look. Magnificent handmade ships and boats where displayed in glass cases around the room.

The one he was working on sat prominently on his workbench.

'Just a bit of a hobby of mine,' he chatted as he poured them a drink.

Normally Kayden would have refused alcohol as they still had a lot to do but he was too annoyed with how this had all gone down and needed something a bit stronger to drink. Woody had resumed control with the men and was holding it together for Kayden's sake. His composed authority was helping him keep his mood in check.

Captain Rogers grinned as he handed the drinks around. 'That girl of yours is a little powerhouse. I watched you on satellite and noticed her injuries. I hope she's well.'

'Yes, Cassie received a slight injury and is having it attended to. I'll pass on your kind words,' Kayden said, not wishing to discuss private issues with the stars. 'The danger is over for now. If you wish to put in a personal complaint towards the Raven or Leon, I'll send Woody back later with some papers for you to sign. Otherwise it will be in my report and as normal, be dealt with by the authorities at Alpha site.'

'Kayden, it's not the first time you've helped me out and I trust you to proceed as usual. You are so much better with detail than an old seadog like me. My days of keeping logs are well over.' He sat back in his chair, lighting his pipe.

He motioned to Woody to hand around the cigars and sat back comfortably, giving them the details of what he knew of the argument between the perpetrators. Woody could see Kayden was in no mood to deal with petty bitching so he engaged with the captain and left the boss to his thoughts of Cassie and Conom.

Woody nudged Kayden when they'd finished the cigars and the drink, letting him know they were itching to move on. Kayden stood up, taking his glass over and placing it on the tray. 'I'm glad your world is safe, Captain Rogers and when we're not so time-poor we'll pop in for a more enjoyable chat. I'll draw up papers and have them dropped off for your signature. This wasn't a direct hit on you; nevertheless the nova could have caused you much damage the way it was so out of control. You'll be asked to testify when the perpetrators are asked to answer to the charges if that's not too much of a bother.'

He was a jolly old soul. 'It'll be a pleasure. I'd expect it out of the cunning Raven but was shocked Leon was involved. He definitely needs to rethink his friends or he'll make more enemies up here than just me,' he croaked out with annoyance.

Next stop was Hydra, the home of the water snake that may have received some slight damage after Cassie had been snatched from them. His men cleaned up all but a couple of chunks and those he had seen head for Hydra. He needed to check out the damage, if any.

Zaine was now the ruler of Hydra. His father had been accidentally killed in an attack many years ago. Zaine was the spitting image of his dad and had the makings of a worthy ruler if he would stop following his father's stubborn views. However, he was only young yet and even though sometimes a little foolish, Kayden liked his strong will and ability to get on with the job. Knowing him well, he knew that Zaine would be getting a little impatient waiting for their visit.

Arriving on Hydra, they had spotted from above that there had definitely been some damage and it had caused a fire in the bushlands. The fortress had no apparent harm done to it that Kayden could see which made his job a little easier. Claiming damage to structures was always so messy and at times dragged out for years. Materials used in the constructions in the sky were so very expensive. A lot of the castles and palace furnishings were of solid gold and decorated in a selection of diamonds and special gems.

Woody joined Kayden as they walked around assessing the damage. From the air they'd already spotted where the nova portion had landed. Where it had exploded, it had left a crater of black and smouldering terrain. The flames had jumped the river, heading up towards the fortress. Even though the fire was now contained, smoke from smouldering embers floated in the air. Zaine came up to them. He had black smeared all over him where he'd worked beside his men to extinguish the flames before they caused any damage to his home.

He was annoyed with whoever it was that had taken Cassie. She had blasted every piece before it reached them, bar the one that did this damage. He was hoping to meet her to thank her personally. He said it would have been a hell of lot worse if she hadn't hung in there with her injuries to protect them.

'She was cut pretty badly on her right arm and shoulder and is getting her lacerations seen to,' Woody intervened, seeing the look on Kayden's face.

Each time Cassie's name was mentioned, guilt plagued him and worry for how she was consumed his thoughts. Not wanting to discuss Cassie further for fear that he might just get back on Zoltan and do what he really wanted to be doing which was to search for his wife, he tactfully changed the subject.

Speaking to Zaine, Kayden found that even though he was upset about the number of water snakes destroyed by the fire, he was taking it extremely well. He wasn't too concerned about the burnt bushlands either as they normally did a burn at that time of year. He was just a bit peeved that he hadn't had time to move the snakes further down the river before the final blast hit them.

'I'm going to be claiming this time, Kayden! I've had just about as much as I can take from that damned Raven.' He was annoyed but in control. Kayden realised he was finally starting to grow up and knew his dad would be proud of the hard-working man he'd become.

Kayden smiled and shook his head. 'We have talked about this many times, Zaine. There is only one thing that will end this feud between the two of you and that is to let the Raven visit the cup every now and then. Otherwise this argument will continue to simmer and blow up intermittently as it has been doing, for many years to come.'

As usual he felt like a broken record, repeating himself. However he put a little jest in his tone, not really wanting to fuel an argument. Today was not a day he wanted to spend revisiting the topic and spending the next four hours debating it. He told Zaine he'd be back in the next few days. That would give him time to take stock of his losses. Then they could go into it more thoroughly once he knew the exact extent of the claim.

'Bring your female Cloud Rider back with you, Kayden. Join us for dinner and a night of festivities if she's feeling up to it. It's been far too long since we enjoyed your company,' he offered as they mounted their rides and left.

Chapter Fourty-Nine
Ophiuchus Palace

Covin was leaning beside the fireplace, viewing them as they came downstairs.

'Cigar, Lepius?' Covin asked, opening up a box on the coffee table and offering one to him and then to Conom. They had enjoyed many a night, just the three of them. Covin would be hoping that by relaxing Conom with a drink and maybe a cigar, this would hopefully help them make sense of what this was all about. Give them insight as to how he ended up caught up in a relationship with Cassie, putting him in deep trouble with the Cloud Riders. Considering they were on totally opposing sides, none of this made sense to either of them.

Lepius lit his cigar and sat at the table with Covin and Conom while the butler poured them a drink each. Conom refused at first. 'Cass might wake and need me. I don't want to go up there smelling like a bloody brewery and frighten the life out of her,' he said, aggravated.

'Trust me, Conom. With the painkillers I loaded her up with she'll not move until morning.' He prodded him on the shoulder with the glass and made him take the drink.

Conom drank it down in one quick movement. 'Crap, I can't think straight,' he said, getting up and pacing. He sat back, sipping the second.

Dinner came and went. During the meal, even though Conom ate very little, he entered into their conversation every now and then if something took his interest. Later they sat outside on the lounges and even though the maid kept a good eye on Cassie, Conom still checked on her himself a couple of times before he started to relax, realising that Lepius was right.

'She's barely moved,' he said after he came back down the third time. He was becoming approachable and actually sat down, confiding in them the whole story. They were stunned to find out that Aldebaran had a daughter.

Covin leaned over the table with a warning gaze. 'Jeez, Conom, you're bloody game taking the wizard's kid and knocking him out in the process! Why not take her back in the morning, apologise, and take on the chin whatever he dishes out. Leave it too long and it'll be far worse. Stop being so stubborn, man.'

Conom leaned forward towards Covin so they were almost touching and Lepius felt by the glare between them, they might just have a go at each other. Not that it would be the first time his hot-headed Commander and Conom hadn't gone at it.

Conom hissed. 'They do not deserve her! She's not going back to them until they can promise me that they will keep her out of danger. I don't give a toss what they do to me and I told Ald so when I called him earlier.'

Trying to defuse the two hotheads, Lepius intervened, putting a different spin on it. 'What do you think Cassie's going to do when she realises she's a captive and you won't take her home? Will the hate in her eyes not be worse?' Lepius asked, trying to make him see his actions were wrong on so many levels.

He spun his head around and considered the question, then breathed out heavily. 'Then so be it. Sooner she hates me than be dead.' He sounded exhausted and agitated. His voice had a lethal undertone. He put his glass down, stomping off back up the stairs to be with her.

Lepius looked at Covin and shrugged. 'We can't push him much further. He's at breaking point and too worried about her for anything to make sense. Maybe I should call Ald and at least let him know she's okay,' he suggested.

Covin shook his head. 'Stay out of it, Lepius. If Ald finds out she's here he'll bring an army and then I'll have to protect us. Someone could get hurt. Let's just play it out and see what happens. You said Cassie seemed more than what she looked. Don't underestimate her. After all she is a Cloud Rider and as is their code, will want to sort this out peacefully. That's what they do and they're damned good at it. Kayden wouldn't have had her join his team or married her because he's only in lust. He is no fool. There is definitely a lot more to Cassie than just her good looks. Don't get me wrong: Kayden's going to be stewing good and proper and won't be impressed with what Conom has done, but will have full trust in his soldier as I do in all of my men. It's a different world she lives in. Just do what you're doing. Give her a protected haven here to work through it.'

Covin was right as he always was when it came to matters of strategy. She'd have to be not just good at what she did, but outstanding for Kayden to have her join his elite team. He grinned at Covin. 'Out of all the planets and stars he had to pick my door to knock on. As if we haven't enough problems of our own!'

He shrugged. 'Ah well, one more won't hurt.' He tried to stay good-humoured.

'You got it in one, Your Majesty,' he stirred him. 'You have big shoulders and a sucker's touch. Just like you to drag in another security risk. I'd better call the other officers together and get them to make sure we're doing everything we can in the event of an invasion. Christ knows what Aldebaran's sorcery will conjure up if he knows she's here. You better hold on, King Lepius, we could be in for a bumpy ride.' He was almost excited and looking forward to a test of their strengths.

Lepius raised his glass to him and laughed. 'Just the way we like it. Bring it on, I say. This may be one fight worth fighting for: a woman.' Covin laughed with him as they both sculled their drinks.

Covin went to organise his officers and Lepius went to bed. He wanted to be bright enough to deal with whatever was going to go down tomorrow. He stopped at the door, not surprised to see Conom had dozed off in the chair. The maid had been kicked out. However, he had left the door open to let them know he meant nothing by staying at her side. He was at least being honourable with her.

Lepius looked at Cassie in the shadows and thought how innocent she looked, just like a child. What did a man like him ever see in such innocence? It was all too hard to imagine. He walked back into his room and left his door open just in case she needed help in the night, then threw himself on the bed fully clothed. *How have I ended up getting mixed up with a bloody kidnapping with one of Zoren's team members? I must be crazy.* He mumbled silently into the night before drifting off to sleep.

Lepius woke to the sound of quiet sobs. He jumped up and walked quickly into Cassie's room. Conom was sitting in the chair and she had wrapped herself around his neck, sobbing so sadly that it even broke Lepius's heart. Conom looked at her helplessly, his eyes glazed with emotions.

Lepius knelt down. 'Cassie, are you in pain? Do you need some more painkillers?'

She looked up, tears running down her face and nodded.

He went and grabbed his bag and gave her another needle, this time only with a pain reliever, not something to knock her out. She calmed within minutes. 'Feel better, sugar?' he asked and she wiped her face, giving a slight grin and nodded.

Even I'm doing it! She's been here all of five minutes and she has me wrapped around her little finger. Even so, he felt so much better now that she did. *The little bitch has me under her spell as well as Conom.* He leaned up against the wall, understanding now. 'I think I get it. You're linked to her somehow. I feel it too,' Lepius commented.

Conom shrugged. 'I can't stand the thought of her being hurt or sad and yet when she's happy she brings everyone around her alive, me included. I can't explain it.' He pulled her hair back off her eyes.

She smiled at him as he gently touched her.

'She joked that she had a machine and it sucks out all the mean stuff from our hearts and she jumps in there and takes its place. You're a little stealer of hearts, aren't you, little one?' he chuckled. She kissed his cheek and hugged him.

She was delightful to watch now she was happy, and all his questions were just answered in that single moment. 'Well, little stealer of hearts, do you feel like a bath and then some breakfast?' he asked, ruffling her hair.

She seemed shy. 'I'll need help,' she said, touching her arm and moving it a little.

'Give me a minute to organise a couple of maids to come up and help you. Us two can shower in here and you can have my room. The bath is all ready to go. But Cassie, absolutely no use of that arm today and no getting it wet, okay? Doctor's orders,' he said firmly.

She nodded and stood a little shaky, walking gingerly to his room with the help of both the suckers that she'd pulled into her game. *Conom can't see it, yet it is as plain as day to me. I am part of her plan as well.* Maybe it was to let her stay there, yet she needn't have worried. He wouldn't have let Conom take her anywhere else anyway.

'Your bath!' she said, delighted. 'Unreal! You just walk down into it. That's no bath. You have a swimming pool with petals in the middle of your bedroom. This is so cool.'

They watched her face and both grinned at her reaction. *Yes, I am now a part of whatever has hold of Conom.* He shook his head at how easily she could make him feel so much joy. *Now I also want to protect her and keep her from harm.* This girl had powers so far beyond anything he'd ever seen in his lifetime and he wondered when she left, if he would miss her dreadfully or if the spell would be broken.

Two maids arrived and they left them to it. Conom paced and finally only had a shower because Lepius told him he stank and that she wouldn't want to be anywhere near him.

'What if they hurt her?' he growled.

'Then I would say that the way you're connected to her, you'll feel it and then you can panic. Until then, chill and wash that bloody cigar and booze odour off yourself,' Lepius insisted. Reluctantly he went in and cleaned up.

After breakfast they both sat out on the patio. He noticed that not once did she ask why they were still here or ask for Kayden. Instead, Cassie ran her hand down Conom's face and took his hand, gently stroking his fingers to relax him, telling him a story of a little princess who had special powers. Her wicked stepfather locked her up and then like Cinderella, it was many years before the princess met her prince. She fell asleep while telling him and he put her back in bed allowing her to rest more comfortably.

That night after dinner he again pulled her over to him and smiled. 'The story—you didn't finish it.'

Cassie began the story exactly where she'd left off. Lepius also listened with interest as she sat happily and relaxed with him and he lay back, listening to her words as if they were all he could muster himself to hear for now. The story continued, telling how the princess ran away to the city and found a job at the casino. She was a very resourceful princess, she told him. Cassie kept telling the tale with so much emotion that Lepius was also wrapped up in her yarn until she yawned and cuddled into him and fell asleep. After taking her up to bed, it was only then that Conom came out and finally had a drink and a cigar with him.

The next morning Cassie seemed so much brighter at breakfast and as they sat chatting to her she glowed and a white light surrounded her. Lepius must have looked stunned because Cassie grinned and touched his hand. 'Don't worry, I'm not an angel, far from it. That's just the Cloud Riders sending me some healing. The magic gets stronger as I get better. You'll see today, when you check my wounds. They should be nearly healed,' she said, getting up, and playfully nudging Conom. 'Tonight, boy, game on. No excuses now I'm better.' Cassie chuckled and he went off after her.

Lepius followed them out to the pool area where they sat around on the outdoor lounges. 'What did that mean, game on?' Lepius asked and sat down with interest.

'Cassie is a little gambler, a professional card player and we have an ongoing feud. I hate to lose so she keeps winning. Today though is different. Today I'm feeling lucky and my opponent has no chance,' he said good-humouredly. He told him of the first time they'd met. 'Her antics just about had me twisted in knots trying to keep my hands off the little minx.' He laughed again with her as they reminisced, telling Lepius the whole story.

Now, I get it. He's fallen in love with a side of Cassie that was just an act and that's why she's telling him her story. It is herself she's talking about. The terrible childhood was not fictitious at all but is why Cassie is as she is.

As Lepius thought it, he could tell that Conom too, finally understood the gist of her story. It was as if they had just both been woken.

'Tell me some more story. What did the princess do when the prince forced a kiss on her in the spa?' Conom asked.

'I didn't think you were even listening. Okay then!' she smiled and continued with the tale. .

When Cassie finished he asked. 'And now the princess has found her real father and a new best friend, how does she feel?'

Lepius could see that if Cassie didn't say what Conom needed to hear, hell's doors were about to open. Cassie bent over, kissed Conom's cheek and smiled beautifully. 'Complete,' she finally said.

Conom closed his eyes. Lepius heard him breathe out heavily and knew Conom was finally happy where he was in Cassie's thoughts, knowing he'd made her life complete would be more than he had hoped for at this stage. 'You are that princess, aren't you?' he asked, opening his eyes.

Cassie nodded. 'That princess would be heartbroken if her friend from the stars did anything that would harm his relationship with her.'

He sat for a few minutes and nodded. 'I understand now why Kayden gives in to you so easily. He's lost you twice and it must have been hell for him. With your drinking and dangerous line of work, I thought he was reckless with you and put you in harm's way. I was angry and yes, bitter that you did not want to stay with your dad and me. I understand now though. You have to experience life to grow and as much as I would like to wrap you up in a cloud so you never get hurt, he understands your need and loves you enough to let you experience it. I've been so blind!'

She touched his cheek and ran her fingers gently through his hair, playing with the curls, looking sad. 'I've been blind too,' she admitted. 'I know I'm just learning and am making huge mistakes like now, nearly getting myself killed. I feel so bad that I never learned to be careful. But I have now. I can't just think I will be fine and not worry. That's not good enough anymore, now that I have so many around me who love me. Someone can get very hurt with that attitude and if that someone is me, I end up hurting everyone.' She breathed out heavily. 'You see, I know I'm not strong like the guys I work with, or you. Nevertheless, I'm smart, I learn every day and I love what I do. I've had all these powers all my life, not understanding why and now I'm able to use them for good and not bad. That makes me feel like I'm someone and not just a nuisance. Conom, I can't have all this energy inside me and not use it. I felt like I was dying inside until Woody showed me how to channel it properly. Don't hate me for what I am. I couldn't stand disappointing any more people in my life,' she said and quiet tears rolled from her eyes and splashed down her cheeks.

Conom was choked up. He coughed. 'Don't you think for one minute you have ever disappointed me, Cass! God, no! I am so proud of how you sat on that horse with blood pouring out of your arm and not a tear in your eye, still staying to fight whatever came your way. I just didn't understand why, until your story, and now I do. I realise I was being far too over-protective and no better than your mother. I wanted to lock you up with me as well so none other could hurt you or take you from me. I'm so sorry, Cassie. I've really mucked up where you're concerned. I can't seem to get this friend thing right.'

She hugged him, sat back and watched him. 'You know, we both need help in that department. I know that if I muck up, Kayden has promised he will always be there to catch me when I fall. Therefore when you muck up, I will always be there to catch you too. But fall gently, I'm not as strong as Kayden,' she playfully teased him.

'What did I ever do to deserve you?' he said, gently holding her hand.

She smiled beautifully at him. 'You loved me and I knew you could never hurt me. That's all I needed to know.'

He frowned. 'But I've hurt the others by being selfish.'

She giggled and smoothed out the wrinkles on his forehead. 'My man will know I'm in good hands. Pops, well that's another matter. He may lock you up in a horrible old dungeon and then, well, it will be my turn to save you.'

Lepius wasn't sure why Cassie had dragged him into their private time together but from the first day she'd arrived, she'd had a hold on him and it was only now he felt it release. He shook himself awake, finally being able to get up and walk away. *Maybe she held me so I couldn't ring Ald or maybe something will unfold in time and this is a lesson I need to learn for some unknown reason.* His thoughts ran as he guessed only time would tell. He could ask her but he didn't really think she knew what she was doing. There was one thing he was sure of. *Damn, she's good at what she does. That was so calculated and clever. With so much love in his heart, she settled Conom without sending him into a rage and left their strong friendship intact.* That was definitely not the outcome he was expecting. Kayden Hunter had found himself a true gem and it was time to let him know where she was.

'Kayden, its Lepius. I think we have a treasure here of yours that you may want to come and collect,' he said.

'Thanks, Lepius, I'm with her father. We'll be there shortly. I assume she's sorted it out with Conom.'

'Mate, you would be proud of her! If you'd just witnessed the last twenty-four hours with her you would have seen how clever she is. She even had me locked into it, holding up my willpower until she had sorted it out. You're one lucky man, Kayden!' he said, ending the conversation.

Covin came in with some guards, even though Lepius didn't feel it necessary. Conom knew Lepius had called Kayden and took Cassie up to her room for a sleep. He came back down and waited to face the music, knowing he would be in for it but also knowing that he had armed guards protecting him until he left the palace. He was a lot happier now and just grinned when their eyes met. There were no hard feelings. Gone was the angry ground-shaking fear. Cassie had replaced it with love and respect. Stealer of hearts: very fitting, he thought as he grinned back at Conom.

When Kayden and Ald arrived, they were shown in. Kayden took one look at Conom, saw his happy face and smiled. 'You all right now, mate?' he asked Conom.

Conom nodded. 'I really stuffed it up, Kayden. I thought you were reckless with her but now I understand you are letting her live. I thought locking her away would keep her safe yet I was being no different to her mother and stepfather. I was an idiot and she has made me see that in the sweetest possible way.'

'Conom, I understood why you took her but if you ever want to see her again it has to be with respect, not only for her but for both of us. I appreciate that you saved her but I would have made it in time as well. Please try and just trust me a little more too.'

'I do, Kayden. I went crazy and I'm really sorry. You must have been out of your mind with worry.'

'See, that's the difference. I trusted you straight up with her. I would never have let you near her otherwise. It's you, Conom, who had to learn trust, and I am pleased it was a quick lesson because I have to admit I missed her like hell. Where is she?' He looked around.

Lepius gestured to Covin. 'Take Kayden up to see his wife. I think Ald and Conom need a minute on their own,' Lepius said, seeing the way Ald glared at Conom with eyes that wanted to squash him like a grape.

Lepius watched Kayden take the steps two at a time, not wasting any time in getting to Cassie. He turned, smiling as he led the other two warring parties outside where they could do no damage if it came to a fistfight. Once out on the patio, he poured them a drink and offered cigars all round. Fumes were pouring out of Ald and Lepius doubted if a cigar would help but he offered him one. He took it and lighting it up, walked away from them both. He had something else on his mind other than Conom and they both felt it and sat down, waiting.

CHAPTER FIFTY

My Sweet Love

C assie heard Kayden's quiet voice and felt the touch of his hand and she rolled towards him, putting out her arms. *Finally, he's come for me.* She felt relieved as he gently scooped her into his arms, kissing her.

His kisses were such sweetness. She closed her eyes and let him sweep her away. She was dizzy from emotion by the time he released her.

'I've missed you, gorgeous.' He reclaimed her lips, sweeping her back into that joyful space where only he could take her. Pulling himself up on his elbow, he smiled down at her, tracing his finger around her mouth. 'I have to stop kissing you, honey, before I forget where I am.' Then he frowned and seemed concerned. 'Not only that but your father is here and is very anxious about you. I should take you down there before he and Conom go at it again. You know Conom nearly put your dad through the castle wall. He was so angry that you were hurt.'

Cassie jumped up. 'Jeez! Quick, get me to them before Pops turns him into a bug and squashes him, or worse!'

Kayden laughed, swung her up in his arms and had her downstairs in a flash. Putting her down and letting her walk the rest of the way, he chuckled. 'Not sure what could be worse than being squashed like a bug, honey, but we're here. Go do your peace-making thing.' He smiled, gesturing to go with the flutter of his fingers.

'Make haste, woman. Come find me when you are done because I have other plans for you when you're done, sexy girl.' He chuckled and she winked, turned and swayed her hips, her butt she gave a wiggle, making him laugh more.

Cassie decided to quit stuffing around and went in search of her father. He wasn't hard to find. All she had to do was follow the smell of cigar smoke. She knew Aldebaran would be somewhere close to that. Out on the entertaining deck, her father was standing with his back to Lepius and Conom. He seemed to be looking out into space, deep in thought, the tension around him thick. Conom, Lepius and Covin were sitting on chairs pulled in tightly at the table as they quietly discussed something together: probably how to get Conom out of trouble with her father. He did seem in an unapproachable mood.

But I'm his daughter and he'll talk to me whether he likes it or not. 'Hi there, Pops,' she said.

He swung around and gathered her to him, holding her with one arm while he used the other to find where she'd been hurt and to run his hand gently over her scars. There was barely a mark left and in a couple of days there might not even be that. He found them anyway, caring in such a way that it made her fret for all the times she had missed this type of concern as a child.

'Pops, I'm okay really,' she whispered.

He hugged her and growled. 'I've been such a damned fool.' His voice was deep and moving. 'If something had've happ—' He choked and let it trail off.

She squeezed him tighter. 'See, I knew you still loved me, you big old grumpy bear.'

He threw his head back and laughed, letting her know she'd broken his mood. 'Cassandra, you had me terrified. Next time if you're going to get hurt in the line of duty, at least keep a wound so I can do my fatherly thing and fuss a bit. Your powers are taking all the fun out of it!'

It felt so good to hear him be just her father again and to be getting his warm, loving hugs. His worrying just proved what she had felt all along, that he did love his daughter.

'My powers weren't that tough,' she grinned. 'I cried the next morning and if you had've been here it would have been you I blubbered all over. The doc had to give me another needle.' She showed him the bruise from the needle. 'That's how big of a sook your little girl was. It was Kayden and the team who healed me. I have nothing on my own in that department. In our future there will be plenty of scrapes I will need you to fuss over.'

He smiled again. 'I love your tears as much as your smiles so I'll look forward to going all paternal on you.' He stopped smiling and scowled. 'I hope that child-stealer has learnt his lesson and won't pull a stunt like that again.'

She nodded. 'You and he are so much alike, Pops. You both want to wrap me up in cottonwool. I think between you and Conom stealing me you have given my husband a few extra grey hairs.'

He held her for a minute, thinking. 'I did the same thing, didn't I?'

She chuckled. 'You're both naughty and terribly guilty of loving me just a little too much but I adore you both immensely for it.'

'I thought you would hate me after how I acted when I saw you last. I've been standing here, worried about what you might say when you saw me. I didn't even feel up to whacking Conom, which may I say is all I've wanted to do for the past couple of days! I'm so sorry I hurt you, Cassandra. I keep doing that, don't I?'

'No, Pops, you only hurt me if you don't do what we're doing now, and that's to talk it through. You're just like me, you're learning about something new. Let's face it, I'm not your normal run-of-the-mill daughter. But then you are not a normal run-of-the-mill father either. Sometimes we're bound to stuff up. That doesn't mean we don't love each other anymore, does it?'

Aldebaran grinned, pleased. 'No, it doesn't mean that at all. I love you more than I have loved anything else in my whole life, although I do need to come to terms with the fact that you aren't a little girl and are all grown up. I just wish I hadn't missed all those important years. I know you would have been a delight.'

'Don't worry, Pops. Wait till I start popping out the grandkids. You'll be sorry you ever wished that.' Cassie knew Kayden had told her it would be up to the gods if she were to fall pregnant. *But stuff it! He needs a bit of shaking up. Get moody with me, the bastard!* She chuckled under her breath at the look on his face. *Perfect payback!*

He laughed aloud this time. 'Don't you dare, Cassandra!' he said, still laughing. 'One of you has been quite a handful so far. Don't scare me by making me do this over again.'

She wrapped her arms around him and hugged him now that he was happy. 'Not now, but maybe in the future I'll make you a grandpa. Mark my words, you aren't getting out of it that easy. You may have been cunning enough to stay out of my childhood but I'll not be letting you escape grandfather-hood that easily,' she joked with him.

He laughed again. 'You better stop threatening me, young lady or I'll hand you back to Conom to save me.'

'And he'll make an excellent uncle for my kids, seeing as they won't have any real ones,' she said, leaning back in his arms. 'Grandpa Ald and Uncle Con … com.' She chuckled.

'That's it, young lady,' he said, picking her up as she wiggled and squirmed, enjoying his good mood. He took her over and plonked her in Conom's arms. Cassie looked at the stunned Conom.

'Here, you deal with her, Uncle Con … com,' Aldebaran laughed. 'I am going to have a drink and a cigar with Kayden. We deserve it.' Still chuckling, he walked over to Kayden and put his arm around him. 'She's your wife,' he said, teasing still.

Kayden laughed and joined in. 'She is your daughter.'

Conom looked down at her, smiling. 'She's my girl,' he said, putting her down.

She took his hand and dragged him back over to her father. 'You were naughty, Conom, so say sorry to Pops.'

Conom screwed up his face at her and she put on a stern expression. Aldebaran just stood looking at them with amusement in his eyes. The words seemed stuck in Conom's throat so she nudged him. 'Conom!' she growled sweetly.

He sighed. 'Sorry, old friend. I lost it—but I can't promise I'll never do it again. This daughter of yours stirs me up like no other woman I've ever met.'

Dad put out his hand and they shook hands. 'She has us both a little rattled. I think it's time we discussed more serious issues.'

He turned to Kayden. 'Give us a minute and I think we'll be requiring your expertise.' He touched her face. 'Don't stress, little one, it's just time for me to become a real father.'

CHAPTER FIFTY-ONE
Lepius Spellbound

L epius and Covin sat back and watched as Cassie worked her magic on the two most notorious rulers in the galaxy.

'Check her out now, Lepius,' Covin said quietly as he poured them another drink.

You could have bowled them over with a feather as Aldebaran picked her up, laughing, and came over to them, playfully dumping her into Conom's lap. How the hell she had turned Ald's mood around so quickly was beyond them. The mood he was in when he arrived, Lepius felt sure it was going to be on for young and old. Now they watched as she dragged Conom to Ald and was making him apologise.

No, surely not! I must be hearing things. Is that Conom saying sorry? Lepius was gob-smacked. She was amazing and they found it hard not to admire the power of such a little bundle of joy.

'Well, Lepius,' Covin grinned and held his glass up to him. 'To the physician and his home. Well done!'

Lepius shook his head, still trying to work out how easily that went down. 'If only our other issues were so easily solved. Maybe Cassie might work with me and melt some of my enemies for me.'

Covin coughed and nearly choked on his drink. 'That ain't going to happen so forget it. If you went all soft on me like Conom's gone, I'd have to knock some sense into you to toughen you right back up again. He's walking on both sides now and you, my king, had better stay right away from that little stealer of hearts,' he warned and even though he'd said it in jest, the underlying tone told Lepius he was deadly serious.

'Maybe. I just wish I had a Cassie of some sort to work beside me like she does with Kayden. I'd give my right arm to have a relationship like that. She's his soldier, his lover and his wife. I've watched her work so hard for him over the last couple of days as she's broken down one of Kayden's biggest threats in the universe. They're enemies out there and yet look at them here. She has them eating out of her hand and it's not false. I can feel how deeply she cares for them too. Her dedication has left me shaken. You know, not once did she ask to go home or did she mention Kayden. Conom was all she saw, yet look how in-love she is with her man.' He watched her eyes melt under Kayden's gaze. 'I have no idea why for the second time in two days, she has captured me to learn her secrets. I can't seem to look anywhere else and I'm fascinated by her. It leaves me to ponder why and wonder if I will ever know.'

Covin sat back in his chair with that faraway look he sometimes had. 'I've always thought you were destined for a very powerful woman. Maybe your Cassie is out there but she is going to have to be a lot more powerful to handle a bloody heartless brute like you,' he said, amused.

Lepius laughed loudly. *Covin knows me well with women. There's no way he'd leave me alone for two seconds with a sweetie like Cassie.* He raised his glass, grinning at Covin. 'Touché, my friend.'

Kayden and Cassie came in, sitting to have a chat. He had always found Kayden very entertaining. The two of them complemented each other and he found he was enjoying himself immensely. Even Covin relaxed into the mood once Ald and Conom had joined them and there seemed to be no hostility.

After a loud night of cards and booze, they woke up around midday, all suffering from the night before.

'That was some night.' Lepius sipped on a strong coffee.

Cassie and Kayden bounced down the stairs, Cassie looking as pretty as a picture. Kayden kept mucking around and twirling her about, dancing with her and making her laugh.

Ald growled at them in jest. 'Will you two stop showing us up? Bloody kids, those two never get hangovers,' he grumbled.

She giggled at her father and walked past Conom who was drinking a coffee and reading the paper. She ruffled his hair as she passed him. 'How's the coffee, ace?' she asked.

He looked up and grumped at her for annoying him. 'I was enjoying it,' he mumbled. She leant over him and whispered something in his ear and he started to laugh. 'I'll give you getting old!' He stood and threatened to throw her in the water. She squealed and wiggled so he put her down. With a flick of her hand, not even touching him, she used her powers to throw him into the water and dove in after him. Kayden and Ald were laughing while Kayden peeled his shirt off and went in after her. Still playing her game, she called out for her father to join them. 'Come on, Grandpa. Don't tell me you can't handle your booze anymore either.'

He growled like a big ferocious bear and flew in after them.

That's devotion, Lepius thought and then recalled another little girl that came to stay with them most weekends and how with her, Covin and he acted the same. Their Angie, who came to play in his palace, was still only very young and not powerful like Cassie was. He couldn't believe how she just threw Conom in the water. He was beginning to think there was so much more to her than the eye could see. *Is this another message?* He nudged Covin who was also watching, intrigued. 'The magic of some females.' Lepius glanced at Covin who agreed. 'Angie.'

'Well, if we can't beat 'em, I reckon I just might join them. Feel like a spa, old boy?' he asked, enjoying the good mood she had them all in.

Covin put his drink down. 'Why not? You know I haven't taken time off in weeks. I'm with you! Shytzer, she has such a bloody hold over me too—has done so since last night. Damned if I can fight it, so might as well give in to it and just enjoy myself.'

It was a quite some time later before the others settled and joined them in the spa. Conom mentioned he was hungry and that set Cassie off again and it was kitchen detail for them all. She kicked the servants out and had them all mixing, baking and making coffee.

They laughed and fooled around so much that Lepius was astounded food even ended up on the table. Although there they sat, consuming homemade cheese scones with butter, apple and cinnamon muffins, and pancakes with butter, lemon and icing sugar.

'Yum, these are really great, Cass. You're going to have to give the recipe to my staff,' he said, enjoying every mouthful.

Kayden laughed. 'Don't bother. Unless you make them with her they never taste the same. We've all tried.'

Cassie looked so caringly at Kayden. 'The recipe includes me to complete the mix,' she smiled at him.

There was barely a crumb left by the time they finished and settled back with fresh cups of coffee. Kayden said he needed to make a move; that Conom and Ald had him working today. Cassie went quiet for the first time all day. Every one noticed and watched her. *How does she do that?* Every mood was reflected in each of them.

'Okay, Pops, 'fess up,' she said quietly after a deathly couple of minute's silence.

Ald put his head down and Lepius could tell it was not easy for him.

'You've made a truce, haven't you?' she said, a bit unsure.

He nodded, looking up at her with those fatherly eyes that took away the dark pits of anger they were so used to seeing. 'I want you in my life and I can't have that while I continue to fight against you. Conom and I worked out a deal and your husband's going to take our proposition to Orion. If he accepts, it is over as far as we're concerned.'

She looked over at Conom and back at her father. 'So, you won't be our enemies anymore? We can hang out whenever we want to?' she asked them with tears running down her face. 'I love you both so much. Thank you, thank you, thank you.' She gave Ald little kisses all over his face, making him laugh. She hugged him and sobbed into his shoulder. 'You really love me, don't you?' she sniffled. 'Even though I'm a big sooky babe.' She continued laughing now and wiping her tears.

'Yes honey, with all my heart.' He held her with the tenderness of a true father. 'Even the sooky bits.' He grinned at her.

'We have to have a drink to celebrate, then. What are we still doing here?' she asked, getting up.

Picking up the plates from the table, she had them mesmerised as she almost danced around, cleaning up and talking. 'We have to go back to your house, Pops. What say we go play loud music, drink and celebrate until we drop? We can invite some friends and put that new magical ballroom to good use. What do you think?' She excitedly wrapped her arms around his neck. 'Well, say something!' she giggled.

Ald shook his head and looked over at Conom.

Conom grinned from ear to ear. 'She had me at drink and celebrations.'

Ald and Conom transported them all over to his place and the servants were summoned to get the ballroom ready to receive guests. The Cloud Riders were there waiting for Kayden's return and were beside themselves to have Cassie back with them. Woody, Kayden and Ald all went off to visit Orion while Covin and Lepius helped Conom with the invites, calling the list Ald gave them. There was no way Cassie was letting go of them just yet, so they rode the waves and enjoyed the energy from her as did all of those who surrounded her.

The guys arrived back with the truce and the drinks started flowing. Before they knew it, guests started to arrive and once the news of the truce spread, there were guests turning up from all over the galaxy. Even Zoren, Kayden's boss stopped in to have a drink with Kayden and Cassie, congratulating them on another successful outcome. Covin and Lepius watched at one stage as Cassie walked around socialising, still having them by the balls, so to speak.

A very slender, stylish lady arrived, escorted by a strange winged man she called Garuda. He had a really strong, male, golden body, a white face, red wings, an eagle's head and beak and to top it off, a crown on his head. She made him wait outside while she entered to enjoy the night.

Cassie went up and introduced herself and they heard the lady say her name was Aquil from the home world of Aquila. Lepius knew that the Aquila constellation is the sign of half-man, half-bird, now understanding the appearance of her bodyguard.

She spoke very seductively. Her style was similar to the type of woman he would go for in a minute. Lepius wondered what Cassie was up to as his tongue hung out in lust for Aquil while Cassie was engaging her in conversation.

She grabbed Aquil by the hand and took her over to Conom who was standing, checking out the ladies with Woody. Who else? he thought.

She introduced Conom and put the woman's hand directly into his, not giving him a chance to ignore her. Conom's eyes lit up as he held her hand, seemingly unable to let it go. They spoke for only a minute before he walked out on the dance floor with her, still holding her hand. Conom was no fool. He nudged Cassie on his way past her. She had even found a woman to suit him. Words failed him. It was a gift from the heart for saving her and no doubt loving her.

Woody chuckled and it was obvious that he knew Cassie well and put his arm around her. He whispered something to her and she started to laugh with him, pushing him playfully before making her way over to Kayden who stood nearby, talking to a couple of his team members. 'All done now, honey?' He looked down at her and smiled lovingly.

She nodded, looking so frail, just as Lepius had seen her that very first day. She wrapped her arms around his neck and hugged him the same way their Angie did when she had enough of something and was letting him know she only wanted him now.

The transformation to what he had just been watching was startling to say the least. Her job completed, the only people she needed were now around her. Her protectors, the Cloud Riders, now all stood guarding her like knights, all of a sudden looking huge and threatening, even dangerous. Their guard was up while hers was down.

Lepius noticed guests move in a fearful manner from the barrier you could feel radiating from them.

'Well, team, our girl has had enough. Ready to go?' Kayden gestured to Ald and he came over, the Cloud Riders only moving enough to let him through.

Ald smiled. 'My sweet Cassandra has finally worn herself out, son. I'll give you a few days to get her strength back before I visit.'

Lepius heard her speaking, her voice quiet and exhausted as she told him she looked forward to it and asked if he could come for the whole weekend as he and Conom had apparently promised to do. Ald's laughter was melodic with joy as she suggested it and after kissing her goodbye, he went off happily.

With that they left, flickering glances around the room, their worry for her safety apparent. There was an electric barrier working around them. Ald came over when he saw how confused Lepius and Covin looked with the sudden change in her team members.

'What just happened, Ald? What did we miss, what was the threat?'

'Cassie is very powerful. She could turn us all to dust with a flick of her hand and needs no protection when she's on a mission. However after her work's done, Kayden is all she wants. She trusts him like no other and now she isn't on duty, she's just a woman in love. She can be herself, nobody special, just his for the keeping. What you are seeing is all Kayden. While her powers are down he will destroy anyone who comes within inches of her. He's not only deeply in love with her but she is a precious commodity to the universe and he will protect her now until she has her strength back and can fend for herself again. Our boy is no fool and he's the only reason I'm able to now let her go and live her life. She chose him, fighting off every power I threw at her and then showing me why.'

Ald smiled to himself and Lepius searched his features, waiting. He wanted the end of the story; needed it like a drug.

He turned to Lepius and put a hand on his shoulder. 'She holds the ones she loves in her heart. She holds the man she's in love with deep in her soul but me, her father? Well, I'm the one who gets to hold her. She's eternally here with me even when her body is not. I can close my eyes and she's right here in the circle of my arms and if I need her I can even feel her jump into my arms and wrap hers around me. That's her gift to me, a reward for ending the war with Orion and I only just figured it out tonight. She gave it to me days ago, obviously knowing the choice I would eventually make.'

'Then what was tonight all about? I thought she was excited and like us, had only just found out.'

Ald pointed to Conom and the new girlfriend he was cozying up to in the corner. 'This is all about him. He's now one of her knights and she's rewarding his gallant efforts to save her. Mind you, if it was up to me the only reward the kidnapping twit would be getting from me is a good boot up the backside. However, my Cassie, she saw through the love-struck-romeo and only saw his loyalty and devotion.'

Covin and Lepius laughed at his attack on Conom's virtue. 'We thought you were taking it all too well, Ald. Not like you at all. Glad to see the love for your daughter hasn't blindsided you.'

'No way,' he chuckled. 'I respect the fact that he is now very important to my little girl. I won't kill him but my God, he will pay for cracking my head open like a damned watermelon! Tonight though, for Cassie's sake I'll allow him her gift but tomorrow is another day and he and me, we have a feud to settle and he knows it.'

'Hope you're both quick healers! You have a date together with Cassie in a few days.' Lepius slowly shook his head, smiling.

Ald grinned back mischievously. 'I'll use magic if I have to but by the time I've finished, if he ever runs off with her again he will remember to take me too.'

Covin and Lepius cracked up laughing. 'Hey, if you need a referee, we can stay,' Covin offered, excited to see a brawl.

Ald opened his arms. 'Ain't going to be no rules and it's not the first or last time me and fancy-pants have gone a round or two. Last time we ended up so smashed, a week just disappeared. We traced our movements and apparently had a blast down on earth but it's not much fun when you can't even remember it.'

A commotion at the front entrance snapped them out of their

enjoyable conversation. Their mate Conom had just spotted the Cloud Riders leaving and was confronting them, demanding to know where they were taking Cassie. The guys were looking meaner than serpents ready to strike and Conom, as brave as ten men, wasn't letting them leave without an answer.

Lepius made a move to grab Conom in an effort to prevent him getting an arse whipping when Ald held his arm. 'Watch.'

Through the cloud of confusion came a glowing light so bright they all held their hands up to their faces. Conom took a step back and as the light dulled slightly they could see Cassie standing before him. She took his hand and placed it on her heart. She touched his heart and they both glowed brightly together. When the glow dissipated, the smile he gave her was as angelic as hers. He bowed and stepped away from her as Kayden swept her back into his arms. The crackle of the guard that the Cloud Riders snapped up around her this time made even Lepius shudder. They were taking their girl home and God help anyone who tried to stop them.

Conom stood, shaking his head and smiling, oblivious to those around him.

'What happened, man?' Ald said to him, trying to snap him out of his trance-like state.

He turned slowly to Ald, his eyes glazed with unshed tears. 'I feel her now. This is how they are all with each other. They have the power to feel each other's emotions. That's how they knew she was safe with me. They can feel her and now she has given me that same power so I don't worry about her.' He threw up his arm and punched the air. 'And my God, she's so happy!' He put his arm around Ald. 'Let's go party, man! Just us. It's what she would want us to do. Stuff the woman unless there are two of them.'

Ald laughed joyfully. His friend was back and all the hostility in him that they'd seen a few minutes ago was gone. Could she have guessed what was going to go down with them and once again worked a last bit of magic to prevent an eruption of discord? *Man, she is good!*

Covin and Lepius just grinned and shook their heads.

When she'd first come to them a few days ago they would have thought Conom was a goner—totally in love with a married woman and about to have his life ended by a young girl who looked too innocent to even know what was going on. Now, not only had she turned it around and healed all their hearts, she had also given them all exactly what all living creatures crave: love.

A heavenly tone whispered in the air around them.

King Lepius and your friend Covin, warriors of the universe, you have both already been chosen. When your goddess comes she will need the man she loves and the man she is in love with forever by her side. Take care of each other while she is gone and when her mission is complete she will come home to the ones she has entrusted with her heart and soul. Trust me, face your fears and jealousies and be there always to catch her when she falls. I promise the reward is worth every hardship you go through without her. Never forget my lesson, my sweet new friends.

And here ended the lesson as Covin and Lepius both felt Cassie release them.

Personal Message
(From the author)

Thank you for purchasing my book.

If you enjoyed it, please take a moment to leave me a review at your favorite book retailer?

To discover more about the

Magical Comos Collection and my other books
visit:

www·debbiebehan·com

A new adventure starts with:

Catlin

Goddess of Peace

Cheers!

Debbie Behan